"The realized nightmare of every parent, written in a strong, unique voice with a striking use of black humor to soften the unspeakable. Heather James is definitely a suspense author to add to your must-read list. Is there honor in revenge? You'll have to read to find out."

—Jordyn Redwood
author of The Bloodline Trilogy

"Crafted with the poetic precision of a master, *Unholy Hunger* will keep readers turning pages into the wee hours of the night. Not only has Heather James delivered a deeply emotional story, she has included plot twists and well-researched details that will ring true for those who have endured the tragic loss of a loved one. No doubt, a legion of new fans will be eager to read more from this stellar debut author."

—Julie Cantrell
New York Times and *USA Today* best-selling author of *Into the Free*

"Heather James's incredible writing strikes the heart, chills the bones, and brings triumph to the spirit. A page-turner to the end!"

—Cindy Martinusen Coloma
best-selling author of twelve novels including *Orchid House* and *Winter Passing*

LURE of the SERPENT · BOOK 1

Unholy Hunger

A Novel

Heather James

Kregel
Publications

Unholy Hunger: A Novel
© 2013 by Heather James

Published by Kregel Publications, a division of Kregel, Inc., P.O. Box 2607, Grand Rapids, MI 49501.

ISBN 978-0-8254-4291-9

Printed in the United States of America

13 14 15 16 17 / 5 4 3 2 1

For Charles,
Ethan,
and Aidan

Prologue

Yes, I wanted to die. As long as my daughter's murderer died with me, I was ready to go. I was already three quarters of the way there after the blow he had given to my head.

Everything turned black for a moment as the sudden, slicing pain radiated into numbness. Black then gave way to a white, heavenly blur, and I strained to see past the world closing in on me. I saw a brown shirt, faded jeans, blackened eyes . . . oh, there he was; there slouched the monster against a kitchen counter. He was clutching one side of his chest, futilely trying to seal the singed bullet hole and cupping his warmed blood before it all bubbled out to the cheap linoleum below.

I fought to see more, to take it all in deeper and beyond the fuzziness of my depleting consciousness, but something oozed over my left eye. More blood. My blood. I blinked, but that made it worse, further welcoming the dark, sticky stuff to seep in from my open wound.

His mouth moved; his lips puckered in and out trying to say something. He looked like a fish plucked from the ocean and left to die on a pier caked with bait and spilled guts. I wondered what he was trying to say, or maybe even ask. Perhaps the question of the day for him would have been a big fat, "Why?"

If he had managed to ask that, I knew how I'd respond: "You want the *Why*? Join the club, you dying carp."

ONE

Blame the Darkness

It all started with Eve and a piece of fruit. They call her deed original sin for a reason. Besides, I think the world is used to blaming others, and I'm no exception. I might as well go back to that first finger pointing before I try to explain why a God-fearing girl such as myself thought nothing of chasing down a bad man for what I thought were good reasons.

At the dawn of time, there stood Adam and Eve in that perfect little number God called Eden. God said to them, and I'm paraphrasing, "Here's the line you two can't cross. You just stand right there and come no farther. You have vastness and plenty to your left, to your right, and even behind you. But you can go no farther. Do not touch that tree."

Of course, Eve touched the tree.

She did it first, and God would have punished her first, too, but Eve wised up and pinned it on that sneaky little serpent who had come slithering out of that tree. And that's fair. He was the one who tricked her; he was the one who lured her.

God doled out the first punishment to that belly crawler, and he took it. He took it because even he knew he was the one to blame. Then, God cursed Eve because it doesn't matter who put the idea into play, the only pair of pants we can wipe our dirty little hands off on is our own.

Suffice it to say, I am a daughter of Eve, and I didn't hesitate all that much when it was my turn to take a bite of that apple—partake in the forbidden when I heard the right words and felt the right sort of entitlement. The one thing I didn't do as Eve had, at least not until it was too late, was point the finger at that stinking serpent and shift the blame where the blame was due.

My name is Evelyn Barrett and in my old life, I was an attorney. I came of age during the advent of runaway hit legal shows on television and, believing what I saw to be an exciting and sexy career, I joined up. I can't say there was either excitement or sexiness in destroying groves of trees to flood my opponents with paperwork in the hopes of frustrating them, or tainting my once perfect 20/20 eyesight when my opponents did the same to me, but I still thought I was cool and elite. Better yet, I found the facade of what others thought my job to be like dependably amusing.

Then there's the fact that I made a bunch of money doing it. Millions to be exact, and that kind of dough is quite a perk. I struck litigation gold when a friend of a friend received a paralyzed son, along with the daily grind of changing pee bags, because said son did a flying somersault off a fishing pier and into a city-built lake.

City management's decision to minimize cost and maximize aesthetics created a shallow lake of only four feet deep, with the banister of the pier topping out at ten feet from the bottom. The boy's spine snapped against the cement bottom after he completed what his friends called an eight-pointer.

At the onset of the lawsuit, the human side of me asked myself why anyone would somersault off anything from ten feet up, especially if they don't know how deep the water is. But the lawyer in me victoriously argued—to the tune of $68 million dollars—that the city should have put a sign up to warn adventurous and lively young men that there is imminent danger and shallow water ahead.

Live and learn I used to say. Especially to losing defense lawyers.

The verdict set me up for life, and I knew I wouldn't have to work so hard anymore. That was all right with me because, soon after, I found Eddie—a gorgeous, blond-haired, blue-eyed guy who stared at me for months before he built up the nerve to ask me out on a date. When I asked him what took so long, he answered, "Because I climb telephone poles for a living and you're wearing a six hundred dollar suit."

I had actually blown eight hundred on that particular suit, but I had no interest in correcting him.

His friends had told him that I wasn't the right type of girl to marry if he coveted keeping his family jewels—metaphorically speaking, of course. But what I do for play and what I do for work are two different things. Eddie knew that, and I treated him right. He was always the man in our family because he was the right kind of man to begin with.

After we married, he insisted on keeping the job that asked him to climb telephone poles but succumbed to letting me provide him with the lifestyle to which I had become accustomed. That involved a fancy SUV with tinted windows and a house on the seventh fairway of the Copper River Golf Course, family jewels intact.

I may have been the type of lawyer who ripped open a paper cut to spill a pint of my enemy's blood on the floor, but I was a woman first and foremost who enjoyed being his wife and the mother of the little girl we had together, a little girl who looked just like her daddy.

Corinne took a sweet pride in the fact she looked just like Eddie. She used to run around and tell anyone who would listen to her that she had *lellow* hair, like her daddy.

Lellow. It's hard to say, even now.

It was one of Robert Bailey's triggers. He'd sit on a park bench and when a cute little blonde thing came skipping by, he'd ask her, "What color is your hair, darling?"

If she said *lellow*, then she was a winner. A winner for him and no one else.

Not for my Corinne. Not for Eddie. Not for me.

If you ever wonder if anything good can survive after the murder of your child, well forget it. Just blame the darkness, blame the serpent . . . just like Eve did. It's what I should have done.

TWO

Flesh on Fire

Corinne had a nanny. She was great until she was stupid. Great until she fell asleep on a park bench and let someone take my child.

One Tuesday in early May, a soft spring air lulled the nanny to sleep while my four-year-old Corinne played nearby in a sandbox. Nanny didn't admit this, of course. Another mother at the park came forward and gave her statement to the police.

"I told that little girl to wake up the lady on the bench because I was leaving, and I didn't want the little girl to be left unsupervised," the mother told the police. "I thought the lady was the little girl's mother, but when I asked, the little girl said it wasn't her mommy, it was her nanny. Then she told me that her nanny didn't like to be woken from naps.

I told the little girl to wake the nanny up anyway. And when I was pulling out of the parking lot, I saw the little girl walking to the nanny. That's the last thing I saw. I thought she was safe because I thought the nanny was about to be woken up."

Personally, I don't know the details after that. Strike that—I don't know the *exact* details after that. All I know is that someone took Corinne after that mother had left and before the nanny woke up on her own to realize my child was most certainly no longer in the sandbox.

It was 10:12 in the morning when the nanny called me, telling me that Corinne was gone. It's amazing how simple English words like *gone*, *missing*, and *taken* can be interpreted in any which way by a mother reluctantly facing the reality of a definition.

"Gone?"

"Yes, gone."

"What do you mean gone?"

"Gone, gone."

It was a twisted Abbot and Costello routine during the worst day of my life.

I started looking everywhere, thinking that my desperate desire for it all to be untrue would span around and beyond me, covering and searching the entire metropolitan area and its 400,000 populous for the one tiny girl on the face of the earth who called me Mommy.

And Eddie, he went straight for the police. He sat in their stucco fort, answering questions and holding a picture of her from the previous Christmas.

A janitor at Mercy Hospital found Corinne later that day as he was taking out trash. Someone had left her outside one of the medical buildings outlining the hospital campus, near a rarely used staff entrance to the building.

That's what a detective told me when he used Eddie's phone to summon me to the hospital, and it was the way he said it—with a heavy, sympathetic voice—that induced panic. But because he didn't specify whether she was dead or not, I clung to the hope she had simply been misplaced by a rotten, lazy nanny. I went to the hospital as quickly as I could. I don't even remember how I got there: my car, a police vehicle, running, or on my hands and knees, crying out to God not to find a dead child at the end of my route.

It was disheartening when I found the interior walls of the hospital spinning wildly around me. My God, my God, even the very walls knew what I couldn't imagine being true. Spinning. It all kept spinning—faces, white coats, door upon door, and an eternity of scuffed linoleum. They swirled around me, taunting, mocking until I screamed.

My shrieks directed themselves first at the faces perched above white coats, then other, nominal faces in decorative scrubs, then only at the linoleum because it was the only thing that didn't lie to me and tell me it'd be all right.

It didn't take the staff very long to come up with the idea of sedating me. An older and rotund black nurse came to help me. Those were her words, "to help." But because she immediately pinned my arms down to my side, she was nothing more than a bouncer, R.N. Her arms were big and strong, but more threatening were her oversized breasts. I tried to push past her on several occasions, and she used her chest as an effective, yet wholly inappropriate barricade. She pinned my torso down on a bed, my legs and head flailing for freedom, and told me, "Settle down now, child." Her Jamaican accent tried to lull me into acceptance, but she was a liar too. I saw, I felt, the lying in her eyes, eyes that wouldn't even look into mine.

That's when I knew. I knew that a garbage-wielding janitor had found my daughter, forever depleted of her God-given breath. Dead. Corinne was dead. Going from missing to dead is like going from doused in gasoline to flesh on fire. And that was only a fraction of the pain I felt.

There went life as I knew it, the only one I really enjoyed being a part of.

Then a quiet hum transcended my being, and the world around me spun faster, so fast that it was nothing but a big, white blur. I saw a barren canvas of life ahead of me.

"Sedate her," a voice behind me said. The blur, the pain, refocused and narrowed upon an angry doctor who was constantly looking over his shoulder to see who I was scaring with fitful hollering I couldn't even hear myself belting out. After he said it, I saw a reflection of myself in a window—mouth open, head shaking, veins protruding. I guess I was screaming.

I didn't see it coming, but I heard the rustle of plastic and paper ripped apart by quick hands. An injection was coming, something to knock me out. I attempted one last breakaway from the Jamaican nurse, freeing my arm and aiming to punch her in the neck, but she blocked me and held me down again. "Sorry, child. It's for your own good."

I wrestled with a dream during my sedation. It was a replay of an incident a month earlier where Corinne had been pedaling on her bike. She was going too fast, leaning too far to the right, and one of the training wheels bent and broke off. Down she went against the asphalt. It sounded worse than it was, and I assumed she'd be scrape-free, especially since she was wearing jeans and a light jacket.

Still, she came weeping and gasping toward me, begging me to take off her jeans and look at her knee. Sure enough, there was a tiny drop of blood where her skin had slightly torn, even though her jeans remained intact. She wailed for five minutes straight. I held her, rocked her, loved her, and found a slight comfort in the fact she was so melodramatic. To me, it meant boo-boo kisses would have a long lifespan in our house. And I liked giving boo-boo kisses to a young lady who otherwise made me work for her affection.

Then my dream turned to a nightmare. One where I envisioned Corinne at the park, wearing the pink sweater I put her in that morning, playing in the sandbox until she was taken, stolen, hurt.

If she cried for five minutes over a drop of blood from a tumble on her bike, how much more did she cry when someone abused her?

I awoke from my sedation at the very moment my mind tried to explore the depths of Corinne's torment at the hands of someone I could only assume carried an absolute evil within his frame. I screamed again. I screamed for the doctor, I screamed for Eddie, I screamed for boo-boo kisses, and loudest of all, I screamed, "Where is my daughter?"

A man younger than me, not yet thirty, came into the room I lay in, wearing a dress shirt, a thin tie, and Docker pants. He came in closer, eyeing the restraints the nurse had put on when I was asleep. He, like the others, avoided eye contact.

"I'm Detective Thatcher," he said. "Are you feeling all right to talk with me?"

I didn't think I had much of a voice left from all the hollering, but I replied, "Where's Corinne? Is she safe?"

He finally looked in my eyes. I wouldn't have thought it could be so, but it was worse. Enough said. Eye contact was worse—far too much pity in that one, simple connection.

I rolled to my side, away from his stare and moaned, "Where's my husband? I need my husband."

"Mrs. Barrett," he started.

"Go away."

"I'm afraid I can't."

"I'd rather hear it from my husband. I know that it's true, but if someone is going to say the words, I'd rather it be from him."

Silence etched between us. It filled the room so completely that I thought the young detective had left. He hadn't. He was still and smooth as stone, now looking at the floor.

"He asked me to tell you," was the detective's response.

"Oh, God," I cried, rolling away again. "Then just say it. I already know. Just say it and leave."

"Your daughter is dead. I won't share the details with you unless you want me to. But the worst that can happen in these circumstances happened."

Still feeling groggy from the sedative working itself out of my body, I was certain he *had* just shared the details with me. And since he had already spilled most of it, I went for the final piercing of my heart. "How did she die?" I asked.

"Asphyxiation."

Medical terms are good. Smothered with a pillow—which I later learned is what actually happened—would've been too hard to hear at the time. The medical term seemed so uppity, far removed from the haunting image that a stranger's, an evil man's, hands were the cause of the "asphyxiation."

I pulled my arm over my face, blacking out the lights as it rested heavily on top of my eyes. There had to be a way to go back in time and stop this, to fix this. But there wasn't. My powerlessness coupled with Corinne's ultimate fragility drove me mad, so much so that in the darkness of covering I saw a pair of beady and lustful red eyes staring back at me.

Someone was going to pay for killing my child. Of that, I was sure.

But first, I had to bury my daughter.

THREE

A Departing Line

I'd like to say I was wholly there at Corinne's funeral, but only a dim, dark shadow of me arrived. A few people, the good kind, told me I was holding up well; the great ones gently squeezed my arm and said nothing.

Then there was my mother.

When life gets scratchy for her, a habit of hers is to lower the barrier between mind and mouth. I thought I had built immunity to her poor choice of words at the wrong points in time, but in the week that led up to, and including, Corinne's funeral, I wasn't on guard for obvious reasons.

But I should have been. That way, I wouldn't have had to suffer the collateral damage from when my mother said she never let a nanny watch my sister and me when we were younger, and we had made it to adulthood, hadn't we? So there, take that. After that comment, I realized that she not only lowered the floodgate but also torched it and intended to blow the ashes in my face.

I tried my best to avoid her at the funeral, but Eddie—who hadn't stopped crying and seeking sympathetic shoulders—was the great embracer and asked my mother and her late-in-life boyfriend, Gordon, to sit beside us in the front pew of the church.

After she gave Eddie a motherly hug, she stretched her arms out to me. I pretended not to notice her, looking instead at the wooden cross bolted in the center of the altar.

"This is not the time for your tough girl act, Evelyn," she said, still waiting for me to rise and give her a hug.

Don't respond, I thought to myself. Don't respond, don't respond, don't respond.

She stayed in front of me while I scooted closer to Eddie on the pew, hoping to hide behind his solid, muscular form, even if he was a despondent mess.

"Come on, now." She bent over, staring at me eye-level. Then her voice lowered. No one could hear except Eddie and me, and I wasn't sure Eddie was even listening. I knew it was coming: another puff of ash blown into my face.

"There's no need to punish me, Evelyn," she said. "We all make mistakes as mothers. Naturally, not as grave as the one you made, but that's still no reason to punish me. I'm here to help you pick up what's left of your life."

My body went into rigor. Eddie immediately stood, took my mother's hand and said, "Here, Kathryn, sit on the opposite side of me. Let Evy have her moment of quiet."

I guess he was listening. It was the first time in this aftermath that Eddie felt like Eddie to me. My shield, my rock, my man. I had been starting to resent him of late for being the weeping shell he had become. All he did was hide and cry in the back rooms of the house, rather than help me bark at the police, the nanny, her family, the hospital, the mortician, the mailman, etcetera, etcetera, and ad nauseam.

After my mother took her seat, I spent the rest of Corinne's service staring at the right side of the altar, holding a tissue from my nose down, so no one would see my open mouth panting for air in a world I didn't want to be in anymore. I kept my eyes fixed on a wall socket near the church's organ; I didn't want them to wander over to the small, closed casket under a heap of pink gerbera daisies. I don't even know why we had the casket—and Corinne inside of it—on display. How in the world is a mother supposed to look at that?

It was bad enough that earlier in the week a jelly-bellied mortician with slicked back hair took twenty minutes to describe casket liners and linens to me in a way that implied it was my fundamental obligation to bury my child in style.

Style?

Right. Style. Pay no mind to the fact that a sadistic monster killed my daughter; I had more important things to worry about, like whether Corinne's small, lifeless body rested on silk rather than taffeta, and how, in his opinion, little girls liked lavender more than orchid.

"Really?" I had asked him, wanting to tear him limb from limb. "You think little girls like lavender better? What's your point of reference for that? Did you ask living, breathing girls their casket preferences after warm milk and bedtime prayers, or did you temporarily cross over and powwow with the dead ones on the inferior attributes of orchid?"

Ultimately, Eddie made the final decision on the particulars, choosing orchid silk, but only after I kicked over a floor vase and stormed out of the mortuary, disgusted with old jelly belly.

Toward the end of the funeral service, my mother leaned over Eddie and his hunched shoulders and said to me, "We're getting close to the end, dear. Remember, people will expect you to face them when they come to the front and give their condolences in the . . . oh, what's that thing called . . . Gordon?" she asked, leaning back to refer the question to her boyfriend.

Gordon stared off in the distance, unaware my mother was talking to him.

"Gordon?" she asked again.

He made eye contact with her in response.

"I was asking what the line is called at the end of the service, where everyone tells Evelyn and Edward how sorry they are."

I leaned away, as far as I could, pulling Eddie with me and inadvertently digging my nails into the flesh of his forearm. I whispered in his ear, "Make her go away, Eddie. I can't . . . I can't . . . deal."

It took him a moment to respond to my request. He must've been back in the land of weeping and woe—the fool glanced at the casket the *entire* time.

He turned his face to me and kissed my forehead. I felt the wetness of his tears; solitary drops of outpoured pain, pooled atop his upper lip. He didn't even look at me when he responded, "I can't either. Please, don't make a scene."

He, of all people, knew that was as good as daring me.

"Like a receiving line at a wedding," my mother continued, "but I don't think it's called a receiving line because this is certainly not a wedding."

Gordon shook his head at her. To shut her up, I think. But she didn't.

"More like a departing line—"

I popped out of my seat with fury, like a person possessed. If the scene were from an old-time cartoon, I would've had smoke blowing from my ears and nostrils.

Gordon shrunk back in fear, his eyes darting to the nearest exit at the side of the church, but my mother gave me this innocent, well-meaning look.

"Oh, dear," she said. "Don't embarrass yourself any further," she whispered.

"Stop it, Mom!" I shrieked at her.

People were looking at me; even Eddie noticed they were looking. He came out of his daze for a moment, taking a quick switch of roles from grieving daddy to crazy wife wrangler. He reached his hand out to me to pull me back down to my seat, but he didn't have the constitution to reel me back. I knew it, and I was sure he knew it. I sidestepped his grasp and went for my mother, hoisting her up by her arm. Eddie slouched back against the pew and shook his head, looking past me at Corinne's casket.

The first mourners making their way to the altar stopped and looked at me, eyebrows raised. I looked back at them, still holding onto my mother. A few of them shook their heads.

They were all full of pity. The inclination to tell them what they could do with their so-called pity overwhelmed me, but instead, I looked at Eddie. Maybe he'd try to stop me again. It was one of the many reasons I had married him; I was the fire, and he was the hearth. I burned better in the confines of his restraint. But the flood of his tears and woe sought to smoke me out, and thus, I had to burn freely.

Worse yet, I don't think he cared about it anymore. His blue eyes looked eerily calm, like the sea ultimately unaffected by a brewing storm.

Forget them, I thought. Forget them all.

I turned back to the altar. It was the first time I'd bothered to notice the pastor officiating, even though he had been at the front the whole time doing the service. He reached out his hand to me, to join him rather than continue in my anger.

No. Forget the pastor.

With my mother still in my grasp, my gaze went to the same exit sign that Gordon spotted earlier. I tightened my grip and dragged her toward the door. That's when she started to put up a fight.

"Evelyn, Evelyn, what in the world are you doing? Evelyn." She planted her feet, but I was strong, and we kept moving. "Evelyn. No! You're making a scene."

A sliver of a consciousness returned. A tiny light shone, and it came with its own handy bell—*ding, ding, dinging* me back to reality. What will all these people think of me? How do I explain myself for this?

Answer: I'm grieving. Free pass. Loophole.

And out Grandmommy went, shoved through the exit before I turned back to face my audience.

Mourners from the back of the church stood now, trying to get a better look at the ruckus up front. All looked at me except for Eddie and Gordon—who went down the aisle toward the rear of the church, presumably to meet up with my mother outside.

"I'm sorry . . ." I started. "I just . . ." I took a shaky breath in. "I can't . . ."

What was the point? Why even bother explaining myself? It didn't matter what they thought of me, I'd still have a dead child at the end of the day, wouldn't I? All I wanted was to collapse on the floor in the fetal position. My knees agreed and started to buckle. I anticipated letting it all ride, right down to the floor, until an arm came quickly around me and held me up.

It was Madeline—Maddie. My sister.

"What Evy is trying to say is that she can't feel normal right now. Could any of us? And sometimes our grief gets the better of us. Right, honey?"

I nodded numbly at Maddie's words.

"Please continue paying your respects. This day is all about our beloved Corinne. Evy and I are going to take a moment outside."

I whispered something into my younger sister's ear. She nodded, and then said to the attendees, "I'm sorry, please excuse Evy from the rest of the service. She very much appreciates your being here. I know you'll understand and forgive her. Thank you."

Maddie took me outside. The day was too bright, too alive. Where were the clouds, the rain, the lightning and thunder to crack open the earth? I just wanted darkness.

My sister led me to a stone bench, and I collapsed on her, my head in her lap. She swept my hair from my face and tucked it behind my ear as I cried, tears dribbling off the tip of my nose and onto her black cotton skirt. I remembered the history of the skirt, and the tears plopped faster. Everything Maddie did had meaning, had substance. We had bought matching black skirts when she graduated from college, six years after I had. Every girl needed to wear a black skirt, and this way, no matter where life took us, we'd always have an opportunity to wear the skirts and think of each other. Hers was soft and faded now, sending me all sorts of the right kind of messages.

"Are you going to make me apologize to Mom?" I asked.

"Yeah, right," she responded, rubbing my shoulder.

"That was bad, huh?"

"Would you be mad at me if I said it was amusing?" she asked.

"No, not if you said it."

"Okay, it was amusing." She didn't giggle when she said it, but if we were anywhere other than Corinne's funeral, she probably would have. "You sure you don't want to go back in?" she asked.

Tears fell, more than I felt comfortable shedding. "No." I stifled the emotion rising in my voice.

"But she's in there, Evy. Corinne's in there," she pleaded with me.

I sat up, pushing off her lap, and shook my head.

"No, she's not," I said, biting down on my lip, turning my head away from her. "Maddie, she's not there anymore. What's left in there is just her pretty little vessel, and that vessel has come to an end. No more—" I gasped, fighting back a torrent of pain and tears. "No more hugs, no more kisses, no more nothing." My face fell into my hands. The tears snaked through my fingers.

I realized I looked like Eddie. Surely, we both couldn't be messes. We couldn't both be sob-ridden babies. Besides, I still had anger. If Eddie gave up the sobbing, he'd have nothing left and then what would he do? Implode?

No, I'd let him have the monopoly on tears. I could cling to the fits of rage. I'm better at that anyway.

The back of my hands streaked across my cheeks, drying up my show of weakness. "Sorry, Maddie, I can't stay. All I'm seeing in there is my husband drowning himself into oblivion and our mother acting like a wild, heartless animal."

"You know she means well."

"I don't care if she means well. I need her to *act* well. And right now," I stood, feeling the anger bubbling, "I need something to be well because nothing else is."

"Okay, sis. Okay."

"No, Maddie!" She startled at the boom of my voice. "It's not okay. I don't know how to handle this. I don't know how people survive stuff like this. I can't . . . I don't even want to. Even if I'm still breathing when this all passes, my mind, my hope, my very being will all be smoke and mirrors at best and an insane asylum at worst.

"She's not around anymore. She'll never be around anymore. I don't get to hold her, buy her bows, send her off to school, eat ice cream with her when some jerk dumps her, go wedding dress shopping. I don't get anything because she's dead. No, no, not *just* dead, she was murdered. *Murdered.* There's just so much more that goes along with that, there's just so much more to swallow than if she had died in some freak accident."

My voice started to shriek out of control. "To know that someone made some sadistic initiative to snuff her life out . . . I feel . . . I feel out of control!" It's as if I couldn't notice small, necessary things like sunlight and food anymore because I wanted my vengeance. I couldn't handle it unless I had my vengeance. I was shaking now, pacing with adrenaline and terror.

I spun toward her, seeing the concern in her eyes, "Maddie, take me home. Please. Take me home. I have pills there."

"What pills, Evy? What are you going to do with them?" she asked.

"Valium. I got them last week at the hospital. To . . . to help me settle down. To help me sleep."

"Okay, I'll take you home and give you a pill. But I'm taking the rest of the bottle home with me."

I shot her a look of confusion, then contempt, knowing what she had implied.

"Go ahead and hate me for it, but I won't entertain any suicidal notions. Not now. Especially not now."

Let her take the bottle, I thought. I knew I had another stashed away.

I turned to walk to my car, hoping she'd follow.

"What about Eddie?" she asked, still sitting on the bench where I had left her.

"He'll manage," I said. Actually, he wouldn't. If I left him behind without recourse, he'd likely be sitting in the same pew come morning.

"Do you think Ben can bring him home?" I asked, inquiring about the availability of her husband.

She nodded. "I'll let him know to do it, hold on." She opened the small satchel she'd been carrying and pulled out her cell phone to send a text message.

She walked several paces behind me as I sprinted to the car. Off to my right, Gordon had finished putting my mother in one of the cars and then turned back to the church. I hoped neither he nor my mom had seen me. Looking back over my shoulder, I wanted to shout back at Maddie to hurry, but I figured she was dragging along for a reason. She was probably trying to buy time for me to change my mind and choose not to put my grief and anger above the only opportunity I had to bury my child.

We might've owned the same black skirt, but we weren't the same people. She didn't understand. No one understood. Why sit on my laurels and cry when there's a killer to find? And I wanted to find that killer. I was sure of it. First, I had to push down and eradicate the grief. It was a pesky thing, standing in the way of my fury being top dog in my heart.

It really was a good thing I had that extra bottle of pills. One way or another, I was going to stuff down the grief.

FOUR

Before and After

Eddie and I spent the next week hiding in our house. Even though we were technically within the same four walls, we only saw one another in passing. He made the couch in the den his new best friend, and I repetitively took a ride on the tranquilizer train in the master suite.

It was the eighth day after Corinne's funeral, and I only knew that because I had run out of Valium. Without its effects—the constant lull and seductive whispers enticing me to lay my head down on a pillow, the floor, or even a countertop—coffee seemed like a good idea. Thus, I stood in my kitchen, leaning against the granite-top center island, and wondered what in the world I had subsided off of over the last two weeks. I didn't remember even being in that kitchen since before . . . since before . . . Oh, God, would it always be like that? The time before and the misery after?

I put my hand over my stomach, feeling around to my ribs. Bony. Very bony. I guess I hadn't been eating much at all. I tottered over to the countertop next to the sink, where our stainless steel coffee machine rested. Coffee brewing was part of a long-standing joke in the house—at least it was before. I was the big coffee drinker of the two of us, but only Eddie knew how to operate the Cuisinart.

He had been dutifully brewing my morning coffee for years. I'm not entirely sure how the routine started, except I was extremely thankful for his assumption of the chore at the beginning of our marriage, in a way only a new bride could be. Then, over the span of time, I lost either the interest or the knowledge to make a cup of coffee as fine as the sort Eddie could whip up, and thus, didn't bother.

He put up a fuss one morning, years ago, and that's how the index cards inside the cupboard came to be. He thought he was being terribly clever when he taped a three-by-five card labeled "Coffee Making Instructions" on the inside of the very cupboard I used to store my mugs. The idea was that by seeing it every day, I'd eventually get the inkling to make my own pot of coffee. Instead, I tore the card down.

That's when the game started, our own little inside joke. He put up another card, and I'd tear it down. The more often he had to make a new card, the simpler he left the instructions—only specifying the last steps of the process because he conceded to "start me off." Of course, I viewed truncating the instructions a landslide of a win, with total victory imminent, but I always underestimated how long my husband could hang from a cliff with only one finger gripping to the ledge.

I opened the cupboard above the coffee machine that morning, that eighth day after the funeral, and saw his shortest "Coffee Making Instructions" yet. It had been up for almost half the year because I didn't have the heart to rip this one down. It was, after all, his last finger on the ledge.

The card read: "Push Button."

On any other day before, when Eddie prepped the grinds and filled the water to the requisite level, perhaps that's all it would've taken. But not today. Not after.

I was fumbling with a coffee filter, trying to align it so it wouldn't fold over when I closed the basket, when I heard a slow, drawn-out dragging noise down the hallway. Eddie. What in the world was he dragging?

My eyes stayed on the entrance of the kitchen to see what he was bringing down the hall, but when he appeared, all he had with him was a pair of vacant, tired eyes, decorated with purple rims. Then I looked at his feet. Just socks. It sounded like he had been dragging cinder blocks, but they were only socks.

He rubbed his eyes when he saw me, and then looked harder, seemingly unsure that I was actually in front of him.

"Evelyn?" he asked.

"Hi, Eddie."

"Are you making coffee?"

I turned to the Cuisinart. "Yes," I said with my back facing him. "I even tried to 'push the button,' but it only hissed at me."

I thought I heard a small chuckle come from him, but I didn't want to turn around to make sure.

"Do you want some coffee?" I asked him.

"No. Just some milk."

I looked at him again. He yawned, swaying back and forth slightly as he did so.

"Are you sure you don't want something with a bit more of a pick-me-up?" I asked. "You look tired."

He sighed and shook his head. "I am tired. I haven't been sleeping." He stepped further into the kitchen where daylight was beaming through a nearby window. When he passed through the brightness to get to the refrigerator, the beaming light made his darkened eyes look more severe, more disastrous, than they looked in the shadows.

"What are you doing, then, if you're not sleeping?" I asked. "I know you're in the den all the time. What else is there to do in there besides watch TV and sleep?"

He chuckled sarcastically. "When you say 'all the time,' do you mean the few minutes in a twenty-four hour period that you're conscious?"

"Oh, that's nice," I said.

"I'm sorry," he said, but I was no longer facing him and couldn't tell whether the expression indicated if he meant it or not. "I'm just really tired," he continued. "I wish I *could* sleep, but I can't."

"I was going to call the doctor again today and get another prescription. You want some?" I asked.

"No!" he snapped, having grabbed the carton of milk, setting it down on the center island. I turned to him, glaring.

He took a deep breath in, and then said, "I'm sorry. No, thank you. I don't want to go down that route. I think it's better if I feel this. I need to feel this. Sleep . . . well, I'm hoping that will come eventually."

"And if it doesn't?"

"Then it doesn't," he said matter-of-factly.

"Do you think less of me because I use pills to sleep?" I asked as he filled up a glass with milk.

"Honestly?" he asked.

My fists balled. "No, not honestly," I hissed, then turned away from him. "Just go away, Eddie. Go back to your little hole."

I soon expected to hear the heaviness of his dragging gait again, making its way back to the den, but there was nothing. He hadn't left the kitchen yet.

"Look," he said, "I want to block all this out too, but I know I shouldn't."

"And I shouldn't either, right?"

"Evelyn, have you seen your office?" he asked. He was talking about my home office—a five hundred square foot separated structure, across from the pool in the back.

"Why? What's wrong with it?"

"You don't know what's wrong with your office right now?"

"I haven't been in my office since . . ." My eyes wandered, my tongue wanting to utter that I hadn't been in there since before the funeral, but something made me think it had been much more recent than that.

"Last night?" he finished for me. "You've been in there every night this week."

I shook my head. He was wrong. He had to be.

"See? That's part of your fog that I want nothing to do with," he said. "So, thanks, but no thanks on the Valium offer." He yawned, looked down the quiet, empty hallway, and went back to the den.

When I heard the door close, I hurried out to my office to see what Eddie meant. I found the office door unlocked. That was highly unusual for me. I couldn't ever remember leaving it unlocked for the night.

Pushing the door back slowly, my first assessment was that the shambles within the room explained why the door had been unlocked. Someone had broken in and trashed the place.

I did a quick scan to see what was missing, but everything was still there, most of it hidden under papers thrown about, but still in top condition. I stepped carefully and lightly over the cacophony of disorder—two chairs had been toppled, the wastebasket thrown aside, paperclips everywhere, unused file folders ripped and scattered, and the sheer volumes of paper crumbled and tossed would likely make someone at the Nature Conservancy cry into a recycled tissue.

"Like I really need this right now," I muttered to myself, making my way to the phone so I could call the police and report the break-in.

"Nine-one-one—What's your emergency?" a stoic, bored voice asked from the other end of the call.

"Someone broke—" I started, only silencing myself when I saw what was hanging over my desk, something I hadn't noticed until just then.

"Sorry," I said to the operator. "I've made a mistake." I hung up the phone and left my mouth agape. I guess I had been in my office recently. And, Eddie was right, I had been in there a lot. In front of me was a map of the city, littered with big, red Xs over the canvas, and a nice little motto on top, in my handwriting, of course. *He's out there. Find him. Kill HIM!*

It all came back to me. I had thought they were only dreams, dreams where I was solving Corinne's murder and hunting down her killer. Now I saw the reality. That map was a masterpiece of my mayhem, a Valium induced frenzy where I had put red Xs over a number of spots in the map that coordinated to a file on my desk that read: Xs—names and addresses. Skimming through quickly, I realized I had also been a frequent visitor of the Megan's Law website of late, printing off the web pages of every sex offender in a twenty-mile radius.

A knock rang out against the opened door. I spun around quickly, gasping in panic. But when I saw Eddie standing there, slumped over and looking like a ghost who should keep to the shadows, I relaxed.

"You scared me," I said, trying to block the map as much as possible with my head.

"Sorry. I figured you'd come out here, and I wanted to see your reaction."

"Reaction to what?" I asked.

He guffawed, pointing at the paper-strewn area. "This. Your reaction to what the Valium did to you. I mean, Evelyn, you've been in here every night trying to track down all these pedophiles. And God only knows what you're planning to do with them. Have you taken a good look at that map? Look what you wrote on the top."

He was referring to the motto. Kill HIM!

"Yeah," I admitted, feeling a sense of failure.

"So, are you still going to call the doctor and get another prescription?"

I pulled out my desk chair and sat down. "No. You're right. This is all out of control. If I hadn't been on the Valium, I think I would've found the right guy by now instead of only getting as far as a bunch of targets on a map."

His brow furrowed, and his jaw clenched.

I was aware that it wasn't the realization he had wanted me to come to, but I was glad to have come to an epiphany, regardless. I said to him, "Admittedly, this production is far below my typical work standards. No wonder there's paper everywhere. I must've been spinning myself in circles thanks to that fog you were talking about in the kitchen."

"That's not what I meant," he said, shaking his head.

"I'd ask you to help me regroup and organize, but I doubt you'll oblige," I said. I turned my back on him, looking square at that beautiful map. "And if you won't help, then go back inside. I don't need your lectures."

"This isn't your responsibility, Evelyn. You can't go after her killer. *Vengeance is mine, says the Lord.*"

"Don't quote Scripture to me, Eddie, or I'll start with all the ones that'll tell you to dry your eyes. Despondency doesn't suit you. It doesn't suit anyone."

"How would you know? Have you even cried for her?" he demanded.

I grabbed the stapler next to my right hand, spun around in the chair, and chucked it near Eddie's head. He ducked as it dented a chunk out of the wall.

Right after the stapler bounced on the floor, I found Eddie looking at me as if I were a stranger, an invader occupying his wife. "I don't know what to do with you, Evelyn," he said. "You're out of control. I don't see how this behavior is going to work out for you, so I'm not sure I can stand by and watch any of this play out. So, like you suggested, I'm going to go back and hide in my hole."

He closed the door on his way out. That's when I noticed something small and black on the floor, previously hidden by the open door. I stood, walked over to it, and bent down to inspect. It was a small revolver. Eddie had insisted we buy it a few years back, after our neighborhood had been a target of some burglaries. I must've brought it into the office from the master closet sometime in the last week.

I smiled. "You might not get to see it, Eddie, but you are helping."

FIVE

Withholding

The line between bestowing fake confidence in someone and then covertly verifying they didn't mess things up is a tough one to walk. Then again, I had sacrificed plenty of manners since Corinne died, so when it came to dealing with the two detectives assigned to Corinne's case . . . what line?

Detectives Pete Shaw and Brian Thatcher posed as a veritable cop comedy—if I had been in any mood to laugh. Pete Shaw, a glum forty-six-year-old, married man with indelibly furrowed brows, partnered with Brian Thatcher, a twenty-nine-year-old who typically kept his right hand on top of his holstered gun and probably signed up for the force because he thought it was a *muy, muy* macho thing to do.

Detective Shaw asked me to call him Pete, and Detective Thatcher said that his friends just called him Thatcher. Either way, I didn't trust them. With Thatcher, it was because he was six years my junior, and with Pete, it was because he acted as if he trusted me less than I trusted him.

With both the Valium and, I hoped, crippling grief behind me, it was time to shift gears and dump everything I was capable of into solving Corinne's murder. My firm had given me a month off, two weeks of which had already expired. That gave me two more weeks to put a fire under the detectives and make them work for the justice I already wanted to taste. That's why I made an impromptu visit to the police station.

"These things take time," Pete said to me as I sat off to the side of his desk. Thatcher's desk was a few feet from Pete's left. He was close enough to hear our conversation but still far enough to pretend to ignore us.

"I know certain things take time," I said. "It's called life. Life at the Department of Motor Vehicles or the doctor's office, but in a homicide investigation, it's not the time to say, 'ho-hum, we'll wait and see what happens.'"

"We're not ho-humming, Mrs. Barrett," he said, leaning back in his brown desk chair as it creaked and groaned under his weight. "We're carefully going over everything we have before we move on to the next step."

"To me, that's ho-humming. If you don't pick up the pace, then you're nothing but a bunch of wild Indians running circles around the scalped and dead. Now is the time to gather your ponies, move on to the next wagon, and set that one aflame."

Thatcher, who still pretended he wasn't listening, shook his head in protest and gave a small chuckle.

Pete shot him a disapproving look, but it was wasted. Thatcher had already gone back to playing Texas Hold'em on his computer. His screen was angled just enough for me to see the game.

Pete lifted up a small pile of folders on his desk and pulled a yellow legal pad from the bottom.

"I know one surefire way to speed things up, Mrs. Barrett. You can answer some questions for me. I've called your home, and your cell phone, and your husband's cell phone multiple times, without any answer or return call, except one time from your husband."

Eddie had talked to the police? That was news to me.

"But, I understand how tough a time this is for you two," Pete continued. "Not only do I have the displeasure of seeing several families a year go through similar losses, I've got three kids of my own. I'll be the last person to judge a grieving parent, even if they do compare me to a scalping Indian."

Thatcher looked at me for that one and smiled.

Yeah, soak it up, chucklehead.

"So, Mrs. Barrett," Pete started, "let's create an extensive list of every adult, both male and female, who had any contact with Corinne. We can start with strangers in passing and work our way up to close relatives, or we can start with the relatives."

"Relatives?" I asked. "You mean like Eddie and me?"

He shook his head, sitting forward in his chair and crossing his arms over his desk. "Originally, we had to treat the two of you as suspects, but we've since cleared you."

"Yay," I mocked.

He ignored my sarcasm. "But, as far as other family members go, we still need to dig into each of them."

"You mean my family, right? Because Eddie's practically an orphan.

He only has his mother, and she's hooked up to an oxygen tank in Oklahoma."

"Yes, your family. Then we need to get at everyone else that comes and goes in your life, from friends to pool cleaners to kooky strangers whose eyes lingered a little too long on your daughter."

"If you've already talked to Eddie, didn't he tell you any of this?"

"Um, no. I had called him about something unrelated. Besides, as even you pointed out, it's your family. I also thought that of the two of you—no disrespect to your husband—you're the one who notices more since you get paid a few hundred dollars an hour to pay attention to details. What's the going rate for a highfalutin lawyer like yourself?"

"An arm and a leg, and currently, I'll even accept the offer of your first-born," I told him, sneering.

He laughed, almost unsure if it was the right thing to do. "Well, my firstborn is in college, so she comes with a hefty price tag."

"I'll take a college kid over a buried one."

And that's when the banter died. Especially since I was never speaking lightly anyway.

After we made the list, he wanted me to supplement each name with answers to the following questions: Who seemed to show an unusual interest in Corinne? Who had opportunity to be alone with Corinne? Who hasn't been quite the same since her death? Was there anyone who showed any unusual interest at the funeral, or was someone absent from the funeral who should've been there?

The funeral-related questions threw me off. I didn't want to admit to Pete that I had at least a foot and a half into the realms of la-la land at the time and didn't remember much about the funeral except throwing my mother out and my cowardice in leaving.

"I don't remember," I answered.

"Please, Mrs. Barrett, I'm sure you do."

"I don't."

He leaned back in his chair again. *Creeeak.* The sound implied that the chair was about to break. I tilted my head to see the chair's four-pronged, wheeled base, assuming something was going to snap, and soon.

"Yeah, I know," Pete said, having seen my wandering glance. "It's a piece of junk. But I stopped complaining about this chair after I took a trip over to the county jail. Now those suckers have it bad. I swear, every unsatisfactory piece of office equipment or furniture somehow ends up at county. I knew we were having budget issues, but the mayor has taken the term 'recycling' to a whole new level. Ah, those poor correctional officers get the worst of it. It amazes me that the very men and women responsible for holding our convicted offenders at bay are the ones who constantly get the bottom of the barrel for resources."

"Maybe that's because the state is trying to send a message," I said.

"What message would that be?"

"Stop locking up criminals."

Pete's brows furrowed so tight that the center of his scrunched-up forehead turned white from lack of blood. "What would we do with them, then?"

"Summary executions come to mind," I said. "Like in the old days."

Thatcher was looking at me again, but this time, with great interest.

Pete responded, pointing quickly at Thatcher, "That's right up his alley. I told him, though, to keep his piehole shut about that stuff. He's still learning. Where were we?" he asked. "Oh yes, the funeral."

"Like I told you, I don't remember much. I was sort of in a . . . fog, as my husband likes to say."

"I'm going to need you to remember. I can't help you if you won't help me," he patronized.

"Yeah, we all need something. You want to know what I need? I need time to reverse itself, so I no longer have a dead daughter," I sneered.

He sighed, tore off the page he had been writing on, and pulled a file from the top of his pile in front of him. When he opened the file, I saw the name *Barrett, Corinne* on the tab. My body tensed and froze. Would things about Corinne always be this jarring? I was sure they would be.

Pete put the page of names into the file, closed it back up, and put it back on top of the pile.

"How long before you move my daughter's case to the bottom of the pile?" I asked.

"Hopefully, never. I'd much prefer to solve it quickly than scoot it down the line."

"What's in that file, then, to speed things up?"

"Right now, I have a list of those names you gave me."

"That's it?" My voice rose. "That's all you have? What have you been doing for the last two weeks? And if you tell me that you've been waiting for my cooperation, I'm going to toss that pile of yours on the floor."

"Mrs. Barrett," Pete started, "I'm not going to belittle your pain by getting upset at your outbursts, but you'll have to work on keeping your cool. Do you understand?"

I shut my eyes, squeezing them until it hurt. Breathe in, breathe out. Don't yell, don't knock stuff over, at least not in the police station.

I spoke through my clenched jaw when I said, "Please tell me you have at least *some* lead to finding her killer."

"Mrs. Barrett, I can't discuss potential suspects with you right now."

"Why not? Because you've only started thinking about interrogating someone since I've been here?"

"Hardly," Thatcher piped in. "We've been sitting on a guy of interest, seeing if he messes up."

Pete stood with ferocity. "Let's have a little chat, shall we, Thatcher? Mrs. Barrett, please excuse us for a moment."

Someone of interest? They knew of a guy and hadn't told me? And instead of pursuing him, they're asking me to point fingers at my own circle of friends and family? The anger seeped back in, slowly at first, and then with a hot, scalding coursing through every inch of my body.

Pete was withholding information, and the moment my mind and fury wrapped themselves around that detrimental tidbit, my eyes widened at a great but dumb idea. The file. Corinne's file. It sat there on Pete's desk, alone and unguarded, just as my precious girl had been when someone took her. And that someone's name was in that file. I knew it was.

I looked over to Pete and Thatcher. They were still talking, mainly Pete to Thatcher, and I started to understand the nature of their partnership. It was more of an old guy, young guy mentoring thing, which meant it wasn't a discussion back there, but a lesson. And while lessons took longer, I knew I only had seconds left to decide if my idea was more great than dumb.

Yes, yes it was.

I grabbed Corinne's file and ran out of the station.

My BMW squealed out of the parking lot with Thatcher getting smaller and smaller in my rearview mirror.

I couldn't go home; that's the first place they'd look. The office. My real office. It was downtown, only a few blocks away from the police station, and I could make copies there. But what if they found me while I was doing that? Not only would they get the file back, they'd take the copies too.

Because I was a civil attorney, rather than a criminal one, I wasn't too familiar with the thousands of misdemeanors in the state of California. Still, I was pretty sure I'd done something bad. Oh well. If the future of this murdering pedophile panned out the way I intended, I had to chalk up the current misdemeanor of file-borrowing as a preview for the main act. Still, I couldn't be careless about this. Surely Thatcher had hopped in a patrol car by now and started a pursuit.

That's when I spied the Hall of Records. From going there to get Corinne's birth certificate after she was born, I knew it had a barren underground parking lot. I pulled in and found a spot closest to the door, near the only other cars in the lot to look less conspicuous. First, I'd do a quick review of the file, and then I'd go to my office and sneak in a back door to the firm. Any number of secretaries, clerks, or paralegals would gladly make me copies while I hid in the emergency stairwell.

Opening the file, the first thing I found was the yellow piece of paper Pete had just added. I crumpled it up and tossed it on my floorboard. Why bother these people if the cops already had a guy?

Then I found more yellow sheets from Pete's legal pad, which were full of Pete's notes. This is where it got good. He had summarized various complaints from other parents in Fresno, all documented within the last few months. They all said the same thing: a man who didn't look like he belonged at a park was loitering around, talking to little girls if they got close enough to hear him whisper to them.

Pete didn't have the details of the parents' statements, but at the bottom of one of the pages, a notation held my interest. The notation read: *They were all young and blonde. He asked them if they knew what color their hair was. Of the three that answered the stranger, only one got a plastic butterfly ring from him after the answer. I reinterviewed each little girl to see what separated the one from the others. I asked them all the same question, "What color is your hair?" Two of them told me, "Blonde." The one who got the ring said, "Lellow."*

It felt like a knife twisted into my gut.

Pete had underlined "Lellow" twice and put a circle around it. There was also an arrow pointing to the circled word, and when I followed the line of the arrow to another part of the page, Pete had written the following: *Called the Barrett house. Mr. Barrett answered. He said yes, his daughter pronounced yellow as "lellow." He told me she liked to tell people that she had "lellow" hair like her daddy.*

I didn't know whom I hated more at the moment: Pete for withholding this information from me, or Robert Bailey, the man triggered by lellow hair who had a copy of his driver's license in my daughter's murder file.

SIX

A Bad Feeling

It was 1:30 in the afternoon when I hiked up to the fourth floor of my office building and slowly opened the back door to the law firm of Wagner, Beardsley & Reese, LLP. Or, as we attorneys lovingly called it, Dewey, Cheetum & Howe. Well, at least it was funny to us.

The back door lay juxtaposed between the copy room and the kitchen. It was a hub for the support staff, and that's exactly what I needed—someone to quickly copy the file and then fax them to my home office to avoid confiscation. It had been an hour since I bolted from the station, and I didn't put it past Pete to send out an All Points Bulletin for my detainment.

I saw the copy machine but the only secretary around was Claire, and she was playfully tossing Cole Stratton's hands off from around her waist. If the firm was a frat house, then Cole was the BMOC—Big Man on Campus. He was the senior partners' darling new attorney, even though they had hired him two years earlier. He was charming, charismatic, and had a smile that won the hearts and verdicts of juries. I would've worried about him stealing my hard-earned rights on the big civil cases the firm let me handle, but he only did criminal work, wealth above the law sort of stuff. In that arena, when money bought freedom, his smile came in handy more than I'd care to admit.

I looked farther down the hall to see if anyone else was around. Phones were ringing, voices over intercoms demanding, and keyboards clacking in large measure, but I couldn't *see* anyone other than Cole and Claire. Just my luck. No one was around except the pair playing touch and tickle in the copy room.

"Hey," I whispered out. They both spun around, hands quickly at their sides. When Cole saw that it was me, he stepped away from Claire.

Claire took one look at the expression on Cole's face as he looked at me, huffed, and walked away. It was no secret that Cole had had a crush on me since he started at the firm. He repetitively told me as much, even referring to me as his cougar, though I was only four years older. I reminded him that I was married, but he was a man infinitely assured of his appeal to the opposite sex. He repetitively told me that too.

He liked to say, "It's almost impossible to stay married these days, so I'm just biding my time, setting up the foundation with you."

Oh, the irony of it.

"Evelyn, hi. How are you?" He cocked his head gently to the left, looking at me with softness and concern. "You poor, beautiful thing," he said. "How are you holding up? Can I take you out for a late lunch, hold your hand, give you a shoulder to cry on?"

I motioned for him to come closer. He stepped inside the stairwell with me and quietly shut the door behind him. "So, that's a yes?" he asked.

Ugh. "No, Cole, I need some help."

He opened his arms and wrapped them around my shoulders. "Oh, I feel so bad for you. Such a tragic loss."

I wriggled out of the hug and held him at arm's length with my hand pressed against the flat of his Italian silk tie until I knew he wouldn't advance again.

"I was at the funeral you know?" he said.

"No, I didn't know. I was . . . well, I suppose if you were there, then you know how I was."

"Don't worry about it. I've seen you do worse to a witness on cross-examination. Anyway, what's up? I thought you weren't coming back for another few weeks."

There were two ways to answer his question: the short version or details. "Do me a favor? Stick this pile of papers into the top feeder of the copy machine and make copies of them."

"You came down here to make copies?" he asked. "Why don't you make copies at your house?"

"Because I'm already downtown. Please, Cole. I need you."

My poor choice of words brought a smile upon his face. "That's what I thought. You came down here for me to console you. And don't think I didn't want to do that at the funeral. Your husband seemed a bit detached and—"

"Cole." If I hadn't been hiding in a stairwell, my frustration would have been voiced louder than a forced whisper. "This is not the time for your tramp-ridden ways. There are many, many reasons why you shouldn't flirt with me right now, so can you please just make the copies?"

"Is it because I was playing with Claire? She's nothing more than a less sophisticated version of you, a wilting flower compared to—"

I squished his cheeks together with my right hand, squeezing them until his lips puckered and he stopped talking. "The main reason that comes to mind, *Cole*, is I've recently lost my daughter. So, please stop flirting with me and make the copies."

He pulled my hand off his face and stretched his cheeks by making circular motions with his lower jaw. "Fine," he said.

He left me in the stairwell for a minute, but then came back to ask, "Do I push the purple button or the green one?"

"The green one, I think. Oh, I don't know. Go get Claire."

I wasn't surprised to find a police car parked on my street when I arrived back home. The afternoon was still burning bright, the kind of day where a shadow would have trouble hiding, when a small, twitchy officer swimming under the weight of his gun belt got out of his patrol car and demanded I hand over the file. When I did, he told me either I could wait inside for Detective Shaw to come over and speak with me or he'd have to handcuff me and take me down to the police station.

I remembered the coursing feeling of power that had come over me when I had held Cole's bunched cheeks in my hand. This officer couldn't have taken me if he tried. I was feeling stronger and stronger each day. Hate and anger will do that to you, I guess. Thus, I had to make them my closest companions, achieving more strength, more toughness. It was the only thing that kept the sadness stuffed way down into the form of a fuzzy memory.

Still, I chose to wait for Pete.

"Let's cut to the chase," Pete said after he stormed into my house. "You don't trust us to handle your daughter's case, and I can no longer trust you to act like a mature adult. I can have another team take over the file, but before you decide whether you want that or not, you should know that I head up the Crimes Against Children Unit for a reason."

"I still can't believe you stole a police file," Eddie whined in the background, pacing back and forth in front of our large living room window. The sun was beating through it, silhouetting his hunched form.

"It's not just a police file, Eddie. It's our daughter's file and I deserve to know what's in it."

"That's a distinction you won't hear me make," Pete said. "You took *my* file, and you most assuredly should *not* have."

"All right, Pete, you want to cut to the chase, then let's do that. Robert Bailey. He killed Corinne and you know it."

Eddie's head spun, seemingly waking up for the first time, and walked over to the couch I was sitting on to stand next to me.

"And have you arrested him?" I asked. "No. He's out there right now, probably lining up his next victim. Someone else's daughter, Pete. You and that Thatcher. You're incompetent fools! How dare you come after me when you're letting a killer run loose."

"You know who killed Corinne?" Eddie asked, pain trembling in his voice.

"No," Pete answered. "Both of you need to settle down, *right now*. First of all, Thatcher had no business telling you we had a person of interest because what happens afterward is this type of panic. I'm going to stress the fact that when Thatcher said 'had,' that was the operative word. *Had.* Robert Bailey has bothered a few little girls of late, but that's all. And, since the description of those little girls matched your daughter's description, we put him at the top of our hit list. However, we cleared him quickly because he has an airtight alibi for the time surrounding your daughter's abduction. He was at work, with video footage and time cards to prove it. But just to ease your fear, we've been keeping him under surveillance anyway, because something about him doesn't sit right with me when it comes to him. Not as it relates to your daughter, however."

"Yet he's still roaming the streets. What if he used someone else to take her while he lined up the perfect alibi? And later, the accomplice hands over Corinne and it's Bailey who rapes and murders her?"

Pete stared blankly at me, either trying to find a rebuttal or because he had already given up trying to explain his reasoning to me.

"You should arrest him," I demanded.

"For what? For giving me a bad feeling? I already told you that we're watching him. That's enough for now. In fact, it's not enough *right* now because I pulled the men watching him to help find you because you stole a stupid file."

"It's not a stupid file!" I shrieked. "It's my daughter's file."

"Fine. That's enough," he said. "We're done here. I'm not going to cite you for anything because like I told you earlier, I try my best not to fault grieving parents. But you are crossing the line, Mrs. Barrett. Keep it up, and I'll make sure the only way you get to step foot into our station is with an armed escort. And you," he said, pointing to Eddie, "keep some control over your wife."

"I can't," he muttered.

"Can't or won't? Man up, Mr. Barrett. Man up. In my experience, a wife only frazzles when the husband cuts the cord that binds them together."

Pete's cell phone rang. He looked down at the caller ID. "Excuse me," he said before he turned his back on us. All we could hear were the strained questions Pete asked in response to the person on the other side.

"What? Where? How long has she been gone? Is she a bl—" He turned to look at me. My eyes recognized the fear in his. With that one look, I knew what had happened. When children suffer, it's the worst time to be right. He turned his back on us again and continued, bluntly, "The color?"

He sighed when he heard the response. He ended the call and said, "I have to go. You'll be hearing from me shortly."

"Another girl with *lellow* hair is missing, isn't she?"

He walked out the front door, leaving me without an answer.

SEVEN

Finger Pointing

I watched that evening's news with anticipation, to clue me into what Pete's phone call had been about, but all I saw was typical Fresno stuff: it was hot and smoggy, some punks vandalized a building, and there had been a fatal car crash thanks to teen drinking. Whatever the call to Pete had been about, either it wasn't newsworthy, or the police had done a good job at suppressing it. When I watched the news again in the morning, I realized it had been the latter. Another young girl's body had been found.

She too had been violated. And, I was right, she too had *lellow* hair.

By the time I arrived at the police station for the second day in a row, there were civilians and reporters thronging against the reception desk where a disgruntled officer barked out, "Stand back! Stand back!"

He was an old, sour-looking bean who looked like he was due for a retirement party last year. "You think *I* woke up this morning wanting this to happen?" he snapped.

You and me both, buddy. You and me both.

A particular heat slammed into me the moment I stepped through the door, but it wasn't merely rising body temperatures and tempers, it was the fiery dance of everyone's frenzy. Men and women clamored against each other, filling the station's foyer with anger, fear, and of course, ever-loving panic.

But, no civilian could aggravate the officer the way the reporters could. And they did. They shoved their handheld recording devices into the officer's face, a sea of tiny red indicator lights all saying at once, "Yeah, we're on."

The reporters shouted out their questions, even over the head of the officer up front, hoping to make eye contact with anyone who'd give them the time of day.

"Do we have a serial killer on our hands?"

"Do the parents of young girls need to be warned to keep their daughters at home?"

"Do you have any suspects?"

No question received an answer. Just another round of, "Stand back," and an occasional, "Shut your yackers for a minute." Yeah, he definitely was a sour bean.

I pushed my way to the front. The civilians gave way, but the reporters wouldn't have moved if I had drawn blood, even their own. Still, I had more of an interest in getting answers than they did, so I pushed and shoved until I found myself at a stalemate of flesh, bone, and press badges. I realized I'd have to pull another card out of my crazy hat to make my way through. I had seen the benefits of how a loss of decorum got me what I wanted, and I wasn't about to stop now.

But what would it take this time?

One of the reporters repeated a question from earlier. "Do you have any suspects?"

That was it. That was the card to pull from the hat. "Yes, they do!" I hollered above the pulse vibrating around me. A swish in the air hissed around the crowd as the heels of patent leather shoes spun toward me, the handheld devices too.

Why, hello little red lights. Are you ready to catch this?

"They have a suspect, and they've *had* a suspect, but did nothing about it," I said.

A loud roar followed, a frightening thing, even for me. The reporters wanted more, more, more. So much so, that I couldn't differentiate one question from another until one Amazonian redhead pressed herself against me, the front of her thigh glued to my hip. She spoke, shouted really, into my ear.

"Who are you and what do you know about the murder?"

I grabbed her recorder out of her hand and put it to my mouth. "I'm the mother of Corinne Barrett, the first little girl murdered by the very man the police allow to roam free and kill again."

Quiet descended. In their sudden hush of horror, the floor seemed to bend inward to me where I stood, making me a precarious bull's-eye. A few let their mouths drop open in stupor, while the others, including the redhead, bore twinkles in their eyes as the full weight of what I'd said cuddled up by the warm fire of their journalistic dreams.

The redhead pushed closer against me, "Who?" she asked. "Who is this man you're referring to?"

I scanned their eager expressions; anticipation spread on their faces like a July brush fire, my lips ready to form the name Robert Bailey, but I stopped. If I did it, wouldn't it be like giving away the last cookie in the cookie jar? I wanted Robert Bailey. Isn't that what I had been planning for over the last week? If I gave the name, then any Joe could take care of Bailey for me. No, this was my cookie.

I looked over at the reception desk to find the officer, but he was gone. Likely to get help. It was time to make my case, and quickly at that.

I opened my mouth, to string them along, when I heard, "Whoa, whoa, whoa!"

A husky voice interrupted me. A couple of cameramen blocked my view to see who it was, but I knew the voice. It was Pete's.

"Move. Move now!" the voice boomed at everyone blocking him. "Let me through to Mrs. Barrett," he said.

The sight of Pete busting through the reporters made me feel nervous in a red-handed sort of way. I had to shake the feeling. Pete would see my guilt and capitalize on it. I imagined redhead would too.

Pete took a hold of my elbow, leaned into me, and said, "Back to my desk. Now," he growled, slightly baring his teeth. He pulled me along about a foot when he stopped, grabbed the handheld recorder I still held from redhead, and threw it back at the crowd of reporters.

He forced me into the visitor's chair at his desk but hadn't let go of my elbow. Instead, he watched the foyer where the reporters continued to shout out at us and stretch their recording devices in our direction.

He tried to pull me by the elbow again, to get me out of the chair, and move somewhere else. It was my turn to bare *my* teeth. I was brimming with the conviction that my bite was plenty more painful than his was. I turned to him and said, "Get your hands off me."

He scoffed and then let go.

"You can ask me to move," I added, "but don't you dare manhandle me."

He squinted in anger, then looked back at the frenzy up front. "Let's go," he said. "You first. Down that hallway and go through the first door on the left." He pointed off to the side.

"Let's discuss your theatrics back in one of the interrogation rooms," Pete said from behind me as I walked forward. "Just you and me, Mrs. Barrett. We'll have some privacy in there."

"I want Eddie here," I said.

"I bet you do. But right now, my beef isn't with him. It's with you."

Pete led me to a closet of a room. Its only design theme was to see how many different shades of green an 8 x 8 room could sport. Some leprechaun-loving person must have had a field day with the floor, the walls, the chairs, and even the reflective glass. There was a small rectangular table pushed into a corner, a camera in the corner facing the table, and just enough open space for some dramatic pacing.

Fatigue overcame me as I sat down. How long would I be in here? Was this the end of my game? Would Pete throw me into jail, or worse yet, an insane asylum? Truthfully, I think Eddie would be the party responsible for the asylum. Pete sat and sighed, burying his face in his hands, elbows propped up on the table.

"I thought I was a patient man," he said. "But you . . . you push me to new limits." He dropped his hands and placed them on top of the table. "You know all those stereotypes they have about lawyers never knowing when to quit, never knowing when to stop before they cross the line?"

I rolled my eyes.

"You make them so miserably true," he added.

"And let me guess," I said. "You're overweight because of donuts."

He leaned back in his chair and patted his belly. "No. Pedro's Tacos."

I stifled a smile. I didn't want to lose my severity on the moment.

"Why don't you lay out for me all your gripes, right here, right now, so I can address them. Because I assure you, we haven't done anything wrong to you for you to come in and mess up someone else's investigation."

"Oh yeah, you haven't wronged me, only the other little girl who's dead as of this morning."

"I know you think that has something to do with your daughter, but it doesn't."

"How doesn't it?" I demanded. "Even the news report this morning said her body was found at the back of the hospital, just like Corinne's."

Pete sighed again and leaned forward. "I'm walking a fine line here with you. On the one hand, I don't owe you a single piece of information on this new homicide because it doesn't involve you. I could even be in some serious trouble if I tell you anything. On the other hand, you're a time bomb these days. If I don't provide you with reasons why I think Robert Bailey didn't kill your daughter, you're likely to go around breaking more laws. And, since everything points to the pattern that you're escalating in your crazed desperation, who knows what lies ahead?"

I knew. But I was right to keep that to myself.

"Because of Robert Bailey's time cards and alibi," Pete started, "we didn't think he abducted and killed your daughter. Yes, the blonde hair and the age similarities were telling, but the man has an airtight alibi. Also, at the time, Robert Bailey hadn't touched any of the little girls whose parents filed reports. A guy can be as freaky and creepy as he wants, but if there's no touchy-touchy, our hands are tied. Now, here's that line you're making me walk: Robert Bailey might have had something to do with this new murder, and if he did, it works against your theory that he killed your daughter."

"How do you figure?"

"Because the guy who killed this new victim did leave the body at the same place where your daughter was left, but he didn't do it anything like the other drop-off. This is a psychological aspect of crime solving, of course, but we rely heavily on it. Many details of finding your daughter were suppressed in the media. One of the reasons we do that is to prevent copycats. And, we think this new offender was trying to be a copycat. He picked the right location to leave the body, but without going into specifics with you, the two *different* men who have recently used the hospital as a drop point, have two different styles.

"You'll be happy to know, if such a thing can exist in these circumstances, that your daughter was treated with much more delicacy than the monster who killed the other girl."

I lifted my face to the ceiling, trying to hide the welling up of my eyes. It was an ugly world. An ugly, monstrous world.

When I took a hold of my weakness, taking a small, measured breath in and out, I asked Pete, "How do you know that it's not the same guy who's simply escalated?"

"The department pays a lot of smart people on staff—psychologists, criminologists, you name it—to decipher these things. They can be wrong, but most of the time, they're not. They've seen both crime scenes and they've told me that even if someone wanted to assume it was the same guy, and even accounting for escalating circumstances, there are still too many differences for them to conclude anything other than we have two separate murderers on our hands."

"And you think Robert Bailey might be a suspect for the new girl but not for my daughter? Didn't you tell me yesterday that you were keep-ing an eye on him? If it was him, how did he manage to get a little girl yesterday?"

"Well, now, I don't know any other way to put this without attribut-ing blame, but sometimes, I've got to call it as I see it. The only time we haven't been watching Bailey this last week was when I had seven patrol cars—including an unmarked that was stationed near Bailey's house downtown—canvassing the area for you after your file-grabbing stunt."

A lump bobbed in my throat. It was warm, suffocating, and I could've sworn it had thorns. As best I could, I swallowed it down.

"Are you saying it's my fault that little girl is dead?"

"No. I'm saying that it's your fault we had to pull the car from Bailey's neighborhood."

"I didn't ask you to make that decision!" I stood, yelling at him. "What real danger did I pose by taking the file? It's information you should have shared with me, anyway."

"All the same," he said. "When a car got back to Bailey's place, the only thing they saw was Bailey coming back home at night. He slipped out for something when no one was around to tail him. What did he do when he left? He says one thing, but he might've gone after that little girl. Either way, I doubt he could've used the restroom yesterday without us knowing it if not for having to pull that unmarked on account of you."

The room closed in on me, and there was hardly any breathing room to begin with. I looked up at the camera in the corner, doubting it was on, or even that there was someone viewing this on the other side of the glass. This was between Pete and me—two people pointing fingers at one another because they both felt the blood on their hands. And for what? A murdering, abusing demon? For what *he* did to two small children?

"How dare you pin this on me," I said, my lips quivering, giving away the lack of my resolve. "I didn't kill that girl. It's not my sick, twisted mind that ended her life and did God knows what to her before she died. And what kind of monster are you, suggesting that a mother who just lost her own daughter to a pedophile has anything to do with it happening to another girl?"

The first sting of a tear ran down my left cheek. I quickly wiped it away. It wasn't from grief; it was from raw anger muddled with guilt. I relayed one opinion to Pete, but deep inside I knew I shouldn't have made the police's job harder protecting other children because of my trust issues.

Pete was looking away from me, squeezing his hands together, and then wringing them.

"If you're here wasting time with me," I started, sincere, "who's with the new girl's parents right now?"

"Thatcher."

"He's not good at the things that come right after when parents realize their child is dead. He's too blunt. It sucks."

Pete chuckled once. "Sorry. You're right. That was a mistake on my part, sending him in to you. I typically do the first interview, and Thatcher sort of keeps them on the burners, if you will, until they're ready. Last I checked in on them after I put them in the chief's office, they're not ready. You know how it is for them right now."

I nodded. Then I bit on my lower lip and fought back tears. "Sedation. Now is the time for sedation."

"Well, not everyone needs—"

"No, Pete. Don't. Let me have that one."

He stood and went to the door, opening it. "Are you going to behave? Can I let you go back to your house while we try to juggle both of these cases and *solve* them?"

"Are you going to arrest Robert Bailey?" I asked.

"If the evidence lines up."

"If the evidence—" I huffed at his response. "What more do you need? Another dead girl?"

"No, I was thinking along the lines of DNA or a connection between the victim and Bailey."

"What about the sample you got off Corinne? Doesn't it match Bailey?"

"I don't have Bailey's DNA. We tried to match it with the DNA in the system and got nothing. We don't have anyone else to match it to yet."

I huffed again, clenching my fists.

"If you can, Mrs. Barrett, have a good day. I need to get going."

I left the station even more convinced that Bailey killed Corinne. He likely used an accomplice to abduct Corinne, but with the new victim, he was solo and unhinged. That's why he was more brutal to her. *More* brutal. Ha. Corinne still suffered. I almost felt the demons taunting me with the images and fear at night, poking at me to fight back or go crazy.

And Eddie had thought the Valium put me in a fog. The Valium had nothing on the haze that came with a reality where sin incarnate stole my only child away.

I didn't know why Pete hadn't locked up Bailey before he struck again, but it was clear Pete felt guilty about it. That's why he blamed me. And yes, I deserved some of the blame. *Some.* But, I had garnered valuable information from my little stunt. I had a copy of Robert Bailey's driver's license. I knew his face and I knew where he lived. It'd be a shame if getting that information contributed to the latest victim, but then I did nothing with it to right the wrong.

I could argue more with Pete to go after Bailey, maybe even poke at Thatcher a bit. I could, but I wouldn't.

Now was not the time to argue. Now was the time to shut up and plot.

EIGHT

The One-Eyed Bird

After I left the station, I went home and realized Eddie was gone. His car was still in the garage, but he was nowhere around. Then, at a quarter to six in the evening, a car pulled up to the house and dropped Eddie off.

"Where have you been?" I asked.

"Work."

"You've gone back to work? Why?"

"I need the distraction, I guess."

He hung his utility belt on a hook inside the hall closet and then sauntered to the couch, falling and sinking into its depth. He laid his head back on the top of the couch, with his eyes closed and mouth open from what seemed like fatigue. But it was more than that. We both knew it was more than that.

"The den isn't doing it for you anymore?" I asked, sarcasm brimming in my voice.

"Don't pick a fight with me, Evy. It was a rough day."

"That's seems like the exact reason why you shouldn't have gone back."

He popped his head up to look at me but only held my glance for a moment before he looked past me, staring off into the kitchen.

"It's harder to sit here all alone in this house, knowing that you're off pushing someone's buttons or maybe even breaking some law, than it is to deal with work," he said.

"When we are here together, you don't want anything to do with me. Now you're saying because I've been absent for a day or two, you're lonely?"

"That's not exactly what I said, but sure, let's go with that," he said.

He dropped his head back and closed his eyes again. A moment passed before he asked, "Would you mind turning off the lights in here? It's pretty bright."

I had only turned them on ten minutes before he got home.

"You want to sit in darkness?" I asked, remaining in my chair, unwilling to get up.

"Yup. It's soothing."

Soothing was the last thing I would have said about the darkness. The more nights I had to endure and the more darkness I had to tread, the more suffocating it felt. Darkness now represented to me where Corinne lay in the ground and the force of evil responsible for putting her there.

Only because I knew Eddie's eyes were closed, and would stay closed for a while longer, I sneered at him. We didn't see anything the same anymore. Anything. He'd rather take his punches by rolling into the fetal position and minimizing absorption, and I'd rather take them ready to fight dirty with a sock full of pennies swinging from my hand. Then there was to work or not to work—I had been seriously considering the notion of never going back—and now, the preference of darkness over light.

To be fair, I knew Eddie well enough to realize it wasn't a spiritual thing, or lack thereof, creating the draw to sit in a blackened living room. Rather, it was a fear thing. I had it and he didn't. And yes, that bothered me. Of the two of us, why did the one who likes to bring a sock full of coins to a fight have to be the same one who needed a night-light?

I didn't use to be so full of contradictions, and the problem with them was how Eddie had a way of making me see them, even without trying. It was as if he was my personal mirror, under fluorescent lights, no less. I used to love that about him; he made me incredibly self-aware in a beautiful, loving way.

Now, it grated me.

I stood and left the room without turning off any of the lights. Before I disappeared around the hallway corner, he said, "Hey, Evy, I take it you heard about the other little girl who was killed."

"Yeah," I replied, holding on to the wall next to me so I could push off from it and make a quick escape if need be. "What have you heard?" I wanted to know whether he knew Pete blamed me for giving Bailey access to take a child.

"I heard briefly that another girl was dead. That's it. That's all I could handle. The guys at work were cool about not discussing it in front of me. I can only imagine what's going on in your head. So, what I want to know is whether you went ballistic again."

"Define ballistic," I said.

He sat straight up and turned to me. "Did you bother the police, yes or no?"

"Define bother."

He shook his head and sighed. Grumbling, he pushed himself off the couch and made a quick tour of the living room, turning off all the lights. It was still light enough to see his form, thanks to the large living room window still letting in a bit of white light. But the contrast made the living room that much bleaker. Maybe it was the contrast, rather than my mounting disregard, that blurred him into a shadow as he plopped down on the couch again.

"Have you stopped caring about her?" I asked him, the stillness and peace of the air around us trying to teach me by example.

He shook his head in disbelief.

"I promised myself that I wouldn't do this to you, so I hope you won't do it to me," he answered.

"Do what?"

"Equate our different ways of dealing with grief with a lack of love for her or each other."

I looked around the room at the growing absence of light as the day drove itself further into evening and shuddered.

"You have no idea what you're doing to me," I said.

Stepping quickly down the hallway and entering the master bedroom, I flipped light switches left and right, as if it were a veritable sanctuary of illumination likened only to a cathedral at Christmas. Then I closed the door, locked it behind me, and pulled my copy of Robert Bailey's driver's license from the bottom of my bra drawer.

On my way home, I decided I would give the police the rest of the day and evening to arrest Bailey. If they drug their heels any longer, I was going to intervene.

A slew of conversations and arguments swirled in my head, taken from the last week's activities. Round and round they went until they materialized into something my imagination could fly better with—they materialized into a bunch of vultures scavenging for fresh meat. Each scavenger was a different size and had their own name: Anger, Blame, Misery, and then there was the big boy boss. He wore a thick, silver chain around his neck, with the name Vengeance etched in blood upon it. That bird looked tough. He was even missing an eye.

The birds flew and circled, trying to find a nest within any one of the cogs that made up my psyche. I had an agenda building up, and the pieces could only drop into certain places for that agenda to come to fruition.

Shuffle this, shuffle that, keep this, disregard that. Shuffling, shuffling around, and then finally everything found a fit—a workable fit.

The vulture named Misery, with his brooding face, reminded me of Eddie. Get to the back of the pack, bird. Anger and Blame, you're going to be big boy's wingmen. And if you do a bang-up job, then you might get your silver chains too.

Of course, the one-eyed cretin named Vengeance landed right on Robert Bailey's driver's license copy.

Good birdie.

Hours later, creeping into the barest moments of the night, I awoke, seeing all my lights still blazing in the bedroom. A dull ruckus from the den had interrupted my sleep. With the copy of Bailey's license in one hand and a red pen in the other, I sat up in the bed and looked down at the copy. I had used the red pen to draw my vision of Vengeance on the blank area of the page, sporting his chain and eye patch.

The noise echoed again. I left the picture and pen on top of the bed and walked carefully to the door, opening it without a sound. Down the darkened hallway, I saw a wisp of blue light leaking through the bottom of the den door, flickering in rhythm to the sound of overlapping and boisterous chatter.

Eddie must be watching more reruns. Oh well, let him. I went to shut my door again when I heard a loud, singular shriek.

If I had thought I was past being emotionally crippled and falling to my knees in excruciating anguish, I was wrong. My hands braced themselves against the frame of the door to prevent me from buckling over. The shriek sounded again, and I felt a cruel, bony hand rip my heart from my chest. What was left of it, anyway.

I knew that shriek.

It was Corinne's. It was her young and delightful squeal of delight.

But I buried her, I told myself. She's not here. It can't be her.

Suddenly, a loud, clear chorus of *Happy Birthday* rang above the rest of the noise, ending with *Happy fourth birthday, Co-o-o-ori-i-i-inne, Happy birthday to you.*

Too much. Too much pain. I didn't even realize I had been holding my breath.

Eddie had broken out the home videos. It was inevitable, I suppose. I rested my body against the opened door, surprised on two counts: one, the thirst and lust for vengeance seemed to subside when the *real* memory of Corinne was thrown against me, and two, I hadn't been the first one to play back the home movies.

Why hadn't I? I had watched them almost regularly over the last four years, especially near her birthdays. She used to sit by my side to watch with me, asking me a million questions that would answer themselves if she'd simply simmer down and watch long enough.

Yup, that's why, I thought. That's why I hadn't broken them out yet. It would be too painful. I couldn't bear one tiny, little shriek. How could I muster watching the countless hours of her videos when they would remind me not only of the joy behind the recorded moments but also of the joy in watching those recorded moments side by side?

I felt the contents of my stomach sour—and a solitary puddle of coffee from twelve hours earlier sours in the worst sort of way.

I turned my back on the hallway, simply wanting to lie back down in my bed, when I heard my voice coming from the television speakers.

"Where's my baby?" I asked playfully. "Someone tell me where my sweetest baby is."

"Here I am, Mommy."

My eyes filled with tears as my body involuntarily trembled with things not meant for the human heart to bear—all from the utterance of that one phrase, "Here I am, Mommy."

I was no longer a mommy. No amount of loss has ever, or will ever, strike me as viciously as that painful truth. My child was dead. She can't call me mommy anymore.

The video, like the embittered breath of my forsaken life, continued.

"What? No, I can't find you, where are you? All I see is a frosting-covered monster," I had said, teasing her.

She giggled. "No, Mommy, it's me. Here I am."

"No. It's not you."

She giggled again, the type of bouncy laughter where she had to catch her breath at the end, causing another little squeal. "It is me!" she shouted.

"Well, then who covered my baby in chocolate frosting?"

My mind went back to that birthday scene from eight months earlier. I didn't need a video playback to remember that gorgeous and happy scene. She had attacked her cake with fervor, shoving bites into her mouth that were far too big, causing frosting to smear all over her face, even as far up as her cheekbones. It was a big, fat, and utterly precious mess.

"Silly, Mommy, I did it. I put da frosting on my face." Giggle, giggle.

"No way," I replied. "Since when did my princess girl start eating like big ol' messy Daddy?"

"Hey!" Eddie protested on the video.

Both Eddies laughed—the Eddie behind the camera that day, and the Eddie behind the den door that helpless night. However, only one of the Eddies didn't sound strained in their laughter; only one still laughed as if they had a child to laugh with.

The cyst of my life was full of decisions to make. A part of me realized there was a modicum of safety in Eddie's way, of bathing in the fuzzy memories until I reeked of despair. But another part of me realized I functioned better when I was stronger, even if it meant a world of illogical, even unethical, rationalizations and justifications. Which would that birthday girl want? A parent who sat on the couch and cried, or a strong parent who brought her justice?

It was silly to ask questions of her. She wasn't around anymore. In and of itself, however, that seemed to answer the question. Either way, that one-eyed bird was leading the way. Another chain dripped and clinked from his long, fierce talons. That one was for me. The name on it was Avenger.

NINE

Tightening

Robert Bailey's house was a hub of police activity when I arrived the next morning. Well, kudos to you, Pete and Thatcher, you did your job.

I was on his street, parked four houses away and spying from my car. He lived in an older neighborhood, an existence left to rot from the happy bubble of the 1960s where people didn't seem to know they needed to slap on a new coat of paint every fifty years, nor that they had a child killer on their street.

The two white vans parked in front of his house had a blue logo on them, specifying, *Crime Scene Unit*. Far too many hours of my *before* life had evaporated on the sexy version of the crime scene profession depicted on television. I could tell instantly—from the white cargo vans to the navy blue bargain windbreakers the investigators wore—that this was no Hollywood production. This was Fresno. Even the investigators were Fresno. Every few minutes, an investigator would come out to grab an item from the van, or come out to show snapshots from their digital cameras to Pete, who was standing in Bailey's driveway. The investigators I saw were a handful of men, far removed from the beefcake actors on television and probably only cool online with screen names like DNA-STUD and CSIHOTGUY.

Then I saw the female of the bunch. She was on crowd control, and by crowd, I mean reporters. She didn't seem interested in dispersing them, although I was certain that's what Pete had told her to do. Instead, she was working her tight pants and highlighted hair to get the eyes off the house and onto her, perhaps so she could see herself on the evening news. A reporter said something to her and she flipped her long hair over her shoulder, flashing the male reporter a smile.

Then I watched as she propped one of her feet up on her toolbox. I spied a pair of boots on her, the streetwalking kind. I looked through the pair of binoculars I had brought with me to double-check. Sure enough, snakeskin boots with three-inch heels.

Man alive, I thought to myself, was this woman at Corinne's crime scene?

The thought of those boots walking around my daughter's lifeless body, occasionally taking pictures but more interested in press time, made me sick.

I reclined in my seat to take my mind off Ms. Snakeskin Boots. I was glad I parked in the shade of an overgrown pepper tree on the opposite side of the street from Bailey's house, as the day's heat would otherwise bear down, trapping itself in my car. How long would Pete and Thatcher be? All they had to do was throw Bailey on the ground, kick him a few times, and then slap some cuffs on him. Fine, read him some Miranda rights too. I just hoped they wouldn't pass up on the kicks.

But maybe they had already arrested him, shipping him before I had arrived.

Before I knew it, lunchtime arrived and tangled, pushy clouds bore into each other in the sky, daring me to intervene. I didn't. Besides, I knew I wouldn't have to wait much longer because a date with lunch is something a civil servant rarely misses, including each and every civil servant processing Bailey's house.

One by one, all the vehicles, including the two white crime scene units and the media vans, disappeared. Thatcher and Pete eventually came out, sans Bailey. They had to have had arrested him earlier. Yes, they had to have. It was done.

Relief washed over me. At first, it was because the wheels of justice had finally started to move on Corinne's murderer, and I hoped those wheels were a part of an 18-wheeler. Splat, Bailey, splat. Thereafter, as I went to reach for the side of my seat, to return it to its driving position, I was relieved that I no longer needed to do what I had planned on doing.

Bailey was done for, and I didn't have to risk incarceration myself.

My seat hummed and moved with the push of one button, and as my feet came into position to reach the gas pedal, I watched Thatcher turn around to the house, point back, and bark something to whomever was standing inside the open door.

Was he angry with a fellow cop? A crime scene investigator who didn't do their job right? I did a quick scan of the remaining vehicles. No more police cars. If all the cops and investigators were gone, then to whom was Thatcher talking?

A man with thinning hair and a face that belonged on the footsteps of hell came out on the front step, yelled something back at Thatcher, then turned and slammed the door.

Of all the police incompetence. Robert Bailey was still a free man.

Normally, I'm a planner. But since I hadn't planned on losing my child at the hands of a monster like Bailey, I wasn't going to get myself hung up when the time came to freewheel it.

I made the decision to go into Bailey's house. For what purpose, I didn't know. The earlier feeling of being glad I didn't have to confront Bailey had diminished.

A hush fell around the outdated and unkempt neighborhood. The only thing I heard was the pounding and throbbing of my heart. It shook my eardrums, my breathing, and even my mind. It was time. He was all alone. And so was I. This was it.

I held my palms up to cover my ears; my increasing heart rate deafened me, pulsing with vibration after vibration to the center of my ears. I couldn't do this. Seriously, what did I plan on doing? Killing him? No. I couldn't. That was just a theory, an angry, pained theory. It's something everyone says they're going to do, but we're not all animals like Bailey. Are we?

Still, I had to act in some way. Pete and Thatcher had just walked away. They walked away!

What had Pete said they needed from Bailey? DNA. Did they get DNA off Bailey? What if they hadn't? Well then, that's what I could do. I could go in, talk to him, and then grab something of his and stuff it in my purse.

Yeah right, I thought. How would I get inside? Then it hit me. Oh, God, bless Eddie. Bless Eddie and his overprotective ways. I squeezed my upper body through the space between the passenger and driver's seat to reach under the former and grab the survival kit Eddie had put there. I reached as far as I could, trying to avoid letting my head rest on top of Corinne's pink flowered booster that I hadn't yet taken out of my car. I fought back tears then. Everything was a reminder. All the more reason to get that survival kit because inside, there was a bunched blue windbreaker Eddie packed in case I had to wait somewhere in the rain.

But today, it was for entry into Robert Bailey's house. Now I was simply another crime scene investigator, coming back because I had forgotten something. Hopefully, he wouldn't ask to see a badge. If he did, then I would have to rely on my other badge to get me inside, Eddie's gun from the house. I had brought my own survival kit.

After I pulled out the windbreaker, unrolled it, and put it on, I opened my black duffel bag on the passenger seat. In it were a few snacks, water bottles, and the gun.

I held the gun in my uncertain grasp, and then cursed my pounding heart for making me feel so weak.

"Suck it up," I demanded aloud. "This is only for protection. The man's a murderer. It would be stupid not to have protection. You're not going to do anything with it, so suck it up!"

I reached for the door handle, knowing that the real deal was upon me. My eyes closed and I swallowed hard, pulling on the cool, metal handle. When I pushed the door open, I felt something on my left arm just as I had tucked the gun into my windbreaker pocket. My head turned toward the small pressure I felt, but there was nothing there. I sat back for a moment, leaving the door ajar and still feeling something holding on to me.

This wasn't the time for my imagination. Not now. My foot closest to the door swung out and planted on the street. The sensation no longer applied mere pressure at that point, but rather, it tugged me with the faintest of movements, away from the door. When it did that, it gave me a bare recognition of its form—both firm and familiar to me.

A mind in my state of emotional warfare liked to play a variety of freak show acts, but I knew that tug. I had felt it before. Twice actually. Once when I was a child and had almost slipped off a two hundred-foot cliff, the second when I was in law school and nearly plummeted down a metal staircase. In both instances, I was younger, innocent, and more acclimated to the saving graces of God. Thus, I walked away from those scares, both times having felt a tugging against my arm, both times feeling an ethereal hand holding and sparing me, believing an angel had saved me. In the latter occasion during law school, with my growing pessimism of the world around me pushing me toward the cusp of disbelief, I inspected my arm an hour after the almost fall. I found an oval bruise. A fingerprint impression came to mind, but since I *was* on the cusp of disbelief, it was inconvenient to assume anything other than the bruise had been there from before.

Now, that same tightening was back, wrapped around my arm as I readied to leave my car.

Then a voice came, a nudging really.

No, it said.

I wasn't sure if I had uttered the word myself, or if someone else—or something else—was in the car with me. My mind played back the message, *No.*

I looked to Bailey's house again. This was a now or never situation. I wasn't planning on doing anything drastic. I didn't need intervention, if that's what was really happening. The gun was only for protection. I tried to shake the feeling on my arm, telling myself it was only nerves misfiring from the onset of stress. Surely, it wasn't possible that the sacred had broken through the boundaries of heaven to stop me from doing the profane here on earth.

Another nudging broke through to my consciousness: *This isn't the way, and you know it.*

That's when I realized that I was, once again, at the crossroads of convenience. Was it convenient for me to walk away and do nothing? No. Was it convenient for me to do what Eddie wanted and cry until the tears dried up? No. Was it convenient for me to reconcile my faith with my anger? No. Was it convenient to recognize the hold on my arm as something from the divine? No.

When I answered that last question, the tightening suddenly disappeared. Curious. Maybe it wasn't even there to begin with. Must've been a muscle spasm.

I stepped out and walked over to Robert Bailey's house.

A Blip from an Atheist

He who fights with monsters might take care, lest he thereby become a monster." That one is courtesy of Freidrich Nietzsche. Despite the fact that I don't normally trust God-haters who suffer mental breakdowns, I think he got it right with that one.

Enter monster.

Red, the Bad Kind

"What do you want?" a man barked from behind the door. Only seconds earlier, I had seen the white, illuminative dot of the peephole turn black, knowing Bailey now stood in front of it, looking back at me.

The question he had asked marched slowly through my head—What did I want? I couldn't exactly say, "Justice, you mouth-breathing demon," so I thought of something else.

"One of our tools was left behind. I've been sent to retrieve it."

"You've done your invasion of privacy. Just go away," he said.

Play the role until you get inside, I told myself. "I'm afraid I can't. It's an expensive piece of equipment, and if you don't allow me inside to retrieve it, then an officer will have to come down and arrest you for theft." Amongst other things, I wanted to add.

"Unless you have another warrant, I'm not letting you in. Tell me where you left it and I'll get it for you."

Sometimes, many times, it paid to be a clever lawyer. "Afraid I can't let you do that. It really is an expensive piece of equipment, and quite delicate too. You're going to have to let me in to retrieve it. You can do it now, or I can come back with some uniforms. Besides, if you read the warrant carefully, it said we're allowed reentry, if need be, within twelve hours of the initial search."

I didn't actually know what the warrant said. Like I've said, I'm not a criminal attorney.

"I'm calling my lawyer," he said back at me through the door.

"You don't have a lawyer yet," I said, breaking cover for the first time and letting the smart-alecky Evelyn out to play. "No one would be fool enough to take you as a client until you were actually arrested." I couldn't believe I had blurted it out, and when I thought about it, I did know one lawyer who *would* intervene. But, based on the look of Bailey's house, there was no way he could afford Cole. "But you are getting closer to an arrest if you don't open up and let me get my colleague's tool."

The bolt unlocked and the door pulled open. I didn't count on my gag reflex as I, for the first time, stood within two feet of the man who killed my daughter and ruined my family forever. Expecting Cujo and finding only a thirtysomething-year-old man with a brown shirt, faded jeans, unresponsive eyes, and a few days of growth on his face, things blurred for a moment.

I felt my composure dwindle when I thought of those very eyes on Corinne. Don't go there, I reminded myself. It'll only hinder you. I stood in front of him, looking at him as if I were both deaf and dumb, and called upon the reservoir of wild hate I had for this man. It was the only way for me to find strength.

"Don't you usually come with a parade of fools and reporters?" he asked smugly.

"N-not right now," I stuttered. Everything about his presence ensnared me. Those were the eyes . . . the mouth . . . the hands that . . .

"It's just me today. Let me by."

I started to charge at him to get into the house, but he stepped back and out of the way. He left the front door open and it occupied most of the short, narrow hallway where I stood. He stood only four feet away in his kitchen, right off the front door.

"You're pretty brave coming into my house all by yourself," he said.

My eyes narrowed and air hissed inward through my clenched teeth. "Are you threatening me?" I demanded. "How could I be scared of a monster who only likes to feed on little girls?"

He rolled his eyes at me, leaning against his kitchen counter. "Get your fricking equipment and get out of my house. The next time one of you idiots accuse me of something, it better be in front of a judge."

Something let go inside of me. I didn't want to admit what was prompting it, but I knew. It was hate. Hate had taken over. All that backpedaling, the thoughts from earlier that I didn't *really* want to hurt him, sizzled up and ashed away. It was an epiphany really, when I stood there and realized that hatred was an able-bodied entity with hands, feet, purpose, and logic. All it needed was an empty vessel, and I had been making room for weeks now.

I walked backed to the front door, closed it, and locked it.

That's when Bailey laughed at me. He threw his head back, letting his laughter rise to the ceiling and bounce back at me like hundreds of tiny, sharp darts.

When he lowered his head, he said, "You're no cop."

He laughed again. His sarcastic merriment distracted me just long enough that I didn't see the beer bottle in his hand until he had brought it over his head to strike me with it. He was still laughing. The cackling of his voice made it clear to me that he was taunting me, showing me how stupid he thought I was.

Then his eyes fell to my right hand and they sobered quickly. I knew his change of expression had everything to do with the black revolver now in my hand—the one I had pulled out from my windbreaker.

The laughing stopped. Everything stopped. And for a moment in time, two lives met at the disaster of the human condition. That's when I think we both knew that only one of us, if any, would be walking away.

"Who are you?" he sneered.

"Corinne Barrett's mother."

The second I muttered the name, it was as if God hit a pause button on the world, or at least the pause button on the disastrous little world of Bailey's bare, dinky kitchen and hallway. The air was so still that I even heard the scraping of the world below me, dragging across the soles of my shoes.

His eyes moved to the left, as if he was trying to remember something. As if he were going through a mental rolodex of all the children he had likely destroyed.

"Yes," I hissed. "That was her name."

In a rapid succession of movement, he surged at me with the bottle. I didn't even try to block it because I was too busy pulling the trigger.

CRACK!

All I heard was the bottle breaking six inches above my left eye, and thought I had failed.

Hadn't I pulled the trigger in time?

Everything turned black for a moment as the sudden, slicing pain radiated into numbness. Black then gave way to a white, heavenly blur, and I strained to see past what was closing in on me. I saw a brown shirt, faded jeans, stubble . . . oh, there he was, there slouched the monster against the kitchen counter. He was clutching one side of his chest, futilely trying to seal the singed bullet hole and cupping his warmed blood before it all bubbled out to the cheap linoleum below.

I *had* pulled the trigger.

I fought to see more, to take it all in deeper and beyond the fuzziness of my depleting consciousness, but something oozed over my left eye. It was red. Blood. My blood. I blinked, but that made it worse, further welcoming the dark, sticky stuff to seep in from my open wound.

Yes, I wanted to die. As long as my daughter's murderer died with me, I was ready to go. I was already three quarters of the way there after the blow he had given to my head.

My mouth was drying. I knew it was hanging open because every attempt to draw breath in felt like I was swallowing a cotton ball. Every other nerve and muscle in my face went on strike thanks to the head gash. My legs turned to slush, but I absolutely did not want to go down before that filth of a man. Now that I knew he was leaking blood, leaning toward the land of the dead as I was, I wanted to make sure he went down first.

I leaned against the wall closest to me, to hold myself up, trying to last longer. The minute I went down, it would be over for me. But I was sure I could summon a little fight within me as long as I remained on my feet.

His mouth moved; his lips puckered in and out trying to say something. It made him look like a floundering fish plucked from the ocean and left to die on a pier caked with bait and spilled guts. I wondered what he was trying to say, or maybe even ask. Perhaps the question of the day for him would have been a big fat, "Why?"

If he had managed to ask that, I knew how I'd respond: "You want the *Why*? Join the club, you dying carp."

My face dragged down the wall in slow motion. I couldn't feel it; I only heard the squeaking of my bloody cheek slipping down his white wall.

Hold on, I thought to myself. Just a bit more . . . hold on. For all the movement of his mouth, he only uttered a gurgle. Maybe he'd be able to say something. Maybe he'd say *it*. He just might say he's sorry.

Both my eyes closed. I couldn't help it. My head swam with numbness and brutal things that eyes have no business seeing. I knew the entirety of my being was about to crash down on Robert Bailey's floor and I took comfort—a strange, strange comfort—in the fact that my baby had probably been here too. Also limp, also fleeing from the world.

That's when an eerie surge of happiness descended upon me. I thought we would be together soon, my baby and I. We'd be in a place where I could chase her around, following after her bobbing and shining curls, while she led me through the fantasy world of princesses and tea parties. We'd enjoy long days together where I would never be too busy for her, never have to think I let her down, and never, not ever, say good-bye. I wanted it so badly. I wanted to hold her and feel her small little head come to rest against my chest. But most of all, I wanted to tell her I was sorry.

Yes, I wanted to die. As long as Bailey died with me, I wanted to die.

I embraced the longings, ready to go. Then I heard Bailey gurgling again. I tried to ignore him and simply slip away, but something beckoned me to open my eyes one last time. His face, still only visible in the eye that wasn't swimming in blood runoff, appeared to me and I saw his mouth. It still moved like that stinking dying fish, but this time his voice came with it.

"Not me," he strained.

He buckled at the knees, fell to the floor, and plopped open in a spread-eagle fashion, face up, with one of his arms outstretched toward me. A few of his bloody fingertips landed with a gentle thud on the tip of my shoe.

I slid off the wall and landed in the crook of his arm. The bullet hole in his chest seeped his gooey, hot blood out on to me as my eyes shut for good and I drifted off into utter darkness.

The one thing I remember though, before the darkness enshrouded me, was that someone was still laughing.

Someone was.

When I woke up in excruciating pain, it was my first clue that I still drug my weary soul through the land of child killers and misery.

Out of sheer instinct, I raised a hand to the left side of my head. Even before I got through the sticky and matted mess of my hair, just shifting a few hair follicles brought a burning and slicing sensation that ran all the way from behind my ear to the top of my head.

And, despite the initial warnings my head sent me, as points of precise and sharp pain, I kept reaching until I found open skin and . . . was that skull? It had to be. Smooth and—.

When I came to the second time, I knew better than to try to poke and feel my open scalp again. Besides, my wound suddenly became an ancillary problem to the smell I was sensing from behind me. It seemed to putrefy every pore on my skin, even the ones within the gaping slash on my head.

I rolled over to my stomach, and then braced myself with my hands on the floor to push up with my arms. But they felt like mush. I lay there for a moment, thinking it through. I opened my eyes, and still only could see out of one eye and even with that, everything was dull. I could make out that it was still light outside, but not as bright as it had been earlier.

Another waft of the stench flowed past me and I willed my hands to anchor down so I could finally push up and get away from the smell. I went up and as my elbows straightened, my hands slipped and slid out from beneath me, slipping on something wet. I landed on my chest with a soft thud, but my face dropped onto something hard and rigid. The part of my shirt over my chest started to absorb whatever liquid was beneath me, and I was glad whatever my face had landed on stopped it from getting wet too.

My face was on something . . . something . . . something that felt like an arm. Bailey!

Wetness. Blood. His, mine, ours, and a nothing-will-ever-be-the-same sort of blood.

I pushed myself up again in fervor, but there was too much blood. My hands slipped and I came crashing back down. I held my head up this time, to avoid Bailey's arm, but at great pain. Using any muscle from the neck up aggravated my scalp as if someone was digging their fingers under my skin and pulling.

Determined to get away from the pool of red death, I modified my movement into an army crawl, using my one good eye to find the darker form of Bailey's front door, near where we had both fallen. I wanted away from the blood. And that odor, that unholy odor, was frighteningly thick and suffocating. I didn't have the strength to move far, just far enough.

I tucked myself against the wall behind the door, facing Bailey. He wasn't moving, and his arm had felt like a piece of marble. Still, I feared him. The front of his head was facing me. Eyes open, he looked at me through death, and I felt the contents of my stomach rise in protest. I looked away, trying to focus on something else—the door. I needed to get out of the house, immediately, but I didn't know what was worse: staying in the bloodbath, or taking my half of it outside for the neighborhood to see.

Even when I avoided his empty eyes, the pungent smell exasperated my senses. I was certain it was coming from Bailey but I didn't remember smelling it when I first walked in. I would have remembered something so wretched.

I couldn't do it. I couldn't avoid the physiological consequences of my dirty deeds—the quick churning of my nauseous belly. I gagged and pursed my lips together, my cheeks ballooning to hold the vomit in.

Sitting up against the wall, I put my hands up to my face, a coping mechanism to soothe the vomit from climbing so much as one more inch, but my hands trembled more than my stomach. They were covered in blood. And by the smell of them, it was his blood.

If that were the only reason they trembled, however, then the day had started to improve.

I had killed a man. His blood was on my hands in every imaginable way.

What have I done? I shrieked inside my head.

My hands. His blood. I did it.

I vomited.

It spewed as far as Bailey's body, and broke into gasping sobs. If only . . . if only I had died too. A part of me still hoped I was only moments away from collapsing for good. The pain was searing. If I lay down on my back, maybe I'd pass out, vomit again, and choke on it.

Then surprise, surprise, surprise.

Someone knocked on the door.

I inhaled sharply.

"No," I whispered. The subtle movement of my jaw made my head pound and throb with an angry pain that made me see twinkles of light in my good eye.

Who could it be?

I looked back at Bailey's body. His red-and-black gunshot wound seemed to wink at me as I took full stock of the amount of blood on his floor. He had bled out to the side, but the blood pattern left a larger, cleaner area. A thick, red line snaked around what looked like a trace of my torso, from where I had passed out next to him. Then there were the bloody handprints, fingerprints, and streaks—my clumsy attempts to get up from this hellish party. Even if I could escape whoever was knocking on the door, there was plenty of proof I had been there—puke and prints, just to name two.

Another knock rapped on the door, louder this time.

"Bailey!" a voice shouted. "Open the door. I told you we'd be back. You're ours now, baby."

It was Detective Thatcher. I was only a few feet from the door and could hear the impatient shuffling of two pairs of feet. Thatcher's and probably Pete's. They came back. They said Bailey was theirs. They must've not had enough to arrest him earlier, but then ran some of the evidence and . . . oh, what had I done?

They pounded heavily on the door, again. I could tell one of them was banging a fist on the top, while the other kicked against the bottom with his shoe.

"You got to the count of three, Bailey, before we kick this door in. We also got men at each exit. Let's go!" Pete's voice boomed the command.

"One."

My heart pounded. The door was about to crack the rest of my head like a stomped walnut.

"Two."

I rolled away as quick as I could, starting to see the black pool of warmth spread over my consciousness again from the exertion. I knew I wasn't far enough away from the door, though. Keep rolling, I told myself. Do it.

"Three."

BOOM.

A burst of air was the first thing that sailed upon me as the door flung wide and hit the wall where I had been sitting. Then a soft but vicious shower of splinters came, spitting upon my trembling and bloodied body.

When I heard the last splinter sprinkle to the ground, I lowered my arms—outstretched for protection—and tried to look back at the opened door. Sunlight poured through behind their figures, making them nothing but shadows to me.

"What the—" Pete started.

"Mrs. Barrett!" Thatcher shouted out to me, kneeling down on the floor and holding me by my shoulders.

Everything got blurry again. I wanted to close my eyes. And I did.

TWELVE

Ominous Music Plays On

In a dream, I found myself standing inside my house. I wouldn't have thought it was a dream at first, but things here and there were different, leading me to the belief that I was in sleepy land. One difference was the addition of a parlor, yes, an honest to goodness parlor and I was standing in the middle of it.

A chandelier dripped from the ceiling, while a leggy grand piano beckoned nimble fingers to take a stab at its eighty-eight. The piano was perched next to a flood of large windows that let in a soft cascade of light, dancing between diamond shaped and cherry-colored windowpanes. This room was hot stuff, if hot stuff also meant regal and divine. I walked back to where the parlor and hallway met, just to make sure I was still in my own house.

I saw the kitchen, our dining room, and yup, there was Eddie's den.

So, when did this little number get added to the house, and why hadn't I seen it before? Still with my back to the parlor, I heard music approaching from behind me in gentle waves. I spun around to see the piano, but no one was playing it.

Then humming. Soft, sweet, childlike humming.

Oh no, I thought. Don't do this to me. Don't bring Corinne into this. I can't bear it. I just can't.

I peeked back down the hallway, even stepping down its length a few steps in order to get a visual of her bedroom door—still shut up, shut up to shut out the pain.

The humming continued; it, too, was coming from the parlor. I stepped back inside, perplexed, and sat down on one of the arms of the fancy Victorian couches. I still heard the piano and humming, but I was all alone.

Suddenly, the hum turned into a chorus and I paled at the words.

"Not me, not me, not me."

Oh, great.

I stood and slowly backed up, heading out of the room. Was there a door for this room? I hadn't remembered seeing one, but if there was, I wanted to lock that thing and run.

The soft ivory tinkle of the piano quickened into something more ominous and creepy. It was as if some hunched-back court jester banged away on a dusty and tapered organ nearby.

"Not me, not me, not me." A low voice sang out again.

The sky outside the windows darkened, looking like a storm that'd tear your roof off and then laugh about it. I walked backward, faster and faster, without yet reaching the hallway. I turned to run, the hallway had to be close now, but the moment I did an about-face, I crashed into a wall that hadn't been there before.

Where was the opening? Where was the hallway?

I pounded on the wood-paneled wall, and the organ pounded with me in rhythm, only stifled by a low and rumbled growling. My breathing stalled and I began to sweat. This was the part where I needed to wake up.

I turned around, facing the windows, and saw a black, vaporous shape materialize outside. The longer I stared, the more it formed.

It had a mouth.

Then it opened wide. And that thing . . . it had teeth.

It bit the windows plumb off and then went for the piano. The piano put up a noisy fight, but the black hole ultimately reduced it to timber, melancholy, and nothingness.

Next, it moved to the wood floors, crumbling them like soup crackers. Thereafter, it slowed down, almost coming to a stop. I thought it was over, but I had thought wrong. The beast, the black beast, had only slowed to suck bolts out from the ceiling, the ones bracing the chandelier. Once the bolts were gone, Beastie stopped spinning, grinding, and destroying. When the moment arrived where I could hear a dragonfly land on a glassy pond, the chandelier plummeted to the ground below, crashing into an infinity of broken pieces. It was a visage of hope utterly shattered and that's when I heard Beastie say, "Ah, to crush is to live."

As the very last crystal teardrop ended its bouncing and cracking upon the floor, Beastie kicked it back into high gear and sucked them all up like the garbage he thought they were.

Seconds later, Beastie set his sights on me. Up against the solid wall, it suddenly gave way and I found myself back in my old hallway. Still, I didn't run. Fear paralyzed my legs. Either that or I was too much of a coward to face the hunchback and his organ, which only seemed to get closer and closer to me as he beat the organ's keys in a perpetual *bum, bum, bum, doom, doom, doom.*

Beastie came closer and closer, until I realized he didn't only have one row of shredding teeth but three, and each moved at a different speed from the other, alternating in ferocity like a triad of hellish chain saws. Hoping to wake up soon, I tried to turn my head away, intending to be blind as it devoured me. But something held my head back, letting me know in no uncertain terms, "You will watch this."

I gasped. The teeth were practically on top of me.

If Beastie had a tongue behind those vicious fangs, he would only need to flick it out an inch to steal a taste and say to me, "You're next, lollipop."

I closed my eyes. At least I had control over that. At least I didn't have to watch three rows of sharpened fangs rip me to shreds.

Beastie swallowed me, and the last thing to go into the darkness was my left hand, clawing for anything to hold on to before I was belched up as an after dinner mint. I saw my hand, trying to reach out to freedom, and upon it, my wedding ring glimmered against the fire in Beastie's eyes. He swallowed again and my ring clinked against one of his fangs, ripped off, and bounced to the floor.

My eyes burst open and I found myself in a hospital room, handcuffed to a bed.

THIRTEEN

She's Still Dead

My hand wouldn't lift more than a few inches. The clanking of the handcuffs as I tried to jostle them upward reminded me that even the little things held me back.

If I had woken up any other way than handcuffed to a bed, I would have been happy and safe; finally out of that bloody tangle with Bailey, and awake from a dream I was sure was in my best interest to ignore.

But that wasn't the case. I was definitely in the middle of one of those "Oh, crap," moments in life.

"This can't be happening," I moaned, realizing the police had arrested me.

A machine off to my left let out a steady beep, but the more I struggled, the faster the beep bounced, finally triggering a nurse to come. She was small, soft looking, and had her hair pulled back. The hairdo accentuated her plumlike cheeks. The last time I had seen a nurse was when that Jamaican broad was pinning me down, shooting me up with tranquilizers. There was no way this little sprite could take me. I wasn't planning on giving her a reason to, but things change quickly, and everything in my sad, miserable life seemed to accentuate that on a daily basis.

"How long have you been awake?" she asked with a simple, clear voice.

"Too long." My voice sounded raspy.

She chuckled at that.

"You'd rather not be awake?" she asked.

I lifted up my right hand again as the bottom cuff clinked and pulled against the side rail of the hospital bed. "No. And this," I said, shaking the handcuffs, "is just one of the many reasons."

She sighed. "Hmm. Then, I guess you won't be happy to hear that there's a police officer sitting outside your room." She pointed to a slump of a man sitting in a chair reading a magazine directly across the hallway from the opened door.

"Yeah, that . . . that's not bringing me any joy."

She smiled again. "At least you have your sense of humor."

"I do? I thought it was simple sarcasm."

"Whatever works," she said. By now, she was over at the heart monitor, pulling out a small, thin strip of paper to check the journey of my heart rate.

I had only glanced at the officer in the hallway for a moment, but I didn't recognize him.

"My constant visitor, huh?" I asked the nurse, speaking about the officer.

"Who, your husband?" she responded.

"Huh? No, the officer . . . what about my husband?"

"You said your constant visitor, so I assumed you were talking about your husband. He's been here since they brought you in."

"Where?"

She pointed over my head and I turned over my shoulder to look. In the corner of the room, against the wall that led into the hallway, was a floor to ceiling window where Eddie's tall, solid frame stood. He made the window look smaller than it was as the absolute despair and betrayal on his face took up every inch of it.

With my unbound hand, I motioned for him to come in.

"Sorry, sweetie," the nurse said. "He isn't allowed in here. Only your doctors, nurses, and the police."

I turned toward her with both surprise and anger.

"But he's my husband."

"Sorry. Police orders. But that's why we gave you this room. It's one of the few that has that window so he can peek through from the hallway."

I looked back at Eddie who seemed unaware of anything else in the world other than sending me disapproving messages with his eyes alone.

He had let his facial hair grow out. It looked soft and rugged and reminded me of our honeymoon in an overwater bungalow in Bora Bora.

I wondered why I even bothered thinking about Bora Bora straight out of unconsciousness. But the alternative was conjuring up the last thing I had experienced in life: blood and Bailey.

My mind was happier, therefore, if it went back to my honeymoon, when Eddie had forgotten his razor. And instead of asking the hotel for another, he decided he'd experiment with stubble.

Maybe because it was Bora Bora, or because we held hands together in a baby blue lagoon, or because we had waited until we were married— when Eddie swept his arm to scatter flowers and palm fronds off the puritanically white bedding to first make love—but Eddie's stubble always, and I mean always, turned me on.

And if it could do that to me while I was chained to a hospital bed as he shot me looks of betrayal, then that said something.

I heard the nurse sigh and looked at her. She shifted her weight to one side and propped one hand on her tiny hip. "He just stares at you the whole time." She was looking at Eddie, and then added, "Not as severely as he's doing now. Wow," she added, cocking her head. "He looks mad."

"Of course he's mad," I added.

She looked down at me and said, "Well, I guess I'd be mad too if my husband almost got himself killed."

Oh yeah, I thought, there was that. I reached up to the side of my head and felt pounds of gauze wrapped around it, with a particularly large mound over the area Bailey hit.

"How long have I been out?" I asked, putting together the length of Eddie's stubble with the medical gauze.

"Three days. Welcome back," she said with a smile.

"Three days? And you said that I almost died?"

"Technically, you did die, but a paramedic brought you back to life on the ambulance ride over. Then, you were touch and go for a bit because of brain swelling, and that's why the doctor induced a coma, but I'll have to let him fill you in on that."

"Does Eddie know?"

"Of your condition? Yes. Like I said, he's been here the whole time. He may not be allowed in the room, but he's been in constant contact with your doctor, even reminding everyone who'll listen that there's no way he'd ever authorize terminating life support if it came to that."

I looked back at my husband. He was still looking at me with his hot and bothered intensity. I shook my head and asked the nurse, "Did it ever come to that?"

"Not entirely. But, you're awake now so it doesn't really matter. Focus on the good. It'll help you heal faster."

I looked over my shoulder, at the window again, but Eddie was gone. I found him quickly, though, sitting in a blue hall chair a few feet away from the officer.

"He hasn't gone home at all?" I asked.

"Not that I know. He eats here, showers here, sleeps here. We have a few rooms for family members to do that when they've got a loved one in critical condition."

"That's stupid," I said.

"Our rooms?" she asked, shocked.

"No," I said. "That he hasn't left."

She reached over to me. I thought she was going to check any of the several wires and tubes running over my body, instead she rested her small hand on my forearm and said, "That's not stupid, sweetie. That's love."

I blew out a hiss of air in debate and then pulled at my handcuffs again. "So, what's the status on my freedom?" I asked her.

"Uh-uh." The nurse shook her head with pouted lips. "I'm not the person to discuss that with. I make sure your heart goes beep, beep and that your bandages are tidy. You have a six-inch gash there on your head, and the doctor put in thirty stitches. You also suffered a fracture on your skull, but it'll heal up. The biggest problem was the brain swelling. That's the part we always worry about because that's the part that puts people to sleep forever."

"I wish," I said.

She looked sharply at me. "No, you don't."

But she didn't know. She didn't understand.

"Anyway," she continued, "you're awake now, so that's a very good thing. You'll have to take it easy for a while, but you're definitely healing. In fact, I think the doctor had it on the agenda to take the gauze off today, regardless of if you were awake or not."

She checked my heart rate one more time, squeezed my hand, and then walked out. Eddie stopped her in the hallway. I couldn't make out what he was saying, but I heard the nurse ask in response, "Well, is it normal that she acts feisty?"

Eddie turned to me, eyeing me with careful disapproval, and then nodded to the nurse.

"Then, yes," the nurse said. "Other than being physically weak for several hours, maybe even a day, and having to take it slow for a while, she's perfectly normal."

The nurse left Eddie standing near the doorway, with the officer monitoring to make sure he didn't take a step inside the room. His face froze in the same hard misery he had when I first saw him through the window.

"What?" I croaked loudly at him. It brought a tugging, piercing pain to the side of my head.

He opened his mouth to say something, but then closed up and walked away.

The officer gave me a quick look before he leaned forward to watch Eddie's progress down the hall. After, he went back to reading his magazine. His police presence—even if it only consisted of reading a magazine—reminded me that Pete and Thatcher would be coming soon.

How long had the nurse said I had been in the hospital? Three days? I guess that meant Robert Bailey was gone and buried somewhere, maybe even cremated if no one claimed him. It seemed fitting, but then again, I should probably just shut up about that since I'm the one who killed him.

My stomach churned when I thought back to that day. What had I done? He was a bad man, yes, and an evil one to be sure. He liked to hurt and *kill* children. But, the whole affair made me feel as if I had wrestled with a rosebush. It was a sweet thing to know I had eradicated a particular evil, but, man alive, the thorns! Bloodshed was not my right. Hadn't Eddie tried telling me that too?

The biggest pebble in my shoe, if pebble also meant bone-crushing boulder, was the realization that killing Bailey still wasn't good enough. I hated to admit it—I'd rather peel my skin than admit it—but Corinne was still dead and the pain, well the pain hadn't lessened at all. In fact, it felt aggravated thanks to Eddie's hard stares and the stinging thought that he had already known going after Bailey wouldn't make Corinne any less gone forever.

He couldn't have suffered any loss of love for Robert Bailey, though, so why did he have those blue eyes filled with the proliferation of such misery? The way he looked at me, it made me feel so . . . guilty.

There was something else there, though. I thought on it. I shut everything out, even the constant beeping of the heart rate machine next to my head, and let my handcuffed wrist lie so still that I almost forgot about the cold metal clamped against it, just to think about it.

It was the betrayal. He looked at me as if I had betrayed him. That was a response I had never seen him muster in all our years of marriage, so what could I have done to establish it now?

You put yourself in mortal danger.

"Huh?" I asked aloud. My sudden interjection made the guard stir. I pressed my lips together and turned my head to the wall, away from him.

The conviction wasn't audible, but when its sender imprints it on your soul like a searing brand, it sometimes feels that way. It felt like the same urging and nudging I received before I went into Bailey's house.

I rolled to my side, mounded gauze facing up, and put a pillow over my head to cover my ear. Even the weight of the thin hospital pillow made my scalp throb.

That won't work. You'll still hear.

"What?" I mumbled. Not only had the world stripped me of my family, but now, I was also losing my mind.

Well, the loony bin seemed all right if I could get my own room with a small window that faced east, a soft bed with white linens, and a plethora of books.

I removed the pillow, and rolled over to my back just as Pete and Thatcher rounded the corner into my room.

Pete looked all business, but Thatcher looked surprisingly happy to see me.

"Nice shootin' Tex," Thatcher said, firing off fake bullets from his extended index fingers. "*Ghostbusters*, ballroom scene," he concluded with a bigger grin.

Pete spun around to his partner. "Knock it off, kid. No playing, no movie quotes."

Thatcher jerked his shoulders up quickly and blew Pete off. He walked to the far side of my bed and gave me a wink right before he leaned in to me.

"You have no idea how much you're my hero right now," he whispered. "Just thinking about how many things could've gone wrong if Bailey went to trial, with all the dumb lawyers and their ridiculous motions—no offense."

"None taken," I said, eyeing him with uncertainty.

"So help me, Thatcher," Pete said. "Keep your opinions to yourself."

Thatcher sighed and leaned up against a nearby wall.

"Mrs. Barrett," Pete started, "as you may have already figured out, you're under arrest."

I raised my cuffed hand again, letting it pull and clink. "And this is because you thought I was a flight risk while in a coma?"

"Standard procedure," Pete replied.

"Yeah, for real criminals," Thatcher added.

Pete's eyes darted to Thatcher's. "I've already talked to you about this. By the book, Thatcher. A man is dead."

"Correction, a murderous pedophile is dead. You won't catch me shedding a tear. And I know you—"

Pete threw a hand up for Thatcher to stop, then pulled out a small notepad from the inside breast pocket of his blazer. He set the pad down on my bed, next to my leg, and dug inside the pocket again, presumably for a pen. He came out empty-handed. Thatcher then pulled a pen out from his back pocket and handed it to Pete, winking at me again as he reached over the bed.

"Okay," Pete said, "let's cut to the chase. Why were you in Robert Bailey's house?"

"Because he let me in."

Thatcher found my response humorous. Pete didn't.

"No games, Mrs. Barrett," Pete said, his eyes darting to the gauze wrapped around my head.

"If only it were that simple," I stated.

"It is," Pete replied. "Just answer the questions. None of your lawyer stuff here. You don't get to wait for the perfect question before you offer the perfect answer."

"That's cheating," I said. "You have to earn the upper hand, not ask me to give it to you." I was surprised at myself for playing cat and mouse with them. I was unaware I even had the energy because my head still hurt, and my heart felt like a moth-eaten wardrobe. But, I guess my attorney instinct kicked in: shuffle and dance, shuffle and dance—until the inquisitor's aim is diverted—shuffle and dance.

"Last time, Mrs. Barrett—"

"Wait, wait," Thatcher interrupted, putting his hands on his hips. "She's right. Let me take a stab at this." He reached over the bed again, reaching for Pete's notepad and the pen.

Pete protested and turned away so the items were out of Thatcher's reach.

"Swear, buddy. I swear," Thatcher said. "By the book, I promise."

Pete relented and gave him the pad and pen.

Thatcher clicked the pen a few times. "Have I ever told you my old man was a lawyer?" he asked me.

I wanted to shake my head, but couldn't.

"Yeah, so I know a few of your tricks," he said with a hearty smile. "Mrs. Barrett, what motivated you to go to Bailey's house?"

"Curiosity."

"Vengeance?"

"Curiosity."

"How did you find him?"

I looked at Pete, then back at Thatcher. "I stole your file, remember?"

"So, you found out where he lived and you marched right up to his front door?"

"Yes."

"Where did the gun come from?"

"It's my husband's."

"Did he give it to you?"

I forced a chuckled. "No. I took it."

"You take a lot, don't you?" he asked.

"Your current method seems like a good reason you're a cop rather than following in your father's footsteps," I said to Thatcher.

Pete finally chuckled. It was more like a rumbling snort through his nose since his lips were clamped shut.

I looked away from the detectives and toward the far windows in the room, which gave me a view of an expansive, smoggy sky. Freedom was out there . . . somewhere. But not in here, because in here, Corinne was still dead and I was handcuffed to a bed.

"All right, let's try it this way. Did you shoot Robert Bailey in self-defense?" Thatcher asked.

"You skipped a lot in between there," Pete interrupted.

"It doesn't really matter if the end result is self-defense," Thatcher said.

"We'll soon find out, won't we?" Pete said. He shifted his stare to me. "Since you're awake, the DA is having you added to the arraignment calendar in three days' time. Your doc says you'll be able to travel down to the courthouse by then. He grabbed the notepad and pen, clipped the pen onto the pad, and tossed both on my lap. "What you get charged with is now up to you. If it's self-defense, you better start writing because the District Attorney's office is starting with murder unless you give them a reason not to."

I wouldn't have been able to write my initials if I wanted to. With the little skips in reality my vision was making here and there during the conversation, I had to keep reminding myself there was only one Pete and one Thatcher talking to me at a time. Still, I wasn't going to let them in on that, for fear they'd stay longer to help write something out for me. If I had to, I'd get the nurse to help me. She seemed like she'd be all right with gilding the lily on my behalf.

Pete then fumbled in his pockets for his keys and went for my hand-cuffs. "Don't make me regret this," he said, putting the unlocked cuffs in his back pocket.

"But I'm leaving the guard."

FOURTEEN

A Tough Thing

Pete came back three days later holding an electronic monitoring device.

"It's either this or handcuffs and a waist chain," he told me after I rolled my eyes when I saw the device.

"What are the exact charges?" I asked.

"Second degree murder and illegal possession of a firearm," he answered, making sure the monitoring device wasn't too tight around my ankle.

Pete must've lived, breathed, and eaten procedure for the sake of procedure alone. If he thought I were the type of accused who actually warranted a device, he wouldn't have made it loose enough for me to slip out of with a little bit of leverage and baby oil. Still, because some rule in some book told him he had to, he did.

"Illegal possession, huh? Are they going to throw in loitering and trespassing too?"

Pete went out to the hallway, pulled one of the blue plastic chairs into my room, and then sat down. He had already released the other officer saying he'd be watching me until after the arraignment. "You know," he started, "you don't seem worried enough about what might happen to you."

I snorted. "What's the worst that can happen? They put me in jail for the rest of my life? Oh no. Who will raise my daughter while I'm in the slammer? Wait a minute, I don't have a daughter anymore."

"Hmm," he muttered, leaning back into the chair, trying to get comfortable. "When you get out of this—and my money is on the District Attorney dropping the second degree murder charge since you two belong to the same country club—I should take you down to the jail. You might think you're a tough little cookie when you're fighting in your own doings, but you won't be so tough when you're fighting in their doings."

"She won't have to fight in their doings because she's as innocent as a bleating lamb," a voice announced from the door. It was Cole Stratton, my colleague from the firm.

He glided over to Pete, grabbed his hand, and shook it. "Thanks big fella, I'm her attorney, so give us a few minutes, okay?"

Cole was already pulling Pete up from the chair, to speed up the process of his exit. Pete forcibly withdrew his hand, stood tall and glared down at Cole. If the size difference had any effect on Cole, he didn't show it. He looked up at Pete and flashed his million-dollar smile. Seeing the contrast between Pete's face and Cole's, I could see now why Cole's adversaries hated him. It wasn't just because Cole won, it was because he let you know he was going to win the minute he met you, through the cockiness brimming in that first flash of his pearly whites.

Cole patted Pete on the arm. "All right, guy, time to move. It's the law. We get our one-on-one together."

"Easy, Cole," I said.

Pete looked at me and said, "Thatcher and your husband are on their way over, with some goodies to get you ready for court." He then left the room, closing the door behind him.

Cole came to the side of my bed, picked up my hand, and kissed the back of it.

"Evelyn, my dear, may I be perfectly blunt?"

I groaned and turned my head.

"What were you thinking?" he asked.

"I don't want to hear a lecture on morality from you, Cole."

He lowered the side rail on my bed and sat down next to me. "I wasn't going to give you one. I was talking about killing a potential client," he said with a smile.

I sat upright and considered slapping the smile off him. He saw the intensity flaming in my eyes and said, "Whoa, whoa, whoa. I'm kidding, sweetie. Geez. Remember?" He pointed back and forth between the two of us. "We like to kid with one another. Below the gut punches. Remember?"

Falling back against the inclined bed, I sighed at his response. He raised his hands in defeat.

"That was too below the gut. I get it."

I doubted that.

"Do you know the charges?" he asked me.

I nodded.

"Good. I'm almost there in convincing the DA to drop the murder charge because, let's see—" he pulled a file out and flipped through it. "One of the detectives who found you in Robert Bailey's house said the scene struck him as self-defense. The only other thing the DA's office needed was your statement, and an initial forensics report to make a decision on dropping the bigger charge. They got the report yesterday, about the same time they got your statement. All you and I need to do is go over the 'Why,' as in, why were you even at Robert Bailey's house. And don't say selling Girl Scout cookies. I already used that one last week." Cole closed his file, put it behind him on the bed, and then extended his right arm over my legs, making a sort of bridge over me with the side of his torso.

"Which detective said it looked like self-defense?" I asked. "Thatcher?" He had seemed like the one fighting for me earlier.

Cole grimaced. "You're going to make me open the file again, aren't you? I was just getting comfortable."

I brought my knees up, bouncing Cole's reach off me.

"Fine," he relented, opening the file. "No, it was, um . . ." he flipped two pages down, "Detective Peter Shaw."

"Really?"

"Yeah. Which one was just here?" he asked.

"Pete."

Cole straightened his back, and out of habit alone fixed his hair. "I just snot-nosed the cop who's going to trash the only shot the DA has at a murder charge?"

I nodded.

"Oh, well," he added. "With or without him liking me, I got this one in the bag. We'll get that murder charge dropped, and the DA's office has already agreed to do probation for the possession charge. We'll talk about why you were at Bailey's house later. I'm not sure it'll even come up. I was thinking about going with the deranged, grieving mother thing, going door-to-door demanding answers. So, with that, we've reached the good news/bad news section of this talk. The bad news is that you'll likely be disbarred from the practice of law."

I hadn't thought about losing my license to practice law. Contemplating quitting—and it was very high up on the to-do list—was one thing because it still gave me a comfortable amount of control over my life; but having the state intervene and tell me I wasn't good enough to practice law was another. It was all the same, I supposed. I wasn't a good enough mother because I entrusted my child into someone's incompetent hands, I wasn't a good enough wife because my husband continuously pulled himself away, and I wasn't even a good enough vigilante to realize you need to at least bring your own, registered, gun rather than steal your husband's. What difference did it make if now I wasn't good enough to practice law?

Everything had blown, or smashed, into dust. Except Eddie. I still had time to put it back together with Eddie.

"Did you hear me, Evelyn?" Cole asked.

"Huh? Sorry," I said. "What did you say?"

"I asked if you wanted to hear the good news?"

I wanted to ask him if the good news involved a do-over. Instead, I simply nodded.

"The good news," he started, pulling my legs back down so they were straight on the bed again, and then putting his arm back over, "is that you're getting top-rate legal representation at the bargain basement price of one dinner with yours truly."

I looked at the closed door, shocked at his inability to read any situation outside pacing in front of a jury box. Here I was with gauze bandages wrapped around my head, having woken from a coma a few days earlier, and he's hitting on me again. "How about I write you a check?" I asked.

A knock rapped on the door and we both startled. Before either of us could offer admittance, the door opened, letting Thatcher, Pete, and Eddie all pour into the room. Cole jumped up quickly. If it were only Pete and Thatcher, he wouldn't have given them a courtesy glance. But for Eddie, he walked over quickly and extended his hand.

"Hey man," Cole said. "It's been a while. How are you?"

Eddie, holding a bag in each hand, looked down to Cole's extended handshake and curled his lip a little. Then, he sidestepped Cole and put down what he was carrying at the foot of my bed. "Here's your makeup bag and," he held up a garment bag, "your suit." He added in a low, hushed mumble: "Your favorite."

"You done with your little chat, counselor?" Pete asked Cole.

"Yes, thank you, Detective," Cole said. "I appreciate your giving us a moment."

Too little, too late, Cole. That one has already made up his mind about you, and it's not good.

I saw Eddie heading for the door. "Where are you going?" I asked, sitting up in the bed. "Why are you leaving?"

He looked at the room's window, then at Cole, and that's all I needed. Great. He'd seen Cole getting up close and personal. He'd always been bothered by Cole. Said he didn't like the way Cole looked at me when Cole assumed Eddie wasn't looking. It was a total of three times, three times too many—today and the last two office Christmas parties.

Then Eddie answered, "I promised I'd give your mother and sister a ride to the courthouse. I have to go pick them up. I'll see you later."

A quick glance at a big purple vase near the window, filled with orchids and stargazer lilies, as well as Get Well balloons and a handwritten banner, reminded me that my mother, my sister, and her two sons had visited me yesterday. Well, they visited the nurses' station, at least. The guard allowed them to leave the goodies before turning them away on account of Pete's orders. Maddie made a squawk, even shouting down the hall that she loved me, but the absence of my mother's typical biting tone—summoned for anyone who would dare to stand in her way—made me think she was relieved to do the one-eighty.

Eddie moved closer to the door.

"Wait, no," I said, feeling far too many eyes on me. "Can you all give us a minute?" I asked the other three men.

The cockiness returned to Cole's voice as he said, "Actually, we have a few more things to go—"

"Leave," I interrupted.

Pete, Thatcher, and Cole filed past Eddie, as Eddie looked after them with longing, almost like he wished he could fall in behind them and leave. Thatcher started to close the door, but Pete voiced something about how this was only allowable if it stayed open. Eddie took to standing near it, as far away as possible. Something between the two of us was slipping, and going down fast.

"Why won't you even talk to me?" I asked.

"What's there to talk about?" he said, putting his hands into his pockets.

I scoffed. "What's there to talk about? Really? How about how I shot a man, or, I don't know, how I almost died?"

"You didn't talk to me before you did those things, so why should we talk about it after?"

I pushed my head back into my pillow, searching for the right thing to say, searching for words that would at least end the ridiculous onslaught of rhetorical questions. Eddie and I sucked at fighting. A pair of village idiots could get to the heart of the matter faster.

I closed my eyes in an attempt to block out his linear facial features now bunched with emotions he normally didn't know how to wear.

"Suffice it to say, Eddie, I realize I made a mistake and honestly, I don't know if I can go over the many, many ways in which I've failed right now. But I do know that it would be great . . . no, epic, for my mental well-being right now if you'd stop looking at me like I've done something bad to you."

The silence that fell when I finished my words accumulated deep in my throat, choking me with the belief that he didn't think I was worth an answer. When the quiet persisted, I even thought he left. But when I opened my eyes, I found him standing right beside me, looking down on me as I lay in the bed.

"You have done something bad, Evelyn." His eyes quickly darted to the ceiling, holding back tears. When he composed himself a second later and looked back down at me, he said, "All I've ever done is adore you from the moment I saw you." He let out a low chuckle. "You came all stomping up to the AT&T phone yard, demanding a supervisor because one of the techs blew off a deposition you had scheduled. Most of the guys were hiding behind their vans, hoping you wouldn't make them be the one to finger out the boss."

"But not you," I added, giving myself over to a well-needed smile, even if it was only a third full of happiness. The other two-thirds were smart enough to recognize the severity in Eddie's voice, and that trumped the warm, sweet shot of recollection.

"Right," he said. "Not me. I walked you inside and made up some ridiculous legal question to get you talking to me. You shot me a hoity-toity look—"

I looked at him then, wondering where he was going with this.

"Yup, that's the one." He chuckled again. It sounded even more strained than the first. "And that's when I knew I had to do one of two things: put you in your place or marry you."

"And now you're wondering if you made the right decision?"

He turned from me, walked a few steps, and stood in the middle of the room. "I don't want to say this, Evelyn, but I have to. You're selfish and self-absorbed, and I—" He swallowed, struggling with the next words.

That's when I knew this was the second "Oh, crap," moment of this adventure.

"I feel that I'm at the verge of hating you for it." His eyes went up to the ceiling again, but tears fell anyway. He wiped them away and went closer to the door, turning to say, "All you've thought about since Corinne died is what you need to do: *your* vengeance, *your* hate, *your* way of dealing with things. But what about me? Have you forgotten that I lost a daughter too? You asked me to help you hunt down this Bailey guy to help you grieve, and all I've wanted for these last few weeks is to lay my head down in your lap and have you run your fingers in my hair. For crying out loud, you could have at least taken three minutes out of your crazed fury just to lie to me and tell me that I still hold a part of your life.

"If you had, I would have believed you. Instead, you go and put yourself in harm's way, almost losing your life, and all I can think about is how it just proves you're not thinking about me at all; that I have no part in your world. If I mattered to you at all, you would have stopped to think that even though I'm not scared of a tough thing like you, there's no way on heaven or earth I could have survived losing my daughter and my wife in the same month."

I had already looked away, finding comfort in a sterile hospital wall that I was sure had seen worse than the end of one romance.

Eddie inhaled and I could hear the bounce within it, grasping for resolve. Almost a minute expired in silence, but I already knew what my response was going to be.

"Evy, if ever there was a case to stake your life on, this is it," he said, breaking the silence and opening the door.

"I don't want my mother or sister in court. I don't want you there, either. This is my problem and I'll face it alone. Just go away."

FIFTEEN

A Daddy Done Wrong

"Am I hurting you?" the doctor asked me, cutting through the stacked gauze on my head. He had small, fragile hands and reeked of cigarettes. I wanted to ask him the point behind a smoking doctor, but then remembered I was a law-breaking lawyer.

"No," I said. He likely asked the question because he saw I was crying. A drop here and there, but I couldn't hide the leakage—Eddie had only left five minutes earlier and I was still lying in the hospital bed wondering why I was such a fool.

The white bandages were off and the cold air pressed itself against my wound. I imagined a portion of my hair gone, shaved before they fixed me up. It would account for the cold sensation.

I wiped a tear that had pooled on my lower lashes and asked the doctor, "Can I touch it?"

"I'd rather you not, but do you want a mirror to look at it?" he asked.

"If the next few months involve a comb-over, I'll pass."

He smiled. "Skip the comb-over and go for a hat or bandana." He held out the small mirror to me, forcing me to hold it. "Do you want me to send in a nurse to help you get ready for your court appearance?"

I took the mirror, set it down on my legs, and sighed. "No, thanks. I can do it on my own."

He put his hands in his lab coat, shuffling cards and pens around in each, and pressed his lips together, thinking about something. "Nah. I'll send someone in. Have you even stood up today?"

"No."

"Then make me feel better and let a nurse help you."

I nodded. When he left the room, I stared at the back of the mirror he gave me, its reflective side against my kneecaps. Two things scared me about picking it up: one, to see what sort of Halloween costume my head looked like, and two, I hadn't looked too long into my eyes since before Corinne had died. I wasn't exactly sure who'd be looking back.

Several minutes later, the pixie nurse came back—the one who helped when I had first awoke.

"Lookey, lookey, what I got you," she said cheery, holding up a cloth headband. "When I first heard you'd have to go to court today, all I thought about was your poor head. Girls don't want to go around with a chunk of their scalp showing."

Oh, great, I thought. How bad was it?

She continued, "So, I asked around and one of the nurses had this black headband she uses to hold her hair back, and since you can't put anything other than sterile gauze on the cut, I got that right here on the inside." She flipped it inside out for me to see a thin white line of gauze taped to the inside of the headband.

"Here," she said, "let's see if it works. I promise I'll be careful." With both hands she stretched the cloth band as far as it'd go, making sure she didn't tug anything she shouldn't as she slipped it over my head and down my neck. With utmost precision and the tip of her tongue clamped between her teeth, she pulled the front up until she had it placed at the top of my head.

"What do you know?" she said. "It fits perfectly over the scar. I hope you're a headband wearing girl, because it's the perfect thing to hide the long scar."

I couldn't refrain any longer.

Holding the mirror up and avoiding looking back into my eyes, I searched the left side of my head. Even with the headband covering whatever the nurse said it was covering, it was obvious I was missing a good chunk of hair—almost a six-by-four-inch rectangle over my ear. But, she was right; you couldn't see any stitches. Then the money shot: I lifted the headband to see what it was hiding.

The second that the full power of fluorescent lights hit the purple, red, and puffy line of disgust, accompanied by black and pointy stitches, is the same point in time that I let the headband fall back into place while dropping the mirror back on the bed.

I picked the mirror up again, but only to thrust it toward the nurse. "Take this, please," I said.

She did, and then dropped it into a front pocket on her scrubs. She

straightened the headband and said, "It'll look better after you've showered. Let's go get you cleaned up and ready."

Showers are good, but not that good.

The worst thing about cleaning off was the dried blood. I hadn't
noticed it earlier, but I still had caked-on blood in a few places: my hands,
arms, and neck. It could have been something to say about the hospital's
level of care, but the nurse had given me a headband to wear to court.
Enough said.

I scrubbed and scrubbed. The fullness of washing the blood from my
hands overtook me, metaphorically . . . literally. I let hot, voluntary tears
commingle with the trickling water because even I couldn't tell which
was which.

As I tried to convince the knot in my belly to unwind—it bunched
tighter and tighter from the thought of killing Bailey—I kept asking
myself: Did I really tell Eddie to go away?

The nurse reminded me we were on a schedule. To me, that meant to
stop crying.

She helped me get dressed and apply makeup, making comments left
and right and reminding me why I don't like chitchat. "Now I *know* your
man loves you," she said to me during the makeup stage, digging through
the cosmetic bag Eddie had brought.

I didn't even know where to start with my rebuttal.

"Look at this," she said, tilting the unzipped bag toward me. "A lady
like yourself must have a bunch of makeup, in all sorts of colors, but he
only brought one shade for you. And this shade—in my mind—goes best
with that navy pantsuit he also brought. You've got different shades at
home, right?"

I nodded.

"Where did you find that man? Does he have a brother?"

I took the bag out of her hand, zipped it back up, and said, "Let's skip
the eye shadow and lipstick, okay?"

"Did you have to teach him to color coordinate, or was that factory
installed?"

That one made me smile. A little. Then I remembered there really
wasn't anything to smile about anymore. Even if Eddie had put in the

effort to bring my things the way I'd want them, I had told him to go away, and he did.

Pete and Thatcher walked into my room, finding me ready to go and meet my legal fate. Pete gave me a look of approval when he saw me, but Thatcher crinkled his nose, especially when he saw the headband and a quarter of my hair missing. Based on the reactions alone, it wouldn't take looking at their ring fingers to tell which of the two was married.

We walked through the emergency room, Pete and Thatcher flanking me. Our first destination was getting to an unmarked patrol car waiting outside the ambulance doors. It hadn't occurred to me it was a strange thing to do, going out via the ER, but Pete made a point of telling me it was the best exit for our purposes.

"Those darn press people are all over the place, setting up shop at every exit," Pete said. "They'll be out here, too, but they keep getting pushed away every few minutes because of the ambulances. We'll catch them on an outgoing wave."

Pete was wrong. But I was too petrified to gloat in his miscalculation.

Reporters were outside. Several of them, and their flashes were already lighting up the ambulance carport they stood under.

Thatcher leaned into me and said, "It's not as bad as you think. Many of the press are hailing you as a hero."

I turned to him and found him smiling, already looking toward the doors and straightening his tie.

"I still don't want to go out there," I said. My hesitation could have been because of the partially shaved head, the gauze already tucking out from the headband, or the fact that I wasn't a hundred percent sure I had scrubbed all the dried blood flakes from my cuticles.

"I'll try to get them to move," Pete said, walking off without us.

"Want me to put something over your head?" Thatcher asked me.

I reached up to the side of my head. "It's bad, isn't it?"

He shot me a confused look, then squinted. "Well, yeah, it does look bad, but that's not what I was talking about. I can throw a blanket or something over your head so they can't get a good picture," he said, pointing to the reporters.

I opened my mouth to protest that a blanket over the head is only for guilty people when my eyes popped at something else.

"Oh geez," I moaned, covering my nose and mouth. "What is that smell?" I demanded. "Oh God, it's . . . it's that smell."

Thatcher looked at me puzzled. "What smell?" he asked. He looked around, even sniffed a few times, then took me by the elbow to urge me forward because Pete had gotten the reporters to back away.

I jerked my arm back. "No. Wait."

I dared not speak what was coursing through my mind, what my eyes inevitably conveyed—panic. The very smell I'd found in Bailey's bloody kitchen was now in the ER. I was too scared to look, but I did. I made a complete three-sixty, searching the entire room, looking for Bailey's body. It was ludicrous. Even I knew that. But that smell . . . Maybe some morgue intern had left Bailey's body to rot in the hallway.

"Mrs. Barrett, we have to move," Thatcher said. "I don't know how Pete made the reporters go away, but I'm pretty sure they'll be back any moment."

"Don't you smell that?" I asked, my voice raising and my eyebrows pressing together so hard that they were inducing a tension headache.

"I smell . . ." Thatcher paused, inhaling through his nose, "that typical Pine-Sol they use to clean people's blood and snot off the floor. Is that what you're talking about?"

I wanted to faint. Or run. Or stick my head into a freshly bleached hospital toilet. Anything that would disconnect my olfactory senses from my brain.

Pete walked through the doors and barked out Thatcher's name. Thatcher responded by waving him off and asking him for a moment.

I didn't think it prudent to tell Thatcher that I smelled Bailey's corpse, because even I didn't quite believe Bailey was nearby. But the smell was coming from something . . . someone. I looked at every man, woman, and child in the ER, even the ones with bandages covering their faces.

Then I saw them. A father and his son. The son, sitting on his father's left, was holding his right arm tightly against his chest and leaning, ever so subtly, away from his father.

I took a few steps toward them, but Thatcher protested.

"What are you doing?" he asked. "Don't you see Pete rolling his hands over and over for us to pick up the pace? Next comes the shouting. You don't want the shouting."

"Give me a minute," I demanded.

I took a few more steps closer to the pair. The father, unaware of my approach, threw down a magazine on the empty chair to his right. As the magazine slapped the chair, the boy shuddered; and when the father reached over the boy for a fresh magazine, the boy flinched, keeping his eyes closed until his father sat back.

The boy's arm was likely broken based on the way he was protectively gathering it in his other arm. He leaned farther away from his father, and as he did, the bad elbow tapped the wooden armrest. He uttered a small howl of pain—understandable considering the break, but the kid's father didn't seem to be as understanding.

The dad leaned over to the son, got up against his ear, and I could swear, no I *knew*, that when the dad opened his mouth to tell his kid to shut up, that foul odor amplified.

Yes, it was him. He was the smell. A father who beats his son, breaks his arm, and curses him for not being able to take it.

Suddenly, I had forgotten the nightmare I had lived in Robert Bailey's kitchen; I had forgotten that my husband was falling out of love with me; and I had forgotten that a judge was waiting for me. I walked right up to the father and asked, "Does junior have a frequent visitor plan here?"

He looked at me and smiled with charm. Naturally. He could turn on the charm all he wanted, but if his stench had an image, then he had green fumes escaping through the small gap between his front teeth. "I'm sorry, what did you say?" he asked me, still smiling.

Thatcher came up from behind and put his hand on my shoulder, trying to tug me back. I grabbed his hand off my shoulder and held it down by my side, squeezing it—I think for strength—because I was about to utter fighting words without really knowing if I still had any fight within me.

"You know what I mean," I said. "I'm asking if your son has a frequent visitor plan at the ER for all the times you beat the crap out of him. I'm sure the hospital can put you on some sort of discounted program. Although my idea of a discounted program for a piece of filth like you would be chopping your hands off rather than chopping your hospital fees."

His smile faded. "I don't know what you're talking about," he said through clenched teeth. "But you got a lot of nerve suggesting that I hit my kid. I ought to hit *you* for talking like that in front of my kid. Now beat it."

I looked at the boy. He had a look of terror and warning in his eyes, trying to convey to me that his father meant what he was saying. Thatcher pulled me back a couple of feet. "Are you accusing this man of beating his kid? Where is this coming from?" he whispered in my ear.

I didn't have time to explain it to him. Pete was already marching toward us, and by the look on his face he intended to drag Thatcher and me out by our ears. There was a nurses' station to my right and I caught the gaze of a middle-aged Hispanic nurse behind the counter. She was desperately trying to hold my attention, nodding at me and pleading with her entire face, wanting to send one message: Yes, do it. Do it. Save the boy.

Pete had approached and was lecturing Thatcher in a forced whisper. What I was about to do was going to physically hurt me, probably even bust out a few stitches, but I had to do it. I raised my voice and shouted, "This father beats his son!"

"Oh, for the love of—" Pete said, exasperated. "Are you serious?"

I turned, only for a second, to look back at Pete, when Thatcher sailed past me and blocked the father's fist, inches away from striking me in the back of the head. Thatcher was squeezing the man's fist within his own. Then, from that position, Thatcher twisted the man's arm, pulled it down, and flipped him to the ground.

Helloooooo, Thatcher! Now that was something to make me smile.

Thatcher came down on the father, getting a knee into his back, and said, "Bad move, man. You can go on and keep kissing that floor while I cuff you."

By now, the boy was on his feet. The conflict in his eyes made me want to stomp on the father's head, or at least his ugly, calloused, beating hands. No child should have to be put in that young boy's position—feeling sorry for the man who made his life a pit of torment and fists. I walked over to the child and stood in front of him, blocking the view of his father while Thatcher pulled the dad up and sat him in one of the chairs.

"Where's your mommy?" I asked the child.

"At work."

That was a knife. A knife right through me. But it wasn't about me. It wasn't.

I took a deep breath in, fighting back a gag reflex hitting me from the smell emanating from that horrible father.

Thatcher said to Pete, "Call dispatch, and then you two go to the arraignment. I'll stay here until uniforms come for this one."

Pete rubbed his fingers through his hair, looking like he wanted to rip every one of his shiny follicles out. "What in the world for?"

"Just do it, Pete."

"You don't get to tell me what to do, Thatcher," Pete said, sneering

"Not now, Pete. Not everything always works out when you follow the book. Sometimes you got to go with instinct, and I'm telling you that something's going off right now in my gut. Look at the kid, Pete. Forget procedure for a second because even you know the ER doctor is going to call this one in later today. So, either we do this now, or we do this later."

I stepped aside to make sure Pete could get a look at the child. The poor thing looked like he dodged shadows just to breathe.

Pete was unmoved. "You can't—"

"Well, I will," Thatcher said, tightening his jaw. "Get her to court. I'll call this one in myself, then."

"Fine, knock yourself out," Pete said.

He led me through the ER's sliding doors and then left me standing by the back door of his vehicle.

"Get in," he barked.

SIXTEEN

Still Falling Down

A part of me wanted to protest sitting in the back of a police car like a criminal, but then that part caught up with reality. For all intents and purposes, I *was* a criminal. Besides, Pete was in no mood for company in the front.

The warm, dirty streets of Fresno buzzed by as Pete raced us to the courthouse. We weren't late. I supposed he only thought we were because of the incident back in the emergency room. He shot me glances every now and then in the rearview mirror, his eyes narrow and his brows furrowed.

I welcomed the silence within the car. I was still trying to figure out what had happened in the ER. Was that father related to Bailey? Is that why they both poured forth the same putridity? A common genetic cesspool that made one's skin reek of . . . of . . . what was that smell anyway? It was awful. It was beyond awful. It was the epitome of wretched, debased, and atrocious. It was unholy.

I dared to break the silence. "Pete?" I asked. "Did you happen to, um, smell anything in the ER?"

He gave me the brows again. Good mercy, I thought. He should practice a new look in the bathroom mirror at home.

"What was I supposed to smell?" he asked.

"Something like a rotting corpse left in the sun," I said. "Even after the buzzards had fed and then died on top, also rotting. And then maggots upon maggots rotting on top of *that*, all like a maraschino cherry of death and decomposition?"

His eyebrows arched in astonishment. Either that or he was flexing the pair to get circulation back into his forehead.

"No," he said. "I think I would've noticed something that drastic and unfortunately detailed."

My face turned to the window, the city still blurring by. "Did Bailey have any family here in town?"

"Why do you ask? Are you going to write an apology?"

I scoffed. "I just want to know if there's anyone else like him out there. Could that guy back in the ER be related to Bailey?"

He shot me another look. "No. Bailey's got some family in Minnesota and that's it."

Must've been a fluke, I thought. Then again, I don't remember smelling anything that foul in my entire life. The first time I smelled it was after Bailey slashed my scalp open. Could it be a by-product of the head injury? Like the creation of a heightened sense? Did everything smell worse?

I leaned forward to Pete and smelled.

Nope, just a faint presence of Irish Spring and a musty room smell that he carried over from the police station.

We were now on Van Ness and I saw the courthouse ahead of us. Pete took a sharp right into the parking lot, cutting into the turn and having the back wheel jump. I bumped up in the back seat, letting out a distressed grunt for the added pain it brought to my head.

"Sorry," he said.

Many of the other official vehicles were near the back door of the courthouse, illegally parked, but Pete found himself a spot near the front, in a properly designated spot.

When he opened my door and helped me out, I asked, "Am I in or out of custody?"

That would make a big difference for any defendant. One involved the chain gang through the back halls and a seat in the jury box, the other involved gliding through the front doors with the facade of freedom.

Pete closed my door. "Well, someone posted your bail, so you get to walk in on your own," he said, holding out his arm to steady me. I opted out of taking a wheelchair with me, and I'm sure Pete was glad for it. He'd be the one pushing the wheelchair. "Here, let me help you. It's a walk. We're going to Department 11."

Great. Eleven was a felony courtroom. That meant one of two things: the murder charge was still on the table or my illegal possession charge counted as a felony rather than a misdemeanor. Worse yet, it could mean both.

Before I walked onward, I asked, "Who bailed me out?"

"Who do you think? Do you ever talk to your husband?"

Outside the courtroom door, my mother and Maddie sat waiting for me. I guess Eddie dropped them off anyway. Either that or they came on their own. Maddie jumped up to greet me with a hug.

"Not so tight," I said.

"Sorry, but oh, Evelyn, what were you thinking?"

I could've sworn it was a given that I wasn't thinking. I guess I hadn't clearly expressed it to everyone else as much as I had to myself. Over and over again.

"That seems to be the common question," I answered.

"How is your head today?"

I shrugged. "At least I'm up and walking. The doctor said that's a few days ahead of schedule. I didn't want Pete to roll me in here in a wheelchair." I turned to see him checking his watch. "He might've pushed me down a flight of stairs," I added.

"I wouldn't have," he rebutted. "I don't make rash decisions to hurt someone because I'm upset with them."

Maddie's mouth opened in shock. She was gearing up to set Pete straight.

"Ignore him," I said. "It's a thing he does. I'll get him back later."

I turned again to Pete, narrowing my eyes, but he was already looking through the wall of windows in front of him.

Maddie grabbed my hands and tugged. "Evy, why?" she asked, pleading. "I don't really want to ask you this because I'm so happy you're okay. But being here in court is different. You might not come out a free woman. So, before that happens, if that happens, I want you to tell me why this happened."

My mouth opened, but that didn't necessarily mean I was going to offer her an answer. I simply wanted her to know I was aware she was due something, even if I wasn't going to pay up just yet.

"You know what, don't answer that," she said suddenly. "I'm sorry. I'll wait until you're ready. Right now, you have other things to worry about. I don't know a lot about legal stuff," she started, "but there are some nasty looking people inside, wearing orange jumpsuits and shackles. And you're going into the same courtroom, in front of the same judge. What's going to happen, Evy?"

Another one of her million-dollar questions. I shrugged again.

"The bailiff has already come out and told us we're not allowed in," she added.

"Sorry," was all I said, despite being glad that was the case.

I looked over Maddie's shoulder and saw my mother, her hand over her open mouth, as she stared at the side of my head. I might as well get this over with, I thought.

I walked over to her and lifted the headband where it covered the stitches.

"Oh my," she said. "That's horrible. Does it hurt?"

"Not enough to make other things hurt less," I answered.

She had been crying. More so than Maddie if I had to put my money on it.

"Are you hurt that I did this?" I asked her.

Her lips trembled. Then she sucked them inward for emphasis before she spoke again. "I'm horrified!" she said, looking relieved for having gotten it out. She took my hand and made me sit next to her. Pete immediately protested.

"Two seconds, Pete," I said. "You said 2:00 p.m., and it's ten until the hour."

Pete sighed, then sat down too.

I looked back at my mother who was by now digging her nails into my hand. "Don't get me wrong, Evelyn, I wished I could castrate the . . . the—"

"Easy, Mom," Maddie interjected. "We're in public and Evy's actually being charged with doing something to him."

"All the same," Mom continued, dismissing Maddie, "you can't go around acting like a wild animal. You have your family to consider."

I pulled my hand out of hers. "My immediate family? Or, do you mean you?"

"I am your immediate family," she said, the shock rising in her voice. "Do you know what your little escapade has done to my life?"

Maddie darted over to Mom, looking down at her, and said, "You promised, Mom. Keep it light, okay?"

"You go back and keep Eddie company," my mother said, trying to shoo Maddie away with a used Kleenex in her hand.

She had said Eddie. Had he come too? I looked up and down the hallway, eventually spotting him. He stood at the far end, near the stairwell. He was too far away for me to see the expression on his face, but he was likely sulking.

"And that reminds me," my mother started again, "your behavior has not only ruined my relationship with Gordon, but it's also ruining yours with Eddie."

"Mother!" Maddie said, her eyes opening in anger.

My mother put the Kleenex up to her nose and gave it a quick wipe. "Oh, Gordon," she said, weeping. "Evelyn, can't you think of anyone but yourself? Gordon has left me because of you."

The shame seared me. I turned around to see how much of this drama Pete was picking up. He looked away as I turned.

When I looked back to Maddie, she was shaking her head at our mother. Then she saw me and said, "Sorry, Evy. I asked her not to bring that up because it doesn't have anything to do with you."

"Oh yes, it does," Mom said.

"No, it doesn't, Mother. Gordon was a freak anyway."

My mother gasped.

"Well, he was," Maddie continued. "I've never liked him and you know what else? I don't think he even liked *you*."

Mom stood, facing off with Maddie. "Just when I thought I couldn't have a more disastrous daughter than Evelyn, you go and top her."

That was my cue. I stood, tapped Pete, and motioned to him that I was ready to go in.

"Mom," I said before I walked away. "Sorry I made Gordon dump you, or whatever."

"He told me he didn't want to be drug down in a family of drama and sordidness," she added.

I patted her on the shoulder. "Yeah, because that's what I alone bring to the table."

I gave Maddie another hug. "Thanks for taking the wrath," I whispered.

"What?" she asked. "It's true. I've never liked Gordon."

"You've never liked any of her boyfriends."

I looked down the hallway again, still trying to make out Eddie's expression. But, just as my vision adjusted, Cole popped in front of my face. He took my hand and planted a kiss on the back of it.

"Let's dance, sweetheart," he said, opening the door for Pete and me. "I think you're going to like the tune good ol' Cole has got coming out for you. The DA's office has come to their senses and you're going to like my music."

Before I disappeared behind the door, I looked back at Maddie. I wanted to tell her I was sorry—I wanted to tell them all that I was sorry—but something inside tried to slap some reality into me. That reality said: "Save it for the end, baby. You haven't finished unraveling yet, so just save it for the end."

It wasn't a good day to realize I was far from the bottom and still falling.

The wood-paneled courtroom had dim lights and an overhead roar of air-conditioning blasting down from the ceilings. The judge hadn't walked in yet, and the clerk and bailiff were huddled around the court reporter's desk. She was pulling cords up from the floor to hook her transcribing machine to her laptop, while announcing to the other two that if her neighbor's dogs kept her up again tonight, she'd slip tranquilizers into tiny balls of ground beef, and then throw them over the fence.

Once we had come through the doors, Pete walked away from us and sat with a group of similarly severe looking men with buzz cuts and untailored suits—the police officer section next to the bailiff's desk.

Cole led me to the left side of the seating area, in the back where the lights didn't make it all the way.

"Let's talk quickly about the arraignment before the judge takes the bench," he told me.

"Please."

"You're going to want to kiss me after this," he said, smiling.

That I doubted. But now was not the time to burst his bubble.

"After I left the hospital, I had another chat with the deputy DA on your case. I agreed to keep you away from the press and he was surprisingly more cooperative after that. Normally, a defendant isn't going to want the press, but with you, you're a ratings gold mine. Anyway, the DA was nervous that if you spoke with the press, you'd garner a bunch of sympathy, and they'd be pressured to act against the state's interests."

"What are their interests?" I asked.

"Look, no one wants to put a bereaved mother behind bars because she offed a child killer. On the other hand, it's not in the DA's best interest to refrain from any punishment when vigilantism is involved. So, the DA agreed to drop the murder charge because of the self-defense, and is ignoring the aggravating circumstances on the possessions—namely, the death of Robert Bailey. They're treating it as a first offense for possession, with mitigating circumstances."

"What's the grand total, then?"

He smiled and leaned closer. "One year probation. Now, do you want to kiss me or not?"

I wondered if he'd be so flirtatious if he were sitting on my left, seeing the absence of a chunk of my hair.

"You said 'child killer.' Does that mean they now have proof that he killed Corinne?" I asked.

Cole huffed, obviously not wanting to veer off the path of breaking down my resistance. "Corinne? No. When those detectives found you in Robert Bailey's house, it's because they were going to arrest him for the murder of Lauren Huller. They found forensic evidence to link him to her murder from a search they did earlier that day. What you had to do with another parent's fight is—"

"All rise!" the bailiff hollered, walking back to his desk as the judge's door cracked open. "Come to order. Department 11 is now in session, the Honorable Arthur Long presiding."

I watched as Judge Long took his seat, straightening his glasses, and gave us all disapproving looks.

What would he think of me? A lawyer unhinged.

"Does Long have any kids?" I whispered to Cole.

"Seven. Why?"

My eyes expanded at the high number. I looked carefully back at the judge. White hair, sagging cheeks, and probably unaware that he bared his teeth when he squinted to look at every face in his courtroom.

"I'm just trying to gauge my audience," I answered.

"Don't need to," he said. "It's out of the judge's hands now. You'll plead out. It's already been negotiated." He leaned in close to me again. I felt the tip of his nose barely touch the top of my ear as he said, "I wanted to make sure that when you get around to thanking me, that you know I'm the only one who really fought for you."

SEVENTEEN

The Wrong Man

After the arraignment proved that Cole was right, and I'd be a soon-to-be disbarred attorney who has to check in with probation on the seventh floor every month, Pete said he'd drive me back.

Back? I didn't know where back was. The hospital? My home? Maddie and my mother were still out in the hallway after I plead guilty to the misdemeanor, but Eddie wasn't. Maddie told me he had left right after I went into the courtroom, taking a cab home.

When Pete sat down in the car, he pulled out his cell phone and called Thatcher while the car idled in the courthouse parking lot.

I could only hear Pete's part of the conversation.

"Where are you?"

"He's already been booked?"

"Did you make sure the boy had a guardian or rep while he gave his statement?"

"His mother and older brother too? That bad, huh?"

"Why would I tell you good job? Isn't the satisfaction of locking up a child abuser enough reward itself?"

"I'm not interested in how she knew," he said curtly, looking at me.

I rolled my eyes, but the effect was lost on Pete, who was ignoring me.

"No. You can ask her that later. I'm going to drop her off at her house."

So, I was going home. I was happy for my bed, but not excited to deal with Eddie. He made me feel like something was slipping away. It was similar to the gut-wrenching feeling I had been entertaining for the last few hours, that my career had waved bye-bye and had already left a box of my stuff at reception.

"Yup," Pete said. "She got off almost scot-free. Bet you're happy, right?

Although, Bailey would have been your first perpetrator to go from capture to conviction. You were robbed of getting your first conviction." "I guess. Fine, the child abuser will be your first. Good job, then. I'll see you later."

Pete flipped his phone shut and tossed it in one of his empty cup holders.

"What will happen to the boy?" I asked, buckling my seat belt.

"His mother and older brother were victims too. I guess they'll all just keep on keeping on without dear old dad in the picture."

"What did the boy say? What did his father do to him?"

Pete gave me a hard, cold look, even shaking his head slightly in disbelief. "Now why in the world would I involve you in any more of my investigations? Are you going to go shoot that one too?"

"No. I just want to know because I hand delivered this one to you," I said matter-of-factly.

"Well, thank you for your powers of observation in noticing an abused child, Mrs. Barrett, but I'll kindly ask you to mind your own business from here on out."

Was it powers of observation? I wondered. Or was it the smell? The smell had been so thick and strong with that father, like it had been with Bailey when I woke up in a pool of his blood.

Both men were bad men; both were evil, despicable child hurters. They were disgusting inside and out no matter which way you flipped them. They wore their sinful filth like a bad, measurable stench.

Wait.

Wearing sinful filth like a bad stench.

Could it be possible?

There *was* something the father and Bailey had in common—their unholy hunger to shatter innocent lives.

But how would that translate into something I could smell? *Why* did it translate into something I could smell?

I might be able to find something on Google about enhanced senses after head injuries, but how I could potentially smell men who hurt children didn't seem the right sort of thing to look up online.

Our first stop was the hospital—I hadn't officially been released as of yet.

"Well, sweetie," my nurse from earlier, the sprite with the headband, said. "What's the news?" She was leaning against the nurses' station, and had watched Pete and I walk down the hall from the elevator.

"I'm not going to jail," I replied.

"So, you're free," she said.

"Free?" I scoffed, easing off the headband to give back to her. "I guess that depends on how you define free." I extended what I had borrowed back to her.

"No, no. You keep that," she said. "You'll need it for a few weeks."

It would be more than a few weeks if I intended to keep my shoulder blade length hair. Perhaps a bob-cut was in order. Eddie liked it longer, but Eddie was playing hard to reach, wasn't he?

"Now, what do you mean you're not free?" she asked. "There's only one way to define free, and it means you not being in jail."

Clearly she had never lost a child, or heard the demons scratching for your soul in the bitterness of a tear-filled night.

"Not being in jail," I corrected, "is a matter of *not* being incarcerated. Freedom has nothing to do with that. I'm sure many prisoners still feel free in their souls and minds while their bodies are incarcerated, and vice versa."

"Oh yeah," she said. "You're almost all the way back to normal now, aren't you? You're a quick healer. Good for you. Your husband talked to me about you and I didn't think he'd be so spot-on, but he called it. He said once you started with your . . . hey, Betty, what was that word he used for her?"

The gray-haired, mother hen of the pack smiled and said, "Semantics. He said once she started with the semantics then we'd know she's up to speed."

"Yeah, that's it," the sprite said. "Semantics. I'm going to go get your doctor. You should do the semantics stuff with him and you'll be out of here in no time."

Pete took hold of my elbow. "I have to go check on a few things. I'm going to have the nurse call me when you've been released and then I'll drive you home."

"That's okay," I told him. "You don't need to do that. I'll get Eddie or my sister to take me home."

"No," he said, tightening his grip. "I'll take you home because we need to talk."

"I don't want to talk. I'm free, remember?"

"I'm with you on the semantics. I don't think you are *free*. That's why we need to talk."

He gave my nurse the instruction to call him right before the doctor released me, and she agreed.

Between being last on the doctor's totem pole of things to do, and reluctantly complying with Pete's request, it was a few minutes after 5:00 p.m. before we were on our way back to my house. A golden, retreating sun capped the tops of nearby trees. I didn't want the sun to go down on this day. Nothing seemed particularly special or magical about this day—despite the fact I got off with a slap on the wrist from my deadly encounter with Bailey. In fact, I felt rather ambivalent about it all, stemming from the fact that I still wished I *had* died on Bailey's kitchen floor. Maybe that was it. From that day, when Pete and Thatcher found me, until now, the sun looked like it rested in the same spot. The blackness of my coma and everything in between was nothing more than a pause on what seemed like the longest day.

And despite the fact that the sun had risen each day, it hadn't risen for me. I hadn't yet forced myself to contemplate what it meant to live another day, because right now, that's the last thing I wanted.

We weren't on Van Ness for very long before Pete veered off into a covered parking lot attached to a bank.

"What are we doing here?" I asked as his headlights came on. Steering tightly around the first switchback, Pete pulled into a spot on the second level and killed the engine.

"We need to talk. Just you and me. Are you game?"

"Probably not."

"Can you fake it for a few minutes?"

"I'll try," I said, only wanting my bed.

Pete took a long, slow breath in through his nose, and then out again. He tapped his fingers on his steering wheel, looked at me, and then turned away. He did this twice. Otherwise, he let the silence close in around us, just as the darkness of the parking structure had.

Finally, he spoke. "What did he say?" he asked.

"What did who say?"

"Robert Bailey. What did he say to you before you shot him? And, if he said anything after you shot, I'd like to know that, too."

"Why?"

"Because I want to know, that's why. I've cleaned up a lot of your messes thus far, and you owe me."

"You tally things funny, Pete. The way I see it, you owe *me*. You owe me to close Corinne's case. Putting aside the little tangle I initiated with Bailey, and yes, thank you for helping me with it, you still owe me Bailey's name in Corinne's file as the murderer and pedophile."

"Would that make you feel better?" he asked. He was being sincere but it felt like a jab and a blow.

"Feel better?" My voice rose like a torrent of waves. "*Feel* better? Is that all you think this is about for me?"

"You're giving me that impression," he said. "One minute I'm telling you I don't like Bailey for your daughter's death, and the next, I'm seeing you lying on his floor after I almost popped your head in two from kicking open the door."

"Don't leave out the tragedy in between: another dead girl at the hands of that man."

We stared each other down for a stretch of time.

"I could just go round and round with you. I'm sure of it," he said. "Can we skip to the meat? I want to know what Robert Bailey said to you in his house."

I rubbed the bottom of my left eye. It had become watery. I had been withstanding the urge to blink with that one eye because it pulled at the stitches when I did. "He said nothing," I said.

His voice turned cross. "You're lying. What did he say?"

I didn't want to go back to that day. Still, something about it was eating me up. I was trying to forget it, but my conscience wouldn't allow that. Whenever my mind slipped into thinking about Bailey's body in the morgue, or the wormy dirt, or even a pile of ashes in the hospital incinerator, there was a small clanging and beating in the distance, as if some fuzzy and has-been toy monkey clapped his symbols. *Bang, bang, bang, bang.*

Pete's question made that monkey beat faster, harder.

I closed my eyes, mainly out of frustration and fatigue. He'd ask again and again and again. And I think I wanted to tell him anyway. Maybe it would undo that knot in my gut. I thought I had felt wound up because of the looming arraignment, but if that were the case, then it would have released by now.

Yet, it remained. If I told Pete what he wanted to know, if I could remember why my bloodied hands had felt so guilty, then perhaps I could understand why I wanted to find a dark corner to huddle in and cry. My mind went over the statement I had written down for Pete the day before:

I had just wanted to talk to Bailey—I never told Pete and Thatcher I went inside to swipe something of Bailey's for his DNA. Then Bailey laughed at me for pretending to be a cop. The gig was up, and he reached for a bottle. Hate and destruction were in his eyes, I pulled the gun to make him stop. He charged, I shot. Then the wake-up in a blood puddle.

Going over it again was like eating at a greasy spoon restaurant, except I knew I was missing the main entrée, the part of the meal that made sure you doubled over with belly pain.

Fish. I thought about fish. Dying fish, dying carp.

My eyes opened and I slouched down in my seat. There it was. There was the part I had been trying to block.

"He said, 'Not me,'" I told Pete. "When we were both staggering, ready to hit the floor, he kept trying to say something. The only thing he got out was, 'Not me.'"

"Hmm." Pete only uttered that one word while he rubbed his chin and stared at me.

"Does this change anything?" I asked.

"For who?" Pete asked. "For you, I think it does. I know it does. For everyone else, it doesn't change anything. Well, I guess for Bailey it might've meant breathing still, but tit for tat for a guy who would have potentially raped and killed more children on top of Lauren Huller."

"He killed more children?"

"No, I'm saying he probably would have. At least, that's what the station shrink said. He said you put an end to a potential serial child killer."

Suddenly, I didn't feel so sick to my stomach.

Pete continued, "See, there are two types of pedophiles: the familiar abuser, and the unconnected one. The familiar one only preys on children he has direct, repetitive, and familiar contact with. The unknown prefers not to have an emotional or familiar connection with his victims. It makes the after-abuse survival rate plummet because there's nothing that ties the abuser and the abused together. Pedophiles preying on familiar children actually believe they love their victims; killing them is the last thing on their mind, but things do go wrong on occasion. For instance, the threat of a child not keeping it a 'secret' preempts the so-called love.

"The department pegged Robert Bailey as the unconnected type. He had certain criteria—which you know because you stole my file—and when someone fit the criteria, he put things into motion. He's likely been on the prowl, actively, for a few months. That's when we got the first complaint."

He rubbed his chin again. What was left of the light in the parking garage had stolen away as we talked about a dead demon. A car had come by every now and then, its tires screeching through quick turns on the smooth concrete surface, trying to catch up with the rest of the rush hour pack. And now, when I heard the escaped squeal of tires ripping through the dark, silent air, my heart let a squeal rip out as well: You killed the wrong man.

"That's where you came in, or I should say, your daughter," Pete said. "I know you think otherwise, but the only way your daughter was connected to Robert Bailey was that she gave him a reason to finally strike, to do more than bother little girls in the park."

"What do you mean?" I asked.

"I figure Bailey used your daughter's death as a window of opportunity to start his career, if you will. As long as your daughter's real killer stayed out there, and Bailey got arrested for a crime on a different child, he could always use the defense that it wasn't him, since he had that alibi for when your daughter was abducted. It would likely create enough probable cause to spring him."

I turned my face away, looking into the corner of the garage at an empty, dirty stairwell with a wall mosaic of pressed, discarded gum.

"So now, because of what I've told you, you're sure Bailey didn't kill Corinne," I said.

"No, I was sure when we got the DNA back. The sample from your daughter and Bailey's sample weren't a match. He was a match for Lauren Huller, but that's it. I wanted to know what Bailey said to you because I want *you* to be sure he didn't kill your daughter."

I bit on my lower lip, introducing pain to stop the anger and tears from peeking out. Turning back to Pete, I said, "How many free passes in court do you think one mother gets while trying to find her child's killer?"

Pete shook his head in frustration and turned on the car. "I really wish you'd stop surprising me." He threw the car into reverse and started down the winding tunnels of the parking garage.

EIGHTEEN

Alone

It was dark by the time Pete dropped me off at my house. There was a certain comfort in it being night already, despite the fact Eddie liked to sit in the dark these days. At least I wouldn't have to see him scowl at me.

Perhaps it was the recent emptiness and stillness of the house that did Eddie in each evening. There was no laughing or shrieking, and no little blonde thing climbing up his legs faster than he could climb up a telephone pole at work. Thus, he would sit in one of the living room chairs, in the dark, like a man come undone. Eventually, the pull of the night would prompt him to turn on a light, even if it was only the flicker of the television back in his den.

When I let myself into the kitchen, not even the light above the stove was on. Nothing except the faint blue numbers on the oven, telling me it was after seven and Eddie would've, should've been home by now. Either he had come and left, or was having a really bad night, moping in the den. I went for the light switch in the hallway, near the living room, and flipped it on.

I gasped when I saw the back of Eddie's head, perfectly still against his recliner. He hadn't even flinched from the light.

He was facing the large bay windows that overlooked the open, dark fields of the golf course. I tiptoed to the back of the chair and stood quietly behind. I was waiting to hear his breath, waiting for anything. A low, soft wisp of air blew out, then back in.

He wasn't asleep or, God forbid, dead; he was defeated. Leaning over to the end table next to him, I turned on that lamp too.

He blinked for the first time, and then turned his face away from me. At least he moved. Not in my favor, but he moved.

"Eddie?" I asked. He still looked away. I came around the chair and stood in front of him.

His jaw tightened at the sound of my voice. If there were a wager on the ensuing battle I foresaw, it was time to double-down in Eddie's favor. I had a feeling he'd be the victor tonight. I moved farther to my left, trying to put myself in his line of sight, but his eyes were barren. That was definitely worse than a scowl.

There wasn't anything to say that he'd give me the satisfaction of listening to, but I still wanted to try. I'd made a mistake by telling him to go away. I simply didn't want to deal with the pressure of thinking about anyone else at that moment, least of all the only other person on the planet who had the right to be as angry as I was, and yet, who chose not to be.

"Eddie?" I asked again.

His eyes flashed with a hint of recognition. Still, he wouldn't look at me. He held up a hand, palm toward me to stop me from talking. I guess I deserved that. In the morning, he'd feel better. I could wait until the morning to talk to him.

"Fine," I said. "I'm going to bed."

"I'm going to leave, Evelyn," he droned, his flat voice going only as far as it needed to in plucking the strained chords of my being.

I wanted to ask him if he meant leave the room, but no, that's not what he meant. Somewhere during the day, this spat of ours had turned into an unfair game. First, I hadn't known we were playing, and second, I certainly didn't know the umpire had tallied the final score.

"You don't have to get drastic," I said to him. "I'm sorry for what I've done. I'm sorry for pursuing vengeance, and I'm done with it." I hoped that would buy me a solid play in overtime.

He looked at me. I wished he wouldn't have. Eddie's the wrong guy to play poker with.

"No, you're not," he said. "And you won't be done until you find the right guy. They told you today that he's still out there, didn't they? They told me." He sighed, closing his eyes. "I imagine they've told you too." He shook his head, then opened his eyes again, staring past me. "They told you that you got the wrong one and that Corinne's killer is still on the loose. So you'll search again and you'll find others. Each time, you'll think it's the right person, and you may even be right. You might be the one who solves the case. But you might also end up dead."

"No, I'm done. I'm telling you."

He stood suddenly, springing from the chair so that it shook without him in it. He grabbed the table lamp, its cord coming along for the ride, and he aimed the top of the lampshade at my face like an intrusive flashlight. My hands instinctively blocked the light.

"Put your hands down and look at me," he said. "Go ahead. Lie to me again. Lie to me and tell me you won't put yourself in danger."

"It's too bright, Eddie," I said, my chin to my shoulder, cringing from the spotlight, the heat, his face, his truth.

The light went down. Eddie went back to the small table and set the lamp back down.

"Tell me again," he said, his back to me.

"I'm done."

He huffed, then shut off the light. I stood facing his back with only the light from the hallway dimly seeping into the room.

He turned to face me. His head had fallen back and his face was toward the ceiling, as if trying to pull down some sliver of mercy from the heavens. He took one last breath in before he responded. It sounded strained and painful, like a cancer victim grasping for one more ounce of oxygen to anchor that final kiss to their beloved.

It was cold all of a sudden. A shiver spread within me because I had missed something—missed something about my Eddie.

"I'm sorry, Evelyn," he started, "but I don't think I can stay here anymore. If you're going to continue pursuing something that might end up killing you, I'd rather not be the chump husband who sat at home while you did it."

That one hurt. A lot. Then it made me angry. I wanted to push him back in his recliner for hurting me, for quitting on me, because that's what he was doing. He was acting like a quitter. My hands balled into trembling fists, but he turned away and walked to the light switch in the hallway. He flipped it off, leaving me in utter darkness, and then dragged his feet down the hall, back to his den.

I gaped at the thought that he had left me alone in the dark. If this were still a game, I'd kick dirt on the ump's shoes and cry, "Foul! Foul! Foul!"

I bent down and turned the table lamp on again.

"Quitter!" I shouted out to him.

His heavy walk came to a halt in the hallway. A moment later he reappeared in the living room.

"You did it first," he said. The small table lamp only illuminated up to his chest. His face, his pallor, and the bereavement in his eyes hid behind the darkness. "Corinne's death didn't have to mean the end of us, but you made it that way. I think you've quit on life altogether, haven't you? And for what? What else is there in this world that will make her come back to us, Evelyn? What will make all this mess disappear? What's going to fix her death, your anger, my despair, and even our marriage? You think *you* can fix it by going after guilty parties? You're doing nothing but digging deeper holes."

He stepped further into the living room, the light ascending to his chin and then his nose before he stopped. He must have realized I still couldn't see his eyes and took two more steps forward. My head turned away. I couldn't bear his gaze.

"And I'm sick of watching you fall into those holes. I'm sick of falling into them myself."

His words were like a knife blade that had jabbed inward—clean and deep—like a surprise deathblow that pierced my lungs, leaving me unable to take even a final breath in.

He put his hands up to his face and groaned. Almost a growl. "And that Cole," he said. "Twice today I saw him touching you. Do you even know the last time you let *me* touch you?"

I didn't.

"Do you?" he asked, getting louder.

I still didn't.

"At her funeral, Evelyn. Everything got buried that day, didn't it? Ever since, you've been avoiding me the same exact way you avoided watching our daughter lowered into the ground. All alone, Evelyn. ALL ALONE!" He panted. Three times. I counted to distract myself from looking at him and seeing the tears I knew were wetting his tired eyes.

"Just like me," he said. "You're not going to stick with it to the end with me either, are you?"

I faced the bay window, the same one he'd been looking at when I came home. There was a certain calm to the empty darkness outside. Except for the light turned on beside me. It allowed me to see my reflection in the black sea of the window. No wonder Eddie liked the lights off: after the death of a child, a parent's face isn't a pretty picture. It's like a mixture of all the small, quaint features you remember of the child—the arch of their brows, the shape of their nostrils, the flow of their hairline—but shredded in a pain that would make you unrecognizable to that very child.

I turned again, away from the window and away from Eddie.

"I'm going to sleep in the den," he said. "I think I know where you stand, but I'll decide what I'm going to do in the morning." He left and went back down the hall.

After he closed the den door, I quickly packed a large suitcase. Clothes, my laptop, the makeup bag Eddie had brought to the hospital, and a few other odds and ends. I tore off my navy pantsuit, crumpled it, and threw it into the bathtub. It wasn't my favorite suit anymore. I hated it.

It was clear to me that life separated itself into two categories: what I could and could not control. The more I could control, the less chance I'd have to endure a repeat of what seemed to be a constant sledgehammer to my once clean and glassy life—each blow bursting me into a million, tiny pieces with small sentences that meant huge pain. Such as, "Your daughter's missing." Or, as was the case tonight from Eddie, "I'm leaving."

If I waited until morning for him to leave, I'd lose the control. But if I struck first, then I wielded the sledgehammer, not Eddie.

It wasn't as hard as I thought it would be to close the front door behind me. I had made plenty of noise packing up and dragging my suitcase down the hall, but I closed the front door with the smallest of movements and the hush of an unuttered good-bye.

Leaving that house was like walking away from a life burned to the ground. Sometimes, the only thing to get from sifting through the ashes is dirty hands. If I tried to sift it out with Eddie, what if we both found the fire had consumed all, and we had plowed through for nothing?

The end of my marriage didn't exactly feel like the type of circumstance that led to a stay at a nice hotel. Still, I wasn't feeling *so* debased that I found it proper to end up at a place that used their pool as a petri dish experiment.

Thus, the Holiday Inn it would be.

When I pulled into the parking lot, I saw a group of men stumbling out from the on-site restaurant. I decided not to get out of my car until the group disbanded. Besides, I imagined I was leaking. Even though I was the first to leave the house, and even if I pretended I was tough about it, Eddie's decision to discard me had punctured the watertight seal of my heart. I was sure of it. My body wanted to leak emotions like bile.

Thus, when I saw those booze-filled men laughing and slinging remarks back and forth at each other, I thought my insides would burst because I refused to cry.

Too many tears had already been shed by Eddie alone. And for what? Corinne was still dead, her killer was still on the loose, and my husband no longer loved me.

Holding it in, willing everything to stay inside, made me angry and angry was good. Angry made me feel better.

That's when it hit me. I couldn't walk around the world, running the risk of leaking from my wounds. Being emotional didn't fix anything and the only way to stop the leak was to mend the wounds. But how?

I considered a few ways. I could wait on the passage of time to heal my wounds but no, I didn't have any more time to give. I could get the wounds stitched up, but so help me, if one more person pricked me . . .

Then there was soldering. To solder: to mend; repair; patch up.

What could I use to solder those pesky and deep wounds, though? Which tool in the box of my experience was going to do the trick?

Oh yes, my anger. The white-hot fury of my seething anger. That would do it. That would solder the smithereens out of the multitude of wounds.

My teeth were grinding together by the time the men from the restaurant finally moved into their cars. They were hollering at each other over the crowded lot as they walked in different directions. I felt the echoing of their voices on either side of my vehicle until each said their last good-bye.

Before the first car door shut, I called 911.

"Nine-one-one dispatch, what is your emergency?"

"I'm over here at the Holiday Inn on Van Ness, near the convention center. There's five guys who just stumbled out of the bar, clearly intoxicated, and they're all getting behind the wheel."

"Can you give me descriptions?"

I told her everything from hair color to car color.

"We'll send someone right over. Do you want the officer to make contact with you?"

"No. I'm just trying to make sure they don't get away with it."

"Okay. Is there anything else, ma'am?"

If I were up for it, I would have asked, "How much time do you have?" Instead, I replied, "No."

Sure, I saw the irony in calling the cops on men trying to break a rule. I had broken a few rules myself. But just like I had done with the drunk men driving home, I was protecting the public. Eradicating Robert Bailey was protecting the public. If Eddie wanted to be done with me for doing the right thing, then so be it.

There, that felt better. A good old soldering did the trick.

NINETEEN

Endure

Ten minutes after I closed the door to my hotel room, latching it shut, I was sitting in the closet, crumpled up in the corner where my suitcase should have gone.

No crying, solder it shut. If I kept reminding myself, it would take. It had to.

The only thing that got me up was the prospect of a Google search. Accessing the hotel's wireless provider, it didn't take long to verify that one's sense of smell—as well as taste—can be affected by a head injury. In most cases, it lessened, in some, it heightened. A doctor might look upon me sympathetically if I told him that cheese now smelled like toast and ketchup like coffee, but would I be leaving without a straitjacket if I told him that pedophiles and child abusers now smelled like unholy hunger?

I started a new search to see if anyone had experienced the ability to smell evil, but the only things that came up made me fearful to click on the links. I was worried I'd either be converting my faith or joining a cult based on some of the blurbs describing the sites.

Not even on the Internet could I find someone to talk to about it. I couldn't tell Eddie or anyone else. They'd think I was crazy.

Maybe I was crazy. Leaving my husband because I didn't want him to leave me first might have reinforced that, but I didn't want to dwell on that. It was all stress. My life had been a walking nightmare of late. Even without the blow to the head, my brain would have frazzled. I needed sleep and I needed it where eyes weren't on me. Whether they were Eddie's eyes, or the nurses, or whomever else; looking at me, judging me, telling me how *they* would handle it.

But not anymore. Now it was only me, my stiff hotel bed with starchy linens, and the streetlights outside cutting through the curtains. It was a shame the Internet search wasn't helpful. I supposed I'd just have to wing this one.

Besides, I had other things to work through. Perhaps it was simply an unfortunate coincidence that the child-hitting father smelled like Robert Bailey. I didn't smell anything now. I hadn't smelled anything at all for the rest of the day. Now I could throw myself into arranging a new life that didn't make me feel guilty for feeling the way I wanted to feel over losing Corinne.

Never mind I was scared senseless to be alone. The less I was around the things that reminded me of her—including Eddie and the house— the more I could rationally stuff the tears away.

Tomorrow was my new day.

First, I changed my voice mail message on my cell: Hi. I'm on hiatus. Leave a message if you want, but don't be offended when I don't call back. Bye.

Second was a haircut. I wasn't sure if I admired or loathed the woman who cut my hair. She went right after the elephant in the room when I took two steps into her salon. She announced to me that it was her personal mission in life to make me look less like freak-zilla. She brought the length up to my chin and swept several layers forward, hiding the bare area and black stitches, and told me the style made my lips look "pouty."

I wanted to say, "No, it's not the hairdo, it's the barren life."

But half of the barrenness was my own doing, so I kept that to myself.

A day later, and thoroughly tired of the hotel, I decided to find a rental home. Eddie had left a message that day too.

"I assume you're all right. I think this is better for now." He sighed, letting the seconds click by in dead, recordable silence. "I never thought we couldn't work through something together," he continued. "But then again, I didn't think she'd die, or that you'd . . ." Another slow, miserable sigh. "I don't want a divorce, but the time apart will be good. I'll be here. You know where to find me. I'll keep the house up, and the bills, and unless you tell me otherwise, everything will be the same except I'll be sleeping here, and you'll be . . . well, you'll be wherever you are. I'm hoping you'll eventually tell me where that is, but if you don't, at least tell your sister. Take care, Evelyn."

That worked. For now.

I found a real estate agency that assisted in rentals, and gave them my search criteria: small house, small yard, and far away from any park. The goal was to find a neighborhood that a young family wouldn't bother living in.

A woman, the manager of the agency, helped me, saying she recognized me from the press I received after killing Bailey. Jeanine wore her hair in a tight bun, a red blazer burning with color, and kept her face so pinched up, I wanted to hand her a bran muffin.

After she confirmed that I had money—her words, not mine—she interpreted my request in a unique way.

"So, you want a low-income rental? Like in the . . . in the . . . ghetto?" She whispered the last word as if it were dirty.

"No," I said. "I'm not allowed to carry firearms anymore. I fear I'd be underaccessorized in the ghetto."

She chuckled slightly, then looked as if her mind was wrapping itself around the first part of my statement.

"Okay, so a small place in a decent area. Like the old homes from the 40s and 50s."

"Are those popular areas for young families?"

"Oh no," she answered. "The young families love the new developments, all those cookie-cutter homes. Are you thinking of starting a family soon—" Her hand went over her mouth. "Oh my," she spoke through parted fingers. "I'm sorry. I forgot."

I shrugged. What was there to say?

"No. It's just me. Oh, and if there's a place that's furnished, let's start there."

She nodded, looking at my ring finger. I had already taken my wedding rings off and put them in the empty Valium bottle I had saved from that first week after Corinne's death.

There was a house on Tower Street that fit the bill, though it was almost too pretty for my predominant mood. The home had a gray-shingled exterior with a purple door, wood floors, and white wainscoting. It was also partly furnished. There was a queen bed in the master and a blanket-covered futon in the second bedroom. In the living room, there was a low couch and a television stand, sans the television. The owner left the dining room empty except for a built-in dining hutch that I'd likely never use, and the kitchen had a thrift store, two-seater table tucked against the far wall. The laundry room led to a covered back porch, and in there, I found a rocking chair that reminded me of myself: all alone, pushed away in a corner, and nicking out against the walls when someone rocked it too hard.

When Jeanine sat me in her office to sign a six-month lease, I gave her the entire amount of rent, in cash. She counted it, then counted it again.

"Mrs. Barrett," she gushed. "Can I be frank with you?" she asked, leaning into her desk to get closer to me.

I stared blankly at her.

"You're self-made, right? From your legal work? Why are you—"

My hand went up to stop her. "Please don't finish that question. I need a break from things. Let's leave it at that."

"Oh, I think I can understand that. It's hard work bringing undesirables to justice. Have you ever considered how many of them are in this world?" She looked past me, over my shoulder. "You could work with one and not even realize it." Her eyes narrowed on something in the main area of the agency where ten or so agents busied themselves in their cubicles. I turned my head to follow her line of sight but saw nothing except the tops of people's heads—a few incidents of radial balding, and the rest a conglomerate of heavily hair-sprayed coifs.

"Yuck, pedophiles," she continued. "They're everywhere, you know? They're so sick, they're so vile, and they make me just want to vomit."

My first night in the Tower Street house was either an omen for a terrorizing future, or an indicator of my continuing run of painfully bad luck. Despite the fact I thought I'd be done by now with waking up from tear-filled fits, that night was a doozy of dreams turned into nightmares. The worst was when I dreamed Corinne and I were baking Christmas cookies together, like we had done on our last Christmas together.

She got tired, her small legs unable to stand on her little stool any longer, and I hoisted her up on the counter. She sat crisscross-applesauce on some loose sprinkling of flour and I relished the thought that once we were done, I'd get to dust off her little buns. I pushed her back into the middle of the granite island, making sure she wouldn't fall over, and then turned around to put a stick of butter into the microwave—I had forgotten to soften it earlier. Ten seconds would do the trick. My back was to Corinne. She knew better than to go anywhere. What could happen in ten seconds?

Ding.

Butter was ready. I turned back to Corinne, but when I saw the empty countertop, the butter went to the floor. The plate went to the floor too. Shattered.

Corinne was gone. Gone, gone. Two small voids in the flour sprinkles were left, and nothing else.

If only I had planned ahead and softened the butter earlier, I wouldn't have had to turn my back on her. If only I hadn't gone back to work and left her with a nanny. If only, if only, if only . . . then the waking up, screaming, crying, and yup, I'm still alone and I no longer had any baby buns to dust off.

Whenever those dreams came, it was as if she was there, truly there with me, and then she wasn't. Each time, I had to relive the panic and regret that one miniscule change could have made the difference between having a child to hold, and having a child to bury. When it boiled down to such a little variance, it was easier to trick myself into believing that a horrendous, permanent outcome could never be the result of such a tiny twist of fate. So, she wasn't really gone. I'd get a second chance, right? This was only a test to make me suffer a bit before the plot took a twist and she came out of what's behind curtain number two. Corinne wasn't actually gone forever. She was at an extended slumber party, or on a long camping trip with her daddy. Right?

Oh, who was I kidding?

Whenever my mind tried to hold on to the hope she was gone only for a little while, my pessimistic, barely pumping heart knew better. It remembered that not only had I buried her forever but also that I was too much of a coward to have seen it firsthand.

It was a battle, truly, between my heart and mind. Hours passed after my dream, without a lick of sleep in between, because those two parts of my body wanted to duke it out. My heart believed in embracing the inevitable truth: nothing was ever going to be the same again, and that was still all right and survivable. But I wasn't ready for that truth.

So my mind responded by calling my heart an ill-bred liar, then turned its back and slept on the far side of the bed, pulling at the covers just for spite.

I was in no mood to wake up early the next morning, but it was time for my first probation appointment, even if it meant arriving sheathed in despair and destitution.

Once inside the elevator, it was hard to push that particular button for the probation floor because I remembered how I used to react when I wasn't the convict—moving over as far as I could within the metal box, when someone dragged themselves in and pushed button number seven.

The seventh floor hall was dark and carried a scent of bleached toilets. After I rounded the first corner, I pulled a business card out of my purse. It had the name Taylor Bernard on it. He was my probation officer. Room 701, that's where everyone started, room 701. It was one large room that took up almost the entire seventh floor. A waiting area was just inside an opened door, separated by a thin, wooden banister.

I could either stand and hold up a sullied wall, or sit in a hard, orange chair next to even harder looking people, waiting for Taylor Bernard to call my name.

I sat. There were two others waiting beside me. The woman twitching to my right had scabs on her face and knots in her hair. Nope, you're not going to pass this urine test, but thanks for coming in.

The man on my left had a tight T-shirt and droopy pants. My eyes had a constant audience with his underwear band—tattered experience, though it was—because the man persistently leaned forward, with his elbows atop his knees and his face in his hands. Worse yet, he had a wide array of Looney Tunes tattoos up and down his arms. I wanted to know why, but wasn't nearly bored enough to ask. In fact, I wasn't even going to look at him anymore. I'd keep my eyes straight, ignore the melting pot of criminal element around me, and hopefully, I'd be back home by—

"Holy geez!" I shouted out, overcome with sudden and repulsing nausea. That smell.

It was back. Ah, where was my Google search now?

I turned to the doorway, where the smell seemed to originate. He was a small, balding man, with a light blue cardigan and brown-rimmed glasses. It was too hot for a sweater, but he couldn't have weighed more than a hundred ten and his skin looked thin and opalescent, contrasted by his purple veins. Let me guess, sicko, you're going for Mr. Rogers?

I didn't have to think about it for more than a second. It felt conclusive at that point: I could smell a pedophile.

"No!" I said, jumping out of my seat, facing him. "You get out of here."

He obliged, like the little weakling he was.

"Wait, no," I said.

He stopped and fixed his glasses. A churn of vomit rolled up my throat. I swallowed the bitterness of bile back down.

"If you go, you'll just go and hurt another child. That's what you do, isn't it? You hurt children." My hands trembled. I was twitching more than the druggie behind me was. I raised a shaking finger at him, aiming at an invisible point in the center of his forehead. "Oh, I hate you. I hate everything about you. You . . . you . . . you make me sick. You make me want to vomit. You're disgusting."

Jeanine, the real estate agent, sprang to mind. Those were almost her exact words.

"Do you know how bad you smell right now?" I asked him.

He backed up, looking over his shoulder to see how far the elevator was.

"No, no, no," I said. "You're not going back out there. I won't let you touch another child. And that's what you do." I looked him up and down again. "You're too little to smack them around, so you must—" He was so insignificant in size that his victims had to be the smallest of them, like little four-year-olds . . .

My cheeks ballooned, trying to hold back my gag reflex. I had my hand over my mouth for the second time, swallowing the rising bile.

I walked closer to him, breathing only through my mouth to prevent another gagging. "This city's kind of justice isn't good enough for the likes of you. I have my own justice. It involves you without pants, then tying you to a chair with your sweater, and a sharp pair of scissors—"

"Whoa, whoa, whoa," a man's voice cried out, swinging open the door on the wood barrier and entering the waiting area.

He stood in front of me, putting both his hands on the tops of my arms. "Are you Evelyn Barrett?" he asked.

I nodded, looking over his shoulder to peek at the pedophile again. He was still inching toward the elevator.

"Not so fast, Mr. Carlisle," the man holding my arms said without looking back. "If you don't make your appointment, you know where you're going to end up tonight."

"I won't be treated like this," the pedophile said, his voice squeaking like a hungry rat.

"Give it a rest," the man in front of me responded. Then he said to me, "Come on back with me, Mrs. Barrett. I'm Taylor Bernard, your probation officer."

"No," I said. "That little demon needs to be arrested. Don't you know what he does to children?"

Officer Bernard gently nudged me by my shoulders, prompting me forward to his desk on the other side of the partition.

"Um, *I* know what he's done, but what's got me is how *you* know what he's done."

"Because I can smell the filth on him," I said, baring my teeth in disgust.

"As in 'he hasn't showered' filth?" he asked, cocking his head.

"No, as in he wears his lust for children on him like a foul, malodorous stench."

Officer Bernard stopped, stopping me next to him. He was processing what I had said. Then he shook his head and took me back to his desk.

"Here you go," he said, pulling out a chair for me.

Before I sat down, I turned to see the Mr. Rogers look-alike again. I gave him a cold, hard, and angry look.

"You, you shouldn't judge me," he said, only acting tough because I was farther away. Bigger words came when he could safely make it down the stairwell if I came charging. "You . . . you know innocent people don't come up here. So, you're not innocent either," he said, looking only ten percent proud of himself.

"I will judge you. It was a piece of filth like you who killed my daughter."

"And we're going to take a little trip to the officer break room," Officer Bernard said as he stood in front of me, blocking my view of the pervert.

He led me through a small, EMPLOYEES ONLY door.

"Sit here." Officer Bernard ushered me to a round table with plastic chairs. "I'm going to get your file and be right back."

The moment he left me alone, I dropped my face into my hands and felt like dying all over again because I envisioned Corinne's pain on that day. Seeing that pervert outside made it all come back: the horrible, gnashing, piercing visions of Corinne begging her attacker, "Stop, stop, stop. Please, Mommy, please! Make him stop!"

I wanted to gouge out my ears, my eyes, and of course, my nose. I couldn't decide which to start with, and wasn't sure if I'd stop once I started.

I gasped for breath through my hands and heard a small, yet strong, voice echoing inside me.

Endure.

"I can't," I moaned under my breath.

You must.

The door opened again, bringing Officer Bernard back. I pulled my hands down and sat up straight.

"Okay, Mrs. Barrett," he started, opening the file and sitting down next to me, "let's get started." He put the file on the table and looked at me for the first time since he'd come back.

I felt like I had been in a catfight with a cougar. I wished the scratches were only visible on the inside, but I supposed Officer Bernard thought otherwise.

His face softened, and his eyes filled with concern. "You know, I think I'm going to call the detectives from your file. It's not standard to do that, but I've had a few conversations with the two of them and they seem to have a history with you that I can't really interfere with. I'd imagine a lot of your current state of mind has something to do with the fact your daughter's case is still unsolved."

"Please don't call them," I said, forcing myself to make eye contact with him.

"Yeah, I think I am. They know you better and maybe they can help me set up a safer place for you to meet up with me." He shook his head and let confusion wash over his face, closing his eyes and taking a moment to reopen them. "Let me just say, right off the bat, that I'm genuinely surprised at how you knew that man out there was a pedophile, but there are ways to know. Take the Megan's Law website for example. And if you know who they are, and you're going to get worked up each time—rightfully so, I'll add—then we shouldn't meet here. I don't want to add insult to your injury, Mrs. Barrett, but pedophiles are in our frequent visitors' club."

My nails dug into the table.

"Daily," he added. "Mr. Carlisle is not our only visitor."

I turned quickly to my purse behind me and fished through it, looking for something to write on.

"Do you have a pen?" I asked him.

He pulled out the one he carried in his shirt pocket. "Sure," he said, handing it to me.

I was writing on the back of an old receipt.

"Wait. What's that?" Officer Bernard asked. "Are you writing down that guy's name?"

I was. Mr. C-a-r-l— "Wait," I said, bringing the pen up to my lip and tapping it. "Is that middle part spelled with an *i* or a *y*?

"No, no, no," he said, sounding strained. "You can't do that."

"Why not? Am I breaking a law? Violating terms of my probation?"

"Not yet," he said, his voice uneasy.

He ripped the receipt from my hand. "I'm going to call the detectives. You wait right here."

TWENTY

A Partner

Thatcher came.

"I figured it'd be Pete," I said when Thatcher walked into the probation break room.

"Pete has the day off," he said. "Some Disneyland trip with his kids."

"Hmm," I offered. "Must be nice."

"Nice?" he asked, sitting down with me at the table.

I had been waiting almost an hour for someone to come. Officer Bernard offered me a cup of coffee forty-five minutes earlier, but nothing else until Thatcher showed up.

"What's so nice about waiting in line, boring kiddie rides, and a glove-wearing mouse?" he continued. "No, thank you," he said, shaking his head. "Not my style."

"You wouldn't get it until you have kids," I said, already realizing this conversation could be a trip down memory lane that I couldn't afford myself. I found a barren place on the floor, focusing in on a tuft of graying dust. I sighed, letting out a little piece of me I knew I'd never recapture. "It isn't the rides or the mouse, it's what's in your child's eyes when *they* see the rides and mouse."

I wasn't sure if it was worth defending, but I couldn't let Thatcher criticize the place we'd taken Corinne each year after her birthday, the place she'd thought was, "the most funnest place ever, Mommy!"

"So, listen," Thatcher started, "Officer Bernard is done with you for today, and we've arranged for him to come to your place every other Tuesday. Will that work?"

"Yeah."

"Copper River is a drive for him, but he agreed to drive out."

"Hmm? Oh, you mean the golf course house. I don't live there any-more. I'll give him the address to my new place. It's closer to downtown."

"You guys moved?"

"No. Singular. I moved."

"Where's your husband?"

"The golf course."

"Everything all right?"

I stood, wanting to be free from both the seventh floor and the forth-coming explanation of my ruined marriage. "Everything's super peachy, Thatcher," I mocked. "Life is full and brimming, how about you?"

He stood too, looking at his watch. "It's a bit early, but do you want to grab something for lunch? Or maybe a late breakfast? We could talk or something."

I chuckled. "Thanks, Thatcher, but I don't need to bore you with my problems. It's not a big deal. I'm just bothered by that . . . that child molester who was out there, and trying to figure out how it is I . . . um, yeah, never mind. But thanks for asking."

"How you smelled him?" Thatcher asked.

My glance rushed to him and stared until he spoke again.

"Yeah, well, I remember you asking me about a smell in the ER, and then Pete told me that you mentioned the smell in the ER was like maggots and maraschino cherries, or something weird like that, and now Bernard just told me that you mentioned an odor on that guy who got you riled up."

I took a moment to consider Thatcher before I opened my mouth again.

I hadn't really looked at him before, at least not long and hard enough to read him the way I did when I sized someone up. He was an attrac-tive man, in a goofy, yet rugged, way. His wardrobe, which I thought was typical of his work wear, consisted of dark colored Dockers, a fitted long-sleeved shirt, and a skinny tie. And, he wore his hair too long—the back of it hanging over his collar, and his bangs touching the tips of his eyelashes. He definitely wasn't your father's flatfoot cop.

His nose was crooked, and most of the time he breathed through his mouth. The mouth breathing wasn't exaggerated. Somehow, it made the bent nose and long hair work to his favor.

The part that intrigued me the most, the thing that made me think this could be the only individual I know who'd believe me, was the glint in his eyes. They flashed a message: I'm young, I'm a superhero in my own mind, and if the story line is good enough, I'll believe you.

"Yeah, Thatcher, let's go eat. I'd like to discuss something with you."

We walked to a nearby diner; Thatcher said it was one of his favorites. On the way there, he loosened his tie, undid the top button of his shirt, and rolled his cuffs to the elbow. He quickly dispelled the notion he was doing any of this for comfort because he kept checking his reflection in the shop windows we passed.

"What's with the primping?" I asked.

He cleared his throat, turning his face to hide the blush in his cheeks. "There's a girl who works at this place. I don't want to come off as, you know, stuffy."

I smiled. Maybe he'd have better luck than I had. No, strike that. I did have my luck. It just dried up, that's all.

When we walked in, he went straight to a young and lovely waitress wiping off menus near the cash register, and asked if his regular spot was available. She bubbled and gushed, and then said she's been meaning to put a name placard on the table for him.

She told us she'd be over in a minute to take our orders, and then handed us two menus so we could seat ourselves.

I looked back at the waitress. She was fixing her hair by the cubby where they kept a few water and ice tea pitchers, sweating out their condensation.

"Is she at least in her twenties?" I asked Thatcher.

"I hope so. I feel too dumb to ask, but unless I know she's at least twenty-one, I'm afraid to, you know . . . like her."

One chuckle escaped my mouth. "It's too late for that," I said. "I'm pretty sure you already like her."

He didn't find it as amusing as I had.

"Why twenty-one?" I asked. "I was kidding when I mentioned she looked young, but you seem pretty convinced a girl's got to be a set age."

He furrowed his brow and opened his menu, blankly looking over a variety of items he had likely memorized weeks ago. "Hazard of the job," he said. "I've only been aboard six months, but the things I've seen done to young girls . . ." He trailed off, his eyes widening and pretending to look more vigorously at his open menu. He must have been hit with the realization that one of those young girls who brought a hazard to his job was my young girl.

"Anyway, I'm afraid certain images will cross in my mind when I'm with a girl and that's why it's important she's old enough for me. Twenty-one is the age I've limited myself to."

My eyes found the waitress again. She was scribbling on her pad, making sure she found a pen that worked.

"I don't know, Thatcher, I think you might be cutting it close on that one."

"Hey," he whispered, leaning into the table. "Could you ask her for me?" he said quietly, stealing another peek at her. "Girls are okay telling that stuff to each other, right?"

I mocked his enthusiasm and candor, leaning into the table too. "Sure. I could also ask her some other stuff. Like: Does she like moonlight strolls? Do sunsets make her cry? Or, does she spin the toilet paper roll under or over?"

He bought it up until the toilet paper preference, then leaned back and huffed at me.

"Sorry," I offered. "I couldn't resist."

Thatcher immediately straightened and became tense. The waitress had come up behind me. "Are you two ready?" she asked.

I ordered a BLT and Thatcher asked for a patty melt. Brave considering the looks of the place. It was a dinky hole-in-the-wall with folding tables arranged so close to each other, you could hardly notice how dirty the floor was. On top of that, red-and-white checkered tablecloths hid the quality of the tables, and then each tablecloth had enough condiments on top of it to hide the quality of the tablecloths. It was one cover-up over another. I had no real intention of consuming my sandwich.

As we waited for our food, I had second thoughts about inviting Thatcher into my new world. He might be young and anxious, but he wasn't stupid. That's when I remembered Thatcher flipping that child abuser to the ground in the ER.

Thatcher was the man.

I couldn't do anything remotely close to that. Look what happened when I confronted Bailey. I barely walked away alive. And the father from the ER would've knocked my block off if Thatcher hadn't intervened. The Mr. Rogers look-alike from this morning I could take.

Maybe.

Eddie had been right when he told me I was engaging in "dangerous pursuits." I wasn't equipped to handle the execution of justice before I had a six-inch gash in my head; how would I be better now? I had the sense of smell, if that's what it was, but what else did I have? I surely didn't have the muscle, nor the authority, to flip a monster over my shoulder like Thatcher could.

"Thatcher, I want to tell you something."

"Okay, shoot. I'm all ears. Is this about your daughter's case?" he asked.

"In a roundabout way, yes. I wanted to throw something out to you, and I need you to understand a few things before I start. First, if you think I'm crazy for what I'm about to tell you, then fine, think I'm crazy. But don't take it out on Corinne's case, okay? I'll just be the victim's crazy mother, and I'm hoping that you'll have the good sense to keep certain things to yourself. Second, even if you do believe me, I need you to be discreet about this."

"Okay. Are you planning another hit?" He smiled.

"Save the jokes for the end," I said.

"Fine, go ahead. I'll save judgment on whether you're crazy or not to the end. I think I might know what you're going to say."

"What?" I asked.

"About a . . . um . . . smell that certain people let off."

"Are you judging?" I asked.

"Not yet. But I'll admit it's hard to wrap my mind around it. I mean, I know you figured out that father hit his kid, and Officer Bernard told me you figured out which one of the parolees in the waiting area was a pedophile. That to me says something is up. But you know, Pete said the way you knew that dad hit his kid was because you have above-average observational skills. I guess the same could be said about the parolee. I didn't see him, but I know there are definitely people in this town that make you want to lock up children."

He leaned against the edge of the table again, putting his weight on his elbows and looking serious. "But there's more, isn't there? It's not just because you're observant, is it?"

"No, I think there's more. Okay, here's the crazy part, Thatcher: I think I can smell them. And you know what? They stink. They smell as bad as you'd think a sick pervert would smell."

His eyes widened, but it was more of a "that's interesting" widening, rather than a "you're crazy" widening.

I went back to the beginning and told him about waking up on Bailey's floor and sensing that horrific smell for the first time. Then I explained how the dad in the ER smelled the same. I even gave him the non–Officer Bernard version of what happened that morning in probation.

Afterward, I moved on to telling him my plan.

"Between that dad from the ER, and that sicko from the seventh floor,

I started to think that I have some sort of power to sense these freaks. And if I do, then maybe I could save kids from these animals. I don't know how I'd come in contact with these guys, but I could sit at parks for a bit, or the mall, or near schools."

"Now *you're* sounding like a pedophile," he teased, but I was far too entwined in my plotting to smile.

"And you think the head injury has something to do with your ability to smell these guys?" he asked.

"I guess."

"What about Pete's argument?"

"I've thought about it, and a part of it has to be true. I *was* paid to notice and read people. Heck, most of the money I made this last year alone was on expert consultation fees to help other attorneys in Los Angles and San Francisco pick winning juries. And the more times I got it right, the more I got paid. So yes, some of that has to be at play here. But still, that doesn't explain how I want to vomit at the sheer stench of another human. And why only men who hurt children? No one else smells around me. You don't smell, and notwithstanding my recent hiding indoors, I haven't smelled that stench on anyone who doesn't have some sort of connection to hurting children."

I, too, leaned against the edge of the table again, anxious to bring the topic to its head.

"I mean, do you understand the implications of this?" I asked. "If it's real, Thatcher, then we don't have to wait for a kid to get hurt before you arrest someone."

"You're talking about that movie with Tom Cruise. What was that thing called? Um, *Minority Report*," he said with excitement. Then he sobered, shaking his head. "You're the lawyer here, so I'm sure you can better explain why that's not how our system works. We both know that I can't go around arresting people who haven't done anything yet. And don't get me started on what Pete would think of this idea."

I leaned back in my chair, defeated. "Yeah, you're right. It would never work. At best, all I could do is point them out to you if I came across them, and then you'd still have to wait for them to . . . to . . .""—I threw my hands up in frustration—"destroy a child."

The waitress came back to put our food in front of us. I watched as she lingered over Thatcher's food, turning his plate just so, to where his fries were in the top left position.

"Excuse me, miss?" I asked. "How old are you, if you don't mind me asking?"

"Twenty-two, why?"

"Did you know that Brian here can flip a dirtbag criminal over his shoulder, just with the flick of the scum's wrist?"

"Really?" she asked, turning to smile at Thatcher.

He gave my foot a light stomp under the table, trying to get me to shut up. Clearly, he didn't know me from Eve. Most of the time, I didn't know how to shut up. I moved my feet out of range.

"What's your name?" I asked.

"Amanda," she replied.

"Amanda, do you happen to know Detective Thatcher's number, other than his main line at 911?"

She laughed, slightly twisting in amusement. "No," she said. "But maybe he'd like mine?" she asked, barely able to keep her gaze on Thatcher.

"Um, yeah," he said. "That'd be great, Amanda. Maybe I could give you a call and take you out for coffee or something."

"Yeah, that sounds great," she said, exuding softness. She pulled off one of the sheets on her pad, wrote the number down, and then handed it to Thatcher. She looked back at him once after she walked away, Thatcher watching her the entire time.

I stretched out my foot and kicked him back, right in the shin.

"Ow!"

"By the way, Thatcher, that look back she gave you, that means call later tonight. Not three days from now and not in thirty minutes either. Got it?"

He nodded. "Yup, got it."

"And if you ever try to kick me again," I added, then stopped myself. "You know what, never mind. I think I'm starting to like you too much to threaten you," I said, smiling.

Thatcher smiled back and then waved the piece of paper with Amanda's number on it. "Do you know how long I've been coming here to build up the nerve to ask her for this number?" he asked.

"Probably too long. I'm surprised you don't have an intestinal virus from this place yet. This food looks like crap."

"It is," he said, taking a bite. "But the service rocks."

"So, Thatcher, back to my little dilemma . . . do you believe me?" I asked.

"Is there any way to put it to a test?"

"Probably. What did you have in mind?"

"I got a call yesterday about a suspicious guy at a kids' spray park here downtown. I'd like to use your 'consultation' services," he said, smiling.

TWENTY-ONE

Worst Case Scenario

Thatcher and I rode together to the park, and on the way, he lectured me. It wasn't his usual style, but I let him talk. He went into the probability that the tip he had received was from an over-zealous mother who suspected the mailman of being a terrorist, and that in all likelihood, we'd go to the park and simply stare at people.

"You're sounding like Pete," I told him.

"No, I'm making sure you don't . . . well, you know."

"Go crazy?" I asked.

He looked over at me and winked. "Yup, go crazy."

"Fine. I got it. But I don't think you understand this inclination I'm having these days. See, if a mom calls in with a suspicion, I'm thinking odds are she's right."

"Nope," he rebutted. "The odds are she's wrong."

"You know that for a fact, or is that something Pete taught you to believe after you two disregarded a tip that turned into a homicide?"

"Hey," he defended. "I told Pete we should've arrested Bailey from the get-go. But I was confronted with the same thing you spoke about in the restaurant: you can't arrest someone because they rub you funny, or in your scenario, they smell funny."

"Well then, it's a good thing Pete's at Disneyland because I've got a feeling today."

"Wait a minute . . . you *feel* them too?"

"What? No. I'm just putting the facts together. You have the tip from a parent; couple that with a crowded area with kids running around in their bathing suits. How is that not a hot spot for a pedophile?"

"Again," he started, "the city doesn't have pedophiles running around all over the place."

I was sure it did. They were everywhere, every day, and parents let their children wade in the toxic ooze without even knowing it. I stared out the window as we came to a stoplight. A small pack of pedestrians waited to cross the street. I narrowed in on a mother with two children—one was in a stroller, the older stood next to his mother, holding onto her skirt.

Targets. That's all they were to me now . . . targets. Any one of the men standing in the same pedestrian pack could view those children as targets. A shiver ran up my spine. No, it tap-danced up there with spiked shoes. I shook it off with a tremble.

"Are you okay?" Thatcher asked.

"Yeah." Something else occurred to me. "Hey, Thatcher, how did a young detective like yourself get involved in the Crimes Against Children Unit?"

"Oh, well, my older brother . . ." He trailed off, distress creeping onto his face. "You know what? I'd rather not talk about it."

I stared at him. His hands tightened on the wheel, letting the blood drain from his knuckles. He didn't look so young anymore. He had not one wrinkle on his face, or gray hair in his dark colored mop, but he didn't look so young.

He noticed I had my eyes on him. He forced a half-smile in my direction. "Sorry," he said.

"You don't need to apologize to me. I get it, Thatcher. I get it. More and more each day."

His smile turned more genuine. "Cool. You're all right, Mrs. Barrett."

"Yeah, despite what Pete says about me."

"Nah, he likes you. He once told me that if you took all the tragedy and chaos away, you'd be tolerable."

"Ah. That almost sounds like poetry to me," I said, clicking my tongue.

Because Thatcher felt he'd be too conspicuous, he opted to wait in the car when we arrived at the park, twenty yards away from where I sat under a large oak, trying to keep cool in the shade. The wind blew gently against my face, and if there were a smell to catch, I'd catch it under that tree.

Thatcher and I had decided to communicate by cell phone if anything struck me, but after ten minutes, all I could smell was sunscreen and the faint smell of urine around me. The sunscreen was an easy enough smell to place, but I pondered a bit on why I smelled urine. That's when I remembered that the park used to be a stomping ground for the homeless.

Unfortunately, that explained the urine in ways I chose not to let my mind linger on. Instead, I stood and leaned up against the tree.

I closed my eyes and before I knew it, I accidentally embraced tranquility. It isn't as if peacefulness was a bad thing, it just wasn't a "me" thing at the time. I simply didn't want anything to remind me of the fact that life had its redeeming moments—moments like before murder and pedophiles came into my life.

I opened my eyes. I had to think of something horrific and negative to overcome the sense of joy trying to seep through my hard inner shell.

I went back to that day with Bailey. Of all the things that haunt me from that day, it wasn't the sound of the gun, the recoil, or even the tiny puff of smoke when the bullet fired. It wasn't even the look on Bailey's face, as every muscle in his body recognized that death was near. Rather, the most jolting memory was when my hands slipped in his pool of blood. Thinking about my fingers squishing around in his spilled life seemed to be a pit of quicksand for my undoing. That was the place where my anger, my conscience, and my ever-loving need to survive collided, and I didn't know which way was up until I had smelled that smell and found the will to get up, even if it was only to get away from the stench.

Another breeze hit me and I alerted. At first, I thought the memory of Bailey had crossed too far over, making me think I could actually smell him again. But that wasn't it. I was catching a whiff of another Bailey, a different Bailey.

"Windy weather will be your downfall, you demons," I said quietly to myself.

Then I saw him. He was on a bench, unaware his forehead was roasting in the overhead sun. He had on a gray T-shirt and jersey shorts. Next to him lay a pair of child's shoes and a neatly folded SpongeBob towel.

But here was the big mistake—other than the fact that I could smell him—he forgot the sunscreen as a prop. It was a nice touch with the shoes, and the towel for the imaginary kid, but it was a blindingly bright day; by the looks of the man's pasty white skin, any offspring of his would need constant reapplication.

I called Thatcher.

"Give it to me," he said.

"Gray shirt to my left. I smell him."

"The dude with his kid's shoes and towel next to him?"

"He doesn't have a kid."

"Are we talking about the same guy?"

"Yes, those are props."

"How do you know?"

I was about to go into the inner workings of my assumptions, but at that point, I didn't need to because gray shirt's eyes were giving him away.

He fixated on a group of young boys who were wrestling and squirting one another with a play fire hose.

The breeze came again, but this time like an impatient whisper.

"Thatcher, get out of the car."

I gasped as the fingers of evil knocked over the first domino. "There," I said in a rushed panic.

One of the boys, who had been grappling with the fire hose, broke off from the group and went into a bathroom, its entryway on the other side of a cinder block wall. I looked around quickly, trying to see as many of the parents' faces as I could, but didn't find anyone looking after the child. No one was looking at the boy except gray shirt, who had just stood up, holding the SpongeBob towel over his groin.

"Thatcher . . ." I said in desperation, but he had already hung up on me and was running for the bathroom.

As he dashed by me, he shouted back to me, "Call 911. Tell them I told you to."

A mother walked directly in Thatcher's path to the bathroom, and then dropped her water bottle. She bent down to pick it up just as Thatcher hurdled over her, the tip of his shoe knocking the bottle back out of her hand. As Thatcher came down with a thud, gray shirt went into the bathroom after the boy.

My heart was banging in my ears, deafening me to everything except what I imagined was the soon-to-be frightened whimper of that little boy. With one breath, my mind was back to the day Corinne died, when Thatcher said to me, "The worst that could happen, happened."

I tried to move but I only panted with fear and stumbled one foot forward. Thatcher was at the cinder block wall now, about to disappear behind it and get into the bathroom. He gave me one final glance and turned the corner. I could still see the top of the door, begging for the moment it opened again because then I'd know Thatcher made it inside and the boy was safe.

The door didn't move.

Locked. Gray shirt must've locked it behind him. The screeching villains in my mind made me envision that the poor boy had those same scared eyes that Corinne must have had.

This was too much. It was all too much. I didn't want to relive this all over again. Not one more child.

I ran. I took a straight line, blindly cutting through the middle of the waterworks, the sunshine, the merriment, and the absolute unawareness that innocence was crashing behind a locked bathroom door. I was gasping, clinging to what felt like my last breath, and trying to muster the clarity to dial 911.

I hit the nine. I hit the one. Then I heard two gunshots.

I fell to my knees.

Seconds felt like minutes and a part of me wanted to burn the entire world down, as long as it would reduce to ashes anyone who would hurt a child.

Thatcher reappeared from behind the cinder block wall, dragging gray shirt by the collar. The man had blood running down the right side of his face, originating from a busted eyebrow.

"Mrs. Barrett!" Thatcher shouted out to me. "Help the boy."

By now, every parent in the park was on their feet, scrambling to get their children in their arms. Still, no one was left with empty arms; no one was left wondering where their child was.

Where were the boy's parents?

I clambered to my feet, and when I did, I went for the bathroom, running past Thatcher. He had his knee in the thug's back, pulling back on his wrists to handcuff them. Other than the blood trickling from the pervert's split eyebrow, there was no other sign of blood.

"The gunshots?" I cried out to Thatcher, still running to the bathroom.

"To get inside the door!" Thatcher yelled back. "Get the kid."

I wanted to tell Thatcher that I didn't have the strength to help, because God, especially God, knew I didn't. I bit my lip in terror, begging not to find something that would make me want to scratch my eyes out.

But what if it were Corinne? I'd gouge my eyes out a million times to be able to have held her one last time after the horror had taken her.

I went into the bathroom and saw two bare feet stretched out on the ground, coming from inside the farthest stall. They were moving. I looked in the last stall and saw two small, frightened eyes look up at me. With only his bathing suit on—and thank God the suit was still on—he crisscrossed his arms over his chest, hugging himself.

He couldn't have been more than a couple of years older than Corinne. I scooped him up in my arms and held him as if he were her . . . as if he were my baby.

"You're all right," I told him.

"Are those guys gone?" he asked, his voice cautious and fearful.

"Yes. Did he . . . did he hurt you?" I asked.

"Which one?"

"Which *one*?" I asked in shock. "The one who came in here right after you. The one who locked the door and was about to . . . about to . . ." I shook my head. "The first one."

"That guy said he had something to show me, and that I should turn around with my eyes closed because it was a surprise. I didn't believe him, but then I heard those loud bangs. Like firecrackers."

He sniffled. He seemed much more fearful of Thatcher than the man who wanted to take his innocence. The boy wiped a few tears from his upper lip, and then said, "Then that other guy came in with a gun and I thought he was going to shoot us," he cried. His shoulders heaved under the pressure of the scare. "And then the guy with the gun smashed the other guy's face into the wall and I hid in here. I want to go home."

"That guy with the gun came in here to help you," I urged. I stood, pulling the boy up with me. "Where are your parents?" I asked him.

"At home. I want to go home."

"They're not here?" I asked.

"No, they let me come by myself because I'm old enough."

I grunted. "You're not old enough." I bit my lip again, shutting my eyes tight. What in the world were his parents thinking? He couldn't have been more than six. It made me so angry, I felt like smashing my fist through something. But the boy had seen enough today. I didn't need to terrorize him more than he had been. I steadied my anger and said, "You're not old enough to come to a park by yourself until you're big enough to fight off a grown man. Do you understand?"

He simply nodded out of submission. Who knew how much it would actually take to undo the recklessness his parents had already instilled in him? I took his hand and led him out of the bathroom.

"Where's your house?" I asked, once we cleared the bathrooms.

He pointed north to a neighborhood across the street from the park, and specifically, to a small, white house with a beat-up kitchen chair on the porch. Lot of good the chair does if no one is going to sit on it and watch their kid. Even if someone had the smallest amount of common sense to watch from the porch, they wouldn't have been able to see anything. We were nothing but specks to them from that far away. The boy's house was a good eight hundred feet off, across an expansive picnic area.

Thatcher had waited for us to exit the bathroom before he started walking gray shirt to the car. "Did he tell you where his parents are?" he asked.

I nodded.

"Go. Then meet me back at the car so we can take this guy in," Thatcher said, giving the guy's arm a quick jerk.

Gray shirt was still eyeing the boy. I stepped in front of the boy so that my body was blocking the pervert from looking, and what did the freak do? He tilted his head to the right to look around me, to get one last look at what was almost his.

"Get out of here, you piece of filth!" I screamed at him. Thatcher shook him again and it was like he had shaken a sauté pan in a hot kitchen; the stench of that rotten animal wafted near me once again, and I had to put my hand over my nose and mouth. After I recomposed, my arm draped around the boy's bare shoulders. "Let's go," I said. "I have a few words for your mother."

He sniffled one last time, but his tears were quickly drying. "I wonder what he wanted to show me," he said.

I stopped abruptly, my arms falling to my sides. The boy stopped alongside me. I didn't know what to say. How much did this kid know about monsters in the world? Was it my place to educate him? His parents were clearly not doing a good job. They left their kid alone in a park. I mean, a napping nanny is just as worthless, but at least it gave the impression that my child wasn't alone. Well no, it actually didn't, all things considered.

"Do you think he was going to show me something good?" the boy asked.

"No," I said, scolding. "Don't you know there are bad people in the world? Hasn't anyone ever told you not to trust or talk to strangers? You shouldn't even be alone at the park, let alone walking into the bathroom by yourself. That man is the reason parents tell their children not to talk to strangers."

I put my arm back around his shoulders and picked up the pace to his house. The boy told me his name was John right before he bounded through the front door and called out for his mom.

"You better have closed that front door!" I heard a woman shout from the back of the house.

But he hadn't because I was still standing in the doorway. Fear seemed to have sparked in him—or barked at him via that gruff, loud voice we had just heard—because he took off through the living room, cutting to his right and running down the hallway.

From the other side of the house, where I could hear the thundering of a washing machine bang against the floorboards, a woman walked out toward me, wearing lavender cutoff sweats, an oversized man's undershirt, and dirty house slippers.

"Why do I always have to close this door for you?" she asked, head turned over her shoulder toward wherever the boy had run off to. "You want someone to come in and steal our TV?"

She turned to the door, and gasped when she found me standing there.

I wanted to shake her like I had seen Thatcher shake that pervert. Here she was, worried that the boy had left the door open to her house, but by not supervising her child at the park, she had left the door open to her son. A television set you could replace, a child . . . oh, I wanted to shake her something fierce.

She was no pedophile, but in the end, when a child had been destroyed, fault gets splattered all around. I knew that from personal experience and felt it my duty to make sure she knew that too.

"Who are you?" the mother asked.

"I'm Evelyn Barrett and I'm returning your son to you."

"Returning him?" she asked. "Did he run off from the park?"

"No, but—"

She cut me off. "Then why are you returning him? Did he do something wrong?"

"Not him, no, but—"

"Thanks, I guess." She blew out an impatient sigh and tried to close the door on me.

I stuck my foot in the opening and held my hand out to stop it from closing.

"You should let me finish," I demanded.

"I thought you were."

"Your child," I stopped to look over her shoulder to make sure the boy wasn't listening, "was almost attacked in the park bathroom."

"What?" she shrieked. Now I had her attention.

"He went off to the bathroom by himself, and a pedophile went in after him. The man locked the door and—"

"Where is this guy?" She pushed past me and stood on the porch, looking at the park. "Is he still there? I'll cut his—"

"He's been arrested," I interrupted.

"Whew. You had me worried there. Well, thanks for returning him, but if you don't mind, I'm a little busy."

"Busy? Aren't you going to check on your son first?"

"He's alive, ain't he?"

Without thinking about it, I slapped her solid across the face.

She stood there, dumbstruck, with her hand covering her cheek. A flash whipped up in her eyes as she focused on me in anger. It looked like it was a flee-or-suffer kind of anger—if I didn't flee soon, then soon I'd suffer.

But I didn't do either. "Just be glad I slapped you instead of a nurse shooting you up with a sedative because your kid is dead," I hissed at her. "That man was going to devour your child. Devour him. And I'll bet you anything he's been watching your boy for a while now. I'll bet he knew your son didn't have anyone at the park with him. Do you know what you just did? You just offered your child up for worst case scenario."

She tightened her lips as her breath seared through her flared nostrils. She took a few steps backward into her house, then slammed the front door.

I took out my cell phone, walked to the curb, and snapped a picture of the house for reference. Someone else could deal with that mother. Child Protective Services, even Pete if need be.

I was halfway back to the park when my stomach churned. I suddenly remembered that pervert was in the back of Thatcher's police car, and Thatcher was my ride. There's no way I was going to ride in the car with that guy. The smell alone would kill me, and my projection of anger would likely kill him.

I veered in the direction of the nearest freeway when Thatcher pulled up against the sidewalk I was walking on.

"What are you doing? Get in," he said.

I looked in the back of the car and didn't see the guy.

"Where is he?" I asked. "You didn't let him go, did you?"

"No, I called for backup when you were walking that kid back. A black-and-white was right down the street and they're taking him in."

I opened the passenger door and climbed in. It still reeked of the pedophile, which meant Thatcher must've at least sat him down in the back before the transfer. I plugged my nose.

"What did you tell the parent?" he asked.

"That she's a bad parent. And then I slapped her," I said, nasally.

"You did what?" he asked.

"I slapped her. She didn't seem to care."

"About the slap?"

"No, about her kid."

Thatcher laughed, looked at me for a response, and then laughed again.

"Why are you laughing?" I asked.

"I just figure that you're not the right person to spar with."

"You should've figured that sooner," I said.

"I wish I had."

"Well then, you tell that to Pete."

"I'm not telling Pete about any of this," he said, shaking his head.

TWENTY-TWO

Avoiding Nevermore

After Thatcher dropped me off at my car, still parked at the courthouse, it took everything I had to turn the ignition. I'd already been in the car for a minute, and found my breath tapering in a struggle, fighting off the intense heat trapped inside from a stifling Fresno day.

Once the ignition turned and my air conditioner blasted against my face, I realized that comfort was the last thing I wanted. I had saved a boy from an unspeakable assault, yet it felt like another one of my many undoings.

What world did I exist in? What was this place where I had to suffer through the knowledge not only that one man devoured my daughter but that there were hundreds and hundreds of them out there, searching for the next child who saw more of the back of their parent's head than the concern and watchfulness of their eyes? I didn't have to assume they were out there, I could smell them if they were close enough. I *knew* they were out there.

At first, it had seemed a noble task. It was uncomfortable for me to endure, but still no less noble. Now, however, I didn't only have the dark, disturbing images of what may have happened to Corinne, I had that boy's image stuck there too—his weak, small, and scuffed legs protruding out of a bathroom stall. Sure, he got up and walked home, mostly unharmed. But what about the next time I ran into a pedophile? Or the time after that?

I was barely surviving as it was. I didn't need more images to make me want to close my eyes forever into nevermore, nevermore, nevermore.

Thatcher and I didn't make any plans for future escapades. How could we? I didn't think I could handle it, and he didn't know how he'd explain anything more than the one solo pedophile capture to Pete.

I drove home, to Tower Street, and made sure the curtains in the living room were shut. Tight.

My cell woke me the next morning. It was Pete.

"Hello?" I strained, rubbing my eyes.

"Mrs. Barrett, you can either come down to the station in the next thirty minutes, or I'll be at your place in five. Which one do you want?"

"Um . . . neither," I said, swinging my legs to the floor. "Why?"

His voice was curt. "Spray park, pedophile, six-year-old boy, slapping his mother. Need more detail? Give me my answer or it's your house in five."

The anger laced in his voice woke me up. Instead of the usual lure of caffeine I needed to get out of bed in the morning, Pete's sharp demeanor was like an injection of adrenaline. I stood quickly, my toes curling against the carpet. "You can't talk to me like this," I said, releasing the valve on my own fury.

"You haven't begun to see what I can do," he threatened. "I come back from a family trip and find, to my not-so-great surprise, that you've involved yourself in yet *another* one of my cases."

"It's not your case, it's Thatcher's case," I said.

"That's it. I'm coming over."

"No, no, no. Fine," I huffed. I passed by the floor length mirrors on my closet doors, seeing my pajamas. My typical fare, even post-Eddie, was a pair of his boxers and a T-shirt. "I'll be down at the station in thirty minutes," I said.

"If I'm late, don't panic," I added. "I'm just trying to squeeze in a good shower before you yell at me."

When I got to the station, Pete saw me from his desk and waved me over. Not running over and dragging me by the elbow was a good sign. His furrowed brow looked fierce, but I took it as a blessing he wasn't already spitting his chastisement out at me.

"Sit," he said once I got to his desk. His voice was softer than it was on the phone. "I've had about thirty-*five* minutes to calm down. I have—as my wife puts it—deflated the veins in my neck. Now, I'm going to ask you to keep the biting sarcasm to a bare minimum, or eliminate it altogether. Fair enough?"

I smirked.

"Now, Mrs. Barrett, don't take this the wrong way—but make sure you at least take it—what do I have to do to make you go away?"

My eyes closed and I sighed.

"You just keep popping up for new crimes all the time," he continued.

"I would think," I started, opening my eyes and addressing him, "that you'd be at least somewhat pleased that I've brought two offenders to you. That's two criminals that you don't have to chase down," I said, holding two fingers up to him. "And who knows how many potential victims or incidents I saved you from making case files over."

"I haven't gotten that far in the logic, Mrs. Barrett," he said. "I'm stuck on the first part, the part where your hands are messing in unrelated cases. I'm also stuck on the part where you happened to be at the same park as my partner on a routine tip follow-up. And most of all, I'm stuck on what the heck you did to Thatcher, enticing him to play dumb as to the details of your involvement."

"Sometimes the end justifies the means," I said. "If you focus on the end—"

"But I don't like focusing on the end when the beginning and middle parts create reasonable doubt for some blowhard defense attorney to exploit," Pete interrupted. "Any way you slice or dice it, it looks bad when someone other than an officer is involved in bringing cases in."

"Bad for you?" I asked. "Because it doesn't look bad for me. It actually makes me feel that a better job has been done."

One of his hands went up to his neck, pushing in against a bulging vein. With the hand still trying to hide the vein, he said, "Any defense attorney worth his paycheck—even the ones at the Public Defender's office on a county salary—would immediately be able to get one of these cases thrown out of court because of your involvement."

He put his hand down, giving up on the vein and allowing it to bulge.

"And what's the end result of that, Mrs. Barrett?" he asked.

"The guy could walk forever," I answered.

"The guy could walk forever," he repeated, leaning back into his chair, slightly bouncing back and forth.

"You're right, Pete," I sighed, propping my elbow on his desk and then

supporting my chin in my hand. "I'm sorry. If it makes you feel any better, I have no intention of butting in anymore. Yesterday, with Thatcher, it
was too much for me. I don't have the resolve to . . . to . . ." I had to look
out the nearest window, to find someone walking by, or see an awning for
a neighboring business, or even watch the stoplight turn from yellow to
red, simply for the sake of not allowing my mind to go back to that boy's
legs jutting out of the bathroom stall. When my mind went there, those
legs inevitably turned into little girl legs with the same ruffled socks I had
put on Corinne the morning she died.

"Suffice it to say," I continued, "I don't plan on butting in anymore."

"You're not feeling a fire burning in your belly to find your daughter's
killer anymore?"

I wanted to say, "Not today, but maybe tomorrow."

Instead, I shook my head.

Who knew how long my inkling of defeat would last? But for today, I
had the power to placate Pete, and it's what I chose to do.

"How did you find out?" I asked Pete, trying to see if Thatcher ratted
me out.

"That mother, of course," he said, sitting back up and grabbing a pen.
"Just because a woman lets her son go to the park by himself, doesn't
mean she'll let a slap in the face go unreported."

My eyes rolled in disgust. That sounded about right for the likes of her.

"Where is Thatcher, by the way?" I asked.

"Oh, since he did such a bang-up, knockdown job of apprehending a
sex offender, and saving a young boy in the process, I've got him tracking
down every single tip that comes into this place." Pete leaned forward,
grinning while that puffy vein in his neck simmered down.

"Sounds like an important job," I said, meeting Pete's look of self-pride.

"So," he started, tapping the pen on the desk, "what's next for you? I
hear you're getting special accommodations for your probation appoint-
ments—for reasons I'd rather not repeat for the sake of my sanity—and
that you've moved out of your old place. I assume without your husband."

I quickly stood, extending my hand out to him. I didn't want to talk
about my marriage with Pete Shaw. "Sorry again, Pete. Unless you have
something to discuss with me about my daughter's case, I promise you
won't hear from me."

He stood, shaking my hand. "Any plans for work?"

I released his hand. "No. I can't practice law, but I'm good right now, financially. Besides, it's summer in the valley. Perfect time of year to hide inside, unemployed."

His eyes narrowed on me. It reminded me of attempts Eddie had made to read what I was really trying to say.

"Have a good day," I said, turning and walking away before Pete could get his answer.

"Have fun hibernating for the summer," he called out to me.

I turned my head over my shoulder to respond. "And you have fun catching pedophiles the slow way."

"That's why I have Thatcher out there. To do it the fast, and apparently effective, way," he called back.

But Thatcher was missing that effective something. Me.

TWENTY-THREE

Small World

July, then August. Every day almost the same, except for a visit here and there from my sister and an occasional call from my mother. Eddie hadn't bothered with me since his voice mail of resolved separation. I expected to find a manila envelope stuffed in my mailbox one of these days, containing divorce papers and whatnot.

I thought I'd be the one to do that, but I was as comfortable as a lifer in prison, and didn't want to rock the boat. On the other hand, since I could have easily made a name tag up for Eddie when we were first married, to define his role in our union with the moniker, Initiator, engraved on it, I figured he would be the one to start any divorce proceedings anyway.

It was September something. Today was mail-checking day. Tragedy, pride, evil, what have you, reduced my once busy and productive hub of a life into days that I checked the mail, and days that I didn't. But hey, it could be worse: I could still be mingling in society, subjecting myself to the stench of pedophiles. I had tried a few trips out in the beginning and it was clear that even if I didn't want to be in the game of finding child abusers, I could still smell them. Hiding inside my house provided an out-of-sight, out-of-mind mentality and I found a tolerable misery in my self-inflicted imprisonment.

I stood on the inside of my closed front door, building up the momentum to make the trip to the lawn-perched mailbox as spectacular as winning a $68,000,000 personal injury lawsuit. Yeah, the same Evelyn Barrett who was once one of the most sought-after litigators in the Central Valley was going to get the mail today. Spectacular!

A warm cup of coffee was in my hand, too hot for a warm September morning, but I didn't approve of any other way to drink it. I took a sip, set the cup down on the nearby coffee table that I had picked up at a neighborhood garage sale—wanting it to match the other shabby furnishings—and, opening the front door, stepped outside.

If that didn't beat all . . . as it turned out, today was *not* going to be mail-checking day.

Jeanine, the real estate agent who had helped me find my place, was walking up the front lawn.

"Mrs. Barrett," she said. "Good morning." She extended her hand and I numbly shook it. She walked up the steps, and then went past me. Before she crossed the threshold of my open door, she turned and said, "Oh, I'm sorry. Is it all right if I come in?"

She had turned around and walked in before I could answer. I considered going to the mailbox anyway. It was only another twenty feet away. I could even shuffle through the piles of junk mail—it's all I got anyway—and maybe Jeanine would disappear as quickly as she had come. She was wearing that red blazer again too. It must've been her office apparel, like the gold jackets at Century 21.

Still facing the mailbox, I heard Jeanine clear her throat behind me. I turned and saw her standing a few feet inside the door, raising her eyebrows and waiting for me. She probably had already made a kettle of hot water, and used the restroom too.

Oh well. If I moved mail-checking day to tomorrow, I'd have something to look forward to for the rest of the day. And by the looks of Jeanine's colored-in eyebrows, raised high on her forehead, I'd need something to get me through the morning.

"What can I do for you?" I asked, closing the front door behind me. "Is it about the rental?"

"Not at all," she said, waving her hand and sitting down on the couch. "Although I have to say, you've done wonders to the place."

"I haven't done a thing except let the dust accumulate. Oh, and I got that coffee table."

"Marvelous," she said, not quite listening to me.

"What brings you by?" I asked.

"It's a small world, you know?" she said, nodding at me and folding her hands on her knees.

"So I've been told." I couldn't fully agree with the axiom, though. The world certainly wasn't *so* small that Pete and Thatcher had found the one man in the half-million people living in the greater Fresno area who had killed my daughter.

"But, how did this alleged small world dump you on Tower Street this morning?" I asked.

"My daughter, Amanda, is dating a young man, whom I've been told you know. His name is Detective Brian Thatcher."

"Hmm. That is a small world," I said. "Did, or does, your daughter work in a little restaurant near the police station?" I asked, remembering Thatcher's little crush.

"Oh, that hovel? Yes, that's her."

With my lips tightly shut, I smiled a little. It was cute, in a way. And I had something to do with it. Or at least I thought I might have.

I sat on the coffee table while she remained on the couch, and we both nodded at one another, each of us waiting for the other to break the silence. But I was used to the stillness. It was my new best friend. Although, on occasion, it asked far too many deep questions, to spite, I think, its own characterization.

"Well," she started, "she and Brian are getting very close. And well . . . oh, how do I put this delicately . . . he told her something about you, which in turn was told to me. I found the tidbit laughable at first, but now, it has me rather intrigued."

All I could think was, poor, poor Thatcher. If he married this girl, Jeanine—red blazer and all—would be his mother-in-law.

My eyes never left her face. I waited for her to get to the point.

"Mrs. Barrett," she said, reaching her hand out to my knee and patting it. "You're still troubled by the head wound, I see. You're staring at me like a catatonic. Do you realize that you do that? Oh, dear. Perhaps I could give you a name of a good neurologist."

Poor, poor Thatcher, indeed.

"I'm fine, actually," I said to her. "Just trying to figure out where this gets wrapped up. I'm afraid you have me at a disadvantage. It's early and I've yet to finish my first cup of coffee." I reached to the other side of the coffee table and grabbed my now cool cup of coffee. I brought the coffee cup to my lips and took a drink, winking at her while I did, so she could observe that I still possessed a good range of motion on my face.

At the sight of my wink, her lips puckered and her Maybelline painted eyebrows took the appearance of a jack-o'-lantern's crooked smirk.

She had carried a black portfolio in with her and now opened it. She pulled out a loose page on top and handed it to me. It looked like a web page printout of one of the agents in her real estate office.

"That's Paul McMillan," Jeanine said. "At dinner a few weeks ago, Brian told Amanda that right after you had your head smashed by that pedophile, you laid claim to the fact that you could suddenly 'smell' a certain odor a pedophile, or child abuser, emitted."

She shifted in her seat, straightening the bottom of her blazer, yet I felt unclothed in front of this woman. She should not know what she knows about. It was *my* underbelly of a secret to tell, not Thatcher's.

"When I heard this," she continued, "I thought you had a placard at the asylum waiting for you. I do try not to judge those who have large reserves of cash such as yourself, but still, it was an outrageous claim."

I set the paper down, walked to the front door, and opened it. "You should leave. I don't know what Brian Thatcher told you, and I don't know why he'd make up something that ridiculous, but I'm not in any mood to entertain visitors right now."

"Would it help if I told you that I believe you now?" she asked, refusing to get off the couch.

"Probably not. I don't know what you're talking about."

"Then, would it help if I told you that I suspect the agent on that sheet I handed you is a pedophile?"

"You should tell the police, then."

She frowned. "My daughter has asked me not to. It would inevitably end up in front of Brian, and she doesn't want him thinking I'm a paranoid bother."

Better now than later, I thought.

Reluctantly, she stood and walked over to me. "Mrs. Barrett, I don't want to bother the police. You, of all people, are familiar with their, oh, how shall I put this gently, their ineptitude in certain things. Take your daughter, for example: Have they found the perpetrator yet? And who *really* stopped that other one, what's his name, the one you shot?"

She raised her hand and stroked my upper arm. My gaze shot to the unwelcome contact, then I looked at her eyes.

She did not intend to leave without my acquiescence. She'd pull out every card in her hat before she'd even think of giving up. I couldn't imagine which card was next.

"Sometimes, when the powers that be aren't good enough, God raises up someone, or something, to fill the gap. Who's to say that you can't really smell the scent of a pedophile? Who's to say God hasn't given you a special ability to weed out a particular evil?"

That was a good one—appealing to my forgotten faith.

She went back to the coffee table, grabbed the sheet I had left, picked it up, and then walked back to me, holding it in front of my face. "Who's to say that Paul McMillan isn't the man you're looking for? The man who killed your daughter."

And there was her grand finale: the dead child card.

I ripped the sheet from her hand. Half on the verge of tears, and half on the verge of smacking her in the face, I called on a reserve of composure I'd been saving up during my hibernation, for something like this. "You're good," I said. "I'm drawn by your request, yet still feel a choking contempt for you."

She laughed and pulled out one of her cards from the portfolio. "That's why I make one heck of a real estate agent." She handed me the card.

"Come by the office later today," she said. "There's someone I want you to smell. Oops," she said, covering her mouth, "I mean meet."

Paul McMillan was a single man in his thirties, who didn't seem to have an interest in women. That's what Jeanine told me as I sat in her manager's office later that day. She told me I'd get a chance to meet Paul after she filled me in on some of the details. Before I could ask the million-dollar question in regard to Paul having no interest in women, Jeanine replied, "No, not men either."

She had a list of other concerns, and I do mean that literally—she checked off the items as she relayed them to me. He was antisocial; disappeared at the same time every day at 2:00 p.m.—except in the summer and on other school holidays; was jumpy; prone to tempers; and never, ever showed any homes near any elementary schools.

"What is it that you want me to do?" I asked, even though I already knew the answer to that.

"I'm going to bring you over to his desk and introduce you as a potential client. Then, you can do whatever it is you do."

My first impression of Paul was that he was a sad, strange, little man. My second was that he smelled of Old Spice, something orange flavored, and nothing else.

Either my special sense of smell had gone away, or Paul wasn't a pedophile. I was rooting more for the former, but would take either at that point.

He stood to greet me, but didn't offer his hand. Instead, he had them both in his pockets. How in the world did this guy even sell one piece of property? Surely he was in the wrong business if he didn't like to shake hands.

"Hi, how are you doing? I'm Paul. Nice to meet you," he said to me.

"Likewise. I'm Evelyn Barrett."

"What can I do for you, Ms. Barrett?" he asked as his hands came out of his pockets to pull his chair under him as he sat down.

I was about to tell him I was looking for a house on or around Tower Street because the neighborhood had grown on me—what little I had seen of it—but just for kicks and giggles, I told him I wanted to see properties for sale at the Copper River Golf Course. I didn't mention, of course, that I used to live there. I expected to see the Brewer house still available. It had been a bad market the last couple of years, and I figured it'd still be up for sale.

"Here's one you might like," Paul said. He turned the screen to me.

I reached for the monitor so I could see it better, away from a glare coming in through a window. The tips of my fingers almost made contact with Paul's hand, but he made a quick jerk away so that we wouldn't touch.

I ignored the screen for a moment and wanted to tell him I was no leper. Somehow, though, I figured my sarcasm would fall flat on him. He was one scared kitty-cat, and I had never thought of using that phrase on a man until I had come across the likes of Paul McMillan.

A little ache plucked within me for the sad and seemingly damaged man in front of me. He was kooky, I'll give him that, but something else was off. It was almost like he was—my eyes took a quick peek at Paul's computer screen to sort out the rest of my thoughts, to come up with what struck me about him—and then . . . Holy betrayal, Batman!

I saw my house.

The Brewer house wasn't on Paul's screen as a listing, but *my* house was. And yes, it was MINE now and not Eddie's if all he was going to do was put it up for sale. I heard a deep panting. In and out, in and out, before I realized it was coming from me.

"Mrs. Barrett?" Paul asked.

I looked at him, but all I saw was this epic, heaving battle brewing in my mind of what would happen when I got my angry little paws on that Eddie.

What about Corinne's stuff? So help me if he had already packed it all up.

"I guess you don't like this one," Paul said, pulling the screen back.

"Huh?"

"I'll find you another one," he said.

"No," I said. "I like that one," I added. "Can you show it to me? How about right now? I would love to get inside that house right now," I said.

Paul looked at his watch. It was quarter to two. "Um . . . um . . . well, now is not a good time for me. How about tomorrow?"

I remembered that pointer from Jeanine's checklist—Paul left each afternoon when school was in session. There was no patience left in me to deal with Jeanine's ridiculous assumptions. I wanted to jump the gun with Paul and directly ask what was wrong with him and why he disappeared each afternoon, so I wouldn't have to suffer through another surprise visit from Jeanine.

All I wanted was that battle with my husband over the sale of the house, though. Now. Still, Eddie wouldn't be home until later if he was at work.

"Can you show it to me later? How about after six tonight?" I asked Paul.

"Sorry. I don't work evenings."

"Prior commitments?" I asked.

"Yes, prior commitments."

"Fine," I said with a belaboring sigh. I didn't actually need Paul to see the house. There would be plenty of other real estate agents willing to work an evening to get the commission on that house.

As he stood to say good-bye, he plunged both hands into his pockets again. I thought about patting him on the shoulder, but that might've induced a seizure. There was still something resonating about Paul that I couldn't put my finger on. I breathed him in one last time. Once again, nothing but Old Spice and orange flavored candy.

I went for the door, remembering I had seen a RE/MAX office on my way over. That would be my next stop.

Jeanine poked her head out of her office just as my hand pulled on the front door. "Oh, Mrs. Barrett, can you come in for a moment?"

Grimacing, I was sure the following conversation wouldn't be coming up roses. More like pushing up daisies. I considered leaving anyway. All I would have to do is push the door and walk away. I was only a few miles away from what had to be an ambitious agent at RE/MAX who'd show me the house after 6:00 p.m.

Oh, but how quickly I had forgotten Jeanine's persistence. She'd probably made a spare copy of my key in the interim, and I'd likely find her in my kitchen tomorrow morning, holding and soiling my coffee cup with her snotty attitude if I didn't deal with her now. I turned from the door and stepped into her office.

"Before we talk about Paul," I started, "can you explain something to me, in your capacity as a real estate agent?"

"As long as we spend most of this conversation talking about Paul," she replied.

"Well, at least you're honest." I sat down in one of her visitors' chairs, "Now, how does one spouse put a marital house up for sale without the other spouse's consent?"

"They can't."

"Then how is my old residence at Copper River up for sale?"

"Oh yes," she said, recognition glinting in her eyes. "That lovely home on the seventh fairway. I listed that one, actually."

"What?" I shouted. "But you just said it couldn't be done."

"But I had personal knowledge that you weren't living there. I helped you find the rental, remember?"

"So? That doesn't preclude my rights to say whether that house is listed for sale."

"Your husband said he'd get your signature. We were going to wait to put it on the MLS until he got it, but oops, I must have jumped the gun. It's a horribly slow market right now. Extra time on the MLS can only help, not hurt anything."

I stood, putting my palms on her desk, and leaned over to her. "Take the listing off," I said, talking to her as if I owned her. Or, at least, that I *could* own her if I put my mind to it.

She gave me an exasperated sigh. "Very well. Consider it done."

Turning on my heels, I went for her office door.

"Wait, what about Paul?" she asked.

"You're wrong about Paul," I blurted out.

"How so?"

"I don't agree with you that he's a pedophile. He's got some internal freakiness going on, but he doesn't smell like the other men who were offenders."

"Well, I think he smells," she added. "I'm not sure it's the smell you'd be looking for, but maybe you've lost that added sense. What if when your head healed, the smell went away?"

"Hallelujah and amen," I said. "Let's hope so."

She stood, nearly barking at me. "But that means he could still be a pedophile, even if you've been proved worthless."

"Wow, you're a real peach. Have a good day," I said, reaching for the door handle.

There was no need to confront Eddie now. He'd find out sooner or later that the house was no longer eligible for listing. If he had a problem with it, he could come to me. And I hoped he would because I'd much rather be on the defensive than going after him offensively.

Jeanine got my blood pumping again. The cobwebs on my unused temper blasted away as a surge of adrenaline and anger coursed through my body. Somehow, I got to thinking that my existence would be more eventful now. There would be days that I'd check the mail, days that I did not, and then days where I fought.

TWENTY-FOUR

The Sad Little Man

I looked at the clock. It had been four days since my visit to the real estate agency and the blue digits on the microwave told me it was 1:15 in the afternoon. I was leaning against the kitchen counter and thinking about Paul, Jeanine's presumed pedophile. According to her observations, Paul would be gone from the office in forty-five minutes. Where did he go? What did he do? And how was that any of my concern?

But the mail-checking had become woefully dull since Jeanine and her eye-singeing red blazer walked into my house. Which, by the way, seemed even odder to me now that I'd been inside her agency more than once; both times, she was the only one wearing one. It couldn't have been a uniform—probably more along the lines of a symbol representing her self-perceived power.

Before her interruption, I could get by with the solitude and misery. Now, I thought of the most ridiculous things. Notions such as Corinne, if she had a say-so, would be pleased with me if I moved on and found happiness again. And the more I told myself that was crazy talk, another notion would pop into my head like forgiving Eddie. I did still love him, didn't I? I was sure I did, but okay, enough of that. It was time for a distraction.

It was 1:22 now.

Well, I've done stupider things. I decided to find out what Paul did each afternoon, so I drove to the agency.

At 1:58, Paul climbed into his Lincoln Town Car.

"Got to love predictable people," I said aloud, starting my car and following him.

He drove clear across town. I wasn't familiar with the area, and my assuredness that I'd be able to find my way back dropped with each signal we passed and each turn we took. To the best of my ability, I tried to keep track of landmarks, concentrating on directions and streets. But the brain can only hold so much. If I could've deleted other information on command to store the new directions, I would have. Perhaps start with any numerous points of pain, shame, and regret.

Suddenly, Paul pulled over in front of a yellow crossing sign for an elementary school.

He parked on the school side of the street, toward the end of the playground, as I drove past him. I went to the first cross street, turned right, and then circled back, parking on the opposite side, facing him about two hundred yards away. The school was quiet, except for the constant arrival of other vehicles—mothers and fathers pulling up to collect their children at the end of the day.

The walls of the school breathed and panted in anticipation for the final bell as hundreds of young students bounced in their respective seats to be free. What was Paul McMillan doing parked in front of an elementary school moments before the end of the school day?

He was looking at the gate to the school yard, and from what I could tell, it was the only point of egress at that time of day.

My stomach churned. Something bad was about to happen. How had I misjudged him? Perhaps my sense of smell did come to a halt. That was good news for me in terms of reentering society, but bad for any one of the children about to dash through that gate. I could have stopped him. I should've stopped him.

I still *could* stop him.

After grabbing my cell phone, I yanked my purse with my free hand and set it on my lap, digging through it to find Thatcher's card. If his new girlfriend didn't want to involve him with her mother's mania, he was going to be involved now.

I looked back at Paul. He wiped his brow and then shoved something in his mouth.

Was this really going to happen? Was he going to wait by the edge of the fence and grab the first kid that walked by? In broad daylight? With people around?

A riot of dumb questions springing from the mother of a child abducted in broad daylight, with people around.

I found Thatcher's card, said the number aloud to commit it to short-term memory, and then put the card and my purse back. I got to the fourth digit before a shrill, piercing ring went off across the street. School was out and the sudden sounding of the bell made me jerk. It caused me to drop my cell phone between the center console and my seat.

The first few children made their way to the gate.

"Oh, God, no," I muttered, jamming my hand through the divide to reach my phone. I looked down to see it. It rested against the metal track on which my seat slid forward and backward. I could see it, but I just couldn't reach it.

My eyes went back to the gate. The first child, a young boy, was the first through. I shot my glance to Paul. He was leaning forward, hands clenched on the steering wheel.

"No, no," I said, under my breath.

I pushed my hand down harder. The phone was still out of reach.

Scattered groups of children were now approaching Paul's car in happy disregard. Paul was in the perfect position. All he had to do is throw open his door, grab a child, and drive off.

I needed that phone.

Grabbing the door handle, I kicked the car door open and jumped out. I spun back toward the car and landed on my knees, facing my seat and throwing my torso over the floor mat to claw at the phone from underneath.

Got it.

What I had already entered of Thatcher's number had cleared from the phone's prompt. For the life of me, I couldn't recall the particular numbers from the card.

"Ugh!" I bellowed, angry with myself for not having programmed the number in my phone before this point. The business card sat in plain view in the top of my purse. I grabbed it again and haphazardly punched in the numbers. I was more worried over the fallout of being slow in this situation than with dialing the wrong number. The only thing left was to push talk on the phone, but a noise, or a lack thereof, distracted me. Pilfering through like the last moments of dusk were the fading laughter and shouts of children. Fading, fading . . . gone.

The Town Car was still there, doors closed, and all the children were now out of reach.

Paul's fists unclenched from the steering wheel, and he wiped his brow again with his hand. He shoved more of whatever he was shoving into his mouth.

I moved toward the vehicle, slowly and carefully. He saw me coming and froze for a moment. Then he turned his head to his left. He might've recognized me; he might not have. I moved in further.

Stepping up on the sidewalk, I slowly inched alongside his car until I came to his passenger side window, the same way all the children had passed his car. He was still looking to his left, stabbing his gaze at a house across the street.

"Paul?" I shouted through the glass. "Paul, is that you?"

His head spun toward me.

The expression on his face made me realize it was a bad day to get out of bed. He wore a look that was half-petrified for an upcoming dance with the devil, and half-bent on annihilating me. I took a step back from the car.

He opened his mouth to say something, but several faded orange Tic Tacs fell from his mouth. He caught a few and pushed them back in, but the others he let fall into his lap. That's what he must have been shoving in his mouth. No wonder he had smelled like something orange flavored.

A drip of orange-tinted saliva hung from his bottom lip. He wiped it with the back of his hand, squinted at me, trying to place how he knew me.

"Mrs. Barrett?" he asked.

It was too hard to hear him through the glass, but I was sure that's what he had asked.

I didn't answer; I didn't know what to say. But the longer I waited, the more I thought I saw tiny red flames flashing in the depths of his eyes.

Something dark was brewing inside of him, but it didn't occur to me to be afraid. Or, afraid enough to leave. It was only Paul—the sad little man. And the Tic Tacs that came drooling from his mouth only made him more sad and needy in my eyes.

"Paul," I called out to him.

"I'm not working right now," he shouted back at me.

I knocked on the passenger side window, letting him know I wanted him to roll it down.

He twitched and then screamed, "Leave me alone!"

I stood upright, aghast, trying to put it all together. Was he or wasn't he a pedophile? Driving to the school seemed like a big yes, but everything else, including the mixed look of fear, anger, and betrayal in his eyes reminded me of . . . that's what it was. It's what I was trying to figure out when I had first met him: he acted like a victim. A very, very broken victim.

A front door opened and then slammed shut across the street—the one where Paul had been staring. We were causing a scene. A frail and bothered looking old woman walked out of her house. She was all sorts of the wrong kind of grumpy to live across the street from a school yard.

She walked halfway down her front yard and then stopped, looking at me. She said nothing, so I ignored her. I bent back down to Paul's window.

"Paul?" I asked again.

"You a friend of that little jerk?" the woman called out to me from her yard.

I looked at her from over Paul's car, and shot her a puzzled look. The sun beamed down on her, showing the raised veins on her exposed forearms. Her head was shaking with age, but not so much that I couldn't make out her mean old eyes and her lips curled from something other than her wrinkled age. My heart pumped faster and my ever-present pain began to burrow deeper when the anticipation to spar with someone presented itself.

I could fight with her and it'd make my mundane, solitary life seem more bearable for at least a few days. Still, she was merely a stick-figure granny. I knew better than to fight with an elder.

I shook both my head and the inclination to spat with her. Bending over again, I looked in Paul's window, rapping my knuckles a final time upon his glass.

"You got trouble hearing? I asked you a question," she called out to me.

Raising only my head, I said to her, "This doesn't concern you. I'll be on my way soon enough, don't worry about it."

"You have no business with that man. No one does. He's a cuckoo bird. Just let him suck on those stinking Tic Tacs."

A sharpened fingernail—a claw, a talon, even a rusty nail—scratched up my spine until it raised every hair on the back of my neck. I stood fully, looking upon her with such intent that I could even make out the tip of her tongue flickering out to moisten the corner of her mouth.

"How do you know he's eating Tic Tacs?" I demanded.

"Because he's been popping them since he was a child, going to this school right here," she said as she pointed to the school yard across the street.

Her face grew more and more severe as she talked—it was wrinkled and pointed toward decrepitness.

"You know this man?" I asked.

"I knew him when he was a kid," she said, snapping at me. "And other than having to watch him do his stupid Tic Tac thing in front of my house all the time, I have no involvement with him." She raised a scolding finger at me, "And neither should you. This has nothing to do with you, so you should leave."

"Well, what does it have to do with you?" I asked.

I felt something touch my shoulder. I spun around, found nothing, then spun more until I was facing Paul's car again.

Shhh. Quiet.

It was the nudge. That nudge.

Feel. Inhale.

A breeze came. It came from behind the woman's house and tickled past my face.

I gasped.

There was something, I could smell something. It was subtle, very subtle.

Oh, how I wished it had all been in my mind.

Welcome back to the freak show, baby.

I looked to the Town Car. The smell had to be coming from Paul. I guess he had been playing victim like any other person could play possum. I didn't know why I couldn't smell it before, but it was there now.

"Hey kid!" the old woman called out to Paul. "I've put up with your nonsense for years now. Leave and take your friend with you." She hobbled back inside her house, and then reappeared with something small in her hand. She walked to the end of her yard and tossed a tiny container at Paul's car. It bounced off the side door and burst open on the street. An entire container of orange Tic Tacs spilled its saccharin guts on the blackened asphalt.

"Stop leaving these at my door," she said. "Darrel is dead now. If you want him to have them, then drop them off at the cemetery."

She turned, went into her house, and slammed the front door again.

A husband? Was she referring to a dead spouse?

Was Paul dropping off boxes of Tic Tacs like a ritual, a tribute, a sacrifice to keep the monster from feasting, even a dead monster? If so, then Paul wasn't the monster. He who brings the sacrifice is the lamb.

And though the true monster has perished, the lamb still laid himself down, out of habit—out of poor, broken habit.

It would explain the faintness of the smell. It wasn't a living pedophile I could smell, but a dead one. One whose scent lingered as long as the scars he'd inflicted.

I looked back at Paul, popping more Tic Tacs.

Perhaps he gave back to his predator the same way the predator had given him. A cheap, minty-orange goodie to keep his mouth shut. Clean and shut.

My heart sank and I thought of Corinne. A dangerous and painful idea simmered within me. It was a bad one. A stinking, stupid one, which could be something I needed to consider: when the worst thing I could imagine happens, it may still be a grace from something even more tragic. An early death might have been better than surviving and becoming Paul. Because Paul wasn't the pedophile, he was the victim.

I put my hand over my stomach. It churned with the nausea of realizing the depths of the sick, twisted, and long-suffering world around me. Paul, even in his thirties, comes back to his hell over and over again, to lay himself down in a habitual slaughter of innocence.

If it were true that Paul's monster had bought his innocence with a box of orange Tic Tacs, then I wanted to fall down into the fetal position and weep. What if death were better than becoming a tainted adult, with so much impurity that the slime coating became too thick to clean?

I wanted to help him. I needed to help him.

I put my hands against his window, my breath ragged and leaving a teardrop pattern of condensation on its surface. "Paul," I said. "We need to talk."

TWENTY-FIVE

All the Broken Pieces

Paul popped his car into gear and took off.

I gave one last look to the old, embittered woman's house. There was a slight crinkle in one of the drapes on the left side of the front window. She was probably snorting at me from behind it.

Running back to my car, I had little expectation I could catch up with Paul. What would I do even if I did? He didn't want to talk with me. That much was certain. Yet my soul ached for him, for Corinne, even for myself if I was being honest.

In some desperate, foolish way, I thought Paul might be able to answer a question that would otherwise have to be posed to God: Why did You allow her to die?

But if I could figure it out on my own—by chasing down Paul and trying to get inside his head—then I wouldn't have to go to God. Not yet, anyway.

I knew the thought I was beginning to entertain was blasphemy. Blasphemy to both my daughter, and the dreams I concocted for her the moment I felt her flutter within my womb. Still, I had to wonder if she got the better end of the deal when I considered Paul. To have her life over was a tragedy. Every pore, follicle, and nerve ending on my body intimately realized that upon each sufferable day since her death. But then the alternative . . . To embrace the gift of breath, only to whither in the shadow of a devourer, was no way to live.

If she were still alive, would she ultimately turn into a jumpy, twitchy, Tic Tac–popping zombie, returning to her place of abuse as a dog returns to its vomit?

Like I said, it was blasphemy. But I still had to know.

Catching up with Paul was a stroke of luck. I found him a few blocks away, navigating through another residential neighborhood and driving the posted speed limit.

My first inclination was to get him to stop and pull over by any means available to me. I wanted to get him to talk and have him tell me what had happened to him in that house across from the school, haunting him still. My second inclination was to stay back, and I did. Fearing that if he saw me, he'd speed away again.

After a twenty-five minute drive—through what seemed like every imaginable stoplight on this side of town—Paul turned onto Olive Avenue. It was one of the longer stretches of road in town, cutting across Fresno in many ways: it stretched east to west, but also from the part of town many pretended didn't exist, to the green, expansive lawns of the powers that be. Everything in between was left to rot or flourish toward each polarity.

Paul lived in the vast middle, and pulled into a two-story blue and white apartment complex. As he rounded the complex's driveway, my car idled, held back at a nearby red light. I saw him park under a long carport. He scrambled out of his car, still wiping his brow, still popping Tic Tacs, and up the open-air stairwell of building 402. I watched him go into the door at the top right, just as the stoplight turned green for me.

I parked near the back of Paul's building in a guest spot. It was quiet and secluded, giving me an opportunity to figure out what was next on the agenda of my not-too-terribly-thought-out plan.

Walk up to the door and knock? No. That didn't end well for me last time I did that. Ugh, Robert Bailey. I let out a heavy sigh, now reminded of him. I'd been so accustomed to feeling sorry for myself as of late, I almost forget how to feel sorry for such a carnal mistake as ending Bailey's life. Self-pity had its plethora of minuses in the tally marks of my life, but helping me to forget I had killed a man seemed like a plus, and I practiced it every day.

He was a child killer, anyway, so I shouldn't spend too much time feeling bad over it.

It wasn't your right.

Ah, great. It was back. "Shh!" I said aloud in the silence of my car. Though that made me feel nuttier than hearing my heaven-centered conscience.

Thinking of Bailey again, and all the ill-conceived decisions that led up to it, I realized I ran the risk of making similar bad choices here. And that, like running with sharpened pencils, scissors, or flip-flops, could likely result in tears. Or blood, or worse.

Thatcher came to mind again. I should definitely call Thatcher. He could toss people over and split their eyebrows, after all. That knee in the back deal was pretty impressive too. I had, on a couple of occasions, practiced the move in the privacy of my bathroom, though the toilet seat didn't quite deserve it.

I reached for my phone and saw the message indicator icon. Cole had sent me a text message.

> You still owe me dinner. You're lucky I've been too busy with high profile clients to demand payment sooner. Thanks for that by the way. They've been coming to me because of your case.

> Time to pay up. Come by my place tonight. I know you split with Eddie. No more excuses.

Delete? Yes, delete.

Then I called Thatcher.

"Hey, Mrs. Barrett. Long time no hear," he said. "What have you been up to?"

"Prolific misery and shame," I answered

He laughed, but for the life of me, I couldn't figure out why that was funny.

"Have you ever given any thought to *not* saying whatever pops into your head?" he toyed.

"I think I used to do that. But now, I'm down to uttering only a few words a day, so they have to count. Honesty seems to work well."

"Oops," he said. "I think you just hit your quota of words. Should we hang up and try again tomorrow?"

"No," I said seriously.

He laughed again and then said, "I've been meaning to call you and give you a status report on your daughter's case."

The status was likely that there was no change in status. As much as I wanted to hear anything about Corinne's case, even if it rang against my ears like a tired bar song, I knew I had to focus our conversation on Paul McMillan.

"Maybe later," I said. "It's not that I don't want to hear it, but something urgent has come up."

"Should I get Pete to conference with us?"

"No."

"Well, to be honest, he's asked me to do that if you called."

"Thatcher, there's a reason I called you on your cell and not at your desk line. Besides, this has something specific to do with you opening your big mouth to your new girlfriend, Amanda."

"Um," he muttered.

"Yeah, so listen. I need your help with something."

"Have you," he cleared his throat, "smelled something?"

"Yes and no. More importantly, I think I found a victim," I said. "Your girlfriend's mother, Jeanine—"

Thatcher groaned.

"She knows about my olfactory deal thanks to you."

"That's a funny story, actually . . ."

"Nope, not interested. At any rate, Jeanine came to my house last week to tell me she suspected a co-worker of being a pedophile."

Thatcher groaned again, louder.

"She asked me to check him out, by . . . you know," I continued.

"Did you?" he asked.

Something rustled behind me near the carport—a crunch of gravel, or a tread of foot. I turned my head over my left shoulder, then my right. Both times, there was nothing.

"Here's the long and short of it: the guy Jeanine told me about, Paul McMillan, didn't have an odor to him, but he had some weird behavior. So I followed him—"

"You followed him?"

"He disappears each day and goes clear across town to wait outside an elementary school. I saw him, and for a moment I thought he was going to steal a kid right in front of me. Instead, he watched the kids walk by and when they were gone, he glares, and I mean glares, at this house across the street. I went to talk to him, and then the old lady who lives in the house interfered. And that's when I smelled something."

"The old lady?" he asked.

"I think it was her late husband. She said Paul keeps dropping off boxes of Tic Tacs for the dead husband, or at least, some man named Darrel. I think it might be some sort of penance or something."

"But if the guy is dead, I don't know what good we'll be."

"Can't you help Paul? Can't you at least officially note that this dead guy molested him when he was a kid?"

"I guess, but we should let Pete decide what we can do, if anything."

"Ugh. Fine. Just keep my name out of it. You should start with Jeanine and tell Pete you came across Paul that way. It's more or less true, and I would *love* for Pete to meet Jeanine. She'll make me look like a saint."

Thatcher chuckled. He knew.

"Give me what you have, and Pete and I will roll out either later today or tomorrow to see."

"Can't you come right now? Paul's just sitting here in his apartment."

"Don't tell me you're staking him out right now. Are you?"

I didn't answer him. I waited for him to cave in to my request.

"Okay, listen to me, Mrs. Barrett. Wherever you are, go home."

"You should come out now," I said. "This guy is completely damaged, a pile of broken goods. Let me give you his address. It's—"

I cut myself off, my eyes now glued on what I saw in my rearview mirror. Was that . . . ?

CRASH!

A baseball bat smashed through my rear window.

The noise shook me, echoing through my rib cage, and I dropped the phone on the passenger side floorboard. The glass shards separated and shot toward the back of my head like a million jagged pieces of regret.

CRASH!

There went the back window on the passenger side. That's when I saw Paul's face. I could even make out the orange-tinted tongue as he opened his mouth and screamed, "Leave me alone!"

No good deed goes unpunished . . . and all that jazz, as glass bounced off my skin and burrowed into my hair.

He moved toward the windshield, the bat lifted above his head for another blow, but since my car was still running, I threw it into reverse and floored it as the tip of the bat struck the ground below.

My back bumper sailed into one of the carport supports.

"Sorry!" I yelled out, feeling more stupid for apologizing than having been there in the first place.

Paul kept the bat toward the ground, chest heaving, looking like he was done with his Louisville slugging.

I sped away, haphazardly driving home. I wanted to hide both my car and fear away where only I had to look at all the busted pieces.

It was late afternoon when I pulled into my driveway. As soon as I shifted the car into park, I lowered my forehead on the steering wheel. What just happened? And, what, if anything, needed to be done about it other than to call a mobile glass repair business?

Remembering my phone was still on the passenger floorboard, I picked up my head and leaned over to retrieve my cell. Thatcher and I had been on the phone, but he must've ended that call a while back. He may have even heard the smashing of glass.

I had to call him, to let him know what happened. Maybe he and Pete would pay Paul a visit sooner rather than later, but before I could place another call to Thatcher, a car pulled up beside me, coming to a quick halt.

Who in the world would be in my driveway? My driveway wasn't even big enough to accommodate two cars side by side.

I looked at the car next to me. It was a black SUV, but I couldn't see the driver in the vehicle twice as high as my own.

I closed my eyes tightly, lamenting my colossal error. I was outside my old house, the golf course house. Eddie had pulled up next to me.

"Evy?" he asked, coming around the front of his car and approaching my driver's side.

I started the engine of my car and heard him say, "No, no, wait. Don't go. Are you all right? What happened?"

I could hear him clearly through the shattered windows.

I shifted my car into reverse.

"Detective Thatcher called me at work," he said, calling out to me. "He said something happened and we needed to find you."

"What happened?" he asked again.

I hit the gas. What a fool I had been to come back here. I didn't even know I was doing it. It must have been a preprogrammed autopilot feature in my mind.

"Evy!" he shouted out as I backed onto the street. "Stop!"

My tires squealed with friction as I sped away. I didn't want to deal with Eddie, not by accident, anyway. And definitely not after someone smashed out my windows. I was sure I'd get another lecture about my dangerous pursuits.

I couldn't go home; Eddie would come. I wasn't sure if he had procured the address from my sister, but he'd find a way.

I had to go somewhere.

Cole. His text said he'd be home tonight, waiting for me. It wasn't something I had planned on doing; I hadn't even planned to respond by telling him no. It would get him off my back, though, about the dinner thing, and I did want to be free of the shameful reminder of my car. There was glass everywhere—each small, crumbled piece reminding me that I'd be better off hiding somewhere.

"Tell me again how you managed to enrage this guy to the point where he batted out your windows," Cole said as he reached for two wineglasses in his cupboard.

"Are you pouring me wine?" I asked.

"Yes, and you look like you need some."

"Don't bother, I don't want any. But thanks for offering."

My comment did not deter him.

"I don't want to talk about the crazy guy with the bat," I said. "I'm just hiding out for a bit. I'm trying to avoid . . ." I looked at Cole, and decided not to tell him I was avoiding Eddie.

"Never mind." I picked up my purse and tucked it under my arm. "I don't know why I'm here," I said. "I'm a mess right now. I'm sorry, Cole. It's better if I leave."

"No, no, you owe me a dinner," he said, smiling.

"Sorry. That's not why I came here," I said.

"I know why you came here," he said with self-confidence. "You had a traumatic event and you want comfort. I'm actually flattered. I was starting to give up on you."

Traumatic, yes. Comfort? Probably. But if I told him I had subconsciously steered myself to Eddie first, then he might not be so flattered.

He finished pouring the wine I told him I didn't want.

Turning my back on him, I distracted myself with studying his loft. He lived in Fulton Mall, one of the downtown towers that had transformed floors eleven through sixteen into luxury lofts. Cole lived on the twelfth floor.

The place was an elite bachelor pad, and I imagined most of them looked the same. Women didn't often live downtown in lofts like this, and if they did, their biological clocks hadn't yet started to thump like a bomb, or had already wound down.

The five bare windows in the living room were in a warm brick wall, overlooking the Grizzlies' stadium. If this were Chicago or New York, this place wouldn't pass muster for high society. But since it was Fresno, Cole was living the high, single life.

The loft circled around the open kitchen, making it its focal point. And other than hiding in one of the two bedrooms, he could see me wherever I moved. I looked over my shoulder at him and then at the two robust stemware glasses he had filled with dark red wine. He saw me look at him and gave me a wink.

"This used to be all office space, right?" I asked, turning back to the window.

"Yes. It was remodeled for apartments a few years ago. Very happening place. Since you're single and unattached, you should look into one. Wouldn't that be convenient?" he asked.

I dared not turn away from the window again. I knew what sort of convenience he was talking about, and if I hadn't, his tone would've filled in the blanks. Besides, if I saw him wink at me one more time, I'm not sure I could stop myself from sneering.

I shouldn't have come. Hadn't I already decided that? And yet, I remained. I looked down at my car on the street, far below, and felt an oncoming tinge of panic for my vulnerable BMW. Now that it was two car windows shy, I worried about theft and vandalism.

The anxiety heightened when I saw the top of an SUV pull up behind my car. Whoever the driver was, he or she sat there with their lights on, flooding into where my back window used to be. It sent off dozens of sparkles, radiating from the obliterated slivers of glass.

"Cole? This is a safe neighborhood, isn't it?" I asked, still looking down on my car.

"Sure. Why?"

The beams of the SUV turned off.

I couldn't see much at that point, having only the dim orange streetlights to illuminate shadows here and there, and the dread I felt increased. A darkened figure got out of the SUV and approached my car.

He looked up at the building. There was no way he could see me, but I could have sworn I saw a beard. Eddie. Of course. I should have figured it out with the SUV, but I only saw the top. I couldn't tell what make or model it was. My hand went up to Cole's clean window, leaving a warm print of condensation on it. Eddie continued to stare up, searching.

"Can people see up here, Cole?" I asked.

"Are you kidding me? No one can see in. That's why I don't have drapes or blinds."

Next thing I knew, Cole's arm was around my shoulders. "What are you looking at?" he asked, peering down with me.

Eddie stopped looking up at that point, and went back to his car. "Nothing. Just a guy down there by my car. I thought he might be doing something to it, but he's gone now."

He slid his arm down to my waist, wrapping around it tighter. "No, look." Cole pointed to the figure below. "He's walked back to your car. What's he doing? Is he putting a note on your windshield?"

I chuckled nervously. "Ha ha. Maybe he's being a good citizen and letting me know some of my windows are broken."

"You want me to go down there and tell him to back away?"

"No," I said in a rush.

"No matter," he said. "He's leaving now. Adios, guy."

He released his hold on me and went back to the kitchen counter, grabbing the two glasses of wine. He extended one to me. I shook my head.

"I'm sorry," I said. "I have to go."

"Are you worried about your car?"

I was more interested in the note, but the car seemed a valid excuse. "Yes, sorry. We'll have to reschedule." Or not.

"What's the worst that could happen to it down there? Smash your windows? Too late. Come on, sit. Have some wine."

"I told you I didn't want any."

"But I've already poured it."

"I told you I didn't want it *before* you poured it, so that won't change my mind. Look, Cole, I have to go."

Cole set the glasses down on an end table, came to the window again, and looked down on the street. "He's not there, he hasn't come back, he won't come back, and your car looks shipshape," he said with a reassuring smile. "Except for the broken windows." He took one of my hands, pulling me to the couch.

I let him lead me. It would give me momentum to get to the door once I broke away. Now I only had half the room to cover for my escape. When he dropped my hand to move some pillows, I went for the door.

"I'm going to go. See you later," I said, turning my back to him.

"What? You just got here."

He darted past me and blocked my exit.

"Come on, Cole. What are you going to do? Hold me prisoner? Don't do this."

His eyes bore into mine as he contemplated something. He didn't answer me; he just stared at me, thinking.

I shook my head and sighed, leaning against the entry wall and waiting for him to move.

That's when I smelled something.

My eyes widened and I stood rigid. My hands balled into fists. When the scent came, I had been leaning on an entry wall that housed a coatrack. On the coatrack, a hat swayed on one of the hooks.

It was the smell. Not in a diluted or changed formula as the scent from the old lady's house, it was the first smell I had become acquainted with. Something about my expression must've taken Cole by surprise. He was no longer playing battle of the wills with me. He cocked his head to the side and looked puzzled.

"Is that your hat?" I asked, my voice breaking as I spoke.

Cole turned his head to see it. "No, that's a client's. I didn't even know he left it."

"You let clients into your house? Which client left this?" I asked.

Cole opened his mouth to speak, to offer up his answer with ease, but then a flash of realization descended upon him. His eyes narrowed and he cocked his head again, this time to the other side.

He tried to start another sentence, but gave up on that one too. Instead, he moved away from the door. "I guess I can't stop you, can I? That wouldn't be very chivalrous of me."

We faced each other in silence, neither one of us reaching for the door. Wine and wooing were way, way out of the picture, and even he knew it.

"*What* client, Cole?" I asked again. "*Which* type of criminal?"

His lips shut tight. He had pieced my concern together and he wasn't going to offer me a thing. He was a stingy, stingy little rat.

"A pedophile," I blurted out. "You're defending a pedophile, aren't you?"

He scoffed, his eyes giving everything away. "I don't know why you'd jump to that, but all the same, I can't tell you a thing. Attorney-client privilege. You remember how that works, don't you?"

"What a crock. That doesn't apply here. You're not breaching any duty by telling me who he is and what he's charged with. That information is readily available to the public."

"Well, considering your past," he enunciated the last word, "I wouldn't tell you, anyway. Privilege or no privilege, I don't want you to know."

I steadied my breathing, inhaling through my nose until the smell stung the insides, singeing my nasal canals. Opening my mouth to get the rest of my breath, I grabbed the hat and threw it across the room. I don't know how I didn't smell it when I first came, but maybe when the door was open, it hid the coatrack.

"How . . . how could you?" I asked, glaring at him.

"Oh, please, Evelyn." He rocked back on his heels, putting his hands into his pockets. "You know what I do for a living. I'm a criminal defense attorney. It's how I pay the bills."

I took a quick look around his apartment. The nice leather couch, the custom black-and-white prints on the walls, the high quality carpets, and all the extravagant memorabilia—from an ancient Egyptian bust to a signed baseball mounted in a fiberglass case—they were all treasures bought and paid for by the bad boys' club. A club that included pedophiles.

"Would you represent him? Are you representing him?" I asked.

"Who?"

"HIM! The guy who killed my daughter." I screamed it at him, shaking. It came out so loud that I think the mummy winced and the ball popped a stitch.

Cole reached for the door and opened it for me. "I guess you do need to leave."

I didn't budge. "Who is it?" I asked again, this time through clenched teeth.

"I'm not telling you. And I know not telling you will cost me whatever we could have had here, but I think it's better if you leave."

I walked past him, into the well-lit hallway, then turned back to face him. "You were never going to get anything from me," I said. "Never."

"Oh, I think I might've."

"No. You're a coward and you're way out of your league when it comes to me."

He snorted, and then shot back at me with a malicious smile. "Out of your league? Evelyn, at this point, you'd be lucky if someone else wanted you as scraps. I was actually going to ignore all your drama and shortcomings. Maybe it's because I have a soft spot for criminals."

If I had anything other than my purse to throw at him, I would have chucked it.

I turned back to the elevator and heard him shut his door behind me.

On the way down to the lobby, I pushed my anger toward Cole aside, remembering the note Eddie had left on my car. I pushed the Lower Level button again and again, hoping to make the elevator descend faster. I should have stayed at the old house, even if I had arrived accidentally. My stupid pride. I did need comfort right now, and Eddie was the only one, *is* the only one I wanted to give it. I'd go back to the golf course house; I'd go back to Eddie. Clearly, he still cared.

Hurrying to my car, I pulled out the note tucked under my windshield wiper. It had been crumpled once, smoothed out again, and then folded neatly.

> Evelyn,
>
> I think I'm finally catching on. I know Cole lives here, and it's all coming together for me. It'd explain why you moved out so quickly. I never got a chance to tell you before, but I officially give up. Since you won't file for divorce, I will. That will help you out.
> Eddie
>
> P.S. I'm not following you, in case you were worried. We have that GPS thing on our phones and it gave me this address. I'll disconnect that.

I wanted to scream WHY at the top of my lungs, but wouldn't. I couldn't. Cole was probably watching and, besides, I felt a sheath of futility wash over me. I'd spent a lifetime finding any old rein I could hold, pull, and control. And for what? Daughters still died, jobs still ended, and marriages still failed.

I crumpled the note and tossed it in the street, then climbed in my car and drove off. A hundred yards away, I came to a screeching halt and jumped out of the car, leaving it idling.

Running back to the curb, I picked up the discarded note and carefully tucked it into my pocket.

What can I say? Broken people tend to hold on to all the little pieces.

TWENTY-SIX

Falsetto

The next morning I watched a windshield repairman replace my car windows. He was a beefy fellow with the name "Bob" embroidered on his blue shirt. Every time he hoisted his pants back up, fiddling with cleaning up the remainder of the broken windows, his gold wedding band glinted in the sun. Ah, marriage. Supposing he had children, I wondered how long he and his wife would stay together after their child died.

I stood in my small, stark living room, holding back the drapes a few inches, watching Bob. I fell into some sort of trance as Bob and his descending pants vacuumed broken pieces of glass from my seats and floorboard.

The vacuum clunked and clanked along. It was like it was swallowing a cacophony of destruction and demolition, as each piece of glass thrashed against its plastic innards from hose to holding tank. I knew the vacuum could handle it because that's what it was designed for; yet it didn't seem right—nothing should have such jagged things shoved down its throat. It may not be visible on the outside, but that's the stuff deep scars originate from.

That's when my internal pleading asked the real question: What about me? How much more could be shoved down *my* innards? And what, pray tell, did my scarring look like?

Probably a lot like a woman all alone, with no child, no husband, and no future; jealous of Bob, his wedding band, and the nickel slot his wife likely adored. The nickel slot was a stretch, actually. No one liked those. To imagine otherwise . . . I had been alone for too long.

Bob's vacuum roared, and other than that, I couldn't hear anything from the emptiness of the life I had created. At first, this rental and my lack of socialization had been my protective bubble. Now it had become the place I would rot. I imagined the rats in the walls—if they were there—were already drawing lots on which one would get first dibs on me after I died, when I would lie expired for weeks before anyone noticed I was gone.

In the barreness around me, I turned my eyes off Bob and onto the blue sky above. It was the color of Corinne's eyes, of Eddie's eyes, yet it still seemed serene to me although I had just been considering rats nibbling on my deceased face.

I asked aloud, "Are You real?"

Of course I meant God—the One who gives and takes away. The One who was getting harder to deny the longer I scraped and bloodied my knees against the filth of the world.

Wasn't it Him who kept trying to talk to me, to nudge me?

I didn't hear a response to my question. But felt . . . well, felt was another thing. I definitely felt something resonating. Sort of like a piano tuner giving that deep, low A chord a tight, fast pluck, *buuuuuuummmmmmm*. And then I knew the answer.

Yes, I'm real.

I had a feeling, albeit a miniscule one, that someone else wanted me more than the rats did.

"It would've helped if you returned my phone calls yesterday," Thatcher told me when I called him back.

Bob, the windshield repairman, had left over an hour ago.

"I'm fine," I said.

"Great, but that's not why I was calling. After I heard all that commotion, knowing you were at Paul McMillan's place, Pete and I went to go check him out. Mr. McMillan more or less turned himself in, and he's still here."

"At the station?" I asked.

"Yeah, in a holding cell. We were going to hold him until you pressed charges, but in a few more hours, we'll have to let him go anyway."

"I'm not going to press charges, but I'm on my way down there. I still want to talk to him."

"Good luck with that," Thatcher said. "He's got both feet in the nuthouse, if you ask me. But let me ask Pete if you can have a visit with him."

I hung up, not waiting for Thatcher to obtain Pete's answer. Showing up would work out—one way or the other.

The station looked dirtier than it had the last time I'd been there. Summer slipping into fall had a way of doing that to everything in the valley. Crops harvested, fields plowed, fires burning in nearby mountains, and the Santa Ana winds mixing it all up like a cloud of filth with nowhere to go but resting like a halo of pollution over every city in the San Joaquin. The only thing worse than the pollution was the dank smell of manure emanating from the dairy farms.

Pete was expecting me. He had an unusual smile on his face as he came to the front to greet me.

"Mrs. Barrett," he extended his hand. "It's been a while. How are you?"

I wasn't sure it'd be all right to shake his hand. The whole thing could be a setup to get me cuffed and thrown into an empty cell.

"Come on, now," he said, still smiling. "Don't be afraid. I'm not mad at you."

"Why not?" I asked, hesitating.

"Ah, well, come back to my desk and I'll tell you." He turned, leaving me in the station foyer. After walking a few steps, he looked back at me. "I promise I won't bite."

His brows looked softened and relaxed for the first time in my recollection. Something was different, so I obliged and followed him.

"Sit, sit," he said, holding out the chair at the side of his desk.

"So, you've muddled yourself into another investigation," he said.

I sat down and winced. It was coming now; I knew it.

"Oh, calm down," he told me. "It's actually funny at this point. Here, look," he said as he pulled up his desk calendar and showed it to me. He pointed to the following week on his calendar. The entire week was outlined in red marker, with two words written in big, bold letters: EXPECT BARRETT.

"You're early, but you've got to hand it to me that I narrowed it down so well," he said, smiling.

I would have smiled too, except I knew he was serious. The joke wasn't on me but about me. I guess I deserved it. Still, I was in no mood to refrain from slinging something back.

"So, Pete," I began, "you should tell me the magic behind your fiber dosage. It's done wonders for you. You look so happy, relaxed, and unplugged."

He waved a finger at me, "Ha ha. Good one." Then he folded his arms across his chest and looked out a nearby window. "Actually," he said, turning back to me, "I've had some happy changes in my life."

"Really? That's great," I offered, though his admission made me envious.

"Yup. I'm no longer ashamed to admit there was some counseling involved. I've always been the type to think counseling was for whiners. If you couldn't suck it up and move on, then you didn't need counseling, you needed a reality check. Then I found my wife of twenty years standing over me while I slept one night, mumbling unkind words. Scared the dickens out of me, but apparently I enraged her with those very opinions on counseling earlier that evening, when she requested we go to therapy together."

He sighed, looking out the window again, his gaze getting lost. "That was a wake-up call, literally. Whew," he muttered, shaking his head. "I tell you, you ladies may be the physically weaker gender but you aren't without your means."

I put the back of my hand over my mouth to hide my smile. I wanted to change the subject and ask if I could see Paul, but since Pete was in a good mood, it was best to temper myself and let Pete ride his counseling pony out to pasture.

"In a nutshell, counseling is working," he said, looking at me again. "And strangely, you've come up a lot. My wife says I need to go easier on you, and more importantly, the therapist reminds me—and I'm paraphrasing here—that I cannot control the self-destructive habits of stupid people. I can only arrest those who have broken the law."

My eyes narrowed and my lips pouted. Laughing at him was no longer an issue; he was back to making fun of me.

"So, have you broken any laws today, Mrs. Barrett?"

"No," I said, almost growling at him.

"Good. I hear you want to see Paul McMillan. But first, do you want to press charges?"

"No."

"Are you sure?" he asked. "It's not my case, mind you, but at this juncture in time, the station refers to me as your 'handler,' so I'll be passing on the information."

"I don't want to press charges. Can I please talk to him?"

"Nope."

"What?" I said, my voice rising. "Why not? If it's not your case, then why would you care if I talk to him?"

"First, we don't let people off the street go traipsing back in our holding cells. And second, you enraged the guy to the point where there was bat wielding and property damage. Taxpayers pay for this building, and I'm not going to let either one of you get even close to chipping the paint."

"I didn't enrage him," I defended. "The guy's just a broken, disconnected individual."

"All the same. I like the paint on the walls exactly how it is."

My head shook at him in disapproval and frustration. "You haven't changed at all."

"Yes, I have." He straightened his tie, and then smiled at me. "See, a few months ago, if you had come in here and had this discussion with me, I would have been in a bad mood all day, and then carried it around with me at home. That's why my wife was enraged enough to stand over me while I slept. I wasn't being a very good husband. But now, I'm going to go home tonight a peaceful man, give her a kiss, tell her you came calling one week early, and that I was nice to you."

"You aren't being nice," I said, leaning forward, challenging him.

"Me not being nice and you not getting your way are two different things."

"Did you read that on your Fiber One box this morning?" I asked.

"Ha ha. You've got a great sense of humor, Mrs. Barrett. Truly, you do."

I growled, squeezing my fists.

"Listen," he said, "my decision is final, but in case it helps, Mr. McMillan is going to be released as soon as I tell the holding officer you aren't pressing charges. He'll walk out of the back doors to the jail. As much as I think it's a bad idea for you to talk to him, it's like my therapist said: I can't control the self-destructive habits of others."

"You forgot the 'stupid' qualifier," I said.

"No I didn't. I wasn't paraphrasing this time."

"Anyway, did Thatcher tell you how Paul McMillan might be a victim of childhood sexual abuse?" I asked, changing the subject.

"Yes, but Mr. McMillan isn't talking about that, so what can we do?"

"But—"

"But nothing. In the same way nothing will happen to McMillan for busting out your windows if you won't press charges, nothing will happen to this man's alleged abuser if McMillan won't talk. If he was still a minor, then it'd be a different story. But the guy is in his thirties. There's nothing we can do."

Pete stood and picked up a file, clutching it against his chest. The way he held it, it was probably the McMillan file from another officer. Pete was wising up. I'm not sure I wouldn't have stolen that one too, given the opportunity.

"If you are going to wait outside of holding," Pete said, "I'd suggest a helmet. I agree with you on one point: Mr. McMillan is damaged goods."

He extended his hand again and I numbly shook it.

"Oh wait," Pete said, setting the file down. I considered grabbing it, but at some point I had to learn, right?

He opened the top drawer of his desk and pulled out a red Sharpie. "Do you want me to mark you down for a future visit?"

I rolled my eyes, stood, my shoulders sagging in defeat, and walked out.

Two hours later, Paul McMillan walked through the glass back doors of the police station where I was waiting for him, sans the recommended helmet.

"Truce!" he yelled out when he saw me.

I froze. Did he just call out *truce*?

I took a step back. The word confused me, but the shouting—paired with the vivid memory of his bat crashing down a mere foot from my skull—scared me.

"Paul," I said. "Can I talk to you?"

"No," he said, walking sideways to get away without taking his eyes off me. "I want to go home. Or back to work before I get fired."

"It'll only take a minute. I want to ask you a question."

"Mr. Crafton didn't hurt me!" he yelled, coming to a standstill.

"Who's Mr. Crafton?" I asked.

"Helen's husband." Then he shook his head with fury, as if suddenly cognizant he had revealed more than he should.

"I have to go to work," he said, turning his back on me.

"Is Helen the woman from that front yard yesterday?"

"Leave me alone."

"My daughter was raped and murdered by a pedophile," I shouted out to him, the genesis of tears springing up within my eyes from the simple act of confession. That particular confession that would do me in for the rest of my life. Like a steel albatross around my neck, hanging so low that it set off sparks on the concrete as I trudged along.

He stopped and faced me. His chest rose in a monumental effort to display strength. "I'm sorry," he told me. "I am very sorry. I can only imagine how hurtful that is."

My feet carried me closer, each step creating more and more panic that I'd make him bolt again. Yet he didn't move. He held his chin up and watched me with stoicism.

He didn't look afraid of me any longer. He only looked fearful that I would see through his facade; see through the pretense that he was abstractly pondering the cruelty of pedophilia, rather than intimately knowing exactly how beastly it was.

"But you don't have to imagine it, do you, Paul?"

His chest deflated, and his hands darted into his pockets.

"You don't know what you're talking about," he said, his returning anger evidenced by tiny flecks of orange in his otherwise muddled brown eyes.

"I just want to know one thing, Paul. Let me ask my question and I'll never bother you again. You don't even have to answer it if you don't want. I hope you do, but it's a ridiculously intrusive and blasphemous question."

That got his attention.

"Hurry then," he said. "And after, leave me alone."

The sun was blinding me from above as I faced him, and if it had hands, it would have reached down from its hold in the heavens, slapping me silly across the face. For trying to find meaning in something above my pay grade, above my meager philosophies in what was but a breath of my life. I was trying to understand the graces behind evil and that's a ridiculous game to play when we're all just human after all. I should know by now that there was nothing behind evil except evil itself; like I knew without thrusting a hand into a fire that it's hot—just don't touch it, dum-dum.

Still, I asked Paul McMillan my question. "Would it have been better if you had died as a child, rather than to have survived the abuse?"

I had to know. It wasn't the first time my mind had disregarded logic since Corinne died, and it likely wouldn't be the last. And though I knew there wasn't what anyone would call a "good reason" behind Corinne's death, and that she was merely collateral damage to a foothold given over to the devil, originating back in the Garden with Eve and her forbidden fruit, I still wanted to know.

A cheap and repetitious melody burst through the air as an ice-cream truck rounded the corner and moved along its route to a nearby park, interrupting our little talk.

When he heard it, Paul's hands pulled from his pockets and raised halfway up his torso, fingers curled as if he was about to defend himself from something.

The ice-cream truck passed, Paul's eyes following it until it disappeared. By the time he looked back at me, I was sure Paul McMillan had gone bye-bye. His eyes had glassed over, his face pale and creamy.

"Paul? Are you all right?" I asked.

He answered, almost in a robotic voice, "You know what's better?" he asked. "It'd be better if I wasn't a bad boy. It'd be better if I didn't have to take it like a bad boy."

Huh?

"Wh . . . what did you say?" I asked.

He stared past me—way, way past me—and spoke again. This time his voice rose to a high falsetto. "You're a bad boy, Paul, and you're going to have to pay for taking that ice cream."

It sounded like he was impersonating a woman's voice. He continued, "Who spoils their dinner with ice cream? Bad, bad, bad."

"Paul . . ." I started to ask, but nothing else followed.

"I HATE ICE CREAM!" Paul shouted at the top of his lungs.

My eyes widened and my hand went over my mouth in horror. Absolute horror. I took a step back. He did too, like we were two opposite sides of magnets pushing each other apart.

I turned to walk to my car; the answer I wanted from Paul would have to wait, maybe forever.

Paul's high-pitched falsetto came again. "He's a cuckoo bird. Just let him suck on those stinking Tic Tacs."

I stopped to face him. The voice . . . the words . . . the woman across the street from the school had said that very thing.

I didn't understand, or I didn't want to. My eyes lost focus, everything was losing focus. I raised my hands, putting them on my temples to grasp some sort of control. Why was *she* coming back into this? Why was

Paul splitting a personality right in front of me? Despite knowing that I shouldn't have bothered, nor continued to bother, with Paul anymore, his ordeal brought me to what seemed like a final crescendo of my experience since Corinne's death—although I was quite aware of the likelihood that I was merely adding volume to my preexisting dung pile. What were a few more flies buzzing around, feeding on feces?

The answer I sought didn't seem as relevant as the sight of Paul breaking right before my very eyes. Alive or dead, when the beast leaves a child in the wake of abuse, the earth cracked and creaked, and then slipped a little further into the abyss of hell. Paul was on a Slip 'n Slide into that very abyss, through the sharp, tangled fangs that enclosed the front gates.

Still, as soon as I no longer needed the answer, Paul chose to give it: "Yes!" he shouted. "I wish I were dead."

He turned and walked away, his hands still raised to defend an attack.

Yup, the answer didn't make anything better.

She was still dead, and I was still empty. But maybe Paul could be saved.

TWENTY-SEVEN

The Bone and Flesh
of a Mother's Arms

I ran back around to the front of the station and went to Pete's desk.

"Where's Thatcher?" I demanded.

"Mrs. Barrett. How was your chat? Glad to see your head is in one piece."

"Please," I implored, pressing my palms on top of his desk.

He looked up at me once, then went back to writing something on a pad of paper. "Are you trying to find him for some sort of crusade, like the two of you did early in the summer?" he asked.

I held my breath, thinking through my answer. "No," I replied with a calm ease, standing and folding my arms while gently shaking my head. "He has my pen. I want it back. My mother gave it to me at my law school graduation. It's special to me." I smiled at him the moment he looked up again. "But speaking of that crusade," I said, pointing nonchalantly at him, "that's when he borrowed it. You know Thatcher," I said. "Doesn't carry pens."

Pete eyed me carefully, then put his hands on his desk and splayed his fingers, taking in a long deep breath. I was cooked.

"You know what? I don't care," he said. "I don't want to know and I don't care. As long as you don't break any laws, I cannot control your actions." He put on a contrived happy face while the tips of his ears darkened in color.

I wasn't sure if he was helping or hurting the case for therapy.

"Thatcher went on some interviews for an—and I'm really going to stress the next word for you, Mrs. Barrett—*unrelated* case. Give him a call on his cell if you want to find him."

I saluted him and left the station, dialing Thatcher's cell as I went through the doors.

"Thatcher, can I talk to you about that McMillan deal Jeanine told me about?"

"Not now, I'm beat and I need to clear my head," he told me. "I just finished interviewing a bunch of high school coaches on an alleged teenage sex ring. This job sucks. This city sucks."

"I'm sorry." I was, but not sorry enough to oblige by calling back later. Maybe if I let him talk it out, he'd get his head back into my current chase.

"What is it? Like coaches pimping out players?" I asked.

"You don't need to know," he said.

"I'm just trying to lend an ear. You should tell me instead of scaring your girlfriend later."

Silence. At least he was thinking about it.

"Yes," he said. "And the girls are willing."

More silence. I wanted to tap my foot as I sat in my car, parked in front of the police station, but I dared not. Thatcher was chatty. He'd get the rest of it out.

"And do you want to know *why* the girls are willing? You'll never believe why they agree to be prostitutes. Playtime. Can you believe it? They want more playing time on the court or field, or whatever, so they have sex with the coach. And then, they have sex with other coaches who then agree to pull their team's best players, so the prostitute team can win. And do you know *why* they want to win so badly?"

"College scholarships," I answered bluntly.

"Yeah," he said, sounding surprised. "How did you know?"

"Because I'm an ambitious female. Clearly not *that* ambitious . . ." My mind went back to walking into Robert Bailey's house with a gun, driving Eddie away so I could potentially do that to another offender, and oh, there was following Paul McMillan. Perhaps I shouldn't judge.

"I'm sorry you have to deal with that, Thatcher," I said. "Hey, how about you call your girlfriend and I'll take the two of you out to dinner? You seem like you need a break."

"Cut the bull, Mrs. Barrett. What do you want?"

I never passed up an opportunity to get to the point. The words tumbled out of my mouth. "It wasn't just the husband of that old lady that hurt Paul McMillan. The wife, that cranky old bat, she helped. Somehow, she was involved. I talked to Paul after he was released, and this ice-cream truck drove by . . . you know what, never mind. Is there any way you could go after the old lady? My gut is screaming that she's involved. Paul almost said it."

"He said that?"

"In his own way, yes."

"Still," Thatcher added, "if he doesn't talk, we can't do anything."

"But what if he wasn't the only one?" I asked. "What if she's still doing something?"

He huffed. I didn't know where he was, but I could tell he was somewhere out in the open streets because I heard a siren coming from the distance. Louder still until I heard something muffle over from Thatcher's end, as if he put a hand over the microphone, or shoved the cell into a pocket to dull the sound of the rapidly approaching, and deafening, emergency siren.

"Sorry about that. Fire truck."

"Will you talk to her?"

"Yeah, I'll go talk to her," he said.

I heard disinterest, even an attempt at pacification, make a slow crawl into the conviction of his tone. He might not ever get to Helen Crafton's house if he didn't do it today when he was already feeling beaten down and a slave to his job.

"Now? You'll talk to her now?" I asked.

Of course, I didn't want him to lose interest, but worse yet, I didn't want him to involve Pete.

"What the heck," he answered. "It's already been a crappy day."

Twenty minutes after hanging up with Thatcher, he was calling me.

"Hi," I said. "What's up?"

"What's up?" he asked. "I see you, that's what's up."

"What do you mean?"

"Will you stop? I'm looking right at you. I'm parked outside Helen Crafton's house, the house you asked me to come to, and I see you parked in your pretty black Beemer, oh, about five houses down."

"The term is *Bimmer*, actually," I said.

"What?"

"It's not Beemer, it's Bimmer."

"Potato, patato."

"Nope, not even close. Besides, there are hundreds of black BMWs in the city—"

"Not on this street, and not with a chick coincidentally holding a phone up to her ear the minute I called your number."

"I wanted to see," I defended.

"Don't you have a life?"

He uttered a sigh of regret the second it flew out of his mouth.

"Sorry," he added. "But seriously, you need to leave. If you don't leave, I will. And *if* I come back, I'll bring Pete."

"Fine. Bye."

I hung up, started my car, and drove past him, waving with a prim smile upon my face. I made the first left and found an alley I spotted earlier when I drove by. It was behind the row of houses on Helen Crafton's street. One side of the alley contained the back fences of the properties, and the other side had each home's detached garage. I pulled into the alley, parking my car front-first in a space between two of the garages. About a foot of the back of my car stuck out; hopefully, Thatcher wouldn't drive by this way and see it.

When I walked down the alley, I did a gut check. And no, I didn't have the guts. But I also didn't want to go back home to the loneliness, the pain, the rats casting lots. Besides, I had already concluded today that I hadn't made a good decision in quite some time; there was no point starting now.

I passed the third garage on the street, only then realizing that I hadn't tried smelling anything. The air was still. Without the help of a breeze, I didn't think I could smell from afar. When I drove past Thatcher in front of the Crafton house, I had counted homes. Helen Crafton's house was eighth from the end of the street. Five more to go, and then maybe I'd smell something.

Number eight. The garage was a solid structure of wood, with a crumbling coat of white paint. It had a garage door and a small side door with a dirty window in it. I peeked inside, but the dirt covering was too thick. I pulled my long sleeve over my hand and used it as a towel. The dirt didn't budge. Time had caked it on from the inside.

I looked at the entirety of the window, noticing that the top panes of glass weren't as fouled up as the lower, but I didn't have anything to stand on. I jumped and looked, jumped and looked, jumped and looked, until I looked like a spastic fool. Still, I had seen enough.

First, I saw a Toyota Camry. Tan, like the dust all around it. Over against the far wall were a few storage boxes with the name . . . I jumped a fourth time up . . . Darrel written on them.

I again wondered who Darrel was. Was he the Mr. Crafton Paul had referred to?

I walked behind the garage, looking for a rock to use to smash the window, and only after coming up dry did I even stop to consider that Pete would skin me alive if he found out I had broken into a viable suspect's garage. Talk about interfering. That was pure and simple tainting of the evidence. A defense attorney's pie-in-the-sky case.

Coming back around to the front of the garage and into the open line of the alley, a small wind wisped by me. It brought the smell, but it came from farther down.

I had been so sure that Crafton . . .

I walked past the Crafton garage, then another, and then another. When I got to the third garage away, I stopped. Bingo. Here was where the smell originated.

I walked the perimeter of the garage. It had no windows at all. Not even on the side door. I twisted the rusted door handle and found it locked. I couldn't escape the conclusion that since this wasn't the Crafton garage, someone else was in the mix now.

I had wanted to be right about Helen Crafton—not as much as I had wanted to be right about Robert Bailey, because that had held a different prize for me. Still, I'd wanted to be right.

Turning to the house across the alley from the windowless garage, I saw a solid fence and the roof of a one-story home. The fence was the only one along the alley without a back access gate leading to the detached structure. It didn't make any sense. If they parked their car in the garage, they'd have to walk all the way down the alley, and then back up along the front street to get to their house.

I put my hands against the back of the fence, the tip of my nose only a few centimeters away from the worn wood topped with oleander bushes springing from the other side. I smelled nothing from the house.

I turned my head to the side, over my right shoulder to the garage. Disgusting.

Two choices presented themselves: forget propriety and kick in the side door to the garage—it was only filler board with a chintzy door handle—or march around to the front of the oleander house and simply ask. Ask . . . something. I'd iron out that detail on my walk around the corner.

I quickly peeked over the fence and through the high bushes. There was a play set, a barbeque, and a blow-up kiddie pool. I had developed my game plan before I exited the alley. My name was Dana Patrick and I was canvassing the neighborhood to make sure people had registered to vote in the upcoming election.

Thatcher would be so mad at me. Pete would serve me up with a salt rub and cracked pepper.

I knocked on the front door.

A woman, a few years younger than me, answered the door.

"Hi," she said.

"Is that your garage across the alley?" I blurted out. So much for the voter registration scam.

Her brow furrowed in confusion, but then she was sidetracked when a sprinting toddler skirted around her to escape through the open front door. She reached out, hooking him around his torso before he plowed between my legs. As he screeched and wriggled, she lifted him up, tucking him under her arm and holding him there as if he was nothing more than a rolled-up area rug.

I gazed at the child, wanting to lose myself in the ordinariness of his mother's gesture—when she lassoed him like there'd be a tomorrow with her child, and a next day, and a next . . . to hold her child as if it's not the last time to do so.

"Sorry," she said, looking thoroughly embarrassed.

But it was nothing to be embarrassed about. I'd give anything just to hold Corinne again; even if it would be like holding a sack of potatoes. Because in doing so, as the mother before me had, I'd be protecting my child from running into the street toward certain doom. And to have that feeling of purpose, or control, or even conviction, that my arms alone, as small and insignificant as I often found them to be, were still *mother's* arms. A pair of extending bone and flesh that, though physically weaker than a man's, were designed by God to catch more, to hold more, to protect more . . . as long as mommy didn't get too preoccupied flexing her biceps for her own purposes, as I had.

"What did you say?" the mother asked me.

My mind took the express train back from la-la land, where if I had allowed myself, I could've beat myself up until the world imploded. I made an effort to look in her eyes and away from the child, who had now rolled on his back, arching downward in his mother's arms, letting blood rush to his bulbous cheeks.

"Does the garage behind your home belong to you?"

"Um, no. That garage doesn't belong to us. Why do you ask?"

"I'm a local realtor and one of your neighbors is thinking of putting her home up for sale. I'm evaluating the neighborhood," I said. I amazed myself with that one, although I was sure that being able to lie on demand was not a trademark for being spectacular.

She set the toddler down and guided him in the direction of the living room. "Oh, well, I think this is the only house on the street that doesn't have one of those garages. It's an odd story too, but that's how it goes. Happened before we moved here. We got this place at a discount because it lacked the garage, so I can't complain."

"What happened before you moved here?" I asked.

She gave me a half-smile. "The owners before the people we bought the house from lost possession of it because of some debt. I don't really know the details, except which house currently owns the garage." She looked over her shoulder to make sure her son wasn't about to attempt another escape. "But I guess if we want it back, all we have to do is wait for the current owner to die, because that's when the ownership of the garage comes back to this place. It's the old lady who lives three houses down. I know it's a crass thing to say, but we might not have to wait that long. Because of her age," she added.

My jaw clenched, but I forced it open to speak again.

"Are you talking about Helen Crafton?" I asked.

"Is that her name? Is she the one selling? Oh, I hope so. She's so grumpy and . . ."

She trailed off and I balled my fists for fear I'd simply reach out and shake the rest of the sentence out of her.

"And what?" I asked.

"It's silly. I'm probably just being an overprotective mom, but . . . let's just say I'd feel easier letting my son play out front if she wasn't around anymore. It's not just her grumpiness, it's—"

"A certain cloud of evil that hovers over her," I interrupted.

The young mother's eyes widened and she put a hand on the doorknob. "Uh, I wouldn't get that fancy about it, but yeah, something like that."

She stepped back and started to close the door. "Is that all?" she asked.

"Yeah, I'm sorry." It was all I could mumble out. Then, I added, "Thanks for your help."

Before three minutes had elapsed, I had run back to the windowless, smelly garage with a leg raised to kick in the side door. I didn't truly expect to possess the force to kick it in, but by goodness, I was going to try. I balanced myself on my planted foot, simultaneously pushing away the thought that I couldn't even open a jar of pickles without using the bulky end of a butter knife to bang the junk out of the lid.

"I can do this," I said aloud. I went in for the kick just as Thatcher grabbed my calf and swung me around. I nearly toppled over, but he caught me and then put my leg down so I could stand.

"*What* are you doing?" he demanded.

I opened my mouth, unsure of whether the truth or a lie would spill out, but he stopped me.

"Never mind. I think it's better if I don't know. Listen, we need to get out of here."

TWENTY-EIGHT

Paul Stopped

Thatcher walked a couple of paces behind me, making sure I kept moving forward. He had his car parked at the end of the alley, but I stopped at my car and turned to him.

"What did you find out?" I asked.

"I'm going to get a warrant." He looked down the alley from where we had come. "Should I include that other garage you were about to break into within the scope of the search?"

"Yes," I said. "The smell is coming from there."

"But that's not Crafton's garage," he said.

"It is. The neighbor told me it had been surrendered to pay off some debt."

"You've already talked to a neighbor?" he asked.

I didn't answer aloud. Instead, I gave him a look that translated, "Of course I have. What kind of amateur do you take me for?"

"Seriously?" he asked.

I nodded, reluctantly laying my sarcasm by the wayside.

He chuckled. "I think you entered the wrong profession. You should have been a detective."

"And then have to rely on the incompetence of lawyers to run the last leg of the race in a criminal prosecution?" I managed a half-smile and he found it far too funny. I was but a breath away from my honorary police badge.

Thatcher put his hands in his pockets and hunched his shoulders. In a quick pace, he changed the mood. "I'm going to go now," he said. He shifted his weight, hiking his pant leg up on the right. "You can't be involved in this, Mrs. Barrett. You know that, right?"

My brow twisted in confusion. It was times like this that I could imagine the multiple occasions his mother could refer to him as an ingrate. "But if it weren't for me—"

"Yeah, but what does it have to *do with you?*" he asked. "Yes, you found this Paul guy, and yes, you were right about some others"—he pulled his hands out of his pockets and brought them to his chest—"but the only reason I'm out here right now is because you were instrumental in getting Amanda to go out with me. Now, Mrs. Crafton, who, I agree, is fishy enough to make me try for the search warrant, still doesn't have anything to do with you."

"Don't forget about that other garage. My money is on the good evidence being in that garage. That old bat might get off scot-free unless you expand the scope of the warrant to include that garage," I said. "Speaking of which," I started, "how about we go back, and *you* kick in the door. That sort of thing is in your job description, right?"

He smiled and shook his head. "Okay, Lawyer, tell me you see the legal problem in that."

"I've been disbarred. I could care less about legal mumbo jumbo at this point in time."

"You don't mean that."

I put my hands on my hips, pretending the best I could that I *did* mean it. He didn't buy it.

"Okay, I'm going back to the station," he said. "I'll have an uphill battle about this, but my gut is screaming that your old lady friend is hiding something bad."

He turned to walk to his car.

"Well, can't you at least tell me what you guys talked about?"

"No," he said, shouting at the empty air in front of him and still facing his car.

I made it halfway back to the garage before he turned around.

"Mrs. Barrett!" he screamed out at me.

Of course I had bolted when his back was turned. Again, not an amateur.

He jogged over. "Please, please, please don't make Pete's day by making me bring you down to the station in cuffs," he said.

I rolled my eyes.

"Listen, if you walk back to your car, and then drive away before I do, I promise I'll update you. I'll email you," he offered. "Is that allowed?" I asked.

"No. But I'm hoping you'll have the good sense not to let others know I've said anything."

I put my hand out to him and gave him a solid nod to let him know I accepted his terms. We shook, but he didn't budge from his spot in the alley, blocking my access to return to the door I wanted opened.

Thatcher's email:

> I swear, you really know how to pick them. Below is a history of the house, including several cold case files for our division.
>
> Helen Crafton was married to Darrel Crafton, a man suspected in four unsolved molestation cases from over twenty years ago. Four young boys, from 1980 through 1984, reported that an ice-cream vendor, driving a vintage ice-cream truck, had molested them. The details varied between the four boys, but the police relied more on the two oldest children. Both nine years old, they said the truck picked them up one block away from school and drove to a secluded garage in an alley.
>
> They described the attacker as a small man, with light, longish hair tucked into a cap.

A man? I wanted to be right about Helen. I thought I *was* right about her. I kept reading.

> They said the man had a funny, low, almost fake voice, and wore an oversized work shirt with the name Darrel on the breast. Investigators at the time brought Darrel Crafton in for questioning. Time and again, Crafton's boss vouched for him being at work during the incidents.
>
> The investigators also did a lineup. The only person in the lineup who even remotely reminded the children of their attacker was a retired jockey who got picked up the evening before on a drunk and disorderly. The jockey was almost two feet shorter and a hundred pounds lighter than Crafton. Also had the suspects do a voice identification for the boys and none batted an eye when Mr. Crafton spoke.

After that, everything went cold. No new accusations surfaced and Crafton had a heart attack and died three months later.

Paul McMillan wasn't listed in any of the files. But like Pete says, many children don't tell.

Pete's reopening the four files because he thinks the reason the children picked the retired jockey out of the lineup was because the real offender could've been a woman pretending to be a man. That leads us right back to Helen Crafton. Her father used to be an ice-cream man and even owned an ice-cream truck.

Warrant's pending. A title search on the second garage you found showed that the Craftons acquired it in the 60s.

Last thing. Save my job and DELETE this email right now.

It could be, and likely was, Helen after all.

I responded:

What email? ☺ When are you guys doing the search?

Thatcher didn't respond until two days later, a Tuesday, saying the search would take place that Thursday.

Liar.

I was making plenty of assumptions when I drove to Helen Crafton's that afternoon, but the gamble paid off. I found a small group of police officers in front of the house, and a few more in the alley as I drove around. Parking my car a block up, I quietly slipped into the alley, planning to make my way behind the row of garages over to the garage I wanted to know about. A machete would have been helpful, but I was sure that weapon was in the long list of no-no's my parole officer had given me.

There was a cinder block wall four feet behind the back of the garages. Ivy flowed in neglected measure both on and over it. I imagined one homeowner on the other side of the wall had planted it twenty years earlier, and now the whole street had it. It had overgrown so much that it created a foot-deep jungle padding on the ground. I only hesitated on the first step of my trek because my mother had once told me ivy is a haven for rats. But then again, she said the same thing about Congress.

I waded through the drooping, thick ivy, only once stopping to tell myself the crunch I had felt under my shoe was nothing more than a bunch of discarded popsicle sticks from the '90s. Yeah, that was it. Popsicle sticks . . . somehow shaped and curved like a tiny rat rib cage.

Two garages away from the Crafton garage, I halted and listened to the voices ahead of me coming from the middle of the alley. I heard Pete's voice. He was barking orders at the underlings, then followed the barking with a curt, "Please."

Since Pete was around, I'd go no farther. I strained to listen, leaning against the garage where I had stopped.

A roaring engine was coming up from behind me. I waited for it to get closer before I stuck my head out to look through to the alley. It was a tow truck. It slowed not too far in front of me, and then I heard Pete say, "Yeah, thanks for coming. Three garages down. It's an ice-cream truck. Old. I hope you brought the right equipment to tow it."

So that's what was in the other garage: the vintage ice-cream truck.

The tow truck thundered away for a moment longer, and then a beeping rang through the air. The universal chiming: "I'm backing up. Get out of my way or taste my tires."

Sharp, metallic banging and scraping ensued, indicating that the driver was prepping his vehicle to tow the ice-cream truck.

A meowing sounded at my feet. I looked down to find a frisky, bright orange cat making tentative little forays into my personal space.

"Tssst," I responded with a scowl, willing it away.

Meow, the cat replied cheerfully.

I tried to shoo it away with my leg. But that had the opposite effect. Now it was rubbing against my pant legs, purring.

"Go away," I said in a frustrated whisper.

Me-e-e-ow, it cried.

"Oh, you're going to give me away," I said, scooping up the orange fluffy noise box, turning around, and then giving it a quick boost toward a garage I'd already passed, making sure it landed on the ivy pad.

"Too late for that, Mrs. Barrett."

I spun back around, the tip of one of my shoes catching on an ivy branch and making me falter. Pete leaned forward and caught my elbow before I fell sideways. He let me steady myself, then backed away to perfect a scowl of disappointment at me.

"Really?" I asked. "You heard the cat?"

"What cat? The tow truck driver said he saw someone staring at him through the garages."

Figures, I thought.

"Neighborhood lookey-loos, I don't mind," he said. "Heck, I even expect them, but you . . . well, no, never mind. I guess I should've expected you too." He motioned for me to get out of the ivy maze and out into the open space of the alley.

"Go now," he said.

I wanted to assert my rights, even to state my rights to him in full, legal details. But what was the point? I looked over his shoulder and saw the tow truck pull forward and head to the other end of the alley, carrying an ice-cream truck from bygone days.

"I'll leave," I said. "But I'm going to go over to the school, stand two hundred yards away, and watch you arrest Helen Crafton."

"You need a hobby," he said. He turned his back on me and told everyone to wrap it up in the next twenty minutes, before kids from the elementary school got out.

I looked down at my watch. It was 1:50 p.m.

McMillan. He'd arrive soon. He'd park outside Crafton's house and watch the kids.

I went over that whole craziness again, remembering how before the school bell sounded, Paul directed the fullness of his attention to each child that walked by his car. The persistent staring is what had originally made me fly into a panic, thinking he would grab one of the children. But then, when the children had disappeared, moving themselves along closer to the safety of their parents and homes, Paul's glance fired at the Crafton house.

Could it be that the real reason he came back every day while school was in session was not because he was paying some sort of sadistic homage to the abuser but to *guard* others from becoming the abused? Perhaps his vigilance was because the beast still panted, breathed, and licked its chops behind the closed curtains of the Crafton house. And didn't he know it more than anyone ever should?

If that was the case, I thought he'd want to see the police tote Helen off in handcuffs. I hoped twenty minutes for Pete's team to wrap things up leaned more toward thirty minutes. Considering the way they had been and were handling my daughter's case, it'd be more like sixty minutes before they left.

I got in my car and, as promised, went over to the school. The end-of-the day rush of parents filing in to get their children helped me blend in.

Like clockwork, Paul drove up, kept his car running, stared intently at the school gate, and popped Tic Tacs.

The school bell rang. It could have been scripted: more Tic Tacs, more angst, the children scampered. I looked back at the Crafton house. Pete was standing in the window, holding the drapes open, and then turned his head over his shoulder to say something. Likely, they'd wait for the kids to pass before they dragged a handcuffed old lady to a patrol car.

Good. Paul would be staring at her house by then.

Children, going, going, gone.

Paul's glance whipped to the house—if looks could kill and all that jazz. Pete looked out the window again, and then let the curtain fall back. For Paul, more Tic Tacs. His car started to pull forward. The front door on the Crafton house opened.

Paul stopped.

I got out of my car. I pretended I didn't remember telling Pete that I'd stay back. A female officer led Helen Crafton down the front lawn. Paul's car was motionless in the middle of the street. His door opened. I walked forward.

He went to the edge of the Crafton lawn. I stepped off the curb from the school's sidewalk. Pete yelled something at me.

Pretended, still, that Pete didn't exist.

Helen Crafton's hands, handcuffed in the front, rose. She pointed a spindly, accusing, and altogether demonic finger at Paul.

"You. You stupid little jerk. It was you." Her voice then sank and twisted like a cheap carnival ride. It sounded like a contrived baritone—a perfect opposite to Paul's bat-crazy falsetto. "You're the one who killed Darrel."

TWENTY-NINE

Legion's Call

Paul took the rebuke of that pruned beast, letting it wash over him like acid, or the shadows of a thousand fallen angels calling themselves Legion.

He turned to me, likely hearing my footsteps treading toward him on the street. "What did you do?" he asked me, a hollow hurt echoing within his eyes.

I stopped my advance, remembering how quickly his eyes could flash from despair to destruction. Remembering how he took a baseball bat to my car. "The police know it was her," I said. "She hurt a lot of children in her time. She hurt you and she's going to have to answer for that."

Pete slammed the back door of the patrol car shut, closing the free world off from Helen Crafton. The female officer, accompanied by the type of cop who could moonlight as the quintessential finger breaker for a bookie, drove away with Crafton.

Paul's hands plunged into his pockets, watching the vehicle grow smaller and smaller, eventually turning left.

Pete approached Paul, motioning for me to come closer. I didn't. I had my reasons: the baseball bat, the crazy eyes, et cetera.

"I didn't kill Mr. Crafton," Paul offered to Pete, looking down at his shoes and avoiding Pete's face.

"That's neither here nor there," Pete offered. "I've already talked to you before," he started, "do you remember?"

Paul nodded.

"You didn't want to say anything about Darrel Crafton, but do you want to give a statement on Helen Crafton?"

Paul gave a half shake of his head, but then turned toward his car. "I should move my car," he said. He took two steps to the opened driver's door, but Pete called out to him.

"No, wait." Pete motioned for one of the uniformed officers to come over. "Barcus," Pete said, "move that car out of the street, will you?"

"There you go, Mr. McMillan," Pete said. "Now what do you say? A witness statement is crucial in this type of investigation."

Barcus closed the driver's door and drove the car to the curb, parking it parallel.

"I don't like people touching my stuff," Paul said, pointing to his car.

"I'm sorry," Pete offered. "But will you come down to the station?"

"I hope he didn't move my seat. I have my seat adjusted perfectly," Paul said.

Pete's eyes widened and he shook his head; a brazen move in light of the effort he was making to get Paul's cooperation, but Paul wasn't looking anyway. He had yet to make eye contact with Pete.

Pete walked over to me, pursing his lips and looking like he was considering something bothersome. Probably the very idea of talking to me induced the discomfort. I had that effect on people—more and more these days.

He put his hands on his hips, lifting his jacket up as it flared out over both hands. "As much as it pains me to do so, I think I'm going to put you to some use. I'm hoping to take advantage of your abilities in reading and persuading people to do your bidding. And if you succeed, then I'll let you watch—from afar—my interrogation of Crafton. You'd like that, right?"

I nodded.

"I don't know why you would, but I've stopped trying to make rhyme or reason out of you," he added.

He lowered his hands and then folded his arms across his chest, chuckling twice to himself. "Can I tell you my theory?" he asked.

"I think," he continued, "and you'll have to forgive me in advance for the therapy talk, but perhaps the reason you keep interfering is because you subconsciously need to assist in investigations because it will ultimately make you feel more confident in our ability to find your daughter's killer."

That was a good theory; I'd have to remember it, and save it for later when I had more time to dismiss it properly. For now, all I wanted was to see Pete rake Helen Crafton over the fieriest coals known to man.

"What can I do?" I asked.

"If you can get Mr. McMillan to come down to the station and give a statement, I'll let you watch the Crafton interrogation from a monitor in another room."

"How do you get around the tainting aspect?" I asked.

"You can fill out a 1099-I at the station. Today, you're a consultant. I'll pay you . . ." he uncrossed his arms and pulled out his wallet from a back pocket. He opened it and slipped out the cash. Fanning out a five dollar bill and three singles, he said, "eight dollars."

I reached out to snatch the money, but he pulled it back. "Work first, then the payday."

"I don't really need the eight bucks, you know?"

"Why did you grab for it, then?"

"Simple. You're not the offering type. If you're offering, I'm grabbing," I said.

He folded the bills and tucked them inside his jacket pocket. "Convince McMillan." He turned away and walked to Paul, who still seemed more upset that someone had sat in his car than the fact that his greatest monster was finally being taken away.

"Mr. McMillan, we're heading off now," Pete said. "We'll expect to see you at the station. Why don't you follow Mrs. Barrett over? She's quite versed on how to get there."

I gave Pete a forced smirk.

Staring at Helen's house, Paul said, "Are you arresting me?"

"No," Pete answered.

"Then I don't want to go to your station."

"You should reconsider that," Pete said, waving at me.

Pete and the remainder of his minions left, the school had completely cleared out, and Paul and I stood alone, fifteen or so feet away from one another. He stood against his car, cleaning off the door handle Officer Barcus touched, and I was in the street, standing near the curb.

Silence fell on us. First, it was from the lack of movement on the street, then it became a state of mind—so heavy and so pressing that I imagined it was like those last few seconds when a victim gives up, knowing no one will hear the screams, no one will help, and no one will save them.

I had an inkling Paul knew that silence. Corinne probably had too, although she was likely too young to understand the despaired reality that many times in life hope doesn't come, and little girls do die alone.

Why my mind went there, I didn't know. But the silence was killing me. "Paul," I said.

He didn't look at me. The sound of my voice alerted him though, and he seemed to contemplate skipping out. I had to get his attention before he got in his car and drove away. I had to say something that would draw him into staying, and even draw him into going to the station. But suddenly, it wasn't just because I wanted to see Pete take a crack at Helen Crafton; it was because I somehow felt that Paul was as sick of the silence as I was.

"Do you remember feeling helpless and alone in the quiet around you when you realized no one was going to stop the bad from happening to you?" I asked him.

He turned to stare at the Crafton house. A car drove by—the driver oblivious to us, and we, mainly, to him.

"Like you just had to close your eyes, and let the worst happen because you knew no one would save you?" I said.

"You don't know how it was," he said. "I don't like you," he added. "I wish you never came into my life."

"If I hadn't, then you'd still have to come back every day and guard the children. Isn't that why you come back?"

"You don't know," he repeated.

"You choose to guard them, to protect them, because no one protected you."

He shot me a contemptuous look. "I remember now. You lost your daughter. No one protected her. No one saved her."

"Right," I said with tight, bottled emotion. "But if I had the chance, I'd eradicate the monster rather than protect the potential prey."

Paul focused back on the Crafton house.

"Follow me to the station," I said. "End the silence. Right now, you're the only one to help. You're the only one to end this."

"Tell me about the ice-cream truck, and remember, Mrs. Crafton," Pete started, "if you tell me to go you know where again, you'll get another thirty minutes left in silence. Old age and full bladders aren't compatible."

"Can he do that?" I asked Thatcher as we sat together in a media room, watching Pete's interrogation.

"Oh, now you want to act like a lawyer?" he replied.

Helen Crafton sat silent, tapping her hands every now and then on the tabletop. It seemed an overly casual movement from a geriatric woman charged with several counts of child molestation, but then I realized she wasn't tapping, but rather twitching, just as her head did, thanks to her age.

"Why do you think she hasn't lawyered up?" Thatcher asked me.

"Probably can't afford one," I offered.

"But the public defender—"

I scoffed, interrupting him. "Do you think a woman who's escaped criminal prosecution for almost three decades thinks she has to lower herself to a public defender? No way. She'll defend herself if it comes to it. She thinks too highly of herself. I'm sure of it."

"Are you a practical individual, Mrs. Crafton?" Pete asked. "Because I think you are. Someone who can instantly see the situation in full and make the most rational decision. So, let's get down to brass tacks."

She said nothing. Chomped a little with her gums, but remained silent.

"And if you are that type of shrewd, logical person, then you'll see the inevitable," he said. "And the inevitable for you is a rapidly approaching death. What are you, eighty? Ninety?"

Her hand twitched on the table.

"Most people who clam up in here have a certain investment in keeping quiet. They have a whole, long life in front of them," Pete said. "As much as I like the truth, I can respect *why* they don't give it up. Self-preservation. They want to live out their long lives in the outside world, even if they are scumbags."

Pete took a seat at the end of the table, a mere four inches from her twitching hands. "But what are you trying to preserve by holding out on me? How much life do you think you have left? Six months? A year, max?" Pete cocked his head to look at her empty, yet resolved gaze. "Is it hard to make your meals each day? To do the laundry? To remember to pay the electric bill? I bet it even hurts to pick up the pen and write the check to keep the lights on."

I was slightly rocking back and forth in my hard, metal chair, both excited and anxious.

"You like this, don't you?" Thatcher asked, smiling.

"It almost feels wrong that he's doing it to an old lady, but this is awesome. Look at her," I said. "The hard shell of her misdeeds is about to crack. I can see it. He's turning her into a human, and when she's a human, she's only an—"

"Eighty-year-old woman with poor bladder control and arthritis," Thatcher interrupted.

"Yes," I said. "Because I don't care how good Pete is, he's not good enough to conquer whoever I saw that day on the lawn, calling Paul a stupid little jerk, but this, this is genius."

Pete continued. "Because of your age, you'll be treated with a bit more humanity if we lock you up now. In fact, you might even forget that you're *not* in a state sponsored retirement program. It's definitely more than what you deserve but, of course, you'll get some accommodation if you confess, and because you've been reformed for nearly thirty years. You have been reformed, correct? You haven't been messing with children since your husband, Darrel, died, right?"

Her eyes finally rose, looking at Pete with such a frightening intensity, I thought her tongue would fork and slither out.

"Do you prosecute dead men, detective?" she asked.

"Depends. Why? You going to try to let your husband take the fall again?"

"Depends," she said. "How stupid are you? As stupid as the police back in the eighties?"

She scoffed. "But no, not Darrel. However, if you tell me you'll prosecute and convict Simon Satters, I'll talk."

"Who's Simon Satters?" Pete asked.

"My father. He taught me everything I know. Also, I'd like to use the restroom first."

THIRTY

Old Sins, New Day

Pete went back to asking about the ice-cream truck. Helen had a nice story about it. It started out fuzzy and warm, about a girl who admired her father, and ended with a feeling—for all of us who heard—that we had all just swallowed a handful of maggot-infested food. It'd be a long time before we'd feel up to eating again.

That ice-cream truck was a truck of horrors, dating back to Helen's own destroyed childhood. Helen's father, Simon, was an ice-cream man for most of his adult life, with a penchant for unnatural needs. But for whatever reason, he never touched a stranger's child; he bottled the desire until he got home and found his little Helen, a young girl who only wanted to be read a bedtime story by the man she looked up to.

To add insult to terror, Simon preferred little boys. Thus, on top of being constantly molested by her father in the confines of his ice-cream truck, she was constantly beaten for being the wrong gender.

Helen tried to have a normal life after she ran away at fourteen—shortly after she grew even more of the wrong parts. She moved to California, met Darrel Crafton when she was nineteen years old, married him, and set up house. They tried for children; Darrel more than Helen as Helen believed little children were of the devil, created to lead lives full of misery and shame, while giving out a type of love far beyond their control.

Years passed, and no children came into the Crafton household. Darrel pushed for adoption. A litter of boys, he had said. Little boys were the worst kind of despicable, Helen thought. They created a lust within her father that never seemed to be satiated, especially since she was an unfortunate substitute.

"Then he settled on foster parenting," Helen told Pete. "He said we had to foster at least a young boy, or he'd leave. Where was I to go if that happened? You tell me. That's when we got Joe. That wasn't his real name. I couldn't stand his real name. Some ugly name I can't even remember. We called him Joe."

"What did you do to him?" Pete asked.

She folded her hands in her lap and pursed her lips, her jaw still moving, chomping those accursed gums of hers. "On second thought," she said, "I don't want to talk about it."

"You better talk about it," Pete said. "Either we put you in general population where they'll see you as grandma jerky, or we put you in a retirement home with bars and guards. You decide."

Right after Joe's ninth birthday, Simon, the original beast and Helen's father, died. And wasn't he a peach for leaving her his original ice-cream truck in his will? Between the demons that came with the truck and Joe having the right material if her father was still alive, it was a pit of hell ready to bubble over. And it did.

"I saw Joe in that truck one day and I don't know . . . something happened. Something seemed to click for me. It was as if my destiny knew I couldn't have a future until I finished my father's past. He never got his boys until he got them through me," she stressed with familial pride.

My hand went to my mouth. I was trying to stifle vomit. Pete looked at the camera. I thought he was considering turning it off. He mouthed Thatcher's name and the word "monitor," still looking at the camera, and then gave the cut symbol—a quick swipe of his hand near his neck. Thatcher immediately popped out of his seat and turned off the set. I could still hear, but just as Thatcher scurried to transfer the open sound to a pair of headphones he had put on his head, I heard Pete say, "Details, please."

Then silence. Thatcher had his elbows propped on the soundboard, putting his hands over the headphone speakers to cover any escape attempt of what only he could hear in the media room. He shook his head once, and snorted in disgust twice. After a few minutes, Thatcher pulled the headphones off, set them down, and unplugged them. Sound echoed back in our room.

"Do you want the monitor on too?" he asked.

I didn't. Why would I want to look at her face? But there was something necessary in beholding the ordinariness of the package that had begot such an unmerciful hatred and unholy hunger. I almost believed that if I stared at her long enough, I'd see the protruding horns. That's probably how the devil works too. He was surely a pretty little thing who wouldn't strike anyone as being someone who could hurt a fly. But by the time you realized that bad boy had fangs, it was too late; they were already sunk into your flesh.

I answered Thatcher's question: "Yes, turn the monitor on."

Helen continued by saying Joe had left the Crafton house when he was sixteen. There were a number of years, and children, between Joe and the first child who reported the abuse back in 1982. Then Paul McMillan. She spewed forth his name as if *it* and not her demonic behavior was the source of her filthiness.

"Paul was the great toy," she said, again with pride. "Had absolutely no self-esteem. I could basically tell him he owed me, and he'd give in. I caught him the same way I caught the others. I'd give away ice cream two blocks from the school. When I found the right type of boy, of course, they had to look like Joe—did I mention Joe looked like my father? Well, he did." She took her middle finger and wiped at the corners of her mouth. "When I found a good-looking boy, I'd ask him if he wanted to ride with me in the truck. If he got in, I drove him to the garage. I'd say, 'eat as much as you want as long as you can pay for it.' Only the clever ones asked the price. The dumb ones only wanted the ice cream. That Paul kid was a dumb one. He ate far too much. And I told him he had to come back every day to pay, and he did."

"And what was the price?" Pete asked.

"My love, of course," she answered.

Pete looked back at the camera, to us. "What does your love consist of?"

"Well, first I'd get a—"

Thatcher jumped up and turned the monitor off again. "We're going to skip this part too."

I said nothing. I was far too dumbstruck. Was this real? Were there really people out there like this, living amongst us? Yes, yes there were.

My throat tightened because I felt as if I was losing a little bit of myself. That's all I seemed to do these days: lose a little bit of myself here, there, everywhere. It was stolen, really. Taken.

Thatcher had his back to me, hovering again over the soundboard, this time trying to keep his shock to himself. I used the moment to consider how Helen could perpetuate her father's sin. Why would she? And, why couldn't I shake the sense that something else was at play here? Something deeper and darker, like a knife-wielding shadow sneaking up an alley at a quarter past twelve.

I had thought a lot about evil in the last several months. How could I not? It had taken my daughter.

Of course, I was aware that for most people the world still spun, people still fell in love, married, had children, got their promotions, and otherwise felt a certain comfort in the status quo. In this regard, it was easier to believe that evil and sin were catchy words that a pastor threw around to raise money for a new church building, or to scare teenagers from fogging up car windows.

But if the status quo spent a Monday morning with a four-year-old who had asked, "Is it true it only rains when God is crying?" and then found themselves on the next day, a Tuesday, learning that a man had used her small body for pleasure, they'd put their as-the-world-turns lives on hold. Maybe then they'd listen to the pastor, or even to me: there's no middle, only sides. There's the bad and the good; there's God, and there's Satan, and only one of them wants to grind you down to a fine powder. No one could walk in my shoes—NO ONE—and not be aware that evil is a hungry, fastidious enemy.

I remembered that in my old, comfy existence it was hard to see that the devil had my number. Until his fist came at me. And when Corinne died, that's when it started to become apparent that he had not only my number but also my name etched on his knuckles—just seconds before his hand smashed through my teeth.

Was Helen Crafton, and her father before her, evil? Was the man who killed Corinne evil? Yes.

I know we all come into this world, born and bred to be liars, cheats, and selfish little pills, but what about that extra step, the voluntary descent into darkness? That additional depravity that escalates from a little rubbernecking on a school test to jamming a knife in someone's gut. Is evil *born* that way? No. Then what had happened?

Empty vessels never stay empty.

My God, my God . . . was it true? Is all that's needed a vacancy sign in the soul?

If so, then when Helen Crafton's father died, only the vessel perished, and a new one was acquired. Helen Crafton did to young boys what her father did to her, in the same ice-cream truck, in almost the same way.

"Here," Thatcher said, taking his headphones off and turning the monitor back on. "She's talking about Paul again."

"Paul was my last. He killed my husband."

"Still not the case," Pete corrected.

"Darrel came home early one day, about an hour after school got out and I was with Paul. He had been having chest pains at work. He also said his left arm hurt. He came looking for me so I could take him to the hospital. He found Paul and me in the second garage. I was surprised he didn't drop dead right there. He'd already been put through the ringer by the police. You were just a teenage zit back then, I'm sure," she said, motioning to Pete. "I still can't believe it didn't occur to you dum-dums back then that a women could be responsible."

I shook my head, tiny remnants of my blasé conscience—what was left of it—fell from me.

"There was a time there that Darrel thought he'd have to go to jail for crimes he didn't commit," Helen said. "And then he finds me, his wife, was the one behind it."

"What happened after he found Paul?" Pete asked, steering the conversation.

"He slapped me, the jerk. Then he helped the boy get himself back together. We yelled for a bit. The more we yelled, the more nervous the boy got and Darrel knew it. He took him out by the side door—the little wimp was in tears, from the fighting mind you, not the other stuff—and Darrel told him to go straight home and tell his mommy. The little boy shook his head, saying he couldn't tell. And Darrel fished down in his pocket and pulled out a box of orange Tic Tacs—Darrel always had a box in his pockets—and gave it to the boy. He said, 'You can have the box if you promise me you'll tell your mommy.' Still the boy shook his head. That's when Darrel grabbed at his own left arm, then his chest. A second later, he was dead. He fell on top of the boy. I hoped he'd crush him, but that was wishful thinking. I left the two of them out there for thirty minutes. When I came back, I found the boy whimpering like a baby, still under my dead husband. I told the boy to leave because the police were coming to take my husband away and bury him. He finally got up and left. He started coming back to sit in front of the house, oh, I don't know, maybe he was sixteen. Been doing it ever since."

"You left your dead husband in the alley for thirty minutes?" Pete asked.

"Yes. What did you want me to do with him? He was dead."

"I hate that woman," I said to Thatcher, wringing a persistent feeling of filth from my hands. My game plan for that evening was to scour with rock salt and a Brillo pad. "I guess it explains Paul's obsession with orange Tic Tacs," I added. "Sounds like the man who saved him likely gave him his first box."

Thatcher nodded.

Pete asked a final question: "If you want us to prosecute your dead father, why did you follow in his criminal behavior?"

She looked at him as if he were a simpleton—a child wondering why the sky is blue. "Because they told me to," she answered.

There it was. *They.* Legion.

"Hey," I said to Thatcher. "What happened to the foster boy? Do you guys know?"

"Not yet, why?"

"Helen perpetuated what her father did to her, and if Helen molested that foster child, then maybe he's out there doing it to others."

"It doesn't always work that way," he replied.

Still, I saw a vacancy sign swinging and flashing before my mind. What if . . . what if . . . what if . . . ?

Helen stopped molesting children years ago. Could *they* have moved on and found a vacancy in the foster son, supplying the notion of old sins on a new day?

"That would make the foster son, what . . . sixty?" I asked.

"I guess," he replied.

"Will you let me know if you track him down?"

Thatcher gave me a puzzled look.

"Sorry," I said, "but I can't shake this feeling about the foster kid. It's too weird to explain."

"More weird than smelling pedophiles?"

It was, strangely enough. It was more acceptable to me to tell Thatcher about the smell than about the belief that a host of demons moved from father to daughter to foster son, Joe.

"Will you tell me?" I asked.

A few weeks later, the news tried to tell me that the economy was sad. And it was. Sadder still, however, was when Thatcher called me and said

Paul McMillan drove his car into a telephone pole, killing himself. It had only been two weeks since Helen Crafton's arrest. Paul left no note and no explanation. It was telling—at least for me—that the pole he chose to plummet into was a few blocks from the Crafton house, and the incident occurred within twenty minutes of the nearby elementary school ending for the day.

I wondered, then, whether the entirety of Paul's existence revolved around the meaning he found in protecting others. It was the one saving grace that prevented him from being swallowed by the horror of a life thrown to abuse—the steel grate protecting curious little fingers from touching the blue bug zapper.

Even if I thought I had done something virtuous, I had removed the grate; Paul's final breath was drawn to that telephone pole as surely as a mosquito sizzled on a back porch.

Unemployment gave me the disadvantage of thinking too much. Naturally, I spent voluminous amounts of time pondering how my actions led to Paul's death. I *had* meddled, even after a few people, Paul included, told me not to. But I pushed and I pushed and I pushed. Just like I *had* to go back to work after Corinne was born so I could be the richest lawyer in town; like I *had* to poke the sleeping bear of Robert Bailey; like I *had* to leave Eddie so I could escape accountability.

And for what?

Hadn't I embarked on this vindictive—and often nutty—journey to find my daughter's killer? Yet her name was still on a number of to-do lists.

More weeks passed and my anger stilled. Truth be told, I was scared of myself, and fear has a way of mitigating anger. Or, so I'd heard, before life forced me to test-drive the theory.

I was afraid to go back into the world and resume a normal life because I figured it'd be easier to convince myself that I wasn't a pariah if my mind didn't tally a body count when someone asked, "What have *you* been up to recently?"

Would it really matter if I disappeared? What if I pulled a Paul? I don't think I'd be as dramatic as ramming a telephone pole. I'd be concerned about the overeffectiveness of my airbag. At the end of the day, I'd have powder on my face, a cut here and there, a bruise across my torso from the belt, and higher insurance rates.

If I went down that route, I'd use something more subtle. Oh, but who was I kidding? I didn't want to end my life. There was so much more pain and misery to be explored in my current state of mind; more guilt and foreboding to satiate my need to punish myself.

Plus, there were always those divorce papers from Eddie to receive. Any day now.

THIRTY-ONE

Angels Singing

Days turned into weeks and the next thing I knew, it was nearing the end of December. I found my sister, Maddie, banging on the front door early one morning.

I looked through the peephole at her. She looked happy, and it rubbed me the wrong way. It was as if she were rubbing it in my face or sticking her pink, pointed tongue out at me. The joy she bore made it obvious to me that the best days of my life were far behind me: like mementos stashed, buried, and forgotten in a little tin time capsule. But I knew she didn't come in malice. She was Maddie, for crying out loud. My Maddie.

She frowned a bit when I opened the door. A concession toward my mood? No. She was frowning at my pajama bottoms. I was holding them up at my side, preventing them from falling down, because the elastic waistband was shot. A rubber band cinching the excess material usually did the trick, but I had busted the last one in the house last night when I thrashed around with the same old, same old nightmares.

She quickly replaced the disapproving look with another big smile. Then she threw her arms around me. She smelled of cranberries and cinnamon, and to me, that made me painfully aware—especially at this time of year—that she smelled of motherhood, and of baking goodies for children still alive, still needing to be tucked in at night, and still eager to help with Christmas preparations.

"Oh, it's so good to see you," she said, releasing me from her grasp. She looked at me again from head to foot. "I *really* want to make a comment about those pajama pants, but I won't."

"Good," I replied. "I won't make a comment about your bonnet."

"It's not a bonnet," she defended. She marched past me to the farthest living room wall where a picture hung—one that came with the place, and one that had been inappropriately glued to the wall to prevent theft. Although theft wasn't what that print should fear but rather the trash bin. It was a disastrously ugly thing—and far too chipper for my tastes—of a cat family, painted with a style I can only describe as regurgitated Skittles.

But Maddie didn't care about the print. She was checking her faint reflection in the picture's glass frame. She straightened her bonnet, or whatever she wanted to call it, and then smoothed her hair as it cascaded over her shoulders. "It's a cashmere beret, Evy, not a bonnet. Please. This isn't *Little House on the Prairie*. Oh, and get this: the tag called the color Plum Kisses. Isn't that cute?"

I went to the far corner of the couch and sat down, knowing she'd eventually join me. "Beret, bonnet, who cares? It's all meaningless chatter with a darling color name like that," I teased.

She spun around to me and balled her small fists. "Ooooh, I've missed you." She walked halfway across the room and then stopped. "If I try to give you another hug, will you push me away?" she asked.

I wanted to say yes because it was my first inclination, but I hadn't seen her in a while. She was good at giving me my space. Sometimes too good, but I'd never tell *her* that.

"Never mind," she said, not wanting to wait for my answer.

She started talking to herself aloud, circling the room, and observing the lack of human touches in my living space. It was a semimanipulative thing she did—pretending not to talk to you but making sure you heard. "Okay, Madeline, you can't tell your sister that she needs to stop wearing out her frumpy clothes, and definitely don't tell her that you've seen caves decorated better. Remember, if you tell your sister she's looking and living like a furry-toothed hermit, she'd probably take it as a compliment."

I licked the front of my teeth. Nope, no teeth fur yet.

She moved into the kitchen, opening drawers and cabinets looking for something until she shouted back at me, "I give up. Where do you keep your coffee?"

"Are you talking to me or yourself?" I asked.

"You. Where's the coffee?"

"I don't want coffee," I said.

Her head darted to the open space in the kitchen-living room wall with her hands planted on top of the serving counter. "Who says it's for you?" she asked. "I'm trying to get a cup for myself. This cold weather is great.

Makes me want to bundle up, grab a hot cup of coffee, and cuddle up on the couch with my sister."

"Um . . . ," I said.

"Oh, relax, Evy," she said, smiling at me. "But seriously, where's the coffee?"

"The freezer," I answered.

"The freezer? Why the freezer?"

"E-d-d-i-e," I said.

"Eddie put coffee in your freezer? Are you guys talking to each other now?" Her eyes moved to the left, trying to recollect something. "Wait, no. You can't be. He would have told me."

"He would have told you?" I asked, standing up and moving toward her in anticipation of the answer. For a moment, I had forgotten about my waistband-challenged pajamas, but managed to catch them before Maddie saw my underwear. It wouldn't have been the end of the world if she had, but she still didn't need to. I stood on the opposite side of the serving counter and asked, "Why would he have told you if we're talking to one another?"

"Because we're buddies again," she said, winking at me. "Ever since Thanksgiving . . . wait no . . . even before that. About a week before Thanksgiving. Remember? I called you and told you he was asking for the address to this place because you weren't returning any of his calls. He wanted everyone to come together again for Thanksgiving."

I remembered the incessant phone calls. I also remembered not bothering to see who was doing the calling. I remembered Thanksgiving Day, and remembered that the only reason I knew it was Thanksgiving was because the Internet wished me a Happy Thanksgiving on my homepage. It's nice to have inanimate friends.

Finally, I remembered that sometime around noon, someone had come knocking on my front door while I hid in the bathroom. I had assumed it was Ben, Maddie's husband, because whoever it was had been brazen enough to come around the back of the house and knock on the back door too. I'd even heard the person creep around the bedroom window. I never budged. It was the first real holiday without Corinne. I wasn't going anywhere.

But again, I had assumed it was Ben. Hadn't even thought it might have been Eddie.

"Did Eddie come over here to get me on Thanksgiving?" I asked.

She pulled the bag of coffee out of the freezer. It was the only thing in there.

"Yes." She looked at me, filled with disappointment. "I knew it. I knew you were home. Why do you do that? We even had Mom over and she was being so good, so nurturing. In fact, she had fallback reservations at Bonner's for the two of you."

"Which two?"

"You and Mom. She was worried because I had invited Eddie to Thanksgiving, and figured that if you came, it might be too much for you. In that event, she'd steal you away for some prime rib at Bonner's."

I hadn't been to Bonner's with my mother since I told her I was pregnant with Corinne. She loved that place, more than I ever could, but that's what made it such a treat to go with her. She seemed like a lighter, contented individual when she was there; as if nothing else mattered in the world as long as she was sitting in a high-backed, half-circled burgundy booth in a dimly lit lounge with other lonely people trying to find a dark watering hole to disappear in.

"I could've done that," I said. "Bonner's would have been nice with Mom."

"Yeah, well, you'd have to return a phone call every now and then if you want prime rib."

I backed away from the kitchen and sat down on the coffee table. I had suddenly become tired and uninterested in Maddie's bait and switch: she starts with coffee or Thanksgiving and ends with bad, Evy, bad, you need to make more effort. It would only be a matter of moments before she threw Eddie or some other family member in my face again. She got that from Mom, the move where she plays the guilt card like a high roller throwing down that ace, about to bust the house.

"So how is Eddie responsible for freezer-burned coffee?" she asked.

I sighed. I figured if I participated, then this would go along faster. "Eddie said that the coffee stays freshest if you keep it in the freezer," I said. "I tried my might to convince him that since I consumed it so quickly, it wasn't necessary to preserve it, while sacrificing some of the flavor. But he wouldn't have any of it. So in the freezer it goes."

She was silent for a moment. Too silent. I had been looking up at the ceiling when I had spoken, but my curiosity piqued and I looked at her. She was smiling at me. A painfully knowing and mischievous smile.

"What?" I demanded.

"You don't have to follow Eddie's preferences anymore, do you? Yet you do. Why do you think that is?"

I looked away again, just as she tossed the coffee bag back into the freezer without having made any coffee.

"I know why you do it," she added, singsongy. "Cuz you still loooove him. You still waaaant him. You want to touuuuch him."

I jumped up and rocked to the balls of my feet. She ushered fighting words. In a catchy melody no less. I was about to let her have it, but she burst into laughter.

I followed her eyes. My pajama pants were at my ankles.

The original notion that it wouldn't be a big deal if my sister saw my underwear was void. That rationale would have panned out if I were wearing *my* underwear; but since I was sporting an old, confiscated pair of Eddie's that morning, it was a different story.

"Oh, oh, oh," she bellowed. "There's no un-throwing *that* rock through the window." She came over to me quickly, pulled up my pants, and tucked them into the top of Eddie's boxers, giggling the whole time.

"Sweetie, sweetie, sweetie," she said. "There are no other words for me to say than give it up or give it over. Whichever is easier for you."

She patted me on the cheek and I recoiled, taking a seat back down on the coffee table. "What are you talking about?" I demanded.

"You know," she said, chastisement in her voice. "Give up the charade that you're your own little island, or give whatever is blocking your path over to someone who can handle it."

"Like who?"

"How about God?"

"Why did you really come over here, Maddie?" I asked.

"Um, because I love you. Does that not come across from the twenty or so unreturned calls I placed this week alone?"

"I'm not ready." It was the only thing I could offer.

She huffed, balling her fists again, but this time it wasn't for fun. "I don't need you to be ready. No one needs you to be ready. We just want you to be . . . willing."

I turned away from her.

Minutes passed in silence. She stared at me and I stared at the floor.

"Fine," she said, defeated.

I looked up to see her grabbing her purse from the counter and walking to the door. Her beret was truly ridiculous. It had a point at the top. It was a purple frosted cashmere cupcake. The more I could focus on that thing, the less I had to let her words seep in to where she could only hope they would.

"One more thing," she added, opening the front door and letting gusts of cold air into the house. "I also came over today to remind you that it's Christmas Eve."

What? How had I missed that? Oh yeah, I hadn't been on the Internet in a few days.

"I know it's a naughty thing to do, but I'm going to hit you below the belt, because it's Christmas and you blew us all off on Thanksgiving," she said.

I had my back to her.

"My children rightfully assume that you're still loaded with cash. Every Christmas you get them something obnoxiously expensive that Ben and I can never afford. They have naturally come to expect these lavish gifts from Auntie Evy."

I turned around to face her. Was she serious? She was speaking my language, at least the language of the old Evelyn Barrett, but this was fundamentally beneath her.

"We don't mind that you spoil them because it takes the pressure off us . . . of sorts," she said. "I mean, for crying out loud, their letters to Santa this year only asked for small, piddly stuff, because each letter had a footnote that read, 'We're trying not to break you, Santa, because we know Auntie Evy will buy the cool stuff.'"

I tried to suppress a smile. It was difficult. I had forgotten how much I adored those incredibly smart and materialistic nephews of mine. A footnote in a letter to Santa . . . surely, my DNA had made its way into them somehow.

"But who can blame them?" Maddie added. "Their aunt has been spoiling them rotten for years. Two little boys' Christmas will be ruined if they don't get ridiculously expensive toys they don't need all because their aunt forgot what day it was."

"Sounds like a real downer for those little fellas," I said.

"Evy!"

I stood up—holding my pants this time—walked over to Maddie and said, "Fine, I'll pull myself together and blow a wad on some electronics today."

"That's the Christmas spirit," she teased. "Dinner at my house tomorrow."

I shook my head slowly. Presents were one thing, but if the intent was to lure me to dinner—especially if Eddie would be there—I was less apt to comply.

"I don't know, Maddie. I just . . ."

"Just what, Evy? You don't want to be with your family on Christmas? You don't want to remember what it's like to have fun and to smile?"

No matter how hard I tried to be logical about it, no matter how much Maddie or the rest of them pushed me, at the end of it I just couldn't see how fun and a dead child coexisted. I was certain it was either one or the other.

"I'm going to do some Christmas shopping today. We'll play the rest by ear."

"Suit yourself, but you should know I'll have a present for you," she said, winking at me. "And I'll give you a hint." She pointed dramatically at her bonnet, or beret, or whatever it was. "Maaatching!" she belted out with a tenor voice she pulled from deep within her throat.

I shook my head. Yeah, that wasn't going to happen.

Christmas Eve at the mall was super-duper fun. How could it not be? The joy started when I tried to find a parking spot, and then culminated when a jelly-bellied store Santa fought me for the last copy of a popular video game. He won, and I was still seething over it hours later, even after I arrived back at my house after nightfall. If Santa hadn't had that costume on . . . if there weren't children around . . . if one of those children wasn't a curly-haired blonde beauty . . . I might've come home with something for my nephews other than cash stacked on gift cards.

It was so cold earlier in the morning, especially after Maddie had left, that I had cranked my thermostat up. Now, standing in my dark living room after having just reentered the house from outside, it was far too hot. Before turning on any of the lights, I shed my sweater, tossing it in the vicinity of the couch. Left wearing only a pair of faded jeans and a black camisole, I made my way to a light switch in the corner.

After I flipped the switch, I gasped in horror. Instead of the corner lamp turning on, I had illuminated a Christmas tree. It had white twinkle lights, bells, balls, ribbons, and a note pinned smack in the middle of all the accoutrements.

Couldn't help myself. ☺ I'm putting my money on the fact you'll ditch us tomorrow. And if you do, at least you'll have a tree to keep you company. Merry Christmas, big sister. We all love you, Madeline

I could smell the pine now; it was pure and inviting. I was surprised I hadn't smelled it when I first walked into the house. Still, I wanted it all gone: the tree, the smell, and those mercilessly twinkling lights.

Looking away from Maddie's note and steering my gaze to the bottom of the tree, my eyes locked on what she had used for a tree skirt. I couldn't tell exactly what it was other than something dingy and old, so I went down to my knees and pulled it out.

Small, empty thuds echoed where my heart used to be as I realized what was now in my hands. I was holding Corinne's purple blanket—the one she had slept with each night. I was so tired of breaking. It was too hard to find and hold the abundance of pieces my heart was dropping everywhere I went, with everything that reminded me of her. There comes a point where you just can't glue it all back together anymore. Or, won't . . . can't. I'm not sure I would have been able to recognize the difference.

Maddie had been bold breaking into my house and setting up a Christmas tree while I was away on an errand *she* encouraged me to do, but she had gone too far by wrapping the bottom of that stupid little tree with Corinne's blanket.

How had Maddie even gotten the blanket? I was certain Eddie had been involved in this, but I no longer cared. I was getting angrier and angrier. First Maddie's visit this morning, then the sparring Santa, and now this. Something was mounting within me, seeking a path to get out. More anger? No, that was already bubbling visibly on the surface. It was something else. Something I needed to shove back down before it bested me.

I hadn't noticed it at first, but there was a small present tucked in the folds of the blanket. It was a CD case with another note tucked inside. This one said:

I wasn't going to give you this blanket until you were feeling better. But I changed my mind because I think you really need to know right now that they can't take everything away, Evy. Some things remain. It's a promise. Some things always remain.

And the CD is all of your favorite Christmas songs. Twelve

different renditions of "O Holy Night" because I know how you get your mind set on one thing at a time. ☺

Come by tomorrow, if you can. I love you. Madeline

I wrapped the blanket tightly around my right hand, almost as if it were the tape wrap before the boxing glove went on. If I could live out the frustration pulsing through my veins at that moment, a boxing glove was surely needed.

Did I have a child to share Christmas with? No. So why celebrate?

I huffed and hawed for a moment, sitting back on my legs by the base of the tree. Then, mainly to see whether she had actually burned the same song twelve times, I got up and put the CD into the player. I sat on the arm of the couch and glared at the tree. When the third "O Holy Night" rang out, I collapsed down on the couch, unsure why I was letting the CD continue to play.

What a cruel, cruel Christmas. No Corinne, no Eddie, no justice. All I had was an intense emptiness, a pudgy, unwanted tree, and the angels singing, "O Holy Night."

The fifth rendition of the song played. This one was a rock version. The steady rhythm and pulsing beat made it more potent, more powerful; I felt myself getting lost in it. Correction, I felt myself starting to lose it.

The singer belted out, "Faaaaaaaaaaaaaallllllll on your kneeeeeeeeeeees, O hear the angel voices!"

The voice seemed to warp and twist, coming back to me with an unwelcome, but much needed, force. That's when I knew this was no longer about a song. That's when the lyrics came back to me with heaven-centered commentary.

This is submission. This is accepting what you cannot control.

"No!" I shouted back, covering my ears. My emotions reeled with poisonous defiance. "Lacking control is how I lost her. I won't do it."

The song continued, "O night divine, O night when Christ was born."

The music rose with joy, a foreign and distant joy I didn't want to be a part of—the drums, the guitar, the lead singer wailing in triumph.

"O night divine, O night, O night divine!"

There's a reason you like this song as much as you do. You know Me. You know who I am.

I jumped to my feet, pacing. The guitar slowed, even the rocker's tempo slowed to a soft croon.

"Truly He taught us to love one another; His law is love and His gospel is peace."

I wanted something to throw. I looked around but found nothing big enough to calm the snarling beast writhing within me. So my anger started with little things like the blanket wrapped around my hand.

"Chains shall He break for the slave is our brother and in His name all oppression shall cease."

Books flew across the room. I was part fright, part adrenaline, and part cleansing.

"Sweet hymns of joy in grateful chorus raise we, let all within us praise His holy name."

I moved to breakables, but even they couldn't drown out that punk-rocking vocalist.

"Christ is the Lord, oh praise His name forever, His power and glory . . ."

I laid eyes on the tree. It was big enough. And even if Maddie had gussied it all up with lights and trim, it was dead, it was dead, it was DEAD!

". . . ever more proclaim, His power and glory ever more proclaim."

I grabbed the tree. I heard the snap of the light cord as it ripped from the outlet; I heard it even as the music continued to pound itself out. I didn't stop to think whether I had the strength to do it, I just did it. I hoisted it over my head, aimed the base at the living room window, and tossed it. The violent shatter of glass sounded like a harmonious accompaniment to that song . . . that very song that seemed purposed in crumbling every ounce of bitterness I'd been storing for months. It was as if those angelic voices were singing not only about that starry night long ago but also about Evelyn Barrett sweetly breaking tonight, on *this* night.

The tree landed on the ground with a choreographed thud, and I heard a hundred cheap and fragile ornaments explode in the silent night outside. I felt the first cold stings of the winter air seeping through the broken window as I watched the tree bounce quickly up one time, and then back down for its final, smaller crash. Burst, crack, split—more goodies for the trash heap.

The music played on, the singer going back to that sweetly famous line, proclaiming the ending . . . proclaiming the point.

"Faaaaaaaaaaaaaaalllllllll on your kneeeeeeeeeeeeeees, O hear the angel voices!"

My mind went the way of the ornaments. Burst, crack, split. I was broken, I was busted, and I was finished.

But no trash heap for me. That would be too easy.

I had played a whore to both my anger and my misconceived sense of justice. I was so willing, so vacant, that I pushed my husband away and confronted a man with a gun. I was oblivious to consequences. As long as I got paid when it was over, I was willing and vacant. I lusted for that final payment—that self-perceived right that I was entitled to correct the wrong of Corinne's killer. So much so that I exalted it high above everything I used to know that was good and true.

Worst yet, oh my dear God, worst yet, I had let my anger, pride, and vengeance defile the person my baby used to call Mommy.

This is where you yield, I heard in the subtlety of my crashing world.

It was the final stretches of the song, a reiteration of the beginning, of the only thing important. "Faaaaaaaaaaaaaaaallllllll on your kneeeeeeeeeeeeees, O hear the angel voices!"

And I did. And I wept. And then I went from my knees down to my face and wept some more. Then it was finished. The song, that is.

I was sweating by now and it wasn't because I still had the heat cranked up to boil. I did an army crawl over to the tiled hearth of the fireplace, knowing the ceramic would be cooler than the brown, ugly carpet I'd been treading upon like a ghost over the last several months. I choked back on my throbbing sorrow, lying facedown on top of the cool hearth. I wanted my body, my whole existence, to flatten out, to cease. I wanted not to *be* any longer.

But I didn't get the last word on the subject.

Love is still alive. You are still alive. You are loved.

Round six of "O Holy Night" began. It was an instrumental. My eyes swelled shut from both fatigue and my tear-induced fit. Round seven. I was fading. I wanted to sleep. Round eight. It was more than fatigue. Round nine. I passed out.

THIRTY-TWO

Pavlov's Response

I don't know how long I had been out, but I woke to an unmistakable wheeling and ripping sound. It was the sound of tape, packing tape, and someone was in my house using it.

The window. Someone had come in through the broken front window.

I clenched in terror but instantly regretted moving even a muscle. I kept my eyes shut because I could still hear the sound of the tape, stretching from its roll. Whoever had woken me was still working on something, and didn't yet know I was awake. It was best to keep it that way as long as possible.

The thought occurred to me that perhaps the intruder was using the packing tape to bind my extremities. I concentrated upon every inch of my exposed skin, feeling if anything was restricting me, but no part of my body had been bound. I was lying exactly where I had passed out, on the cool tile hearth of my fireplace, not far from the broken window. But now I was feeling a sting of cold from something other than the broken window. Fear had sunk its teeth in.

Reeeeeeeeeeeeeep. The tape squealed.

I then heard a crackling of some sort of plastic material. Oh, please no. Was that going to be my body bag?

Another physiology check: I didn't feel drugged; I didn't even feel hurt. Still tired, yes, but otherwise fine. Whoever was messing with the tape and plastic hadn't hurt me . . . yet. But what if he was preparing something for when I woke up? And he'd eventually figure out I was awake. I knew I had a fight in front of me. The intruder already had the advantage by isolating me in my own home. Now was the time to find a weapon. That was *my* advantage on him.

I knew where I could find a weapon. I moved my hands slowly, positioning myself for a quick dash to the kitchen. Then he grunted.

Just under his breath, he muttered, "Ah, man."

I heard the crunching of broken glass. "This stuff is everywhere," he muttered again.

I knew the muted voice. I'd know it anywhere.

But just to make sure, I lifted my head slowly and turned it to my right. I saw a figure standing on top of the couch, in front of the window I had recently broken. From where I was on the floor, I had a straight shot of his back end. It was dark inside, but the light from the street lamps poured in just enough to silhouette the figure.

Oh yeah, that rear used to be in the possession of Evelyn Barrett via that catchy little vow, "Till death do us part."

Eddie was in my house, trying to put a large piece of plastic over the gaping hole of where a window used to be, trying to secure it against the wall with packing tape.

I pushed myself into a sitting position and cleared my throat.

"Oh, hey, Evy." He jumped down from the couch. I couldn't make out his face but his voice sounded unsure and embarrassed. He walked near me and I balled up, thinking he was coming at me. Instead, he went to the nearest light switch, but then stopped. Before he turned it on, he asked, "Do you mind if I turn on a light? I can finish faster if I can see what I'm doing."

"And what *are* you doing?" I asked.

He turned on the light.

"Well, I'm trying to temporarily patch up this window."

"Yes, I can see that, but why are you doing it?"

"Because from the looks of it"—he pointed to the hole and out toward the front lawn—"you've tossed a Christmas tree through the window."

I huffed, then stood up and folded my arms across my chest. "You know what I'm asking you. Why are *you* here?"

My stare was unrelenting. He turned his back on me, and climbed back on the couch to finish up on the window.

He started with the tape again. "I don't want to fight, Evy. I just want to fix the window, and then I'll leave you alone. It's not safe having it broken like this. It's not even safe with the plastic, but that'll have to wait until after Christmas. I'm going to get the plastic finished, then I'll find a piece of wood. I think I have one big enough back at the house. That's going to go on the outside so no one comes in."

"I don't want you here *now*, let alone coming back later with some wood."

He closed his eyes and tightened his jaw. "Tough. I'm not leaving you with the window like this."

"How did you even happen to be driving by to see it, Eddie?" I asked. I moved my hands to cover what they could of my arms, trying to warm them. I looked across the room at my sweater lying crumpled on the floor. To get it, I'd have to walk past Eddie. I opted for being cold.

He finished the last corner of plastic, double taping it to the wall. He jumped down from the couch and set the tape roll on the coffee table.

"Huh, Eddie? How were you in the neighborhood?"

He unzipped his jacket, slid it off, and held it out to me. "Here. Put this on. You must be cold," he said, pointing to my camisole top.

"No, thank you," I said. The sweater it would have to be. I was only getting colder. I walked past Eddie and just as I crossed him, I felt his touch on my lower arm. I shied back, pulling my arm across my chest.

"Don't," I whispered.

He sighed and sat down on the couch, rubbing his eyes.

"So, you don't want me to come back with the wood?"

"No. I don't," I said.

"Fine, I'll just stay here on the couch then."

"What?" I shrieked, the sweater in my hand. Now pumped with adrenaline, I had no need to put it on. "You can't stay here."

"Why not?" he asked. "Is Cole going to come down from his loft and protect you?"

I chucked the sweater at his face. He scoffed at my less than Herculean effort.

"There is no Cole, you fool. There never was."

"Got any eggnog in this joint?" he asked a moment later.

"Are we switching subjects?" I asked.

He shrugged. "I guess. I just have a hankering for some eggnog, that's all. Besides, the less we talk about a subject you have no control of, the better it is for me. I'm not leaving you here with this window like this. I won't. End of story."

"Get out. There's my control. This is my house and I don't want you here."

He let his head fall back on the top of the couch, looking from below at his window-covering job. He didn't bother to answer me.

"I said *leave*."

His head popped up and he stood, grabbing my discarded sweater.

Before I knew it, Eddie was standing in front of me, reaching out for my right camisole strap. It had slid off my shoulder, probably from when I had thrown my sweater, and hung limp against my arm. He raised the strap back to where it belonged, his eyes soaking in the contours of my chest. After he put the strap high on my shoulder, he didn't let go of it. His eyes came to mine, only briefly to assess my level of comfort, and then looked like he had second-guessed the act of seeking my permission. His gaze lowered again. His hand went with it as the backs of his fingers slid down my bare skin. I raised my hand to shoo him away but he saw it coming and stepped back.

"Put the sweater on, Evy," he said, gently pushing my sweater into my abdomen. "For both of us."

I took the sweater and dropped it on the ground as he walked past me to enter the kitchen.

He chuckled once. "That bad behavior is what made it so hard for me to keep my hands off you while we were dating."

"Get off the road to memory lane, Eddie," I said, a harsh tone tumbling out with the words. I heard him open the refrigerator.

"So, no eggnog?" he asked. "How were you planning to celebrate Christmas?"

I followed him into the kitchen. "I want you to go."

"And get eggnog? Great idea," he said, still looking down into the white, stale emptiness I knew my refrigerator held. "Let me just see what else you need from the store." His head then popped back up above the door, a look of surprise on his face. "Good grief. What do you eat?"

"It's time for you to leave," I repeated.

"Yes, we've been over that. I'm trying to get a complete grocery list first." His head went back down to the refrigerator.

"The only problem," he said, "is that I doubt any store is open."

I charged at the fridge and struck the door, not caring whether he moved out of the way or not. He did, though, and the look on his face made me instantly regret being aggressive.

Of course he had known what I had meant when I asked him to go. He wasn't an idiot. He was determined. And that's how he had originally gotten me to be his wife.

"*Behave*, Evelyn," he said through a clenched jaw.

But I didn't want to.

"No. You should leave."

"No," he answered back at me.

"Why not? Because you want eggnog?" I mocked. "Forget eggnog. Forget it all. No eggnog, no Christmas, and no more us!"

The middle of Eddie's forehead turned red. That was a rarity for him. I had only seen him worked up enough to make the red spot appear on a few occasions. He must've really wanted that eggnog . . . amongst other things.

He took hold of both my arms and backed me up against the refrigerator, pinning me. "I'm not going to leave my wife with a gaping hole in her window. What kind of man does that?"

I struggled in his grasp, only stopping to mince words back at him. "The same man who told me he was leaving me. The same man who said he was going to file for divorce."

"But I didn't, did I?" His fingers slowly loosened their grip, without letting go. He took a step closer to me. I felt the hot touch of his breath on the tip of my nose and upper lip. "I'm sorry, Evelyn," he almost whispered. "Back then, I acted out of my hurt. But right now, I'm not willing to give up," he said, his eyes starting to water.

"You *already* gave up," I hissed back.

I took advantage of his loosened fingers and broke free. He let go of me easily, but I had barely walked away when he reached out to grab me again. He pushed me back up against the refrigerator, his face nearly on top of mine, and the metal button of his jeans pressing into my stomach. He opened his mouth to say something but then closed it tight. In a fluid moment, he took one hand off my arm, buried it into the back of my hair and kissed me.

I tried to shake my face away. His other hand rose and he moved both hands on each side of my face. He forced a hungry, angry, and gorgeous kiss upon me until I stopped squirming against the wall of his strength and build, remembering the magic of melting into him.

I kissed him back, hungry myself. He released my face and wrapped his arms around my waist and back, pulling me harder into him. He stopped to take a breath, nestling his face into my hair, near my ear.

He took a deep breath in, loudly, through his nose. He exhaled through his parted lips, softly, against the side of my neck. I felt the condensation from it and trembled.

He was breathing me in. Eddie always inhaled the scent of my hair and skin immediately before he made love to me. Always. To me, it had become like Pavlov's response. Whenever I heard him take that breath in and then felt the hotness of his exhale, resistance was futile.

Even more so because I still loved him.

I grabbed the back of his head, gently tugging him by his hair, and brought his mouth back to mine. The gesture quickened his breathing and he hoisted me against the refrigerator, lifting me up and holding me by the backs of my thighs. I felt the cold metal of the door against my back and the rugged need of his hands.

He took a hand and crossed my ankles at the small of his back, pulling me away from the refrigerator and carrying me into the bedroom.

When he laid me down on the bed, I turned my head to the side and saw my nightstand clock: 12:03 a.m.

My first Christmas without her. *Our* first Christmas without her . . . together.

THIRTY-THREE

Paw Prints in the Dining Room

I woke up Christmas morning and found Eddie gone. I figured he was making good on his offer to go to the store for me. Sure enough, he came back with a carton of eggnog and a few odds and ends.

"Where did you find an open store?" I asked.

"I had to go several miles out, but I found one."

"You just had to get that eggnog, didn't you?"

"Yup, and you'll soon see why," he said with a smile. Out of a plastic bag, he pulled a tall, skinny carton with images of holly and wreaths upon it and set it on the counter. Seeing the carton made me imagine I could taste nutmeg and the creaminess of whipped eggs upon the tip of my tongue. I saw the craving in it just as Eddie had. Longing for something trivial almost made me feel normal. But then again, maybe it wasn't the eggnog, maybe it was the man who had brought it and set it down on my rarely used kitchen counter.

Why hadn't I remembered how much he meant to me when it mattered most—when it would have helped save us after Corinne died?

He opened the eggnog, put the carton directly to his mouth, and chugged.

"Good grief," I said, shocked at his display of rapid consumption.

"Now, Evy," he started, only stopping to wipe the corners of his mouth with the back of his hand, "I'll give you a head start, but the eggnog has lots of protein and I feel my strength returning. I doubt you'll get very far before I overtake you."

I shot him a puzzled look. A seductive smile stretched upon his face. But most surprising to me was the fact that I ran.

In that small wrinkle of frivolity, I felt a hidden power to sidestep the unforgiving pain of my child's death. The pain wasn't gone, of course, just on pause. And the pause made it possible to smile once again. With Eddie clamoring playfully behind me—pretending to run into walls and trip over my meager furniture—I smiled. Not the smiling smirk I could muster when I found myself clever and sarcastic even on the darkest of days, but a real smile, a real thing of joy.

I didn't clue my long lost grin into the fact that this was only a pause, because if I did, my lips would have plucked themselves right off my face, called a cab, and accused me of wasting the best years of their life.

And if that happened, how would I kiss Eddie?

It wasn't long before I let Eddie catch me inside the bedroom.

We spent the rest of Christmas day talking and relaxing on the couch. For hours, I had my head in his lap while he ran his fingers through my hair, asking me what I had been up to for the last several months. I gave him very little information.

Saying I swam mindlessly and hopelessly through a jagged abyss of darkness would have likely ruined the mood.

On his part, he was much more open. He told me why he had tried to sell the house—mainly to get my attention—and how he wouldn't have actually sold it.

I wasn't ready to tell him about the smelling issue and everything that went with it, but I knew I would. Eventually I would. I was hoping for the day I could speak about it in the past tense. It'd make me feel a little less crazy if that were the case.

Everything else was a brimming bucket of various hurts and night-mares that I didn't want to deal with—each one a little soldier of emotion vying to be the Supreme Being in command. But not now, not today, and not when Eddie mooned over me.

"Don't you want to go over to your sister's?" he asked me.

"Not really."

He twirled a piece of my hair around his index finger, gently tugging on it. "She might get upset," he added.

"Yeah right," I scoffed. "All I have to do is call her and say you're here with me, and all will be forgiven."

"But she went through all that trouble, even bringing you a tree—"

Eddie mentioning the tree triggered a sudden concern. I sat up quickly, and because Eddie still had a finger entwined with a lock of my hair, I grimaced in pain. He immediately unraveled my hair and then asked, "What's wrong?"

"The tree!" I shouted, jumping off the couch and going for the front door.

"I already picked it up," he said with a soft smile, motioning for me to return to the couch.

"When?" I asked.

"Early this morning when you were still sleeping. I figured the neighborhood kids might get traumatized when they ran outside today, wanting to try out their new bikes and roller skates. We can't have a discarded tree on the front lawn ruining a kid's Christmas, can we?"

"No," I said. That was the exact reason I had run for the door. It was a hollow feeling to know that we both had a concern about preserving another child's Christmas when we didn't have a child of our own anymore. It was like our lives were an empty metal bucket under an occasional drip; thinking of someone else's children made a single drop fall and land within us as a cavernous thud, a noise far too loud for such a little thing.

I wanted to ask Eddie regarding the extent of his hurt when he thought of Corinne, but since there was a risk, albeit a small one, that his reaction would be like throwing a flare into a bat cave, I kept my mouth shut.

"Evy?" he asked.

"Hmm?"

"Are you going to come back home with me?" he asked. "We can stay here for today, but how about tomorrow?"

Sitting up, I tucked one leg under the other, fiddling with my big toe, and looking off into the kitchen. Back . . . home. This was one of those hurts and nightmares I'd have to tell Eddie about, and I didn't know how much longer this one could wait.

"I don't know," he said, cutting off my silence. "I guess I'm hoping that we'll go back and start over."

That was the problem for me: starting over. I had. Going back was the wrong direction, even if Eddie didn't agree.

"Eddie . . ." I let out a deep sigh and then looked at him. His demeanor fell. He knew what it meant when I hesitated. "I have started over. Don't get me wrong, I'm glad you're here. I haven't started over or moved on from that." I grabbed his hand next to mine and squeezed. "But there's a certain freedom in not walking down a hallway that inevitably leads to her room. I don't know how you do it. But those walls back at that house—each scuff, chip, or, you remember when she got into the baby Vaseline and submerged her hands in it, and then took those hands and put her paw prints all over the matte finish on the dining room walls?"

His lips turned up slightly. "Yeah, greasy print after greasy print that won't come off."

"See?" I asked. "That's what I'm talking about. You can smile about it. I can't, Eddie." My mind, despite my initial warning to it not to linger, recalled exactly what the handprints in the dining room looked like. Tears sprang to my eyes and I wiped them away. "This," I said, showing Eddie the wiped tears on my fingertips, "this is what happens when I remember. And I already barely survive in a place, this place, which holds none of those memories, like the spots where she learned to crawl or walk." I whisked away more tears. "I can't imagine being back there. I'd go crazy."

I chuckled a little at that. "Crazier, I mean."

Eddie shot me a look. I realized that one would probably need some clarification, but later. "You know," I said, "crazy . . . figuratively speaking."

He turned his head toward the kitchen, rubbing the tops of his legs. "So, are you saying you want to sell the house?" he asked.

I nodded. "And sell or give away everything in it."

"Isn't that a bit drastic?" he asked.

I scoffed and rubbed my hand across my forehead, trying to smooth and ease the headache subtly approaching. "Drastic?" I repeated. "No offense, Eddie, but drastic has taken on a whole new definition for me. The only thing that rises to the level of drastic is someone dying. Everything else is plain and simple life."

"Are you talking about Robert Bailey?" he asked.

Lowering my hand and resting it in my lap, I said, "I am, but I'm not. I don't really want to talk about it. Suffice it to say, there's a reason I left the house and have been living here with bare necessities for months. You, I want. The rest of it has to go."

He leaned over and put his hand on the back of my neck, gently pulling my face to meet him in the middle. He raised his mouth and kissed me on the forehead. In that simple little gesture, I felt sealed. I was under Eddie's protection again and it felt good.

"Sure, Evy. I'll take care of it. We'll live here for now. And then we'll find somewhere new. How about that?" He released me and we both sat back against the couch. His eyes surveyed the room. "You don't mind finding a new place from this one, do you?"

I shook my head.

"Good. Because something tells me there's bad memories here too."

THIRTY-FOUR

Click

"Want me to make you something to eat?" Eddie asked me. "No, thanks. I'm not feeling hungry today."

I heard him rustling a plastic bag, putting the newly purchased groceries on the counter in the kitchen. It had been almost a month since we had decided to sell the house, and he had been back there almost daily either packing stuff up or getting rid of it. He had taken some time off from work—vacation days that had been accumulating for years. After the first two weeks had elapsed, I wondered about the extent of junk we had in the old house. It made me feel bad for not helping, but that's when I suggested hiring someone.

He had said, "I need to do it myself. I'd do it with you since we're the ones who shared the life, but otherwise I don't want anyone else touching or getting rid of the chapter we're closing."

As for Corinne's stuff, I think that's where he spent most of his time. I never asked about the process because I actively tried to keep the moments we'd break down together over her to a bare minimum. Whenever those moments started, we went to opposite sides of the rented hovel. It made me realize that it wasn't as if we had changed, and were thus able to rekindle our love, but rather that we were finding success in being unoriginally infantile, walking away from what bothered us. The way we individually expressed our grief over her was the lead weight pulling down our marriage all those months ago. We didn't want to repeat the mistake, so we gave up trying to impose each other's coping processes on the other.

Still, I imagined there were days, entire days, where Eddie only managed packing up one box. When the sun set on the western side of the house, it would find Eddie on his knees, his hands trembling and his eyes misted, trying to write the word CORINNE on the top of a cardboard box with a black Sharpie.

One box. Her box. That was enough to occupy his strength for a full day.

Fragile would be added too, if I knew Eddie as well as I thought I did—even if it were only a box of pillows and blankets. He probably wrote it small and dainty, an afterthought really.

But by the time he got back to the rental, he was all smiles and warmly composed, just as he was this afternoon.

The rumpling of plastic grocery bags continued with Eddie in the kitchen as my cell phone lit up at my wobbly computer desk. It was an email.

From Thatcher. He was good about giving me an end of the month update, even when nothing seemed to change from month to month. I picked up the cell to open the message when Eddie came into the living room and met me at the desk.

"Look what I got," he said.

I turned around to see him; he was grinning ear to ear and holding a tall, skinny carton of eggnog.

I chuckled. "Are you serious?"

"Yes, ma'am."

"Why did you get eggnog? Isn't it rotten by now? Stores stop carrying it after Christmas for a reason," I said, my arm hanging over the back of the chair. My cell was in the dangling hand.

"Ah, but remember that mini-mart I went to on Christmas? The eggnog carton I got from there said it expired on February fifth, so I figured the place might still have some. The big places get rid of that stuff quickly, but not a mini-mart. And I was right."

He happily showed me the expiration date. He was right: February 5. I put my cell phone on the desk and stood. I'd check Thatcher's uninformative message later. I took the carton out of Eddie's hands and examined it, shaking my head.

"I don't know, Eddie, this disturbs me," I said, smiling.

"Why?"

"No man should be *this* in love with eggnog," I teased.

"Well, you have to think about the mini-mart too," he said.

"Pray tell, why?"

He stepped behind me and wrapped his arms around my middle, just below my bustline, laying his chin upon my shoulder.

"That place looks like it struggles," he said. "So I just helped boost their profits. If I didn't buy this, then they would have never sold it and then chucked it. Bye-bye profit, bye-bye rich and creamy eggnog."

I laughed, tilting my head back to position us cheek to cheek. He still had his beard. He kept it trimmed, but said he hadn't stopped wearing it since finding me in the hospital. As mad as he was that day, he said he recognized the look on my face when I saw him. "Like our honeymoon," he had said recently. "Yes, like our honeymoon," I had replied.

"If you're so concerned about the mini-mart's profits, you should have brought back those hot dogs that have been spinning on metal rollers for four days."

"Oh, great . . . you guessed what I got you for dinner."

I spun around to face him, gave him a kiss, and walked into the kitchen to dig through the bags. He followed. I had to make sure he was kidding about the hot dogs.

"Except, I think the guy at that place has had those dogs on the rollers for more than four days," he said. "You're being generous. I don't think they remove those things from that cooking cage until the bacteria matures itself enough to walk itself and those dogs right out the door."

I smirked at him, then went back to searching through the bags. By now, I was sure there weren't any mini-mart hot dogs.

"Hey, that reminds me," he said. "You'll never guess who I ran into at that mini-mart."

"I don't even feel like guessing, so just tell me."

"I'm really glad you're not this abrupt in every area of your life."

"Strange. I thought I was. It's kind of my thing," I said smiling, and then returned to the groceries to help put them away.

"Anyway," he started, "I was walking into the mini-mart and saw a small, brown puppy on a leash, tied up to the bike rack at the front door. I bent down to give it a pat, and out walked Gordon to untie the puppy."

"Gordon Racobs?" I asked. "My mom's old boyfriend?"

"Yeah. He was at the mini-mart buying dog food for the puppy. He told me it was a birthday present for his granddaughter."

I turned to look at Eddie square in the face. "I didn't think Gordon had children; how could he have grandchildren?"

"He doesn't. Sorry, he actually said the puppy was for his girlfriend's granddaughter."

I heard a small, faint, but strangely measurable *click*. It was as if someone had unlocked the front door from outside the house. I looked at the front door, but it was locked. I must have imagined the sound.

"I found it odd that he was buying a girlfriend's granddaughter a puppy since he seemed so standoffish toward children when he was dating your mother. But maybe he's found 'The One,' and will show lots of interest in her offspring," Eddie said.

Click. There it was again. It was louder this time, but I didn't bother to look at the front door again. I was staring past Eddie, his voice starting to echo out of my immediate consciousness, yet my mind, my very being, processed every single word.

"I wanted to ask him about the new girlfriend and the granddaughter, but he seemed jumpy and eager to leave, so I wished him well and went inside the mini-mart."

Click.

Pete Shaw's face and voice came to me from all those months ago. He had said I'd remember, that something would eventually click.

My mind quickly spun through its catalog of memories. Find Gordon, find Gordon, and pull them *all* out. They came, swooshing fast enough to make a motion picture out of the stand-alone images.

Gordon was always uncomfortable around Corinne; he usually kept his hands in his pockets when we came around.

Click.

My mother had once carelessly remarked to me that she wanted to break up with Gordon because he acted as if his interests were elsewhere.

CLICK.

That swim party, the only one Gordon ever came to, where Corinne was running around in a bikini. We all got up and went inside for lunch, but he didn't. He stayed outside and alone because he said he often liked to sunbathe, and wanted a few more minutes. He said it as I snickered to Maddie, later telling her that I doubted that because of his milky white skin.

CLICK!

The fight with my mother at Corinne's funeral—he started to leave with my mother, but then he went back in. While Corinne was alive, he had never uttered so much as three words to her at a time, but at the funeral *he went back in.*

CLICK, CLICK, CLICK! Family and friends, family and friends, family and friends.

I doubled over, my hand covering my mouth.

Eddie put his hands on my back and asked, "Are you all right?" His words were distant crashes, empty bottles thrown against the back wall of an alley.

I raced to the bathroom and slammed the door behind me. Dropping to my knees in front of the toilet, I barely got the lid up before I vomited.

Eddie came barreling behind me, rapping his knuckles on the door. "Evy, are you all right? What's the matter?"

All I saw was red. Lots and lots of red.

Then, beyond the red, I saw Corinne's trusting face with a man she knew. Of course she went off with him. He had probably promised to bring her to Mommy or Grandma, to take her away from that boring and sleepy nanny.

More red, blood red.

I blindly reached for the roll of toilet paper to my side, trying to grab something to wipe my mouth, eyes, and nose. My clumsy pull spun the roll wildly in disarray until I had a mass of white two-ply in my hands. But it didn't look white to me, it was red. The red of smoldering hate, yeah that red.

I thought of the new little girl, the new little granddaughter. The puppy, the act of his gift, meant one of two things: she was safe because Gordon only ignored the ones he planned to steal, rape, and kill; or she was in terrible danger because Gordon had figured out there was no point in wasting all those potential living moments they could have together if the little darling would end up dead anyway.

My jaw clenched, my teeth felt the crushing pressure of being ground together. I white-knuckled the rim of the toilet seat, imagining that it was Gordon's neck after I crushed the life out of him.

"You're dead, Gordon," I muttered under my breath. "You're dead."

Eddie knocked on the door again. "Evy? Evy? What's going on? Evy? I'm coming in."

"I'm fine, Eddie," I shouted back at him through the locked door. I was anything but. But he didn't need to know that. Humor, I thought. Diffuse him with humor. I wiped the bottom of my nose, trying to excavate humor in that horrific moment. "See, just looking at that bad eggnog made me throw up," I said, forcing a chuckle.

He chuckled too. "Can I get you anything?" he asked.

Let's see, yes. Since I can't go out and purchase a gun or lye or a shovel without raising suspicion under the terms of my probation, then, yes, you go and run to Vigilantes 'R Us and pick me up a few items.

Why now? I thought. Why did this all have to come out now when I finally had Eddie back? Then again, if he wasn't here, if he hadn't had that infernal love for eggnog, and near this neighborhood no less, then he would never have run into Gordon.

I'd still be wondering the monster's name, THAT monster's name.

I was sweating profusely—out of anger, fear, hatred—and things were getting blurrier by the second, except for the thoughts spinning in my mind, the very same horrible thoughts I had when I first learned she was dead. What went through her mind when Gordon had his hands on her? Did she suffer? Did she call out for me? When I didn't save her, did she feel betrayal? Those impossible questions would drive anyone to the edge of insanity. And there I stood, my toes dangling off the rim with a parachute strapped to my back because I thought I could beat the laws of conscience and consequence. I thought I could jump off into the netherworld of a woman gone mad, exact my fury and revenge, and then pull my parachute open and sail back to the safety and love my husband.

I'd crush Gordon's skull, wash my hands, and then put my head back into Eddie's lap and let him play with my hair. It worked that way, right?

Eddie knocked on the door again. "Are you coming out? Are you sure you're okay?"

"My stomach was acting up, but I think I'm okay," I told him. "Let me wash my face, and I'll be out." I was more frightened by the level, cool voice coming from my mouth than the task in front of me, the task I planned to carry out on Gordon. It would likely be a repeat of my encounter with Robert Bailey. However, this one I wouldn't feel sorry after. Maybe that's what the scary part was for me. If I went after Gordon, this would be a choice, a consequence that would have to be as worth it as a crash was for a Kamikaze pilot.

I finally opened the door and stood with Eddie in the hallway. He put his arms around me. "You should lie down. You've barely eaten anything all day and maybe that's why you got sick." He walked me to the bed and helped me onto it, sitting next to my side. I tried to tell myself to settle down, to unclench. But my fingers and toes wouldn't oblige. I could taste my hate bubbling up into my throat and it burned in the way sizzling bile does.

"Geez, Evy, you look so pale and tense," he said. "Are you sure you're feeling better?"

I nodded robotically.

He stood. "We don't have any medicine here, do we?"

I rolled on my side, away from him because I felt a sheath of red color inking over my vision. Bloodred hate and Gordon was his name.

"If you don't mind, I'm going to run out again and pick you up something to help you feel better. You want the pink stuff, or flu stuff, which one?"

I sat up in the bed, almost excited. He was going to leave? Perfect.

"Flu stuff, I guess," I replied.

"Okay." He bent down and gave me a kiss on the forehead. "I'll be right back."

When I heard the door close behind him, I jumped out of bed, only my stomach reminding me I needed to take it easier. "Calm down, you," I said to it. "I know what you want. You want what I want: Gordon," I hissed through my teeth.

I walked to the living room and saw my cell phone, remembering Thatcher's message. The fact that there'd be no new information from the police coursed through me like a toxin of fury—and I needed as much of that as possible for what I had planned.

> Mrs. Barrett,
>
> I'll give you my monthly update later, but right now something came up that I promised I'd tell you about. Remember the Crafton foster son? We found no Joseph Crafton that fits the bill, and then looked under his original name, Gordon Tournay. Couldn't find the right guy on that either. Figuring he might have changed his name, we did more searching and one guy, locally, fits the right age and foster home sequencing. His name is Gordon Racobs. Pete says there's no need to stir up old ghosts for the guy. There was lots of press on Helen Crafton, and since this guy is in town and still didn't come forward, we're going to let this go. Sorry, Brian Thatcher

"No, no, no!" I screamed at the top of my lungs, nearly crushing my phone into oblivion.

My mother once commented that Gordon was like Eddie—the thought alone, even back then, made me shiver—but she was referring to his lack of family. He had once told my mother he had grown up "in the system," but left it at that. It's not something you typically label a sixty-year-old man with, so I never thought about it again until after reading Thatcher's message.

So this is why Paul had come into my life. That whole ugly situation was to get me closer to Gordon in the event Eddie hadn't stumbled back to that mini-mart for some nearly expired eggnog. But two affirmations of the identity of Corinne's killer in a single day?

If that wasn't a sign to go after him, I didn't know what was.

NO.

Yes.

That was to show you who is in control.

Yeah, me.

THIRTY-FIVE

When Evil Calls the Shots

I stormed into my mother's house.

"Evelyn," she said, shocked, springing from the couch. She had been sitting and watching television, but then came toward me, holding the remote and turning the set off. "What brings you by?" She looked behind me and saw her front door left open. "Go close the door, honey. That's just rude."

"No, I'm leaving. I just want to know Gordon's address," I said.

She scoffed, tightening her housecoat and walking around me to close the door herself. It was twilight on a Sunday—a quiet and cold evening in the middle of winter. When I had left the house after Eddie, the sun was setting; by the time I'd get to Gordon, it'd be pitch-black. Just the way I wanted it.

"Why in the world would you want that?" she asked me after she bolted the door. Little good that did now—I had already come in while it was unlocked. I would think she would've wised up about that. As if losing a granddaughter wasn't enough, an unlocked door or window was inviting further sickness to seep into her life when she least expected it.

I didn't want to tell her *why* regarding Gordon's address. She would call me a liar, and then accuse me of being selfish and crazy. Any number of things she could, and probably would, sling at me, including her impeccable ability to judge people, and how she would've never allowed anyone in her life who could hurt her grandchildren. I took off into her bedroom.

"Evelyn," she called out for me. I said nothing in return.

"Oh, well," she said, sighing. "I thought you'd be more back to normal with Edward back in your life. Should I call him, dear?"

"No!" I shouted back to her.

"What are you doing back there?" she asked as I heard the television go back on.

After five or so minutes, I reappeared in the living room. She was back on the couch, watching her show.

She heard me walk past her and asked, "Why would you ever need Gordon's address? That's such an ancient connection."

"I don't need it anymore, Mom," I said. "I just took it out of your address book."

She gasped and turned around on the couch to face me.

"You went snoop—" she started, but when she actually saw me, she switched directions. "Evelyn! Are those my clothes?" she asked.

As quickly as I wanted Gordon's life over, I took a moment to try to be rational and minimize my chances of being caught. Rational and hunting down . . . oxymoron, I knew. But when I was this angry with an ever-loving need to exact something that should have been taken care of months ago, my body coursed with poisonous adrenaline. An oxymoron was too insignificant to slow me down.

The only thing I had to worry about was my hair and fingerprints. I had grabbed her black coat because it came with a tight cinching hood, and grabbed her dark brown driving gloves. Good and good.

"I'm borrowing these, Mom, sorry. It's happening."

I turned to the door and opened it.

"Evelyn," she cried out after me. "What's happening?"

Before I closed the door behind me, I yelled back at her, "And lock this door!"

Timing was everything, and, thankfully, it was on my side tonight. I had just parked my car three houses down from Gordon's when I saw his garage roll open. Throwing myself across the front seat of my car when I saw him back his Chrysler out, I laid low until I heard his vehicle pass.

That made it easier. Now I could break in rather than knock on the front door with a smile. I didn't think I could pull the latter off. Granted, I didn't know where he was off to, nor did I know when he'd be back, but it didn't matter.

All I needed was to be in that house *before* he arrived back, in the dark, with something, anything, in my hand to make sure he never stood again.

With my mother's gloves upon my hands, and her hood pulled tight, covering every strand of my hair, I exited my car. It was a good thing it was a foggy, wet night. I looked normal if anyone happened to look outside as I crossed the street and let myself into Gordon's back yard. Normal except for my snarling lips.

The first thing I touched with my gloved hand was Gordon's metal trash can, stashed just on the inside of his side gate. I carried it to the back door and then scraped it roughly against the back patio, hoping the scratching noise would distract neighbors from the quick burst of broken glass I created when I rammed a rock through one of the door's small glass panes. The rock was small enough to carry with one hand, but big enough to do a heap of injury without sacrificing my fingers through glass, or as I hoped for later, Gordon's skull.

Now with the rock dropped inside my mother's jacket pocket, I reached inside to unlock the door, letting myself in. My blood quickened through my veins, pumping in fury and fear and echoing like a tribal drum. Yet the tip of my tongue flicked out against the sides of my mouth, eager to taste the spoils of justice. Even if my heart rate wasn't ready for this, the rest of me was living large.

Gordon had left a few inconsequential lights on: the one over the stove, a desk lamp in the living room, and a night-light in the hallway. That would help. I had only brought the tiny flashlight I usually kept in my glove box.

Suddenly, I froze at the stench around me. It had been months since I had smelled a pedophile. The back of my gloved hand pressed against my nostrils and I wished the smell were something I had remembered and anticipated. If I had, I would have brought something to shove up each side of my nose—tissue, cotton balls, baby carrots if need be.

I went for Gordon's bedroom, navigating through the dark. It was easy enough to make my way around his place. He had a simple L-shaped ranch style home. Into the kitchen, then the living room, then a long, narrow hallway that ended in a master bedroom. I'd be ready for Gordon when he got back, but in the meantime, it wouldn't hurt to look around. Perhaps I could find evidence, even if it were evidence that would kill me with grief on the spot.

Lowering my hand, the smell proved to be too much. I wouldn't be able to dig through his stuff with only one hand. Heading back down the hallway, I made my way to the bathroom I had passed. With the help of the night-light, and the fact my eyes were rapidly adjusting to its dim orange light, I spotted a tissue box on the bathroom counter. I split one tissue in half and shoved a crumpled wad in each nostril.

Back at the bedroom door, I inched a step forward. My head swirled. This could be the room where Gordon took both Corinne's innocence and her life.

I fell to my knees, gasping for air through my opened mouth.

It was one thing to know your child was dead, but it was another to stand in the place she died. And I knew, in a way only a mother could, that this *was* where she died because I heard a shattering cry that reached my mind, my heart, my soul; every inch of me screamed, "Profane! Profane! Profane!"

This was a mistake that would ruin what was left of me.

I wasn't a big girl. I was a broken girl. I was a girl who had lost her baby, and as much as it felt like that fact ripped at my very core, opening certain doors could only make it worse . . . it had only made it worse.

There wasn't enough resolve within me to do what I had planned to do with Gordon. I should've listened to the pounding of my heart, the conscience God had instilled in me—and from Corinne's death onward, had often used to speak to me.

What was I doing?

Even if I took my revenge on Gordon, then what? I'd lose Eddie. I'd lose myself. Forever. And— and— and she'd still be *dead.*

My hands went to my face and I wept and I moaned and I hated, utterly hated, realizing that vengeance is not mine. I hated it as much as knowing that my child had been murdered, that someone else's child somewhere in the world had been murdered today, and another tomorrow, and again, and again, and again, until the world takes a knee and cries out, "Save us!"

We're not all bad parents; we're just all living in a bad world. We don't belong here. This place is not our home. How stupid do we have to be to blame God for the injustice? Does He pull the trigger? Does He throttle their necks? Does He inflict the bruises? No. People do. And what's the one thing those people all have in common?

Evil.

When does it become obvious that when a player wears his team's colors, he's a part of *that* team? He's following *his* captain's calls.

I heard something creak behind me and I turned my head to the left, instinctually lifting my arm for protection, just as something crashed down. My forearm took the weight of the blow, but he still managed to connect with my head. Right where Robert Bailey had smashed me.

My eyes fluttered open, but that's all I could move. It was too cold to be inside, too wet and too dark as well. The fog, I saw the fog. I was outside and I was lying on something hard.

I heard a shuffling to my right and tried to move my hand. Nothing. I was getting colder and colder, my head swimming between a thumping pain and an automatic response to close my eyes and black out again. I wanted to test whether I could speak, but I was certain that whoever hit me was standing nearby and making the shuffling noise.

Gordon.

Had Gordon come home and found me falling apart just inside his bedroom? I had been crying so loudly, I wouldn't have heard him come in. Stupid, Evelyn, stupid.

I groaned. The sound was an accident; I hadn't meant to give myself away. The moment the groan had escaped, the shuffling stopped.

Footsteps approached near my head. Then a foot gave my arm a little nudge. "You awake?" a voice asked me. It was a man's voice but I couldn't tell if it was Gordon or not.

He nudged me again. Harder this time. I groaned again, but it was really the same soft, whimperlike sound from before.

"Yes, by goodness, you're awake."

I heard what sounded like a wooden ship creaking against a dock, but it was the man next to me bending down to get closer—his knees were the old wooden ship, gravity was the dock. My eyes focused more and I made out the back of his house, then the trees over me in the back yard, shrouded by the low-lying fog. I was face up on Gordon's back patio.

"Evelyn?" he asked. "Why did you break into my house?"

His voice was sweet and curious, almost friendly.

"Should I call the police or should I call your mother?" he asked.

I blinked. Still, nothing else moved. I started to grunt, trying to use my vocal chords.

"Hmm," he said. "Let's start out this way." He seemed to be talking to himself. "No jumping to conclusions, Gordo. Might just be a misunder-standing." He stood up, the creak of his knees sounding again.

"Evelyn, your old pal Gordon has to make some quick decisions here, so I'm going to have to ask you to speed this up. I know I've knocked you something silly on the head, but you'll have to forgive me on that one. I came home to find someone in my house and it was jarring. I picked up the fire poker and defended my house. Then I saw it was you. I've yet to call the police—going to give you the benefit of the doubt. So I need to ask you again: Why were you inside my house?"

Even if I could speak, what was I supposed to tell him? The truth would ring through him and incite his panic while he had me in a very vulnerable position. If he wanted to make sure the truth died, he'd kill me along with it. On the other hand, if I offered him a lie, which would be the right one for him to believe? That I've suddenly turned to a life of cat burglary and what a coinkydink that I hit his house?

Either way, it didn't matter. I couldn't speak.

He huffed, ending the pause of my silence. "This really puts me in a pickle, Evelyn."

He paced the length of my body a few times, each turn getting faster and faster until he stopped next to my hips.

The wooden ship creaked again, but this time he straddled my chest, his knees pinning my arms down in the event I started to put up a fight. He sniffled, sucking up what sounded like clumps of snot high into his nose, and then cleared his throat.

"Evelyn, please understand that if I'm wrong about why you're here, I'm very sorry."

I willed something, anything, to move. Inside, I was thrashing around like someone tangling with a crocodile; on the outside, I was already limp and dead.

"But I can't take any chances, because I *think* I know why you're here—something akin to your pursuit of that poor Bailey character. And I surely can't wait for you to recover your strength to clarify it for me. I'm just an old man. You could probably escape me if you tried. I'm sorry," he said again. "Self-preservation," he added.

He unzipped the top of my jacket, exposing my neck. The cold and darkness covered my bare throat moments before Gordon's hands covered it too.

He squeezed, and I struggled. Again, only on the inside.

My throat was gagging, fighting for breath, fighting to swallow. Where was my strength? Even one muscle. Please, God, just one muscle to start. Anything but lying on my back and dying, the same way Corinne had, and at the hands of the same man.

My arm twitched, trying to throw off his knee. More strength, please, more strength.

His grip tightened and his knees pushed further, boring excruciating holes of pain into my biceps.

My leg kicked up. Just a small movement but he must've heard the sound of my shoe hit back down on the concrete. He squeezed harder, his hands crushing my throat. My tongue felt like it was in my ears, my mind clotted with both lightness and softening pain.

I was milliseconds away from death; I even heard the flutter of angels come to take me away, though their wings sounded like heavy boots on pavement.

A loud, painful "No!" erupted through the whitened hue around me. A whoosh of air sailed past me and I was free of Gordon's weight. I no longer felt his hands on my neck. I no longer felt anything.

THIRTY-SIX

It's Gone

Evy?"
The voice sounded like Eddie's, even when a siren wailing over my head drowned it out.

"Evy? Can you hear me?"

It was definitely Eddie. I panicked, my eyes bursting open to warn Eddie that Gordon was around, but all I saw was a bright light above me.

I tried moving my hands, but found my arms strapped down. Then, I felt an immediate, fiery burn in my left arm. That's when I remembered I had used it to block the blow to my head. I hadn't suffered a broken limb before, and wasn't entirely sure that's what was going on, but the pain from trying to lift my left hand seemed a clear enough warning to stop trying.

"Eddie," I whispered hoarsely. Using my voice was like sipping acid. It burned, it ached, and it was because Gordon had crushed my throat. My body gently swayed as it was strapped down to a gurney.

I was in an ambulance.

"Eddie?" I strained again, gasping at the pain.

"Evy, yes. I'm here."

I turned my head toward his voice. My head throbbed from where Gordon hit me.

"Tell her not to talk," a voice to my left said.

Eddie's face lowered next to me on the gurney. He was crying. "Shh, shh, shh, baby."

I heard him swallow and steady his breath. "Your neck . . ." He lifted his head to look at it, his face twisting in anger and revulsion, baring his teeth in a way I had never seen him do. He lowered his face back down next to my ear. "He almost crushed your larynx. Don't use your voice.

The paramedic said you could damage it more if you talk." His voice trembled, bouncing for air and control, a sign that he had been weeping, that he was still weeping.

"Shh, shh," he repeated, putting his arm over me. "We're in an ambulance," he said. "We're going to the hospital."

"Gordon," I tried to cry.

A latex glove went over my mouth; Eddie's eyes darted over to the paramedic to my left. "Miss, please. You want to talk again, right? You're going to want to tell the police what happened, right? Don't talk. Let the doctor look at you first. We don't want any more damage to your voice. Do you understand?"

I nodded and she removed her hand. She was a diminutive woman with caramel skin and jet-black hair pulled into a bun at the back of her head. She had the longest, most feminine eyelashes I had ever seen, but her cocoa-rimmed eyes were all tough-and-stuff business. When she turned around to reach for something, I looked at Eddie again, mouthing something.

This time Eddie's hand went to my mouth but he quickly pulled it back and hid it in his lap. But it was too late. I had already seen the blood on his fingers.

"Wh—"

The paramedic immediately hunched over me and put her hand on my mouth again. "Okay, I get it. I do. You have a million questions and your brain wants to ask them all right now. I get it." She looked over at Eddie. "I'm going to fill her in, okay? Just what I know. Is that all right?"

"I guess," he said.

She looked back down on me. "If I move my hand, will you promise to keep quiet?"

I nodded.

"You're going to be okay. Your husband, he's going to be okay too. He found you at that house with your attacker on top of you. The two got into a scuffle, but since I personally saw the other guy, I'd say your husband won."

She reached over me and grabbed at Eddie's hands, looking them over. "Yeah, mostly superficial. I'd say the blood is the other guy's, right?" she asked.

Eddie nodded.

I looked at Eddie with pleading, hopeful eyes; biting down on my lip to prevent myself from asking the question aloud.

He leaned back against the side of the ambulance and sighed, tucking his bloodied hands under his armpits. "No, Evy," he said, answering the curiosity in my eyes. "I didn't kill him. He's still alive."

I whimpered and closed my eyes. Anguish came like a wave, bringing with it arms and legs of debris and seaweed, anxious to pull me down and sweep me into the sea. Hot tears made a steady trickle down my face, some pooling in my ears, some making a final descent to the gurney below.

I resolved to save the rest of my questions for later. Sufficient for the moment was the excruciating fear that I had almost died at Gordon's hands, and the overwhelming betrayal that he still breathed.

The ambulance made one final turn, the siren quieted, and the back doors flung open. The pint-sized paramedic helped a male nurse yank my gurney down, prop it up, and roll it away toward the hospital entrance. I shifted my eyes to see Eddie, still climbing out of the back of the ambulance. His bloodied hands stood out under the fluorescents of the ambulance carport. What was worse, though, was the devastating hollowness of his eyes. He looked to me as angry as I had felt after Corinne died. Angry wasn't one of Eddie's shades. He wore spring tones better.

I saw light after boxed light over my head as the paramedic and the nurse wheeled me down the hallway. Eddie had to be following behind; at least I hoped he was. At the end of the route, a doctor appeared at my side as soon as the gurney stopped moving. He took hold of the plastic tubing that ran from the IV bag to my arm, and injected a syringe into it. A sudden, warm flash engulfed me, dancing and racing up my veins.

My little but feisty paramedic objected, "That's not necessary, doc. She's good. She panicked a little when she woke up, but you didn't need to sedate her."

"Watch yourself, Rosa. I'm the doctor. Besides—" He looked over his shoulder at the sound of another gurney quickly rolling in. "I'm being preemptive," he added, using a small jerk of his head to show Rosa what was coming around the corner.

She looked. Then I looked.

I started to thrash and wail, using the points of pain as fuel. If I lost my voice forever, so be it. A mother needs to scream at her child's killer. She needs to.

Gordon was coming. His face was puffed and disfigured, but he wore the same plaid Chaps shirt I'd seen while he was strangling me.

"No, no, no!" I tried to scream. "Not here. Don't bring him here."

The flush of sedation tingled to the far reaches of my body, surging to the smallest of my extremities. Then it took a gentle stroll to my heart. Everything slowed, dulled, and muted.

The last thing I heard was the doctor again. "Get her husband off that man."

When I woke, the light coming in from a window told me it was morning. I struggled against a new set of restraints, but when I attempted to wriggle free, they wriggled back and then wrapped tighter around me.

"Easy, babe. Stop thrashing," Eddie groaned. "You're going to push me off the bed." He was lying next to me on the hospital bed, his arms wrapped tightly around me.

"Eddie," I whispered.

He hugged me tighter, spooning me. "Eddie," I said louder, feeling the strain in my throat. "Get up. He's here. Gordon's here," I said, my voice wrecked and scratchy. At least it still worked. Somewhat.

He groaned again, then burrowed his face deep against the back of my neck. "Don't remind me," he said.

I flung my elbow back to move him, and it felt heavier than normal. There was a cast on my left arm. One that hadn't been there the night prior, and a temporary one at that. At least, I hoped it was temporary due to its shoddy and thin appearance. Eddie only came closer, even with the threat of me elbowing him with plaster, holding his hand tight over my abdomen. I tried to yank it off with my good hand. "I can't just lie here while he's in the same hospital. I can't."

He turned his hand around to hold onto mine, controlling it, and raised himself slightly to put his mouth near my ear. He said to me in a low, forceful rumble, his hot breath sending shivers down my spine, "No, Evelyn. Stay put. We're done with that."

Trying to control my breathing so I could control my voice, I took three quick breaths in. I wasn't trying to be calm as much as I was trying to spare my throat the pain that slid down every time I talked above a whisper.

"I thought I was done. I was," I said. "But then he hit me and tried to choke me to death. Look, he broke my arm." I said the last part too loud. My hand went to my throat to press down the pain, but my skin must've been bruised too because even touching the surface sent pain to the back of my skull.

"Yes, I know," Eddie said. "Trust me, I know."

I thrashed more. He got up quickly, letting me roll to my back, and then came back down on top of me, being mindful of my broken arm and pinning my free hand on the pillow.

"What are you doing? Get off me," I told him.

There was fire in his eyes. Not as much as I had seen last night under the ambulance carport, but they still kindled. "Listen," he said. "It's over."

I fought him some more but his hand was tightly around mine. Then, remembering his bloodied hands from last night, I looked to find them. They were clean now, except for red and purple bruises on his knuckles, and a scratch or two.

"Why didn't you kill him, Eddie?" I asked, tears breaking free. I looked back at his face. "Hmm? Why didn't you finish it?"

Eddie searched my eyes, likely trying to gauge whether I meant it. He dipped his head in defeat, released my hand, and then gently lay to the side of me. He scooted down, putting his head upon my chest, and tucked his arm under my back.

We laid a moment like that, until he moved a hand and rested it on my belly.

"Get off me, Eddie."

He didn't.

"Please. It's starting to hurt. Get off," I added, softer.

He popped up on his hands and knees, still hovering over me, and lowered his lips to my stomach, hidden under a heavily worn hospital gown, and gave it a kiss. When he looked up at me, there was a strange look on his face. It was something I hadn't seen since a different life ago. He looked . . . thankful.

"How can you look like that?"

"Like what?" he asked.

"Like you're grateful."

He climbed off the bed, straightening out his hair. "I am happy."

I almost wanted to hit him. How could he be happy right now? Did I dream everything that happened last night? Were we actually at the rental waking up on any other day?

No. The monitors, the rails on the top part of the bed, the needle in my arm letting me know I was in a hospital.

"How?" I demanded. "How can you be happy with Gordon here?"

"Because he is not my problem anymore."

Now we were getting somewhere. "You . . . you finished him off?"

He gave me a look of scorn. "No, Evy, I did not *finish* him off."

I flung my legs over the bed and tried to stand.

"Where are you going?" he asked.

"To find Gordon."

Eddie ran around to the other side of the bed to stop me.

"No, Evelyn."

I pulled the cold metal IV tower with me as I went to walk around Eddie.

"I want to . . ." I clasped at my throat again, feeling the fire within and unable to complete the sentence.

"You want to what?" he asked, holding me by my shoulders, trying to push me back into the bed. I was weaker than I imagined, but a part of me still tried to convince myself I was a terrible tiger who'd eventually get the upper hand, just as I had thought last night before I went into Gordon's house. But that hadn't really worked out, had it?

"I want to see him, so I can . . ." But I still couldn't finish a sentence. Not because of my throat this time. All of a sudden, I couldn't place the bubbling sense of desperation within me. Was I desperate to kill him? No, I had moved beyond doing that dirty deed myself. I think I had. Although, if Eddie had done it in the course of stopping Gordon from killing me, so be it. Then again, maybe not. I didn't actually want that on Eddie any more than I was able to bear it.

A small harmony of reason said I shouldn't want Gordon dead at all, because such flippant thoughts are how this whole thing started, like how evil and sin belong to people as if it's some sort of entitlement they want to act out—as long as it's done in the shadows.

But if I was no longer rooting for his death, then what? Was I desperate to hurt Gordon? My legs felt wobbly, my throat felt like someone's hands were still wrapped around it, my left arm throbbed against the makeshift cast, and everything about ten or so feet out blurred in and out of focus. What would I be able to do, anyway? Throw a pee cup at him?

Would the result be different if I were in tip-top shape?

I wanted it to be. I really did want to hurt him. I could feel it. It was this tremor of anticipation. I felt it vibrating in my good arm. There was a desire to pummel him. But why?

Because I was angry. And hurt. Most of all confused that this kind of agony, this horrifically painful, gut-wrenching situation, could exist in this world. *My* world.

Life is a good thing. Breath is tops. Then there's love, hope, mercy, and grace; even cutesy little pictures of lions lying down with lambs. But that's not what happened in my picture. Nope. I came back and discovered the lion had devoured my little lamb. He took a bite out of her and didn't stop feasting until she was gone.

And what could I do about it? I know what I had been trying to do, but what about now?

I still wasn't sure. A beat-down on Gordon was off the menu, and I was going to put my reason behind that, on the physical impossibility of the moment. What was left, then? I wasn't sure, but the longing to do something was gnawing at me.

"I just want to see him," I repeated. It sounded trite, stupid even. It's good to "see" friends and loved ones, but the man who killed my daughter, and then tried to kill me . . . "seeing" wasn't the right word, but I hoped it'd get me past Eddie. At least I hoped it'd get me out in the hall.

"It's too late for that," he urged.

"What do you mean?" I asked.

"Sit down," he told me.

I shook my head.

"Yes," he said. "You need to sit. If you could see yourself, you'd notice you're leaning to one side, probably only being held up by that IV tower. Please sit down. I'm sure your head needs you to."

I let go of the IV tower and tried to balance myself, raising my good arm to reach over and feel the left side of my head. I wondered if it had cracked open like it had when Robert Bailey smashed me. The spot was sore, and there was a round, raised circle, but nothing else.

"You were luckier this time," Eddie said, responding to my gesture. "No cut, no stitches, no brain swelling. Just enough to black you out for a bit. Oh, and the broken arm," he said, gently tapping my cast.

Everything hurt more now after having been standing a bit, and I was profusely tired. But sitting in my room and doing nothing was too much to bear.

"Sit," Eddie repeated.

Instead, I tried to push past him. "Don't make me get on top of you again," he said.

"Get out of my way, Eddie," I shrieked through a whisper.

"Fine," he said, moving away. "Here." He took a hold of my IV tower. "Let me follow behind, rolling this along for you. Let's see what you're going to do. Let's see Evelyn Barrett fix the wrongs in this world by doing wrong herself."

My eyes filled with bitter tears, and darned if they took their sweet time to fall, blurring my vision even further. Now, I couldn't even see the ten feet in front of me. "Why are you doing this to me, Eddie?"

"Because you're not God, Evelyn. And neither am I," he said, his eyebrows pinching together in the middle of his forehead. "I might have gotten a little out of control last night when I found him on top of you. But I know I stopped far before I'd actually killed him. His life isn't mine to take."

I sat back down on the bed, undone. Still floored by the injustice of it all, I kept picturing the lion and the bloodied lamb. Whose right was it to take Corinne's life? Why did Eddie or I have to refrain on Gordon, when Gordon didn't refrain on Corinne?

"But he killed her, Eddie," I screeched out. "He did it. He was brought into our lives and then he took our daughter." I put a hand to my eyes, forcing more pooled tears to run free.

"He deserves to die," I whimpered.

"Is that why you went there last night?" Eddie asked.

"Yes, at first," I admitted. "But then I decided not to go after him."

"Why?"

I didn't want to answer. I listened as a cart in the hall rolled past my room and then beyond. If I didn't know any better, I'd say this was the same room I had been in before. If that didn't articulate the old proverb about a dog returning to his vomit, I don't know what would.

I put my arm over my eyes, feeling the tube taped to my arm against the bridge of my nose. "Because I felt God was telling me that it wasn't the way to go. And He had been trying to tell me that for months."

"Did you listen?" he asked.

I lowered my arm, letting it fall limp next to me and giving Eddie a perplexed look. "Well obviously not until after I broke into Gordon's house. But yes, I did before doing anything rash. That's actually how he got the jump on me. I was crying and I guess I didn't hear him come home."

The bed bowed under Eddie's weight as he sat next to me and put his arm around my back.

"Hey," I said. "How did you find me, anyway?"

He chuckled. "Your mother called and said you stole some of her clothing." He chuckled again. "She said that was right after you stomped into her house and asked for Gordon's address. The wheels started turning for me because I had just told you about seeing Gordon at the mini-mart. I figured a guess was better than nothing so that's when I showed up at his place. Your mom gave me the address. I saw your car down the street but there were hardly any lights on inside his house, and then no one answered the door. So, I went around the back and . . ."

His voice trailed off, as well as his eyes, which found a spot on the floor below us.

To finish Eddie's thought: and found Gordon choking *me*.

A new pulse of energy resounded within. It might only last for a minute, but taking advantage of it was at least worth a shot. Maybe this time I could make it to the door. I slid off the bed.

"You're not really going to try going after him again, are you?" Eddie asked.

I looked at the door, trying to convince my weakened limbs they could do it this time. Leaning forward to take that first step, Eddie stopped me with a firm grasp, and then stood in front of me.

"Like I said earlier, Evy, it's over."

I shot him a look of contempt. "What do you mean it's over?"

He wiped the side of his face with his palm, sighing again and closing his eyes for a moment, then reopened them, and said, "They released him."

If the human body could puddle, mine would have. That's what it felt like.

"Re . . . released? They let him go?"

Eddie looked at his watch, and then lowered his head, his voice, anything he could for what seemed an overt measure to mitigate what was about to tiptoe from his mouth. "Or, they're about to release him. The detectives said they'd have him out of here by ten, at the latest. I was hoping you wouldn't be up until long after."

I didn't have the benefit of Eddie's watch, but then I saw the wall clock by the room's window. It was just after 9:30 a.m.

"That's why I'm trying to keep you in here," Eddie added, spreading apart his arms a bit toward me, but not in compassion. It looked more like a defensive measure. I wasn't sure if his plan involved tackling me, but he reminded me of a linebacker. Still, I was fragile and maimed—at least I'm sure that's how he viewed me—so I dismissed the notion he'd actually use any more force than gently holding me back.

But I had to see him. If he was still here, I had to see Gordon. There wasn't a rational explanation, especially since I couldn't envision how I'd react if I were to set eyes on him again, but I wanted to start with seeing if he was still in the hospital. That meant getting by Eddie.

Without looking at it—for fear Eddie would be on to me—I thought of the IV tower next to me. It would only slow me down, from its size, its lack of maneuverability, to its being something that Eddie could grab and use to contain me.

In a quick, unflinching movement, I ripped the needle out of my arm. A drop of my blood flung off and hit Eddie's cheek. It stunned him just enough for me to get through the door and enter the hallway. I only had one chance to choose the right direction but I chose well when I had turned to my left, beelining toward uniformed officers who stood with Pete at the end of the hallway.

Eddie darted after me, but I slowed right before I arrived in front of the officers. As if I could actually play it cool at that point, with my hospital gown flapping open in the back and Eddie behind me, shouting, "Evy, no!"

Thatcher came out of the last room down the hall, quickly closing the door behind him. As Eddie had tried earlier, Thatcher held his arms out to block me. Before I could open my mouth, my body fell to the side and hit the wall as my vision blurred and my legs turned to jelly. Pete caught me before I hit the floor. He propped me up until Eddie took over.

"Take her back, Mr. Barrett," Pete said.

"No, no," I mumbled, holding my head. "I want to see—"

"Don't even finish that request, Mrs. Barrett," Pete interrupted. "The answer is no."

I started to feel my legs again and pushed off from Eddie.

"Why not?" I asked Pete, still holding on to Eddie's arm.

"What point does it serve?" he responded. "In my experience, there's a garden variety of things victims want to do when they 'absolutely have to see their offender,'" he said, throwing up air quotes, "like spit, curse, or chuck something. And while a case could be made for letting one or more of those things slide every now and then, I'd say, given your history here, you've exceeded your 'getting back' allowances." Air quotes again.

"But he killed Corinne! This isn't like before. I know for sure now." My voice throbbed and now skipped, choked up on the floodgate of the situation. It was like being strangled all over again, but this time instead of Gordon's liver-spotted hands, it was an overwhelming sense of impotence that seemed to mock me and tell me I was a weakling if I let my child's killer be forever unaware of what I'd like to do to him.

Not only did I have to carry on in a world where my daughter no longer lived, but I had to share its air and sunrises and absurdities with her killer. I knew that prior, but it felt colder and more vicious when I could put a name and a face to the killer, when I could even see his slow moving shadow creep below the hospital room door in front of me. Gordon. He stood there, likely listening to Pete's rebuke as I let it fall over me like a reluctant bath during childhood.

Maybe Gordon was even feeling safe from Eddie and me. He was the one we all should have been afraid of—the man without the limits of morality, the man who allows himself a killing or two out of convenience. "We know, Mrs. Barrett," Pete said. "We know he killed your daughter. DNA came back this morning. It's case closed."

But it didn't feel that way. Nothing felt closed except that stupid door separating Gordon and me. Safe. That's all I could think again . . . he likely felt safe.

Eddie's grasp on me had slowly loosened over the last minute. I wondered if he saw the creeping shadow, too, and it had paralyzed him. I lunged forward, bumping Thatcher out of the way with my left shoulder and feeling this searing, white pain radiate from my broken arm straight up to the back of my eyes.

I took my good hand and banged on the door with all my weakened might, scratching my voice out like raging desert sand against a speeding windshield, "Why do you get safety? Corinne didn't. Why you?"

The pain buckled me, starting at my feet, collapsing at my knees, and I was still seeing a sheet of white in front of me. But maybe that was also because I knew it was time to quit. It was time to give up. That reluctant bathing was washing all sorts of me away.

I'm not sure if I fell into Eddie's arms or if he simply hoisted me up and cradled me.

Didn't I know I had been buying into a lie? The lure, the tasty sweet of sin, which is nothing more than writhing around in the shadows and pretending it's no big thing to have the claws in our backs and the endless slithering, naked as we are, upon the broken stained-glass window of this world. Where was the real safety for a man who hides behind a door? Where was the safety for a man who preys on children? There is no safety for people who dance with the devil. That destroyer doesn't know how to play nice and he sure doesn't intend to be a considerate dance partner. You're going to be minus something when the music stops. I knew this; I should have always known this.

Eddie carried me back to my room. Based on the hot tears that fell from his face to mine as he had his cheek pressed to my forehead, I guessed he didn't find this business any fairer than I had.

It seemed like only a moment later when Thatcher rapped quickly on the open door to my room. He only said, "Quickly." I didn't know what he meant, only that he meant for us to move.

Eddie had already put me on the bed, and barely got himself to the chair in the corner, near a flood of light coming through the window. He sank into it, turning his face away from me. I figured he was still crying and hiding it from me. What a fool I had been. I wanted to address it, to take it up with Eddie, but I heard several pairs of footsteps ascending the hall toward us.

What Thatcher had meant when he said, "Quickly," suddenly triggered.

I shuffled to the door, dragging my feet and hoping I wouldn't fall because Eddie wouldn't make it over to me until it was too late. Thatcher's arm was stretched out across the threshold, preventing me from moving out, but I rested up against it to get a better look just as Gordon came walking by, his hands cuffed behind his back, and a beautifully crooked, busted nose with a pair of gorgeous black eyes. Such were only becoming to me because my Eddie had created them. I knew it was bad to think that way, but at least now, I knew I would never mention Eddie had done nothing when it came to Corinne's killer.

"Eddie," I choked out, meaning to look over my shoulder and get his attention, but couldn't stop looking at Gordon.

"No, Evy. I don't want to." I heard him say.

Gordon looked relieved. But still scared too.

I guess Pete had changed his mind because he kept Gordon there for a moment instead of walking on. Pete even shook Gordon by the arm to jolt his head up when he didn't have the courage to look at me. I wanted to look away, too, but I wasn't going to if I could help it. I summoned a reserved strength to endure the gaze. Not in an "I'm tougher than you" sort of way, but in a "You didn't win" sort of way, even though I only half meant it since I was still void of my child. Still, the externally smooth masquerade paired with the trembles within caused something inside me to skip a beat, move out of sync.

I had suffered an immeasurable loss. That would be forever with me. Gordon's dirty, debauched fingerprint would always be on the glossy photo of my life, my family.

Then that wash fell on me again, this time cleansing the suds from my eyes. I don't know what prompted it. Maybe it was Eddie crying over in the corner, or the fact that Pete had jerked Gordon's upper body again for him to look at me, but he wouldn't.

I felt my blood, my pulse, my very heart coming to a full stop. The last beat echoed and landed like a dull thud near the back of my ears before starting up again. Everything synchronized once more, and I knew I'd go on. No longer piecemeal this time, saying I was fine but acting like an unhinged lunatic whenever it served my purposes.

I took a deep inhale, waiting for the next audible beat of my heart, but suddenly became distracted because I smelled . . . I smelled nothing.

I inhaled again. Nothing.

"It's gone," I said.

I dared not walk any closer. It wasn't because of Pete, or the fact Thatcher still had his arm stretched across my door's threshold, but because I was stunned. I had heard Gordon's admission, I had even heard Pete say the DNA matched, but if there wasn't a smell . . .

"I don't smell him," I said, looking at Thatcher.

Pete rolled his eyes and then stopped at Thatcher, saying, "You watch her and keep her back. Don't let her move even five feet."

Thatcher turned to me with a puzzled look.

Pete led Gordon by the elbow, although it looked like it was Gordon, not Pete, pulling the lead, especially when he was trying to dash from my room. I seethed at the thought he appeared to be running *toward* safety, but I tried to focus on the fact that it was still running, and running away like a coward isn't a telltale of safety. And since he was fleeing from a broken, banged-up chick like me, it sort of felt right. Almost.

I raised my hand to my head, feeling the goose egg still there. "Thatcher," I started, "Gordon hit me in the same spot. Do you think . . . ?"

"I never knew what to think about it in the first place," he replied. "Are you saying it's gone?"

"I don't know. Maybe."

"Well then, good. You didn't want it anyway, right?"

"Right," I mumbled.

He removed his arm from the doorway, but made sure I could steady myself on my own before he dropped the arm to his side. "Gotta go, Mrs. Barrett. I hope to see you around. Heck, I actually hope we get to work together again." He looked over his shoulder. I figured he was seeing if Pete was still in earshot, and then added, "I actually started to think we could somehow work together as partners. You know, permanently. Pete's going to retire now. I'll need a new partner."

I tried to smile at him but it probably looked like I was in pain. In many respects, and on many levels, I was. "Bye, Thatcher," I said.

Eddie had come to the doorway, helping me back to bed. He laid me down and then rested his head on my stomach, giving it a kiss.

"He's not done, you know," I said to Eddie.

"Who's not?" he asked.

"Gordon. I mean *he's* done, but not . . ." I trailed off, trying to think through what I wanted to say. "Eddie, do you believe in all that demon and devil stuff?" I asked.

"Of course I do. I believe in it so much, that I take it as my own personal incentive to choose the other side, God's side."

Team colors, I thought. Which team color had I been wearing since Corinne died? And what about before she died, when I was living the high life? Even if I had the right colored jersey in my closet, did I actually put it on and wear it for the world to see?

"So, what do you mean about Gordon not being finished?" Eddie asked, pulling me back into the conversation.

"He was a pawn," I said. "A tool of something bigger, something more sinister. Evil. Demonic, even. And if he's locked up, unable to hurt any more children, the thirst that drove him to kill Corinne, it'll go elsewhere. I'm sure of it. Remind me to tell you later about Helen Crafton and her father. About Legion too."

"There's a story in the New Testament where Jesus cast out a legion of demons from a man. After, they scurried to find another host. Is that what you're talking about?"

"Yes, I think it is."

"And you're scared that someone else will take over where Gordon left off?"

"Will?" I asked, raising my head in anguish. "Try has. Someone already has. That part I know. Those sort of pawns are a dime a dozen. There's no shortage of broken people who are open to habitation—so many empty vessels flashing their vacancy signs."

"But not us," Eddie assured. "We're sealed off because we've made the right choice. Of course you veered there for a bit, but I think you're coming around." He looked up at me, flashing a smile. "The ones who should be the most worried," he continued, "are the ones who pretend there isn't a choice to begin with. They're the most vulnerable."

"I don't know about that. I'm feeling pretty vulnerable myself."

"That will change in time," he said, giving my belly another kiss.

"Why do you keep doing that?"

He pulled something out of his shirt pocket and handed it to me. "They gave this to me last night after they ran some tests on you."

It was a small, blurry black-and-white photograph. Any woman, especially a mother, would recognize that paper. It was an ultrasound snapshot. The name on the top, the owner of the womb, was Barrett, Evelyn.

A child. Eddie had given me another child. God had given us another child.

So many things crowded my thoughts. Would I even know how to be a good mother anymore? What if this child died too? I couldn't go through this again, I couldn't. And the betrayal . . . wasn't loving another, new child a betrayal to Corinne? As if we had simply replaced her out of the blue one day.

Eddie stroked his finger across the sonogram picture. The image was nothing really—just a vacuous dot surrounded by white fuzz. Yet, it was still altogether everything.

Acknowledgments

First and foremost, nothing compares to the greatness of knowing You, Lord.

Thank you to my husband and sons. There's been so much sacrifice on your part. It couldn't have been done without your willingness to give. I'm blessed to love you and to be loved by you.

Thank you to my parents. All of you. Mom, for being the type of mother who isn't afraid to push me to do better. Dad, for being the type of father who keeps me grounded until the prize is in my hands. And Karen, for always keeping the cheering section on their toes.

Thank you to my siblings, Erin, Lloyd, and Megan. I'm lucky to have you.

Dana Martin, you gave me everything and you probably don't even know it. Thank you for yanking me from the cocoon.

Stephanie Cline. If anyone dares to think that one adult can't irrevocably change the course of a child's life, say Stephanie Cline.

Thanks to Cindy Coloma for telling me to use my "real" voice. To Sarah Oaklief for pulling me out of the slush pile. To Greg Johnson not only for giving me an honest word and a second chance but for being an agent who is sincere in his support.

Thank you to everyone at Kregel. Thank you for this gift.

Thank you to everyone who prays for me. You've uplifted my spirit countless times.

Thank you to my music makers: Beckah Shae, Barlow Girl, Nate Sallie, Group 1 Crew, Toby Mac, Switchfoot, and pretty much anything heard on www.air1.com.

And a final, hearty thank-you to everyone who has taken the time to read my words. I'd be rambling into madness without you. Again, thank you.